LORI COPELAND

Marrying Walker McKay

AVON BOOKS

An Imprint of HarperCollins*Publishers*

This is a work of fiction. Names, characters, places, and incidents are products of the author's imagination or are used fictitiously and are not to be construed as real. Any resemblance to actual events, locales, organizations, or persons, living or dead, is entirely coincidental.

AVON BOOKS
An Imprint of HarperCollins*Publishers*
10 East 53rd Street
New York, New York 10022-5299

Copyright © 2000 by Lori Copeland
ISBN: 0-7394-1370-8

To my husband, Lance.
Have I told you lately
how very much I love you?

Acknowledgments

A special thanks to Heidi Skurat for her expertise and editorial comments during the writing of *Marrying Walker McKay*. You're a sweetheart, Heidi! Play lots of golf with your dad!

To Micki Nuding, a special editor who makes me think harder than I want to think. Love and appreciate you, Micki. It's a pleasure working with you.

Chapter 1

April 1867
Laramie, Wyoming

"**S**. H., I need a wife about as much as I need a square-dancing bull."

Walker McKay released the steer he'd just branded and shoved his dusty Stetson to the back of his head. What would he do with a wife? He had it made: no female to order him around; no interfering woman to lie to him, tell him what to wear, when to eat, or whom to eat it with. His life was his own, and he had no intention of changing it.

A cowboy galloped in, roped a calf, and then dragged it toward the branding fire. Drovers tackled the calf and held it to the ground while Walker applied the mark of the Spring Grass

1

Ranch: a large *S* with a lowercase *g* intertwined in the bottom. They'd branded close to two hundred head since dawn; it would be close to five hundred before the work let up.

"You're as hardheaded as a blind mule," S. H. complained. Sizemore Horatio Gibson—"S. H." to friends—released a heifer, and the animal sprang to its feet bawling. Realizing she was free, she trotted off to join the others. The grizzly old man met Walker's eyes. "How old will you be on your birthday? Twenty-nine?"

"Yeah. Why?" But he knew why. S. H was on him again about an heir, or rather, the lack of one.

"Twenty-eight and nary an heir to carry on the McKay name. Dang shame. Your papa would set up in his grave and spit if he knew how you were avoiding the altar." S. H. dragged another heifer to the ground.

The dang shame was that Mitch McKay had had only one child. If Walker had a brother, the pressure to marry and have a child would be off him and he would be free to run the ranch. He scowled. He'd have *been* a father by now if Trudy Richards hadn't jilted him at the altar last year. Walker still saw red when he thought of how he'd spent two years convincing himself that he loved that woman enough to marry her; it had taken her less than fifteen minutes to prove him a jackass. He could still smell the rose-scented church; see himself and Pa standing at the altar, dressed in their Sunday best, waiting for the bride. The sea of expectant faces trained on the church foyer. That damn organ playing.

About the time he was making a fool of himself in front of the whole town, Trudy was high-tailing it out of the city limits with a fellow who sold hats—bowlers, no less; a drifter she'd met two weeks earlier at a town social.

Dust swirled around the milling cattle, who bawled when the ropes found their marks and hauled them in. Overhead, clouds drifted across a clear Wyoming sky. Only the unusually warm spring sun, stinging horseflies, and memories best forgotten marred an otherwise flawless day.

Walker laid the branding iron across the next heifer's rump. Disgrace was still a bitter pill to swallow. The scene still haunted him. The hushed condolences as guests stood about, eating wedding cake, sipping punch, and making the best of a bad situation while they eyed him with pity. Never again would he allow a woman to make a fool of him. Not for S. H. or anybody else.

"You can't let one woman ruin your whole life," S. H. remarked, grabbing a steer and riding it to the ground. "You got to get busy, son; produce an heir. Your papa worked hard for this land—nearly killed himself building Spring Grass. It was hard work that put yer momma in an early grave. You don't want to leave the ranch to strangers, do you?"

"I tried it Pa's way and your way, and it didn't work. I'm content with my life and I don't intend to change it—not now, not any time soon."

He had plenty of time to worry about marriage and kids. Youngsters were okay, but in Walker McKay's book, women were good for just two things: lying and bedding, and not necessarily in that order. Other men might put up with being led around by their noses, but he sure as the dickens wouldn't do it. After Trudy's betrayal, it would be a cold day in July before he gave *his* heart to a conniving woman.

"Who's gonna inherit the McKay fortune if you die? You ever think about that?"

Why think about it? He figured he had a good fifty years to settle the matter before his number was up. He wasn't a gunslinger; he didn't pick fights and tempt death to his doorstep. He ran a ranch, lived a temperate lifestyle, and visited town only when supplies ran low or he felt the occasional need for a woman's companionship. He enjoyed hunting, catching a trout or two, maybe reading a dime novel. Hardly the kind of lifestyle that threatened an early demise. He hadn't even had a cold since the winter of sixty-two.

Longevity ran in the McKay family. Grandpa McKay lived to be ninety-two; Great-grandpa, ninety-six. If Pa hadn't tangled with that bull last year, who knows? He might have lived to be a hundred. Maybe by the time Walker was forty, he'd give serious thought to death. Right now, he had his hands full running the ranch. He was responsible—the ranch made a sizable profit each year, and he made sure that his thirty-five ranch hands were the first to volunteer for a barn raising. He took a bath regularly, combed his hair, put on his clothes every morning—all without a woman's help.

"Let me tell you, son. You don't put off what

needs be done today. A man never knows how long he's got on this old earth."

A man S. H.'s age would naturally be worried about such things. "Can't we talk about this another time?"

"You ought to ask Willa Mae Lewis to the Grange social Saturday night." S. H. paused, knocking the dust off his trousers. "Now, that woman is as pretty as a prize heifer and bakes a mean rhubarb pie. Got the hips to birth a cow."

"I have all the livestock I need, S. H."

"Rolene Berry?"

"Too immature."

"Ruthie Gaines—now, there's a fine-looking woman."

"Vain. She'd rather stay home and look at herself in a mirror than attend a social."

"Heidi Watson."

"Spoiled. Get off my back, S. H. I don't *want* a wife."

A drover whistled loudly, ending the conversation. Walker stood and wiped sweat off his forehead. The whistle shrilled again and Walker turned, shading his eyes against the sun. An Angus bull twisted and bucked, crazed with the need to escape the rope. Head bent and bellowing, the animal broke the cowboy's grip.

"Watch out!" S. H. bolted for the fence as the bull charged. Walker whirled around too quickly, losing his balance.

Staggering, he retained his footing, but not before images of an earlier scene raced through his mind. Frenzied cries, the gore, the spurt of bright red blood as the animal's horns sank into Pa's flesh.

"Walker!" S. H. shouted over the milling herd, and others, overcoming shock, joined in.

"He's headed your way!"

"Give him room!"

Before Walker could pull away from his mind and respond, the bull struck him head-on, and Walker let out a muffled yell. The impact propelled him backward and spun him around. Reeling, he struggled to stay afoot and catch his breath.

The animal whirled, paused for an instant to snort and wag his head, then charged again, eyes red with rage as he thundered in for a second strike.

Dropping to the ground, Walker curled into a tight ball, arms shielding his head. He gasped for breath, too stunned to notice the trickle of blood coursing down his chin.

This couldn't be happening. Not to him.

Three ranch hands charged the bull, shouting, waving their arms in an attempt to divert the animal's attention.

Horns caught Walker in the side and he felt muscles tear, then blinding pain. Confusion broke out as other wranglers raced to the rescue, trying to divert the bull as it spun and lunged again, catching Walker in the upper thigh and tossing him like a rag doll. S. H. bolted to the fence where his rifle rested, shouting something Walker couldn't make out.

The bull struck again from a new direction. Walker struggled to stay conscious, trying to ward off the nine-hundred-pound assault. From somewhere past consciousness he heard S. H.'s voice prodding him to produce an heir.

The bull was going to kill him.

I'm twenty-eight years old. I've got all the time in the world. . . .

Coiling into a tight knot, he burrowed his face in the dirt. *His time was up, his number called.* The realization was as certain as life itself had been only a scant minute ago.

Riders galloped in and managed to divert the bull's attention long enough for the men to pull Walker to safety.

Drifting in and out on a sea of pain, Walker opened his eyes to see S. H. hunched over him, getting in the way as ranch hands tried to cut the clothing from his wounds. The old man folded his battered hat against his chest, and tears rolled down his cheeks.

"Come on, S. H.," Walker muttered. "It's just a couple of broken ribs. . . ."

But he didn't need S. H. to tell him it was bad. He could feel blood oozing from his left side. Instead of S. H.'s voice, past conversations drifted through his mind.

I'll think about an heir someday. I have plenty of time.

S. H. knelt beside him, openly weeping, his dusty trousers seeping up Walker's lifeblood. "Didn't you hear me? I tried to push you out of the way."

"I heard you . . . S. H. . . . couldn't get out of the way." Walker struggled to focus, barely able to comprehend or respond now. Men were working over him; the pain in his groin felt like a branding iron.

"Hang on, son, hang on," S. H. urged. "They've gone for the doc . . . don't die, boy. . . ."

I'm twenty-eight—got all the time in the world.

Reaching for the old man's hand, Walker grasped it tightly. S. H. had been with Pa when he drew his last breath, had been with Spring Grass since Mitch felled the first tree. It was right that he would be here now.

"Saw the bull—couldn't . . ."

"Lie still, son." S. H. gripped his hand and Walker felt the old man's trembling. "You can beat this."

"Take care of Spring Grass, S. H. . . . and take care of Sophie. She's a good woman. . . ."

"None of that talk—you're not going to leave us, Walker. Hold on, son."

Walker closed his eyes, allowing the welcoming darkness to pull him under.

"Dadburn it! Where's that doctor!" S. H. bellowed. Sobbing, the old man sank back onto his knees.

He'd thought he had all the time in the world.

Chapter 2

Boston, Massachusetts
Late May, 1867

"I'm dying. It's true, I'm dying, Wadsy."

"You ain't dyin', honeychile. Now hold still and let Wadsy put this cold cloth on your forehead. Lawsy me, you're hot as a poker." The old nanny squeezed a cold compress and laid it across Sara's forehead. "Runnin' off in this cold rain, entertainin' the idea of marryin' some no-good riverboat worker. What're you thinkin', Babygirl? Marryin' some man who'd end up breakin' your heart—you want your papa's dyspepsia to flare up again? He's gonna have a conniption fit when he hears what you been up to!"

Sara, lying on the bed, with arms flung spread-eagled, stared at the ceiling. She'd missed the opportunity of a lifetime. Hank *was* a bit unstable and Papa would point that out, ranting about how she'd known the "scoundrel" only less than a week. But Hank had promised to settle down, to devote himself tirelessly to family life. He'd vowed that he was weary of traveling from town to town, wasting his life on women and strong drink. She'd believed those blue, blue eyes. Unlike Papa, she didn't have to know someone a hundred years in order to judge his character. Hank was handsome and exciting, and other than having an overactive admiration of women and an occasional sip of whiskey for his health, he had shown real promise.

"I was *this* close to getting married, Wadsy." She measured a minuscule distance with her thumb and forefinger. "I could have been a June bride."

Wadsy groaned.

"This *close*! Why did Abe have to come along when he did! Why couldn't that old mare have thrown a shoe any other time but today!"

"You're 'this close' to feelin' the strap of your daddy's belt to that delicate backside, Sara Elaine Livingston." Wadsy lifted the cloth off Sara's forehead and soaked it in a pan of cool water. "Good thing Abe came along when he did or you'd be in a fine how-de-do."

Curling up into a tight ball, Sara released her misery, drenching the silk spread with bitter tears.

"Oh, now, child," Wadsy soothed. "It ain't the end of the world."

"But it is," Sara cried. "All I've ever wanted is

to get married. Just *look* at me. I'm eighteen and an *old maid*."

The heartbreaking admission opened the floodgates. Sara wadded up her pillow and bawled. Her voice was muffled through the crisply ironed pillowcase.

"I'm going to *die* before I ever get to be a wife!"

Nothing *ever* went her way. Every time she got close to the altar, someone nixed her plans. When would she ever escape Papa's attempts to "make things better" and ruin her dream? When would she finally have that husband she ached to care for, or an infant to suckle at her breast? When?

Wadsy rescued the pillow, clucking her tongue and shaking out the creases. "Never seen such carryings-on. Sit up, honeychile; your nose is gonna be red and all uglylike. You'll never find a husband if you have an ugly red nose."

Sara bolted upright, pinning Wadsy with a cold stare. "I'm never going to find a husband no matter what my nose looks like. And who cares? *No* one, that's who." Not Wadsy—she was on Papa's side. Certainly not Papa, who was bound and determined to keep his daughter under his thumbnail until she was old as Methuselah.

Old Abe could have helped today, but no, he had to come by the landing on his way to have the mare shod, spot her boarding with Hank, and drag her off the boat kicking and swatting, knocking the hat off his head. He'd *humiliated* her in front of the whole town. And the worst was yet to come. She still had to face Papa.

She would be dead and buried before Papa found a man "good" enough for his daughter.

"We all care, baby. We just don't want you goin' off half cocked and marryin' the wrong man." Settling her bulk on the side of the bed, Wadsy smoothed Sara's fiery tendrils from her forehead. The Negro woman had raised Sara from infancy; she was the only mother Sara had ever known. "I know how your heart aches for a husband; Lord knows you've clomped around this house with a curtain over that unruly hair, wearin' your mama's gowns, gettin' pretend married since you could toddle. Lawsy me, I've attended more weddin's the last eighteen years than I can count, but marriage is powerful serious, Babygirl. You got to get it right or you'll live with the mistake the rest of your life. None of us want to see you go through that—cain't you understand?"

"Oh, Wadsy." Sara blew her nose into her tightly wadded handkerchief. This time she'd been *so* close to realizing her dream.

Marriage *was* sacred and shouldn't be entered into lightly, but she was about to give up on finding the perfect man. She'd started to think he didn't exist. Papa was rich beyond belief—owned his own railroad, half of Boston, and hundreds and hundreds of acres of abundant cotton land—so he could purchase anything she wanted. Yet he was powerless to buy what she needed: a husband, someone to love and care for, someone who would love and care for her when Papa and Wadsy and Abraham passed on.

No amount of money in the world could buy that kind of happiness.

Over the years, dozens of young men, men

who worked for Papa, had courted her. Something—usually Papa—always interfered with those promising relationships. No one was ever good enough for her in Papa's eyes, though Papa insisted that she was being overly dramatic. Yet here she was, getting older by the minute and not a lick closer to a husband than she'd been the day Wadsy helped Doc Mason bring her into the world.

Life was just plain unfair.

So was Papa.

"Come on, now." Wadsy lumbered to her feet, taking Sara's arm and urging her up. The old nanny was twice Sara's size, her fleshy bulk swaying with the motion. "Suppa's on the table, and there's no need to anger your papa any more than he already is."

Sara dug her heels into the carpet, refusing to be led to the slaughter. She knew that supper would be an emotional scene, with Papa vowing to send her off to Uncle Brice.

She'd *die* before she'd live in Uncle Brice's stuffy old mausoleum. He had long black hairs growing out of his nose; how was she supposed to face that every day? And his humorless laugh sounded like he had a crow lodged in his snout.

She would be forced to listen to one more lecture from Papa on her hooligan ways and how they were a disgrace to the Livingston name. If Papa wanted to bawl her out, he'd have to come get her.

Wadsy's eyes flashed with determination and she pulled, hauling her struggling charge across the Turkish carpet, out the door, and into the hallway. Sara tried to get back into her room, but Wadsy blocked the door and called for Abe.

The towering black man quickly appeared at the bottom of the stairs and Sara's heart sank. She shrank against the wall, trying to avoid his gaze, but the white-haired servant pinned her with a stern look that she knew meant business. His low-pitched bass rumbled deep in his massive chest.

"Come on down now, missy. Suppa's gettin' cold."

"Never! I'm ill—I'm dying, Abe! Don't make me go see Papa!"

"Ain't no use, Abraham. Gonna have to come after her," Wadsy called. "She's in one of her moods."

Stiffening, Sara fixed her body in a rigid stance, keeping an eye on Abe and a hand clenched on the banister as he slowly ascended the stairway.

"I don't want any supper. I'm too sick to eat."

"Makes no difference to me if you eat suppa or not, but your papa wants you at his table while he eats his."

Prying her small hand from the rail, he swung her over his left shoulder and hauled her down the winding stairway as she pounded his back and kicked the air until her skirts tangled around her knees. When the battling duo reached the foyer, Wadsy hurried to straighten Sara's skirts, avoiding the flailing legs.

Crossing her arms, Sara refused to let her captors intimidate her as Abe transported her into the dining room. They might force her to sit at Papa's table, but they'd need a crowbar to make her eat. Or speak. *Or* convince her that Abe's rescue was necessary to keep her from a terrible mistake!

She was *going* to find a husband, with or without this family's support.

Lowell Livingston glanced up when Abe stepped into the dining room, carrying Sara over his shoulder.

Settling her was no easy task. She kept her knees locked straight out and slid out of her chair twice before Abe could get her planted. Then the servant excused himself and backed out of the dining room.

The mantel clock ticked away the seconds like a slow rain as Lowell fixed his daughter with a harsh stare down the long, silver-laden table.

"Exactly whom," he began in an evenly checked tone, "were you about to marry this time?"

Sara pursed her lips, focusing on the gold-rimmed plate. "I don't care to discuss it. I'm dying."

"You're *not* dying. Wadsy says you have the sniffles and a fever from your reckless outing this afternoon. What were you thinking, daughter? Were you honestly going to marry this man?"

"I was. And I'm thinking," she answered in a carefully modulated voice, "that I want to get *married*, Papa!"

Leaving his chair, Lowell paced the room. Sara recognized the stubborn set of his jaw and knew that it meant trouble; she'd stretched his patience to the breaking point—but hers was close to snapping, too. Papa must understand the importance of marriage now that the years were passing her by. She couldn't stay his little girl forever.

"A dockworker? A common stranger? Have you no shame?"

"You make him sound terrible. He's better than most of the others. Name one man more suited for marriage."

"Joe Mancuso, trainmaster. An up-and-coming young man, making a real name for himself at the railroad."

"Mr. Mancuso doesn't want to get married."

Lowell snorted. "You can't know that! You spent one evening—one very short evening, if I recall—with him."

"I asked him."

Lowell paused, looking faint. "You *asked* him?"

"I asked him. He just muttered something and excused himself. I knew what *that* meant, Papa." Lord knows she'd heard it before.

"What about Richard Ponder? A splendid example of a young man going somewhere. His parents are fine people and I talked to them personally before I arranged the meeting. Twenty-six and already a station agent. Youngest man in the division to obtain such a position—you didn't ask *him* to marry you, did you?"

Sara shook her head. "He volunteered the information. His *mother* doesn't want him getting married. Not now and, judging by his tone, not ever."

Papa slapped his forehead. "Great Day in the morning!"

Sara shrugged. He was clearly aghast at her

candor, but how was a woman expected to know a man's potential if she didn't ask? If Papa could be nosy, why couldn't she? He would never understand her need to be a wife and a mother.

At times, she didn't understand it herself, but she did know that Papa's health was precarious. Three heart spells in two years reminded them both of his mortality. Wadsy and Abe were even older, and someday she was going to be completely alone. Alone. With no one to love her, or for her *to* love. If she were married, losing Papa would still be devastating, but she could surround herself with her family and ease the pain.

She'd heard from Wadsy about the way Mama had looked at Papa during her illness—as if he owned her soul. He'd looked back at her exactly the same way, with so much love and want in his eyes it took Sara's breath away. That was what she wanted. Love so strong that even death couldn't tear it away. If it was wrong to want that kind of devotion, then consider her guilty as charged. Wadsy had said she shouldn't depend on others for happiness, but if she had her own home, babies to look after, and a husband to nurture and love, she could cope with the losses certain to enter her life soon. Until then, she would never be happy.

"Sit down, Papa—remember your heart."

"Humph. *You* remember my heart."

The somber reminder calmed her. She did remember, thought about it every day of her life.

"I'm sorry, Papa. I love you and I don't mean to be such a bother. I wish you could understand."

Lowell sat down, allowing Cook to spoon

thick slices of beef swimming in a rich brown broth onto his plate. Doc Mason had advised him that he should eat more vegetables and fruit, and said he was going to die from eating so much rich food—but he wouldn't hear of it. When Cook moved to serve Sara, she waved his efforts aside.

"I'm not hungry, Will."

"May I bring you some soup, Miss Livingston?"

"Nothing. Thank you." She watched Papa lather thick butter on a slice of warm bread, waiting for the inevitable. This time she'd gone too far. This time he would carry through with his threat to send her to Uncle Brice. She couldn't bear even the thought of a dreadful, hot Georgia summer full of long, boring days of trying to keep Brice entertained. Tears of self-pity and hollow remorse threatened to break loose, and she quickly averted her eyes. Clenching her fists, she waited for the storm to break.

"I'm at the end of my rope, Sara."

"I know, Papa. I'm sorry."

"Today's little escapade has convinced me that you will be better off with your uncle Brice."

"Papa—no!" A tear found its way down on her cheek and hung on the tip of her quivering chin.

Slamming his fist down on the table, Lowell glared at her. "Daughter, yes! I can't watch you every waking moment, and you've proved to be too much for Wadsy and Abe to handle. Wadsy will pack your bags and Abe will take you to the train Saturday morning. A year in Savannah will help to refine you and make you see the error of your ways before you drive us all to an early grave."

"A whole year? Papa!" Her thoughts turned from self-pity to anger. "I won't go!"

She'd run away—she'd run so far and so hard that Papa would never find her. The summers she'd been forced to endure living under Brice Livingston's roof were intolerable. His fits of temper kept her confined if she did the least little thing to rile him. Brice wouldn't let a man near her for the whole year. Why, last summer he'd practically locked her in her room every night! Papa couldn't just ship her down South and consider the problem solved.

Her uncle had survived three loveless marriages all ending in separation, and he had nothing but contempt for the bond she held so dear. He would strip her of spirit, do everything within his power to color her outlook on life, love, and, most certainly, marriage. She could not, would not, let that happen.

Staring at her empty plate, she vowed softly, "I won't go to Uncle Brice. I won't."

"You have no choice." Picking up his fork, Lowell speared a piece of beef, fixing her with a hard look. "End of discussion, young lady."

Chapter 3

"**A**h don't like it. Ah don't like it one little bit." Old Abe set the brake Friday morning, then climbed down from the buggy and turned to help Sara. Boston still slept beneath a heavy blanket of darkness. A dog barked in the distance, the only sound in the predawn stillness.

"I'll name my first son after you," Sara promised. If it weren't for Abe's help, she couldn't have slipped out of the house unnoticed, or reached the train station in time to catch a train before anyone awoke.

"The only reason I agreed to bring you here is 'cause I can't bear to see you shipped off to your uncle Brice. That man's the devil if I ever seen one."

"Oh, Abe. You understand what I'm going through. I'm sorry I was so mean to you before supper last night."

"Tha's all right, Miss Livingston. I knows what you was facin'. I wouldn't let a cur live with that man. Good Lord knows you got no business traipsin' 'round the country by yourself, but I reckon if you're not old enough to look after your needs, Wadsy's done a poor job of raisin' you."

Leaning forward on tiptoes, Sara kissed the old servant's shaving-soap-scented cheek. Wadsy would hang us both out to dry if anyone suggested that she'd failed in her duties."

Abe chuckled. "That she would, young'un. She'll not hear it from me." He set the bag down on the ground, his eyes assessing the empty terminal. "I'd carry it inside, but if anyone was to notice—"

"You've done enough, Abe. I won't jeopardize your place with Papa by asking you to take me inside." Giving him a brief hug, she whispered, "I'll write and let you know where I am."

"Yes'm, you do that. We're going to be powerful worried until we hear that you're safe."

"Take good care of my papa."

"I will. You take care of yourself, young'un."

Sara watched him return to the buggy. He drove away, not looking back.

Picking up the valise, she entered the station. A mellow light bathed the deserted waiting room. Ordinarily, she wouldn't have to purchase a ticket. Papa owned the railroad and the Livingston family traveled free. But the sleepy-eyed man behind the ticket counter wouldn't recognize her today. She'd carefully dressed in Abe's grandson's clothing, pulling a hat low over her face. Other travelers would assume that she was a teenage boy traveling alone, exactly as she intended.

"One way to New York," she said, trying to make her voice gruff and manly. The sleepy ticket man didn't even look up. She laid the bills on the counter, smiling. Moments later, ticket in hand, she sat down to await the arrival of the five-forty southbound. Julie Steinberg had a small apartment above her father's Jewish delicatessen. She and Julie had been roommates in boarding school and still corresponded regularly, and Sara was sure Julie would let her stay with her until she could get her bearings.

Her educational skills were above most other young women's; finding suitable employment shouldn't be a problem. As soon as she could find a job, she would bury herself so deep in New York City that it would take Papa months to find her. By then she could be married and settled.

The door opened and a young woman, followed by an older couple, caught her attention. The girl was crying, trying to sop up the stream with a soaked hankie. The older man set his jaw, ignoring the waterworks.

"You'll be thanking us in a few years. Love ain't got a thing to do with happiness, girl."

The young woman shook her head, murmuring a rebuke, crying harder.

Realizing she was witnessing a private matter, Sara looked away, concentrating on the double wooden doors leading to the train platform. In a matter of hours she would be independent—free from Papa's tyranny. She shivered with uncertainty. What if New York men were as boring as Boston men? The thought scurried away as the older couple shuffled past her, practically dragging the girl behind them.

"Dry your eyes, Olivia. Your father is right—you'll come to understand that we only have your best interests at heart."

The girl shrugged off her mother's hand. "How can you and Pa be so mean! I love Rodney!"

Sara watched the struggle from the corner of her eye, reminding herself she shouldn't be so nosy. She had enough trouble with her own papa.

The coarse-looking man took off his hat and ran his hands through his graying hair. "You'll do what we say, Olivia. You're not too big to take a switch to yet, young lady."

"It's my life! I'm not going to throw it away. If you'd just try to understand . . ."

The sound of a train whistle interrupted the heated discussion. The five-forty was arriving. Retrieving her bag, Sara made her way out the doors and watched as the big black locomotive pulled into the station, steam bellowing from its coal stacks.

The young girl followed, sobbing as she continued to argue against her parents' intention to get her on the train. Angry voices followed Sara as she climbed aboard and took a seat in coach. She closed her eyes and breathed deeply. From her seat, the voices of the girl and her parents were only murmurs that faded as the train left the station. She was on her way!

Once it was light enough, she watched the passing scenery, her heart thumping with the rhythm of the tracks. The train wound through fields and farms, small towns awakening to the shrill whistle as the locomotive streaked through the countryside. When her watch hands reached closer to seven, her stomach reminded her that she hadn't eaten since breakfast the day before. Getting out of her seat, she walked to the dining car, struggling to keep her balance against the swaying of the train.

Her eyes searched the bustling dining car, lighting on the young woman who still sobbed into her hankie. The red nose and swollen eyes assured Sara that the crisis—whatever it was—still bloomed. Her heart dropped when she saw there was only one empty seat, and it was across from the young girl. She made her way to the table, trying not to stumble.

"Mind if I sit with you?"

The girl refused to look up. "I'm not good company."

Sara slid into the seat opposite her, then unfolded a napkin. "That's all right. I'm too hungry to be much company, either." The girl finally glanced up, frowning at Sara's appearance.

Of course—she would think a boy was seeking her company! Sara was still wearing Blue Boy's clothes.

Removing her cap, she released the pins from her hair and a cloud of brushed auburn hair spilled over her shoulders. "It's too complicated to explain why I'm dressed this way, but I am a woman. You don't have to worry."

The girl looked out the window. When break-fast was served, she pushed the plate away. Sara ate with gusto, feeling like a bird finally free of its cage. Of course, Papa would send someone after her—probably those same old Pinkerton men whom he'd sent last time. But it would take weeks for anyone to track down her activities, and by then she would be safely tucked away in Julie's apartment—or even better, married.

Sniffing, the young woman turned without warning. "I'm Olivia Mallory. I'm very unhappy."

Who wasn't? Sara reached for a hot roll. "I noticed you've been crying. Is there anything I could do to help?"

"You can marry Walker McKay."

Sara blinked, dropping the roll she was about to butter. "Pardon?"

"Marry Walker McKay. I'm being shipped off to be a mail-order bride, and I don't want to be. My father is making me marry some old dirty Wyoming ranchman so I can produce an heeeeeeeeeirr." Her head hit the table with a dull thud as she resumed weeping. The force of the vibration tipped the butter from the knife to the tablecloth.

Sara's mind churned. Marry? Seriously? She leaned closer to the heaving girl. "Have you seen this Walker McKay? Is he . . . beastly-looking?" She could tolerate unattractiveness as long as a man was clean about his personage. She could even tolerate an older man so long as he was kind. But beastly—having mean tendencies? It'd be like marrying Uncle Brice.

"I haven't *seen* the man—all I know is what Father's told me. He's twenty-eight, recently got sliced up by a bull or something, and now he's decided that he needs an heir to his ranch." Olivia bawled harder.

A desperate man looking for matrimony. Too good to be true! "Can't he marry a local woman—someone he knows?"

Shaking her head, the girl wiped her nose. "I have no idea. I just know I don't want to marry Mr. McKay just so my parents can save their—" She stopped, looking as if she'd said something she shouldn't. "I just don't want to marry him."

Sara absently bit into the unbuttered roll. "What are you going to do?"

"Marry Rodney. He's meeting the train in Denver and I'm getting off. We're going to be married immediately."

"Oh, my." Sara chewed, fascinated by her spunk. "What happens when Mr. McKay meets the train and you aren't on it?"

The girl shrugged. "I don't care what happens to Walker McKay. I love Rodney, and I refuse to spoil my future happiness in order to cater to Pa's whims."

Well, the good-luck fairy was working overtime. First Abe had agreed to drive Sara to the train, and now this. The girl obviously had made up her mind: she wasn't marrying this Walker McKay. And he *was* expecting a bride to arrive. . . .

"I'll do it."

Blowing her nose, Olivia frowned.

"I'll marry Walker McKay."

"But you don't know him!"

"Neither do you."

"You're not serious."

"Perfectly serious." Sara carefully rearranged the silverware. It would be daring and reckless and the answer to her problem. "The reason I'm here, all dressed like a boy, is because Papa and I are having a terrible argument. I had to run away because he keeps ruining my plans to get married."

"Like me and Rodney? Father and Mother think he'll never be able to support me."

"That's one of the things my papa's worried about. He is entirely too picky about men. He wanted to send me to live with my uncle Brice in Georgia, to cool me down, but I slipped out before he sent me away."

"But you're so pretty—or you would be if you weren't dressed in that clothing. Surely you could have your pick of suitable men."

"Thank you, but I can't. The men I know are either married, don't want to get married, or . . ." Howard Winslet popped into her mind. Howard bit his nails and talked for hours about horses. Horses didn't interest Sara, nor did Howard, no matter how much she wanted a husband. "Or their mothers don't want them to marry."

"But Mr. McKay is expecting me."

"Has he seen your picture?"

"No . . . he didn't request one."

"Does he know anything about you other than you're willing to marry him?"

"I'm not willing! My father concocted this crazy plan to keep me away from Rodney."

"What's wrong with Rodney?"

"Nothing that I can see. Papa says he'll never be able to support me, but I can work. I sew beautifully, and I make lovely hats. I'll find work. Papa just wants me to marry Mr. McKay because he's—" She broke off, then said, "Papa likes to run my life."

"Then my taking your place would solve both our problems. I'll be you. I'll meet Mr. McKay, introduce myself as Olivia Mallory, and marry him for you."

"But—when Mr. McKay finds out what we've done—"

Sara bit her lip. This plan had to work. She didn't know how long she could carry off the ruse, but with any luck, long enough for her to conceive Mr. McKay's much-needed heir. By then he would be so completely, devotedly in love with Sara that when she told him about the trick he would only laugh, scolding her for lying but happy that she had. She frowned. Maybe not happy, necessarily, but at the very most, mildly upset for a few days. But when she proved to be a loving wife and mother, he wouldn't hear of her leaving.

"Oh, dear," Olivia breathed. "Do you really think we could?"

"Of course we can. I'll make it work." With a satisfied grin, Sara took a sip of hot tea, suddenly feeling as if a weight were lifted from her shoulders. Switching identities was the perfect solution. Papa would *never* look for her in Wyoming, not under another name. Once she was settled and expecting McKay's heir, she'd write and

inform him of her state of marital bliss. Certainly
Papa couldn't object too strongly to her marrying
a rancher. Her uneasy conscience settled at the
thought of what a good wife she would make for
this Mr. McKay. He would thank his lucky stars
that God had sent him Sara. She would cook and
clean and be the best wife any man could possibly hope for, even if Walker should be—and she
sincerely hoped he wasn't—a bit on the beastly
side.

"What about my folks? They expect me to
write once I'm settled with McKay."

"Go with Rodney and don't write, not right
away. Mail takes a long time; they won't be concerned for a while. Write the letter but forget to
mail it. When the letter returns, several more
weeks will have passed, and you can say you're
sorry it's taken so long to write, but you forgot to
post it and then, lo and behold, you neglected to
apply proper postage and the letter came back."

"When I tell them I've married Rodney instead
of McKay, postage will be the last thing on their
minds."

"I suppose so. But you can deal with that when
it happens." Pressing her lips to her teacup in
thought, Sara murmured, "What are the odds
this might work?"

Olivia gazed back expectantly. "A million to
one?"

"That good?"

"Two million to one? If we can pull it off at all,
it will be a miracle."

Olivia slid to the front of her chair, her desperate brown eyes searching Sara's.

"I have a wedding dress. It's small and you can have it if you can wear it." She looked Sara up and down. "It's nothing fancy, but it would look bad if you didn't show up with one."

"I'll squeeze into it." Even if she couldn't, she could let it out, if needed.

Olivia stared at Sara as if sizing up her seriousness. "Let's do it."

Sara smiled, ignoring the strange lurch in her stomach.

"Done."

Leaning across the table, she shook hands with Olivia Mallory and sealed the bargain.

A gust of hot wind greeted Sara as she stepped from the train at Laramie station. It snatched a lock of red hair from its clip and sent it flying above her head. She tried unsuccessfully to rein it in while holding her skirts.

Stepping from the bottom stair onto the ground, she searched the milling crowd, her heart fluttering wildly.

The station teemed with activity—mothers and fathers greeting returning children; sweethearts embracing, caught in the moment of blissful reunion, unashamed of their public displays of affection. Families bumped against cattle ranchers and farmhands waiting for shipments of supplies. Sara searched the crowd for Walker McKay. Olivia couldn't provide a physical description of the man, beyond the possibility of disfigurement from his recent accident. Sara's eyes leapt from face to face, trying to match the features she'd formed in her mind—tall, strong, and rugged. Unfortunately, the description matched a number of men, all of whom paid her not the slightest notice.

A man, a gun in a holster slung low and heavy from his belt, made his way through the milling crowd, his eyes searching the platform. His cragged features were ringed in dust, his clothes spattered with— Sara recoiled. Horse dung! When his gaze locked on Sara, he offered a tobacco-stained grin.

Drats. Her worst fears realized. Her new husband was grizzly *and* old. Her future husband—not quite the man of her dreams—came to a stop a foot away. He was four inches shorter than she was, and as he removed his hat she saw that he was as old as Papa.

That rotten Olivia had lied! The wench had needed someone to marry this shriveled old pipsqueak so she wouldn't have to. Sara checked her temper, telling herself she could still back out. She'd just admit what she'd done and be on her way.

"Miss Olivia Mallory?" The tender excitement in his voice softened his countenance but did nothing to ease Sara's disappointment. "Is that you, girl?"

Truthfully, she *wasn't* Olivia Mallory. If there ever was a time to admit it, it was now, with the safety of the train and a return trip no more than five quick steps behind her. But the days spent traveling to Laramie would certainly have given the detectives ample time to have located Julie's apartment; traveling back would mean almost certain capture. It didn't take a crystal ball for her to know that Papa would banish her to Uncle Brice's forever.

"Yes," she said, her voice betraying her hesitance.

The old man's smile spread across his worn face, deepening the etched lines. "Y're finally here. And y're even purtier than I'd pictured." He appeared barely able to contain himself as he replaced his hat and reached for her bag. "This way, ma'am."

It took every ounce of resolve for Sara to drag her feet across the station, past the young, handsome men with lovers and wives, past the young children on the platform engrossed with a dead coyote near the tracks. What would her children look like? Former images of a perfect home life with a handsome husband and strong, beautiful children gusted off with the hot wind. How Papa and Wadsy would laugh. Even Abe would tease her about this one.

Then she berated herself for her foolishness. If she started being picky now, she might as well reconcile herself to being an old maid. Her dream, however bittersweet, was about to be realized and all she could see was flaws—a few missing teeth and battle scars. A lot more years than she'd anticipated. She looked at the man, her heart sinking. Could he even produce an heir?

With newfound resolve, she caught up to him as he was unsuccessfully maneuvering himself and her bag into a buggy. She gathered the nerve to ask him how long the ride to his ranch was when a particularly strong gust snatched his hat and sent it skittering into the crowd. Without thinking, Sara lifted her skirts and ran to catch it, following it as it skipped along.

The hat bounced merrily in front of her and she broke into a semi-trot to catch up with it. The hat paused momentarily as if to tease her, then bounced on. A break in the wind lent her hope and she made an ungraceful lunge, propelling herself forward at the very moment a set of dusty boots appeared on the opposite side of the hat. Unable to break her fall, she lurched forward into the waiting arms of a man who caught her with surprising grace and easiness.

Flaming with embarrassment, Sara mustered her composure and raised her gaze to meet two of the clearest blue eyes she had ever seen. Her gasping breath caught in her throat and for a moment she forgot to breathe. Arms—gloriously strong and as stout as oak posts—casually lifted her to her feet and then reached down to recover the hat. Her eyes were held captive by his long, jeans-clad legs, slim hips, and broad shoulders. This was the man she'd pictured would meet her, sweep her into his arms, and marry her.

He straightened and brushed a lock of curly black hair off his forehead. His eyes followed the length of her gown down and back up before he extended the hat. "This must be yours?"

"Oh, it's not my hat," she said, amazed at how just a brief jog across the station could make her feel so faint. The old man caught up to her. She tried to ignore him, but he reached over and took the hat from her. The stranger smiled and looked over at the old man knowingly. "It's his hat," she said, motioning to the older man, who was trying to adjust the unruly rebel back to the shape of his head. "Mr. McKay's hat."

Both men paused, and for a moment she was confused as they glanced at each other and winked. Was there a joke she was missing?

"What a coincidence. My name is also McKay. Walker McKay, to be exact. You must be Miss Mallory," he said in a deep, rich baritone. Sara could do no more than stare at the two men. *Two* Walker McKays? Olivia had lied about everything.

"I'm Sara—uh—Olivia Sara Mallory. But I don't understand. If he's Walker McKay," she said, pointing to the old man, "then you would be . . ."

"Heavens, girl, you must be worn to a nub from the train trip," the old man said, slapping his hands on his jeans and laughing.

The tall, handsome cowboy smiled. "Miss Mallory, I'd like you to meet my foreman, Sizemore Horatio—"

"You can call me S. H., ma'am. Pleasure to make yer acquaintance." The man bowed, sweeping his hat from his head. Sara stared wide-eyed.

"I'm Walker McKay." Electric-blue eyes focused on hers, and Sara thought for a moment that every ounce of energy had left her body.

If this was true, it changed everything. She shook off her shock and reached for his hand, breaking into a wide smile.

"Relieved—*pleased* to meet you, Mr. McKay." She drew a long breath and released it. He had no idea *how* pleased.

Chapter 4

"Is that Babygirl gonna stay in bed all day?" Wadsy glanced at the foyer clock, frowning. Sara was usually the first one at the breakfast table, cheeks aglow, eager to start a new day. It was well past sunup, and the girl was still in her room.

"You can't run after her every time she has a fit, Wadsy," Lowell muttered from his place at the head of the breakfast table. Lifting the paper, he shook it out. "Let her be. She'll be down when she's ready."

Wadsy cleared away the untouched meal, then busied herself in the kitchen until Will's resulting scowl sent her off to the parlor. Keeping an eye on the stairway, she dusted, pretending not to listen for the girl's soft footsteps. By late afternoon the temptation to comfort won out and, armed with Will's fresh-baked biscuits and hot tea, she crept up the back stairs to Sara's bedroom door, careful not to let Mr. Livingston hear her.

She rapped softly and got no response. "Honey, open up, now. Ain't no use a-starvin' to death over havin' to go to Brice's. It won't be that bad, you'll see."

Sara's door remained closed.

Babygirl was determined to make a body suffer. Wadsy balanced the tray on her hip, rattling the door handle.

"C'mon, Sara, open the door. Your mammy wansta talk to ya. I got tea." She cracked the door open to peek inside. The room was dark, the curtains drawn. "Lawsy me, you gonna grow to the mattress, honeychile. Get on out of the bed. Why, it's almost suppa time." Nudging the door open, she set the tray down on the floor and slid it through the narrow opening. "I'll leave it on the floor and ya can eat when you're ready."

Only silence met her efforts.

Straightening, Wadsy rose slowly and peeked around the half-open door. Finally entering, she shuffled to the window and pushed the drapes aside, tying them to the walls with braided gold fasteners. Surely that child hadn't climbed out the window again!

"Sara?" She turned around and found the bed empty. "You hidin' from your mammy?"

A faint breeze fluffed the bottoms of the heavy satin drapes, throwing a flicker of light across the untouched bed. A quick search of the room revealed nothing but absences. The silver brush was missing, as were Grace Livingston's antique ivory brooch and the gingham dress Wadsy had sewn for Sara to wear when she wanted to help weed the garden. The hook where the frock usually hung was conspicuously empty. Babygirl wouldn't leave and take that ole rag with her. Wadsy moved to the closet, where Sara's fine garments hung. Taffetas, silks—nothing plain for Babygirl. Now, why was that gingham gone and the others untouched?

Wadsy made a full sweep of the room. Also missing was the monogrammed travel bag that Sara's papa had bought her when she traveled with him to the opening ceremony for the first California railway station on the line. Wadsy remembered Sara's excitement before the trip as she laid out her best dresses in the trunk at the foot of her bed.

"Imagine," the girl had said with a sigh as she twirled around, a green silk evening gown clutched to her chest, flaming hair in wild disarray, "just *imagine* all the prospects, Wadsy! Handsome young cowboys with spurs and *guns*. Dangerous men on fast horses." Pausing, Sara had carefully laid the dress with the others. "I know he's there, Wadsy. He has to be . . . I couldn't stand coming home without having met my future husband."

"California ain't Boston, doll. Menfolk out there ain't seen a woman in years. Dirty, nasty men ain't gonna touch my Babygirl."

"Oh, Wadsy. I'll never get married if the man has to meet your standards. Don't you think it'll be wildly exciting out West?"

But, as always, Sara had returned unbetrothed.

Wadsy picked up the untouched tray, worried now. Mr. Livingston was gonna be powerful upset when he learned that Sara was missing. She dreaded telling him that his daughter's bed wasn't slept in the night before, partly because of the news itself and partly because she knew she would be reprimanded for taking tea to the pouting girl.

"Babygirl, you're gonna get your mammy in a mess of trouble," she muttered, closing the door behind her. "A *mess* of trouble."

Lowell started at Wadsy's knock, his leather chair squeaking. "What is it?" he asked, swiveling to face her. The nanny came in, carrying a tray of biscuits and tea. "Has Sara come out of her room yet?"

"No, sir, she ain't."

"Ah . . . tea. Thank you, Wadsy, but I'm very busy." He turned back to the mound of papers littering the desktop.

She set the tray on the polished desk and wrung her hands in her apron. "I know you ain't gonna like this, but—she's gone."

Lowell kept writing. "Who's gone?"

"I know I wasn't supposed to go up, but I did, and the window was open and her stuff is gone. Her bed wasn't slept in, neither."

Sighing, Lowell looked up. Sara's rebellion was hardly newsworthy. The chit sorely tested his patience, but he refused to give in to this recent show of defiance. He shuffled a stack of papers, then irritably shoved them aside. There were days when he would give his railroad to have Grace back to deal with this child.

"Where is she this time, Wadsy? Should I send Orville over to her cousin Eleanor's to see if she's hiding out there?"

"I don't know, sir. Do ya think she'da left for good? She was powerful upset."

"Certainly not. She's just out of sorts." He ran a finger along the inside of his heavily starched collar. "I can't buy her a husband, so I can't make her happy. She's got to settle down and have patience until the right man comes along."

He glanced at the nanny, who had been staring at the tea tray since she'd set it on the table.

"Give her until evening. If she doesn't come home by then, we'll start looking." Weary, he reached for a pencil. "Take the tray when you leave. I'm not hungry."

"Sir . . . you didn't touch your suppa or breakfast. A body got to eat . . ."

"Run along, Wadsy. We both have work to do."

Picking up the tray, the old woman shuffled toward the doorway. Before she could leave, Lowell spun the chair back to face her.

"I've tried, Wadsy. God knows I've tried." His face crumbled, bravado slipping. "What more can I do?"

"You're a good papa, sir. Babygirl'll be home in time for suppa—don't you fret none."

"Yes, you're right. She'll come home when she realizes no one loves her like family."

"Yes, sir. No one loves her more than us . . . she knows that."

* * *

Two days later, Lowell paced the study floor, fit to be tied. "Two days! My daughter's been missing for two days!" He'd aged a good ten years in those two days.

" 'Member your heart, sir." Abe poured sassafras tea, wiping a drip with a snow-white cloth before returning the pot to the silver tray.

"Heart, my foot." Lowell drew on his stogie and puffs of blue smoke hazed the room. "She'll be the death of me yet."

Abe fanned cigar smoke away from his nostrils. "Yessir."

Pausing before the window, Lowell watched the falling rain, his shoulders slumped with weariness. "Where is she, Abe? If anything's happened to her, I'll never forgive myself."

Setting a steaming cup on the desk, Abe said quietly, "You're makin' yourself sick, Mr. Livingston. You know the child's tendency to worry a soul to death afore she decides to come home. She'll be back when she's ready and not a minute sooner—no use frettin' yourself sick."

"But two days. *Two* days, and not a word. Are you certain you've checked with all of her friends? Is she with that giggly Liddy Snow? I wouldn't put it past those two girls to try and pull the wool over my eyes. It wouldn't be the first time."

Abe fussed with the cream and sugar bowls. "Orville done checked with the Montgomery girl, sir, and everybody else Sara knows—and a few she don't know. Ain't no one seen her in the past few days, but I feel in my bones she just fine, sir.

Try to drink a little of this tea. Gettin' sick ain't gonna help nothin'."

Lowell drew on the cigar, gesturing Abe's efforts aside. He couldn't eat or drink with Sara running around the countryside doing God knows what. Had she followed that German fellow she'd talked about the week before? He searched for a name but came up empty-handed. Or had she somehow hooked up with that dockworker again? After a while the candidates all blurred, a seemingly endless stream of handsome young swains who hadn't given a thought to marriage, only to what they could get from Sara's innocence.

A new idea hit him.

"The summer Cotillion—she wouldn't miss the Cotillion at the end of the month. Wadsy's been sewing her dress for months—if she misses that Cotillion . . ."

"No, she surely won't miss Cotillion, sir—but if she do, just means she ain't got all her meanness out yet."

"If she's not back in time for that ball, Abe, I'm calling in Pinkerton and his detectives."

Abe glanced away. "Yes, sir . . . you did that the last time."

"And they found her, didn't they? Had to go all the way to Philly to do it, but, by gum, they found her—selling flowers on the street corner like a regular hoyden. Her mama would sit up in her grave and shout if she knew that."

"Yes, sir, Miss Grace shorely would."

Turning away from the window, Lowell snubbed out his cigar. "You're right. All this worrying and not eating is making me sick. Have Will fry me up a couple of fatback sandwiches, and I'll have some of those cream potatoes."

"But the doctor says—"

"Don't remind me of the doctor! I know what the doctor says—he wants me to starve to death, that's what he wants. Go on, now, Abe—and tell Will not to be stingy with the butter on that sandwich."

"Yessir. Slav' on the butter. Be buildin' a pine box tomorrow," the old servant grumbled, turning around to leave.

"I heard that."

"Yessir."

When the door closed, Lowell reached for Grace's picture, which sat on his desk. His features softened. "Ah, Grace, what am I going to do? We've sired an outlaw. I do my best, but Sara's stubborn streak would put your papa's to shame. Doesn't matter what I do or say or buy her; our daughter's intent on ruining her life."

Memories flooded him as he traced the outline of the ornate silver frame, softly chuckling to himself. Sara and her mama were two peas in a pod. Grace had had the same fiery hair, fiery spirit, and ornery zest for life. Many a time Lowell had thrown his young, sassy wife over his shoulder and carried her around the house, singing "Amazing Grace" at the top of his lungs until her temper cooled. They'd have a good laugh, and then she'd look at him with Sara's wide, trusting eyes and the rest of the afternoon would be lost. One time Grace had sat up three nights in a row nursing a sickly newborn kitten—

wouldn't hear of giving up on the runt of the lit-
ter. No one had been more surprised than Lowell
when the weak little animal made it. Gracie had
named the kitten Pertinacity before exhaustion
overtook her and she collapsed in Lowell's arms.
He'd carried her and the cat to bed, where they'd
both slept twenty-four hours through.

Yes, Gracie had had spunk. That was what
he'd loved about her. Much as he hated to admit
it, Sara came by hers naturally.

"Ah, Gracie," he whispered. "I miss you, ole
gal." Absently placing a two-fingered kiss on the
frame, he strode to the double doors and opened
them.

"Abe! I'm not waiting a minute longer! Get me
those Pinkerton detectives. By God, that girl's
gone too far this time!"

Closing the door, he rested his weary bulk
against it. *Sara, girl, where are you?*

Over a thousand miles away, Sara was fully
immersed in wedding plans. Walker had told her
in no uncertain terms that they should waste no
time in courting; the wedding should occur as
soon as possible. There was an impatience about
his request that she couldn't quite place, as if he
thought she might change her mind and return to
Boston. Leaving Spring Grass was the last thing
on her mind. Only two things occupied her mind:
planning a wedding and keeping her secret.

The ranch itself was enormous—thousands of
acres of hayfields and pastures, smooth hills and
gently rolling valleys. The homestead consisted
of the main house, a smaller house for the fore-

man and his wife, a shed, a bunkhouse for the
ranch hands who handled the cattle, a large barn
for horses, hay, and equipment, and several small
pens used for keeping cattle or horses near the
barn. The house itself was grand: a large colonial
with five bedrooms—obviously a house built to
be filled with children. The only part of the ranch
that wasn't perfectly kept was a large flower garden behind the house that stood in disarray. Sara
hadn't asked Walker about it, and S. H. and
Sophie hadn't mentioned it.

Walker's ranch foreman and best friend, S. H.,
had insisted that Sara stay with him and Sophie,
his wife. So far, Sophie had been invaluable to
Sara, who, for all her zest and desire to be married, knew next to nothing about weddings
beyond what she'd read in books. Sophie volunteered to orchestrate the whole affair. Now they
sat in Sophie's tidy kitchen discussing the guest
list for the ceremony, which was only days away.
The register consisted of half the state—all
Walker's friends. Sara was determined they
would be hers, too, in a short time.

Sophie shook her head. "Poor Sadie Miller.
She'll bawl for days when she finds out Walker
chose a mail-order bride over her." Walker's
white-haired housekeeper couldn't contain a
chuckle. "Of course, I'd have to say every man in
the county would make the same choice." She
wrote Sadie's name on a growing list of families
from the surrounding area who would be invited
to attend.

"Why didn't Walker consider any of the
women on this list?" Sara picked up the sheet of

paper, scanning the column of names. "Who's Katie Brown? Is she single?"

"Katie? She's single, and a nice enough girl, I suppose. Walker's known her since the two of them were knee-high to a grasshopper. But I think he considers Katie a friend—more like a sister than a wife."

Sara sighed. It seemed to her that Walker could have his pick of women, yet he'd chosen a woman he'd never even seen. "There has to be one woman in the whole state of Wyoming that he doesn't have sisterly feelings for." She couldn't understand how any woman with an ounce of sense could let Walker McKay get away. Her face flushed and her knees turned to jelly whenever she saw him striding from the house to the barn with long, assured steps, or when she sneaked a peek at him riding out to work in the morning. Her excitement was twinged with worry, too, considering that he wanted nothing more than a broodmare. Since arriving, she had done and said everything she could to reassure him that she was delighted to be at Spring Grass, even gone out of her way to show him she was thrilled and eager to be his bride. Yet she felt his hesitancy—almost as if he wanted to avoid being tangled in love. Maybe he didn't want to fall in love, but she would soon change that.

"You're gettin' a fine man," Sophie said, breaking into Sara's daydream of changing Walker's mind and heart.

"But he could have picked any single woman—"

"He had his pick and he picked you." Getting

up from her chair, Sophie refilled Sara's lemonade, her red, roughened hands proof of her workload.

Sara sighed. "But he really didn't pick me, did he? I mean, he *picked* me, but actually he only chose a mail-order bride, which wasn't really *picking* me. It could have been anyone who responded to the ad, and probably many more women responded than he could shake a stick at, but he *did* pick me— Oh!" The more she talked, the less sense she made.

"Has he been married before?" It wouldn't matter if he had been—right now, she wasn't picky.

"No, you'll be the first Mrs. McKay. Might be best if I told you about Trudy, though, so you won't go asking him and getting him upset. She done a terrible thing to him—he's real touchy on the subject."

"Trudy?" A knot rose in Sara's throat at the thought of a hitch in her plans.

"Walker was engaged to her couple of years back. She ran off with a hat salesman a few hours before the wedding—left him standing at the altar, poor boy. In front of his friends and neighbors." Sophie picked up the wedding list, her eyes running down the columns. "Ran off with a man who sold bowlers, so I wouldn't mention anything but cowboy hats to Walker, if I were you." She tossed the list aside. "Needless to say, we were all shocked. Walker adored her and she humiliated him real good."

How could anyone be so cold? Sara wondered. Walker was ten times better than any man she'd tried to marry in Boston. It would take fifty Joe Mancusos to make one Walker McKay. Desert this man, this handsome, wonderful man, for a hat salesman? Trudy's actions were inconceivable.

"I best warn ya, too, not to go anywhere near that garden behind the house. That was Trudy's garden, the place where the wedding reception was to take place, and Walker ain't allowed anyone near it since the day she left."

"I was wondering about that garden. It's the only part of the ranch that isn't just beautiful. What a shame to let such beauty go to waste."

Sophie sat back down at the table, smiling. "Speakin' of beauty, what about you, young'un? Ya haven't said much about yourself. 'Pears you could have your pick of any red-blooded young man. What made you decide to be a mail-order bride?"

The weight of Sara's ruse was heavy. For days now, she'd considered telling Walker about the switch. But if he sent her away, she would never forgive herself. She was comfortable with Sophie, but not enough to confide her secret. Better to wait until after the wedding, when less could go wrong.

"I've never wanted anything but to be a good wife and mother, to raise children and keep a home for a loving man." She paused, deciding to keep as close to the truth as possible. "But when my dear uncle wrote, telling about his travels throughout the scenic West, I couldn't help but think of how wonderful it would be to raise my children in the country, surrounded by mountains and prairies and oceans of waving grass.

Wyoming has been everything I expected. The whole train ride here—ever since I knew I would be coming—I imagined everything would be big, but it's even bigger than I thought! The ranch is far more wonderful than I could ever dream."

A sweat bead trickled down the back of Sara's neck and into the nape of her blouse. Wadsy, Abe, and Papa all said she had the chatters—talked all the time. Was that true? The heat in the kitchen was insufferable. "The men in Boston are so intent on their work they don't have time for a family and . . . I wanted a man—a rancher—who would love me and his children, and not always be at the office or at the train yard . . ."

She bit her lip. The train yard was almost too much information. What if somehow Sophie linked her to the railroad and to Lowell Livingston? Yet how could she? Sara was no longer Sara Livingston; she was Olivia Sara Mallory, telling Walker that she preferred her middle name because it was that of her deceased mother. Being called Sara avoided confusion and made her feel less like a fraud. She looked up from her hands to see Sophie looking directly at her.

"Are you all right, dear? You look flushed."

"It's very hot in here. May I have another glass of lemonade?"

S. H. breezed in through the back door, removing his hat. "You set where you are, Mama. I'll pour the pretty lady another glass of lemonade. It's so hot out there, trees are beggin' dogs for relief," he said, plucking Sara's empty glass for a refill.

Sophie blushed at S. H.'s kiss on her forehead

as he passed by on the way to the sink. The love between the two had been evident from the first day Sara met them. The couple had spent nearly all their lives in the log cabin at Spring Grass, and were obviously as enraptured with each other as they had been when they first came to work for Mitch Walker forty years ago. It was exactly the kind of relationship that Sara wanted.

How long would it take before she could begin trusting these people enough to let them, and Walker, in on the secret? Her biggest fear was that she would say the wrong thing, or do something that would alert them or Walker to her secret, and she would be sent away. That just couldn't happen. She loved the long days at Spring Grass, the cool nights on the prairie, lying in her soft feather-bed, listening to the murmuring cattle, knowing bright stars twinkled high overhead. She loved the clear blue skies and the courteous cowhands, who were careful to take their hats off as she approached to say hello. Most of all, she found she was already falling deeply in love with Walker McKay, although she barely knew him.

S. H. placed a full glass in front of Sara and she smiled. "Thank you, S. H. With all this planning, and the wedding only a week away, I haven't had time to catch my breath."

The old man grinned. "Don't worry, miss. Sophie and me'll take care of everything. We're just so darned tickled to have you, we cain't sleep for thinking about the weddin'."

"You've both been wonderful," she said, softly stifling a yawn. "Maybe I'll lie down for a while. I'm a little weary."

"You go right ahead, young'un." Sophie got up from the table, swatting S. H. away from the apple pie cooling on the windowsill. "Think I'll go out and see if Potster needs any help at the bunkhouse."

"Potster can feed the men without your help," S. H. complained good-naturedly. "Too many cooks in the kitchen spoil the taters." Sophie giggled.

Sara excused herself from the table and went into the back room.

Sophie watched the girl leave, shaking her head. "What do you think of her, S. H.?"

"I think she's exactly what Walker needs. They'll make a fine baby to take over Spring Grass. Once Walker slows down and pays a little attention, I think he'll notice that."

Frowning, Sophie picked up Sara's glass and carried it to the sink. "You don't think there's something odd about a young woman who's that pretty and well mannered wanting to be a mailorder bride?"

"Now, Sophie," S. H. teased, tweaking her under her chin. "There you go thinking about Trudy again. Miss Mallory wouldn't do that to Walker. Maybe you should be laying down for a while to get those crazy idears outta your head." He stole another brief kiss. "Yore man's a-starvin' and here you are worryin' 'bout Walker. He'll take care of himself. Stop yore frettin'."

"I don't know, S. H.—I'm real troubled about this—" She jumped when S. H. smacked her on the backside. "Go on, now," she yelled, snapping a rolled-up dishcloth at his rump.

He fled, flashing her a grin.

Sitting down at the table, Sophie stared at Sara's closed bedroom door. What was it that had her on edge? The girl seemed warm and honest. Her manners were faultless, her tone that of a woman of higher education. She should be happy that such a find had practically fallen into Walker's lap. Her eyes traveled back to the guest list.

So why wasn't she?

Late that afternoon, Walker watched S. H. from the corner of his eye. They'd been stringing fence for hours, and he could tell the old man was dying to ask what Walker thought of his new bride-to-be.

What *did* he think of her? Sara Mallory was pleasing to the eye, no doubt about that. She'd be pleasing in bed: curves in all the right places, lips right for kissing, all womanly fluff and softness. He found himself looking forward to the marriage bed. But he hadn't changed his mind about love.

The bout with the bull had convinced him that he needed an heir, but the concession hadn't softened his stance about women. Walker refused to say anything about Sara or the wedding, though S. H. was fair to bursting to hear what he thought of her. But S. H. should know that Walker was too much like his pa, not willing to talk about things he didn't find necessary to discuss.

S. H. took off his hat and let a wisp of wind cool the crown of his damp, balding head.

Bearing down on the posthole digger, Walker

twisted the rusty iron through the topsoil and into the hard-packed ground below. The muscles in his arms quivered with the weight of the strain. He grimaced when he knew S. H. wasn't watching, his injured ribs screaming for relief. He wasn't going to let up on his duties, get soft and lie around the house like an invalid. Besides, if the fence weren't repaired before fall, the herd would wander off into the early-winter snow-falls. He'd rather mend the fence now than spend hours slogging through a foot of snow searching for lost cattle.

He let up on the digger, drawing a deep breath. S. H. was staring at him again. The two men's eyes met—one pair brown, older, more experienced; the other, sky-blue clear, stubbornly unrelenting.

Walker leaned on the digger, buying a few minutes of rest. "You've been staring at me for a good five minutes now. Is there something on your mind?"

S. H. threw the hat back on his head and bent over to pick up the post. "Just wondering about the weddin' an' all. You ain't said a thing about her since she got here."

"She'll do." Walker lifted his hat and ran a hand through his sweat-soaked hair.

"What about the weddin'? Her'n Sophie've been working hard puttin' it t'gether. Ain't you gonna help?"

"Nope."

"Ain't you being a little hard-nosed? Sara's a fine woman, looks to me like—"

"Never had a neighbor refuse to show up for our barbecue yet."

S. H. glanced up, looking confused. "You mean for a weddin'?"

"I said for a barbecue." The digger met its mark and Walker pulled it up, depositing the last of the dirt in a pile to the side of the new hole.

"What are you talkin' about? You don't mean you—"

"I mean I'm telling everyone I'm having a barbecue. I'm not making a fool of myself in front of the whole town again." Walker motioned for S. H. to bring the post over, and the two men centered it and drove it into the hole. "If the bride shows up, I'm in fine shape. If she doesn't, the town will never be the wiser. They'll have a good meal and go home."

"If that don't beat all—Sara's a sweet little gal. She's not gonna disappoint you—you got to give 'er a chance."

"I gave the last one a chance, S. H. Look where it left me."

S. H. took his hands off the post and turned to face Walker.

"Does Sophie know about this?"

"She does, but she doesn't like it. Don't see where she has much say in the matter, though. I will not be humiliated again."

S. H. straightened and frowned at Walker.

"When are you going to get Trudy out o' your head? And what makes you think that Sara's gonna let you turn her weddin' day into some kind of country hoedown? I've been on this good earth long enough to know she ain't gonna like having her weddin' turned into a barbecue."

Walker shrugged. His mind was made up. "She's getting married, isn't she?" He drove the posthole digger into the ground again. "That's all she wants. Women don't care what's done as long as they get that ring. I don't expect her to like it. That's why I asked Sophie not to tell her."

S. H. stared at him in disbelief. "Son, you're askin' for a heap of trouble—you know that."

Walker refused to reply as he tightened the line around the post, then moved himself and the equipment down the line.

Chapter 5

Sara caressed the large four-poster bed with its dark, masculine-looking spread. In a scant few hours she would be sharing it with Walker McKay. Her heart thrummed against her rib cage as Sophie stuck the last few hairpins in place.

Her pulse raced feverishly through her whirling head. Today was it: her wedding day. The day she'd dreamed about from the moment she was old enough to whisper the words "I do."

After sliding another pin into place, Sophie loosened a few strands of hair. "There—I think that softens your face."

Sara caught a glimpse of herself in the long mirror. Her eyes shone with barely contained impatience as she prepared to take vows that would forever bind her to a man she hardly knew. Why didn't that concern her? She was marrying a complete stranger, yet she felt as if she'd known him forever. He barely glanced at her over the breakfast table each morning, despite her efforts at conversation, but she watched his lean, tanned hands as he buttered a biscuit, fascinated by their strength. She loved the way that one lock of unruly hair fell across his forehead at the oddest times.

Stepping back to inspect her handiwork, Sophie beamed. "You're about the prettiest thing I ever laid eyes on."

"Will Walker think so?" Sara hadn't seen her husband-to-be all day, and only briefly the day before. Sophie said Walker and S. H. were busy, and it was bad luck for the bride to see the groom on her wedding day. She'd missed seeing Walker at the breakfast table this morning, missed him asking how she'd slept the night before. Not exactly pillow talk, but close enough for her.

She'd awakened to the sound of shouting voices outside her window as the last of the sawhorse tables was erected in the yard, and tablecloths and decorations were arranged. Five hours later, here she was, getting ready, while S. H. was busy a few doors away getting Walker ready for the big event.

Sara flew out of the chair and started dancing around the room, scooping up the dress that still lay on the bed, then holding it to her chest. "I can hardly believe it, Sophie! I'm going to be Mrs. Walker McKay!" Sara stopped twirling when she reached the mirror. Closer inspection of her face and hair set off a flutter of apprehension. "Are you *sure* I look all right?" The gown was simple, yet when she'd tried it on, it had fit as if it were made for her.

"You'll be the prettiest bride this town's ever seen. Any man would be proud to have you as a wife. You're so much prettier than—" Sophie broke off, color dotting her cheeks.

Sara turned to look at her. "Than Trudy?"

"Than Ettie Mae Simpson's daughter. That's a plain girl—even a fancy weddin' dress couldn't help."

Sara barely noticed Sophie's answer. She swayed back and forth in front of the mirror, entranced by her own reflection, imaging the ceremony, the flowers, and the music. Sophie had told her that Walker would take care of that end of the service, and she was happy that he wanted to be involved. It was his wedding, too, and she wanted the occasion to be perfect for both.

"It's going to be the most beautiful wedding ever," she said softly. "I wonder what kind of flowers Walker chose—oh, it doesn't really matter. He'll have lit candles, because what's a wedding without lit candles, and I"—she whirled, clutching her petticoats to her breast—"am the happiest bride in the whole world!"

Sophie frowned when a bobby pin dislodged and swung loosely on a stray curl. "If you don't hold still, we'll have to postpone the wedding, because I'll have to redo that hair."

The thought of anything interfering with her nuptials tempered Sara's enthusiasm, but it didn't stop her from picturing the wedding while Sophia patiently repaired the damage: guests dressed in their Sunday best, little boys in blue suits and spit-shined shoes, darling girls in frilly frocks and dainty footwear. All of them smiling congratulations, an aura of happiness surrounding the festive event. Champagne would flow, and they would dance until the wee hours of the morning.

Then Walker would scoop her up in his arms and carry her through the crowd, grinning at the catcalls, and— She wiggled when she thought of the way he'd looked at her the other day as she helped Sophie with the dishes. He *was* aware that she was a woman, though he'd failed to seize upon it yet.

"Hold still," Sophie complained around a mouthful of pins.

Sighing, Sara tried, but it was impossible to be still today. "I'll walk slowly down the stairs. He'll meet me at the bottom. The whole room will be able to do nothing but sit and stare because we are so perfect for each other—and they'll sense that. Everyone will know . . ." Sara paused. *Would* Walker's friends like her? Would they think that she was a gold digger, marrying Walker because he was rich and handsome? They couldn't be more wrong! What if no one liked her? The only people she knew in Wyoming were Walker, S. H., Sophie, and the occasional ranch hand she'd bumped into on her brief walks around the ranch.

Sara spun around to face Sophie. "Do you think they'll like me, Sophie? I mean *really* like me, not just pretend because it's my wedding and they have to be polite?"

Walker's extensive guest list showed that he was popular among the families who lived within the area. Until today, he had been the state's most eligible bachelor. What if the young women who'd had an eye on Walker were jealous and refused to be friends with her because she was an outsider?

Downstairs, she could hear the flurry of arriving guests. She glanced at the clock, surprised that people would be arriving nearly an hour before the wedding was scheduled to begin. She finished dressing to the sound of friendly voices as men, women, and children entered the house and were greeted by ranch hands and servants. Even the bout of unseasonable heat apparently hadn't deterred well-wishers and their eagerness to witness the McKay marriage ceremony.

A bubble of panic erupted in Sara's stomach. What if everyone compared her to Trudy? But that was impossible. She would never run away from marriage. Besides, whom would she run away with? She silently vowed to prove that she could fit in, that she could be the perfect wife and the perfect hostess. The perfect everything.

Sophie finished repinning her hair; then both women lifted the dress high over Sara's head, careful not to disturb Sophie's work. Sara's uncertainty about meeting the guests faded as Sophie fastened the long line of buttons up the back of the dress. Hooking the last fastener, the housekeeper paused for a moment and both women admired Sara's reflection.

"Simply beautiful."

"Not really, Sophie, but thank you anyway.

Every bride is most beautiful on her wedding day."

Sophie snorted. "Etta Mae's daughter wasn't."

Downstairs, the voices grew louder as guests continued to arrive. Above the din, Sara heard a door open down the hall where S. H. was helping Walker into his wedding attire.

"Sophie?" S. H.'s voice cut through the noise. Sophie rolled her eyes and stepped over to open the door.

"What?" she yelled back.

Sara grinned at the shouted exchange.

"She still here? Walker says he's not puttin' this blame coat on till he's sure she's—" Sophie slammed the door shut before S. H. finished his inquiry.

Sara's smile dissolved as she walked over and sat down on the side of the bed. Tears shimmered close to the surface. How could Walker be so insensitive? Of course they weren't in love, but did he have to be so crude?

She stared at Sophie questioningly. "Was that necessary? Does Walker actually think I would walk out—now? This late? How could he think that I would run away?"

"It may not be Walker, honey. It could be S. H.'s misplaced sense of humor—you know he likes to tease. Don't fret your pretty head none." Sophie rearranged a stray hairpin, securing it more tightly. "Dry those eyes, child. You don't want your face to be all blotchy."

Sighing, Sara got up. She wasn't sure what that exchange had been about, but she couldn't let it ruin the day. Slipping on a pair of high satin boots, she bent to lace them. What was she worried about? In less than an hour she would be Mrs. Walker McKay, and she could start working to win her husband's heart.

Sophie took her by the shoulders when she straightened. "Be patient with Walker. He's a good man, but you've got to bear in mind that he *is* a man, and sometimes he's going to be stubborn and occasionally seem blind." Her knowing eyes were filled with wisdom. "Things might not always be the way you want at first. There'll be days when you wonder how you ever got into this mess, but you'll have to remember that Walker's been a bachelor a long time, been real hurt by a woman and it's still stuck in his craw. Things'll work out, but you're gonna need the patience of Job."

"I'm used to hardheaded men. Papa is as stubborn as ragweed," Sara murmured. For a moment she wished Lowell were here to witness the wedding, to see how happy she was going to be. She didn't expect the marriage to go smoothly at first. There would be awkward moments, especially when she told Walker the truth—but that wouldn't be today. Sara couldn't think of a single thing that could spoil this day, short of the wedding not happening at all. But Walker could relax; she wasn't going anywhere but down those stairs at the appointed time.

The two women turned when they heard the door down the hall open again. Sara held her breath until two pairs of booted footsteps echoed toward the stairs. She glanced at Sophie.

"Just remember, honey, it's your wedding day.

No matter what happens, the Good Lord is watchin' after you."

Whirling, Sara gave her a hug. "Nothing could ruin this day, Sophie."

The housekeeper clucked as the clock in the hall chimed, signaling the hour had arrived. Sara straightened, holding still as Sophie adjusted the crown of flowers over her brow. "You go out there and knock 'em dead, young'un."

Late-afternoon sunshine streamed through the stained-glass window at the end of the hallway when Sara stepped out of the bedroom with Sophie carrying her train. The music faded into clapping as the musicians struck up a tune Sara didn't recognize. She paused, cocking an ear to identify the song. It certainly wasn't the wedding march. She crept down the hallway, Sophie close behind. Her petticoats rustled as she halted at the top of the stairs, drawing a deep breath. Laughing voices floated up the staircase; boots scraped back and forth across the floor. Music swelled and she stepped down onto the top stair.

"Remember," Sophie whispered, "don't let nothin' bother you today. It'll get better, given enough time."

Sara glanced over her shoulder with a hesitant smile. How strange to play "Turkey in the Straw" at a wedding. Was it Walker's favorite? Gathering her skirts around her, she continued her descent.

Halfway down, Sara paused, shocked at what she saw below. People dressed in everyday muslins and calicos were milling about, cups of punch in their hands. Others danced, unaware that the ceremony had begun. There must be a mistake. The reception was never before the wedding.

She spotted a group of men talking and laughing with a man wearing a black collar. The clergy—but his Bible was nowhere in sight. He seemed to be in the middle of a funny story. Shouldn't Walker tell him the service was starting? Shouldn't he know? Where *was* Walker anyway?

She stepped down another two steps, assessing the crowd. Walker was coming across the room, hurrying to meet her at the bottom of the stairs. Now whispers made their way around the room; people paused in mid-sentence to stare.

Walker reached the bottom of the steps as the music died away. The lead fiddler spotted Sara, his bow dropping to his side while he stared. One by one, the other musicians, confused without direction, allowed the song to fade.

The silence was deafening. Sara knew she must look like a wide-eyed screech owl as she met the bewildered gazes of the wedding guests, all equally speechless. The band members had dropped their instruments to their laps.

Sara turned to look at Walker, who calmly awaited her at the bottom of the stairs.

"Keep movin', darlin'." Sophie nudged her forward. Sara started, forgetting for a moment that she was the bride—the center of attention. Her legs had forgotten how to move.

Walker attempted a smile, but failed. Instead, he extended his arm with a hopeful look.

Navigating the final two steps, she slipped her

arm through his, murmuring under her breath, "Why are they looking at me like that?"

"Keep walking. I'll explain later."

"Hey, Walker, who's the bride?" a voice called from across the room.

"Is this a *wedding*? You should have warned us this was gonna be a dress-up occasion. I'da worn my Sunday suit," a second male voice chimed in.

Sara heard her own soft intake of air. Her heart raced as Walker maneuvered her gently through the crowded room.

"They don't *know*, do they?"

"They're starting to suspect."

It wasn't the nicest thing Walker could have done, but Sara thought she understood why. Trudy again. This time he wanted to make certain the bride showed up before he faced his friends and neighbors. Well, the bride was here and more than willing to overlook the slight. So what if folks didn't know they'd come to a wedding? That didn't make the ceremony any less binding.

They drew closer to the stone fireplace, and faces gradually melted away until there was no one in the world but Sara Livingston and Walker McKay.

She couldn't ask for a better man than he. Young, brash, wildly handsome, strong, smart, and ambitious. The road to matrimony had been long and at times had seemed endless. But now she knew what Wadsy had meant when she said, "When that one man show up, Babygirl, you gonna feel it clean down to your toes."

Well, Wadsy, what I feel at this moment goes clean down to China.

Smiling, she tightened her hold on Walker's arm, then whispered, "Coward." She caught his boyish grin from the corner of her eye.

"Invited the preacher, didn't I?"

"Does he know he's about to officiate at a wedding?"

"He will soon enough."

Walker and Sara stopped before the clergyman. Though smiling, the older man looked a bit confused.

"Got your Bible with you, John?"

"Er . . . why, it's in the buggy. Do I need it?"

"Yes, sir. We're about to have a wedding."

Cheers broke out as the startled preacher quickly made his way out of the room. Well-wishers gathered around Sara, vying for introductions. Walker accepted good-natured backslaps and ribbing, his tanned face flushed by all the excitement.

"Didn't think you had it in ya, son!"

"If I'd known I was coming to a weddin', I'd have duded up!"

Women voiced mock complaints about how they weren't able to show off their newest dresses. Smiling, Sara promised there would be many more McKay parties in the future.

"There will be?" Walker asked as she passed him on her way to greet a group of women her age.

"That's all right, isn't it?" She hadn't thought to ask him, but the McKay house was big and roomy, ideal for community socials—and she loved to entertain. The Livingstons' Christmas parties were the talk of Boston.

Reverend John Baird returned with his Bible prominently tucked beneath his arm, and the rather unconventional festivities finally began.

"Good friends, we delight in the marriage of . . . uh . . ." The preacher paused, blushing, and leaned close to Sara. "What's your name, dear?" he whispered.

"Sara," she quietly replied.

". . . in Walker and Sara's marriage today, and let us never forget the seriousness of the vows this couple is about to exchange."

The crowd quieted as the ceremony began. It wasn't the marriage Sara had dreamed about. Outside the window, ranch hands turned the roasting meat over open spits. Household help shooed hungry hands and flies away from the steaming bowls of corn on the cob and parsley potatoes lining the long rows of cloth-covered tables. The smell of baking bread drifted from the kitchen while younger children scampered about on the lawn, kicking a ball as Sara and Walker repeated their simple vows.

"To love, honor, and obey, till death do us part."

Sara knew that when she was very old, she would recall the scent of lilacs blooming outside the window, and remember the exact moment that her dream was realized. She'd recall the slight, uncertain tremor in Walker's voice while he repeated the vows in a deep baritone, the brief warmth of his touch when he slid a simple gold band on the third finger of her trembling left hand.

The McKay parlor wasn't the church she'd

attended since birth. And there weren't a lot of flowers, just a bouquet of daisies that someone— probably Sophie—had placed on the parlor table. There wouldn't be a large, lavishly decorated wedding cake waiting to be cut, or a garter thrown, champagne toasts, or Wadsy, Abe, and Papa in the crowd, eyes brimming with love, wishing her the best.

But it *was* her wedding—the happiest day of her life—and she would do anything she could to erase the uncertainty in Walker's voice, the haunted look in those blue eyes. It wouldn't happen today or tomorrow. But in time, he would love her. She'd make sure of that.

Then it was over. She was married; had the prized gold band on her left hand. S. H. engulfed her in a bear hug, nearly squeezing the life out of her while a beaming Sophie looked on. The whole room was buzzing with congratulations, everyone wanting a turn at the newlyweds.

"Can't say I've ever been more surprised," Tom Howell confessed, pumping Walker's hand.

Walker's smile was modest. "Me neither, Tom."

"Walker." A pouting blonde approached, her quivering bottom lip hung low. Sara felt a twinge of panic. "How could you—a mail-order bride? Couldn't you at least have given the local girls a chance?"

"And have every man in the county mad at me?" He winked at her. "Seth Olson would nail my hide to the barn if I'd stolen you."

"Seth?" Her eyes shifted to the tall, rawboned farmer talking with a group of men. "He doesn't know I exist." But a speculative smile now lightened her face.

Walker moved Sara on to shake hands with the other guests. Before she knew it, she was being whisked away by a man Walker had introduced as Frank Gillens.

"You sure did make a pretty bride today. You don't suppose that you could give Frank a little ol' kiss." When he leaned closer, Sara could smell liquor on his breath.

"Frank Gillens! I been lookin' all over for you." S. H. stepped in, slapping Frank on the back good-naturedly. "Let's go out back and talk some cattle."

"But I was talkin' to the beautiful bride—"

Walker rescued her, giving S. H. a wink. "I'll take care of that for you, Frank."

Drawing her aside, her new husband introduced her to a man who was the exact opposite of the handsome rancher. Small in stature, balding, with pale skin, the man wore wire-rimmed glasses, which he had taken off to clean as Walker and Sara approached. "Caleb, I'd like you to meet Sara Mallory."

"McKay," Sara reminded him under her breath.

"McKay," he said quickly. "Sara, my good friend, accountant, and banker, Caleb Vanhooser."

"Extremely pleased to meet you," Caleb greeted her, returning his glasses and grasping her hand solidly. "You could have knocked me over with a feather when I realized Walker was getting married today."

"Yeah." Walker smiled at his bride. "Me, too."

Shortly after the meal, Sara dispensed with ceremony. Discarding her wedding attire, she donned a calico dress and moved through the rows of tables outside, pouring coffee, offering pie, and being the genial hostess. When Walker saw that, he pulled her aside.

"What are you doing?"

She gazed up at him, wide-eyed. "Serving our guests."

"You're not supposed to 'serve our guests.' It's your wedding."

Reaching for his hand, she smiled. "Yours, too."

Ignoring her teasing banter, he took her arm and ushered her to a chair and sat her down. Sara knew better than to protest, but she had hoped to share a few private moments with him. Women crowded around Sara and her hopes were dashed as Walker moved on, checking over his shoulder to make sure she'd stayed put. Sara watched him disappear, fielding questions from the guests. But the thought of what was to come pacified her, and she settled in to await the coming hours as Walker McKay's bride.

Dusk streaked the reddened sky, and lanterns were lit. Musicians stepped to the wooden platform and began taking their instruments out of cases. The sounds of fiddles and guitars filled the warm spring air.

Standing beside the gazebo, Walker chatted with friends who chided him about the surprise celebration.

"What gives, McKay? All these months and you never let on you had something like her— you old fox!"

"Figured you was bound to stay single the rest of your life."

"Bull changed your mind, did he?"

The men chortled, one reaching out to tap the angry scar still evident on Walker's left cheek.

"Darn near got yourself killed—you're lucky to get a second chance."

"Where have you been hiding this little beauty?"

Walker's eyes followed his bride, being waltzed around the dance floor by yet another man. Bride. Wife. That was going to take some getting used to.

"Safe from you coyotes."

The men threw jovial arm punches. "At least none of us sell bowler hats," Pete Haskell razzed.

Walker took the affable ribbing in stride, his eyes on a radiant Sara. He couldn't dispute the fact that his bride was a desirable woman. Her eyes sparkled, her laughter filling the spring air. Something stirred inside him, something he hadn't felt in a year. Something he didn't want right now. "Yeah, if I knew where that salesman was right now, I'd give him a hundred bucks."

The men hooted, stepping aside as a group of energetic young children burst through the crowd.

"Folks, gather around," S. H. hollered. "Time to cut the cake!"

Walker watched a smile light Sara's face when Sophie emerged from the house carrying a large, three-tiered wedding cake. He silently thanked Sophie for her amazingly adaptable skills. She'd made a wedding cake faster than the average woman could cut one. The smile faded. What kind of groom would have forgotten the cake?

The customary exchange took place between the happy couple. Sara sliced the cake and fed Walker a bite. He did the same, his eyes meeting hers over the tip of the fork.

It was late when guests began departing. Parents loaded children into buckboards and wagons, while others, reluctant to give up, danced beneath the full moon. The musicians seemed ready to play all night, if necessary.

The bride had disappeared upstairs earlier. Walker stood beside the barn, smoking a cheroot, his eyes focused on the lamp burning in the upstairs window. Sara would be getting ready for bed, brushing her hair, putting on a white silken gown.

The preliminaries were over—all he had to do now was produce an heir.

Desire rose strong and unchecked in him. He hadn't been with a woman in months, and he had never slept with strangers. Sara was a stranger— a desirable, young stranger. The ten years between them didn't seem like much until he looked at her. The trick would be to allow her into his life but keep a safe distance from falling too hard and being burned again. A man didn't have to love a woman to live with her. He could spend the next fifty years with her in the house and never give her his heart. Sara was young, innocent—a loaded keg of dynamite if he weren't careful. Still, the deed was done. He and Sara Mallory were man and wife. There was no going back now, even if he could.

Tossing the cigar aside, he ground it out with the tip of his boot. *Show time, McKay.*

When he tapped on the bedroom door, Sara answered with a soft "Come in."

Candlelight spilled over the pristine sheets. His bride was sitting in the middle of the bed, her hair falling to her waist, waiting for him. Her gown left no doubt about her gender—or her intent. Soft, rounded breasts and satin skin peeked through the sheer, gauzy material. Olivia Sara McKay's gaze fastened on him boldly, issuing a silent but unmistakable invitation.

He took it. Closing the door, he stripped off his tie as he covered the few steps to the bed. Darned if he didn't feel like a kid on his first mating. But he wasn't a kid—she was. *Try to remember that, McKay.*

"Are the guests gone?" she asked.

"There's a few still dancing." He glanced at her, unbuttoning his shirt. He was surprised when she watched, her eyes brimming with interest. Peeling the shirt off, he tossed it on the chair atop her wedding gown.

"Oh . . . you have *hair* on your chest."

Self-conscious, he rubbed his belly. "That a problem?"

"No, not at all." She slid out of bed, padding over to him. Meeting his gaze, she smiled. "Here, let me." When he frowned, she explained softly, "It's the wife's duty, isn't it?"

The thought set off a reaction he was power-less to curb. "I believe it is."

Her hand slipped to his belt buckle, gently freeing it from the loopholes. Slipping it from around his waist, she lightly touched kisses along the rim of his jaw. The sensual foreplay had the desired effect. His hands came around her waist, drawing her closer, allowing her to feel his appreciation. Their mouths briefly touched; then his closed over hers fully. Standing on tiptoe, she succumbed, deepening the embrace.

He'd been worried about making love to her; afraid he wouldn't know how to handle an inexperienced woman, but this woman feared nothing.

"Am I too bold?" she asked, hesitancy creeping into her voice.

"No, ma'am," he whispered.

"Good," she whispered back. "I only want to please you."

"I don't think we have a problem," he teased, amazed at the needy breathlessness he'd heard in her voice. And in his. He thought the man was supposed to be the aggressor on the wedding night. Not that he cared—it was nice to have her take the lead. He just hadn't experienced the pleasure that often.

She kissed him again, her fingers working the snap on his trousers. Her agility made him wonder if she was as virginal as he anticipated. When she pulled him toward the bed, he followed like a sheep to slaughter.

He stepped out of his trousers and pitched

them on the chair as well. Climbing beneath the cool, sun-dried sheets, he was aware of the sounds of "The Missouri Waltz" drifting through the open window. He doubted he'd ever hear the melody again without remembering this night and this woman. Olivia Sara McKay was the woman who was about to conceive his heir.

Sara lay back on her pillow, gazing at him.

"What?" he asked, wondering if she expected him to take the initiative now that the ice was broken.

"Nothing. I'm admiring my husband." She sighed. "I am so unbelievably happy—have I mentioned that?"

"Three times during supper, twice when we cut the cake." Drawing her close, he kissed her, long and thoroughly, and with more hunger than he had intended.

"Just want to make sure you know it," she whispered during pauses to catch her breath. "What about you?"

Right now, he wasn't exactly in the mood for conversation.

"Are you happy?"

"I'm about to make us both happier." He kissed the tip of her nose, his hands working the sheer fabric of the gown up over her head.

She sat up suddenly. "Wait!"

He mentally groaned, closing his eyes to the white-hot heat in his groin. Was she turning prudish on him? Or playing hard to get, now that she had him on his knees with need?

Leaning over the side of the bed, she blew out the candle. "There. That's better." When her fingers returned to explore his bare flesh in whispering pleasure, he shuddered, reaching for her. Their mouths met and his last coherent thought seemed odd, even for him.

For the first time, S. H.'s nagging makes sense.

Chapter 6

Sara stirred, shielding her eyes against the sunlight, reaching for Walker. Morning rays fell across the empty pillow where he'd lain beside her all night, his breathing slow and gentle. She smiled, quietly humming "Turkey in the Straw," which had unofficially become their wedding song. She was a wife—and hopefully, she would be a mother soon as well. She raised her head and looked around the room, aware that she was alone. Where had Walker gone so early?

Her wedding dress lay next to his rumpled suit. It was hard to imagine that one day earlier, in this very room, Sophie had been helping her dress for the wedding, careful that every hair was in place. She smiled at the thought of Walker's "barbecue" wedding, recalling the sights and sounds, the guests celebrating long into the night.

At least that part of her dream had remained intact. The only thing more exciting than the wedding had been the wedding night—her first night as Mrs. Walker McKay.

The door opened softly and Walker came in carrying a tray of steaming coffee and cinnamon rolls from the kitchen. When he saw she was awake, color crept up his neck and he mumbled a good-morning.

"I thought you might want to sleep in," he said, setting the tray on a cedar chest at the end of the bed. "You had a big day."

"And night," she teased, eyeing the tray. "Do you cook, too?"

"Sophie left the rolls for us. I made the coffee, though. Hope you like it strong, with cream."

A man who didn't like his coffee black. It was a refreshing change. Propping herself up on her elbows, Sara tucked the sheet under her arms. Last night's activities had considerably diminished her modesty, but she still felt awkward about exposing her naked body to her new husband in full sunlight.

"I like it any way you do." When she first came to Spring Grass, she could barely drink the coffee that was thick enough to spear with a fork. Over the past few days she had gotten used to the murky black liquid, though, and actually started to enjoy her morning cup with Sophie.

She muffled a weary yawn. "Yesterday was quite a day, with the barbecue and all." Their eyes met and she grinned impishly. Walker sat down at the foot of the bed, his shirt open just far enough to reveal a thick thatch of curly, dark brown hair interspersed with red scars. Her throat closed, realizing how close he'd come to death. Sophie had said it was a miracle that the bull hadn't killed him.

"Sorry, I wanted to make sure—"

"The bride showed up?" She sipped the coffee, watching his reaction over the rim of the cup. At least he had the decency to look apologetic. "Wild horses couldn't have stopped me from being there. There was one tiny problem, though."

Walker frowned. "What's that?"

She leaned toward him, letting the covers drift far enough to expose her bare left side, and murmured, "I felt a little overdressed."

Walker responded, meeting her halfway. Their mouths were mere inches apart. "Do you feel a little overdressed now?"

Nodding, she closed the distance for his kiss, sighing with pleasure.

"What should we do about that?" he said between playful nibbles.

She pretended an innocence she didn't have the slightest interest in keeping. "About what?"

Lifting the sheet aside, he lowered his mouth to kiss the column of her neck. Shortly after, he solved the clothing dilemma in a way she'd only dreamed about.

Later, Sara returned the cold coffee and untouched cinnamon rolls to the kitchen, and decided that she would enjoy married life. Immensely. Immeasurably. Really a lot.

* * *

"That chair would look much better over here by this window."

Sophie, a hand on her hip, stood by as Sara bustled around the room, cleaning up the final reminders of the previous day's wedding. She'd been busy as a one-armed wallpaper hanger all afternoon, dusting, polishing, and rearranging. Considering the pinched look on Sophie's face, she was getting on the housekeeper's nerves.

"Can't understand all the fuss. I've cleaned for the McKays nigh onto thirty years. I don't know why all of a sudden things need changin'." Sophie sidestepped as Sara flew past, clutching a broom and a dustpan. "I dust the parlor every morning, but with the extra cleaning lately, I hadn't had time . . ."

"Oh, Sophie, I want to help! It's my home now and I'd feel awful having you do all the work." She swatted an imaginary dust bunny. "Really, don't you think the chair would look better over here?" She stood in the exact spot for effect. "We can go into Laramie and look for material for new drapes; then we could look for new lamps—"

"Whoa! Walker's a generous man, but he hates change. He likes his home the way it is."

Sara frowned. "But the drapes are faded—and those old lamps look awful." She didn't understand Walker's modest lifestyle when he apparently had all the money he'd ever need. New money, Papa called it. Second-generation money, like his. Besides, how much could a new pair of drapes and a new lamp cost?

Sophie dropped into the chair in question—a

large brown leather monstrosity positioned in front of the fireplace. Sara knew it was Walker's favorite because he sat in it every evening to read.

"Walker likes the drapes—and his mother bought his father that chair for a wedding present. Walker's happy with the way things are. He won't want you to change anything."

Sara cocked her head. "Papa says the house is a woman's domain."

"Walker ain't Papa."

Sara couldn't understand why Sophie was being so stubborn about moving a silly old chair a few feet across the room. The more she tried to help, the more Sophie vetoed her ideas. How was she supposed to be a good wife if she wasn't allowed to *do* anything? Sara stared at the chair, determined. It didn't look right where it sat; the light was better by the window.

"Sophie, I'll take full responsibility for moving the chair. If Walker notices and says anything, we'll move it back, but I don't think he will, because it'll look ever so much better over here. He'll be so glad for the change that he won't mind that it's not in its normal place." Sara touched the worn leather lovingly. "Men don't care about furniture."

Once Wadsy had rearranged the whole parlor and Papa hadn't noticed for weeks. Of course, he'd looked a little cross when she lit in on his study.

Sophie snorted, sitting down in the chair and crossing her arms. "Walker'll notice."

"You can tell a lady by the mark she leaves on

her home." Sara began pushing against the back of the chair with Sophie still sitting in it. "Now . . . please . . . help . . . me . . . move . . . this."

Sophie gave up and got up. The chair lunged forward and threw Sara momentarily off balance. She caught herself before she fell.

"Move it, then. But you'll have to do it yourself. I'll have nothing to do with this." Muttering something Sara couldn't make out, the housekeeper left the room, confiscating the broom and dustpan along the way.

With a newfound resolve, Sara shoved the chair to its new place by the window. After several tries at pushing and pulling and coaxing, she got it how she wanted it. When the chair was in place, she lugged a table from the opposite side of the room and placed it just so next to the chair, for Walker to set his coffee cup on.

"Fresh-cut flowers," she murmured. "And it's perfect." She stood back, assessing the newly arranged room with a satisfied smile.

The rest of the day she scurried about the house, polishing, adjusting, and putting her touches on Walker's home. Sophie had barricaded herself in the kitchen, so she couldn't consult her about further domestic possibilities. There were so many things she could do to convert this house from a bachelor's hideaway to a loving family home.

"I'll redo the kitchen," she thought aloud. "It's old and outdated. Then I'll purchase lighter fabrics and recover a few chairs, then convert one of the spare bedrooms into a nursery. By then I'll surely be in the family way." The room next to hers and Walker's would be a perfect nursery for Walker Junior. She could have a wall knocked out, extend the area another twenty feet out the back, build a new closet, paint it a pretty, neutral yellow, put in a water closet . . .

When she ran out of things to say, she sang in a slightly off-key soprano, despite those hours of voice lessons her father had literally begged her to take.

"Black, black, black," she sang, wafting lightly from windowsill to windowsill while waiting for Walker to come home, "is the color of my true love's hair. His lips are rosy fair . . . la-la-la."

When she finished the improvements, she braved her way into the kitchen to see if Sophie had started supper. The housekeeper was standing at the sink chopping something green and refused Sara's help when she offered it.

"Two is one too many in the kitchen," Sophie said.

"But shouldn't I be cooking for Walker on our first night together?" She'd looked forward to this occasion for weeks.

Sophie paused, giving Sara an exasperated look. "I've got most of it done, but if you insist, you can make the corn bread. Be sure and watch that it don't burn. I'm going to see if the men are back before I set supper on the table."

Sara opened the back door for her, bidding Sophie a pleasant good-bye. A minute later, she was dumping cornmeal, flour, egg, buttermilk, salt and pepper, and a wad of grease in a ceramic bowl. Blending the thick mixture, she scraped it into a hot, greased skillet and carefully slid the pan into the oven. Then she hurried upstairs to freshen up and put on the calico dress.

As Sara disappeared up the back staircase, the front door flew open and Walker strode into the parlor, stretching his aching shoulder. Kicking the door closed behind him, he walked slowly across the room, leaving a trail of boot scuffs across the freshly polished floor.

Engrossed in a piece of mail, he headed for his favorite chair, kicking off one boot and then the other. It had been a long day. He and S. H. had worked on both fences in the back field, since the cattle were being moved to greener pastures so hay could be conserved for a predicted early winter. After a long day in the saddle, the coolness of the wooden floor felt good to his sore feet.

He absently walked across the room with the summer issue of his favorite seed catalogue tucked under his arm. One of the ranch hands had picked it up at the mercantile just today. He'd read through it after dinner, but first he'd peek inside. Pausing in front of the fireplace, he folded the letter, flipped open the catalogue, and sat down. Before he could read the first ad, he was flat on his back, seeing stars. The seed catalogue flew into the fireplace, where it rested on ashes. Not yet able to grasp what had happened, he heard footsteps coming down the stairs two at a time.

Sara appeared in the doorway. "Walker? What happened!"

"Where's my chair!"

"By the . . . window."

Walker struggled to sit up and Sara hurried to assist him.

"Oh, my goodness . . . Are you all ri—"

"Who moved my chair? Sophie!"

"Don't yell at Sophie—I moved your chair. I thought you'd enjoy more light when you read, so . . ."

"I want my chair where it was! Sophie!" He shot Sara a dirty look. "Does Sophie know you're moving furniture?"

Sara nodded. She knew, all right. "Change does a body good. You need—"

"I *need* to have my chair *right* here," he said, pointing to the spot where the chair had previously sat.

He saw Sara bristle at his tone. The last thing he needed today was a fight.

"Where's my seed catalogue?" he demanded. Sara's eyes switched to the fireplace and his followed. He grunted and reached for the catalogue. Ashes and dirt fogged the air, threatening a freshly polished table close by.

"You're getting everything dirty!" she cried, trying to intercept the sooty catalogue before he ruined a whole day's work. Snatching it out of the ashes, Walker started to shake it clean. Irritated, Sara snatched it back and swiped it across the front of her dress, leaving a black powder mark but saving the rest of the room. Walker glared at her for a moment, then went to move the chair to its original spot.

When he turned back, he saw tears hovering in

her eyes as she clutched her dirty dress, and his expression softened.

"Look—I'd rather you leave things as they are."

Blinking, she lifted her chin. "I'm sorry. I was trying to be helpful. I thought you might enjoy more light."

Walker uttered an oath under his breath. Women and tears. He'd forgotten how easy it was to hurt their feelings, especially about womanly things. He fell into his chair, removing his hat. "I didn't mean to hurt your feelings. At the end of the day I look forward to coming home and sitting down in my chair in its usual place." He paused, waiting for the tears to let up. "Sophie *knows* I don't want the furniture moved."

"Even if it's a better arrangement?"

"I like my furniture kept in the same place. Okay? If you want to move something, move the porch furniture."

"Who cares about porch furniture? A woman leaves her mark on her house . . ."

"Please leave things alone," he said, more gently this time. "Sophie knows how I like things kept."

Sara's brown eyes snapped. "Sophie's not your wife. I am."

"Sophie's taken care of me for twenty-eight years. You're going to have to live with that." When he saw the tear roll down her cheek, he mentally swore. This marriage thing was going to take some getting used to. "Look, I'm not spoiling for a fight. I only mean . . ." He paused, sniffing the air. "What's burning?"

Sara's jaw dropped. "The corn bread!" Whirling, she raced out of the room and into the kitchen, where smoke was rolling out of the oven. Walker followed her, pitching the smudged seed catalogue onto the table.

Grabbing an oven mitt, she opened the door and snatched the pan of corn bread. A plume of smoke bellowed out of the oven and she jerked back as a blast of hot air assaulted her. Her arm hit the corner of the stove and she yelped.

"Here, let me get that." Walker stepped in and took the mitt away from her, and she rushed to smear butter on the burn. He extracted the corn bread and tossed the skillet on top of the stove. "There. It's out."

Sara burst into fresh tears. Sinking down into a kitchen chair, she buried her face in her dirty dress and sobbed.

Hands coming to his hips, Walker shifted stances. "Now what's wrong?"

"I can't do anything right!"

"You burned the corn bread. It's not the end of the world."

"Sophie told me to watch it and not let it burn, but I was busy arguing with you about that silly chair."

He glanced at the smoking skillet and sighed. "I like burned corn bread."

Sophie came into the kitchen, fanning smoke with her apron. "What's burning?"

Walker pointed to the smoldering pan.

Sophie focused on Sara, who alternately sobbed and dabbed butter on her arm. Sophie's eyes switched back to Walker. He shrugged. Sara couldn't do anything right, and he couldn't say anything right.

"Land sakes," Sophie said, eyeing the damage. "I'll stir up a new batch."

"Set the food on the table, Sophie." Walker winked at Sara. "Tonight's corn bread will make a man appreciate good cooking when he gets it."

"Sara."

Sara opened one eye to see Walker inches from her face the following morning. He shook her shoulder again lightly.

"Get dressed. We're going to town."

Sara propped herself up on one elbow. Walker seemed in an unusually good mood, especially after the humiliating incidents of the night before. After supper, Sara had gone to their room and pretended to be asleep when Walker finally came to bed. She'd been Mrs. Walker McKay one day and already stirred up enough trouble to last a month. Maybe Walker wanted her to get up so he could send her home—was that why they were going into town?

"Why?"

"Errands. Put on something presentable. We'll be leaving in half an hour."

Walker left the room and Sara rolled onto her back. Because of her childish behavior, she'd denied herself the pleasure of Walker's body last night.

Wadsy's amused face danced in front of her. *Done cut off yore nose to spite your face, haven't ya, Babygirl?*

Sara spotted the cup of coffee and piece of toast

on the bedside table. Walker couldn't be too furious with her if he was bringing her breakfast in bed. Of course, he hadn't stayed to eat it with her.

Sara consumed the buttery toast and the thick, scalding coffee, hungry from not having eaten much at dinner the night before. She slipped out of her nightgown and into a plain cotton frock. She hadn't given much thought to clothes in the rush to leave her father's house. She'd brought the dark cotton, an everyday muslin, and a pretty calico that Wadsy had made so she could work in the garden. The gingham now had black soot across the front of it, and she'd worn the muslin yesterday. She dressed and brushed her hair, nimble fingers braiding it into a thick plait.

In spite of the happiness of marriage, her concern over Papa's certain worry cast a heavy shadow. His health would be sure to suffer. Sara scowled at herself in the mirror and bit her lower lip. She'd promised Abe that she'd write as soon as she was settled, and a quick telegraph to home should do the trick. Whirling from the dressing table, she hunted through the nightstand until she found a pen and paper.

Dear Papa, Wadsy, and Abe,

I am sorry for my hasty departure. Be assured that I am quite content and well, but please don't look for me yet. I will send more information later.

Sara

She folded the note and shoved it in her pocket. All she needed now was a chance to go to a telegraph office—alone. How likely was that to happen? And would Papa be able to trace it?

When she came downstairs, both Sophie and Walker were sitting at the dining room table.

"Well, she is awake!" Sophie said, smiling.

Sara wondered if Sophie's happiness came from having her out from underfoot for a day.

"Thank you for the toast and coffee, Walker. I very much enjoyed it. I'm ready to go when you are."

Walker tossed down the last of his coffee and got up. "We may be gone all morning, Sophie."

"Don't worry about me. You two have a good time." The housekeeper accompanied the newly-weds out to the front porch, where S. H. had the buggy hitched and waiting.

"Aren't we going for supplies? Shouldn't we take the wagon?" Sara wondered what would make Walker take a day off just to go to town.

"We don't need the wagon today."

S. H. helped Sara into the buggy and Walker reached for the reins. His secrecy about the unexpected outing puzzled her, but she was relieved he hadn't asked her to bring her valise.

"So your father started Spring Grass?" she ventured, unsure of what he'd find conversational. She held her head high as other buggies passed, proud to be sitting beside her strong, handsome husband.

"Some forty years ago. He and Mother came to Wyoming with a group headed for the far West to find work. Ma loved the land, and Pa bought it for her. Used every penny he had. S. H. and Sophie live in the original homeplace."

"You were born in Sophie's cabin?

"Guess I was. Pa built the new house for Ma years later."

"It must have taken a great deal of money." Sara colored at her forward remarks. She cared not a whit about Walker's bank account. The curse of being a Livingston meant that she had more money than she could ever spend in a lifetime. "Because it's a lovely home," she amended.

A young couple in love, building a home together on the wild prairie! How romantic!

"They earned every cent. And they paid a high price for the land. The hard work killed Ma, and Pa was gored by a bull and died at the scene." Walker fell silent and she wondered what demons he dealt with. They rode for miles listening only to the clicking wheels.

Finally Sara ventured to speak. "You were in an accident involving a bull recently, weren't you?"

Walker nodded, his jaw tightening. "I was luckier than Pa."

"Your folks had a good marriage?"

"Yes."

Sara watched his tanned, masculine hands flick the reins against the horse's flank. She wanted to know everything about him, including his life before he met her. Would he ever love her like his father had loved his mother?

She wanted to ask a dozen things more about him, but the buggy had rolled into town before she could voice them. The newlyweds caught everyone's attention, and once in a while Sara would see someone point and turn to the person he was with, no doubt talking about the "barbe-cue" at the McKay ranch.

The buggy pulled to a stop in front of the mercantile. Sara took in the row of weathered buildings, and her excitement built when she saw a telegraph office not far away. There was a livery, a general store, and a miller to the west. The bank where Caleb Vanhooser, Walker's accountant, worked sat across the street. Overshadowing the other buildings, it was easily the largest structure on the block.

Springing down from the buggy, Walker helped Sara down. Though her feet were now planted firmly on the ground, he still kept hold of her hand. His touch sent off all kinds of exciting sensations inside her. Her pulse speeded up, and she tingled deep inside. Squeezing his arm, she whispered, "Have I mentioned how happy I am?"

With a smile she couldn't quite read, he patted her hand. "Look around in the store. I need to talk to Caleb for a minute."

"Is there anything I should get?" she asked as he started across the street, wondering why he'd brought her with him if he only needed to talk to Caleb.

"Just look around. I'm sure Martha will be happy to help you."

"Hurry back." She waved until he disappeared into the bank. When she was sure he couldn't see her, she scanned the street for buggies and hurried across to the telegraph office. Using the last of the money she'd taken with her from Boston, she ordered the telegraph to be sent and gave explicit instructions that the persons on the end of the line were not to be told where the telegraph had originated. The request caused raised brows, but the clerk promised to adhere to her wishes. "It's your money," he said. His eyes lit up when she added an extra dollar, which he stuck in his pocket.

A lively bell jingled her entry into the mercantile, bringing a tall, slight man with two missing teeth from the back room.

"Can I help ya, miss?" He glanced at the wedding ring on her finger. "I'm sorry. Can I help ya, ma'am? We got some—" He stopped and scratched his head. "Wait a sec. Yer the new McKay missus, ain't ya? Didn't recognize ya there for a minute."

Sara smiled and blushed. This was the first time she had been referred to as a missus, and she liked the sound.

"Yes, and you are?"

"Denzil. Denzil Mitchell. Only got ta meet ya for a second at the barbecue—I mean, weddin'. Quite a surprise for us all."

"Denzil! Denzzzzzillllll! Who's there?" a sharp voice barked from the back room, startling them both. Sara turned in search of the source.

"It's Mrs. McKay, Martha! Walker's new bride." The shopkeeper looked apologetic. "It's the missus," he whispered, as if the marriage were a secret and he'd like to keep it that way.

A tall, rawboned woman lumbered out of the back room, wiping her hands on the front of her apron. She looked to be a little younger than

Sophie, but Sara was no good at guessing ages. Martha Mitchell's round red face looked as if she had been in a smokehouse, with the sweat rolling down her forehead and plump cheeks.

"Well, so it is. Morning, Miz McKay."

"Good morning. Please call me Sara."

"All right, and you can call me Martha." Her greeting faded when she glanced at Denzil, who was leaning on the counter, admiring Sara's hair with an ear-to-ear grin.

"Denzil! Go set up the machine. And be quick about it!"

The henpecked spouse excused himself and disappeared behind a curtain. Martha turned back, a friendly smile replacing her frown, and she looked Sara up and down as if she were a ham laid out for Christmas dinner. Her open appraisal made Sara uncomfortable.

"Well, let's see," she said, taking Sara by the arm and turning her around to study her backside. "Whoever made this dress knew what they were doing. Wasn't you, was it?"

Sara shook her head.

"No, suppose not, if you're here. Well, let's get to work, then. Do you know your measurements, or should I take them myself?"

Sara stared at the woman in disbelief and glanced out the front window. Where was Walker? And why would this woman be interested in her measurements?

Martha Mitchell lumbered around the counter and pulled out a tape measure. "I bet that waist ain't much more than twenty inches. Hmmmm . . .

Last time I had a waist that tiny was right before I married Denzil. Hon, married life will change that waist. Hate to tell you."

Sara smiled lamely. "Yes, ma'am."

"Call me Martha, hon."

"I'm sorry, Martha, but I'm not sure what you're talking about. I came in here to . . ." Why *did* she come in here? Because Walker had insisted, that was why.

"Don't know what I'm talkin' about? Why, I'm talkin' about when ya have babies. You can't expect to keep that figure if you're gonna be birthin' McKay young'uns. Look at me." She patted her round stomach, the apron's fabric stretched full. "Had five myself before Doc told me not to have any more."

Sara looked around the store for signs of children, but there were none.

"They're grown now," the woman clarified, as if reading her mind.

Sara considered quietly backing away from the woman and leaving the store, but the bell jingled and Walker came in, his hat in his hands. Sara wanted to run and tell him about the strange couple, but she supposed he knew. Denzil and Martha Mitchell would be hard to overlook.

"You almost done?" he asked.

"Walker, you got a stubborn woman here. I asked her for her measurements, but she doesn't seem to want to tell me." The woman grinned and brought her hands to her ample hips. "Never seen a girl so fidgety when it comes to getting measured for dresses."

Sara shot Walker a puzzled look. "Dresses?"

"Oh, honey, didn't your man tell you? You're here to get a mess of new dresses. Seems Walker don't want you running around in calico. Never found anything wrong with the fabric myself, but some folks are more picky than others, I suppose." She faked a frown and shook a finger at Walker. "Some's too rich for their own good."

"New dresses?" Sara gasped.

"I noticed you didn't bring many with you. I sent one of my men into town late last night to see if Martha would be willing to make a few." Amused blue eyes rested on hers. "You were busy elsewhere."

Sara blushed.

"Can't have a McKay wearing the same three dresses the rest of her life."

Sara wanted to hug him, but she knew he'd frown on too much affection in public. Instead, she clasped her hands together in front of her and turned to Martha. "So you wanted my measurements because you're the seamstress!"

"The best in town and don't you forget it!" Martha said, beaming. "Of course, Bessie Higgins will swear she is, but don't you believe her."

Martha ushered her into the back room, shooing Denzil back to the front with a wave of her beefy hand. Among a variety of dressmaker's forms and material, the storekeeper's wife took Sara's measurements. When Sara emerged from behind the curtain a few minutes later, Walker was browsing the store, looking at farm implements and supplies.

"Martha said I'm to pick out fabric for my dresses. How many should I choose?"

"As many as you want. Just don't break the bank."

She smiled at her husband, hoping he knew how much she appreciated his generous gesture. If he didn't, she'd show him when they were in the privacy of their own room. When her secret was out and she told Papa about the marriage, he would send her wardrobe to Spring Grass.

Most of the samples on the table were plain, everyday fabrics, with none of the fancy taffetas and silks the dressmakers back East carried. She looked up to see Walker watching her, his eyes dark with desire. She blushed and picked up a bolt of brushed cotton.

"Do you like this?" She held it up next to her face.

"Fine."

She held the bolt at arm's length and studied it. The fabric was a deep red color. "I think it may be too red for me."

She held up another, a light yellow. "How's this one?"

"Fine."

"I don't know . . . maybe it's too bright." She smiled. "Why don't you come over here and choose one for me?"

Walker hesitantly came over to the table and shuffled through the fabrics. He picked up a bolt of light pink.

"Here." He held it up to her. "This one looks all right."

"Not pink. With this red hair, I'd look like a clown."

"Okay—you pick," he said, laying the fabric back on the table. "Order what you want from Martha's selection or special-order something if that suits you better. I'll be out front." He turned to Denzil. "Put it on my account, Denzil."

Denzil looked up from restocking tomatoes on the shelf. "Sure thing, McKay."

Sara scolded herself for being so picky. She'd asked Walker to help and then criticized his choices. Martha came out from the back and approached Sara, who was reconsidering the pink fabric.

"I think I made him mad, Martha. I didn't like what he chose for me."

"Honey, men aren't no good at pickin' fabric. Especially Walker. I'm surprised he didn't pick a saddle blanket." The women laughed, and Sara was reminded of the new saddle and blanket her father had bought her for her last birthday so she could show her horse, Samson.

"I suppose so. But I don't know what to choose," Sara said.

"Why don't you look through the books I have in the back and see if you want to order something special? I have a feeling your man'll pay for anything so long as he don't have to pick it himself."

In no time Sara had picked five fabrics and patterns she liked, thanked the woman, and left to join her husband, who was now chatting with a group of elderly men on the front porch.

"Ready to go?" Walker asked.

"Whenever you are." She smiled back, nodding to the men as she stepped lightly to the buggy.

Chapter 7

"**C**an't we find out where it came from?" Lowell laid the telegraph aside, his face blotched with anger. Two weeks had passed, and the only sign of his daughter was the telegraph that had arrived that morning. He was put out that Allan Pinkerton himself hadn't found time to work on the case. Perhaps he should wire the head of the agency and explain exactly how urgent the matter was. Would this woman detective be able to handle the case as well as Allan?

Kate Warne was a pale woman, and Lowell wondered if she suffered ill health. Her eyes flashed from Mr. Livingston to Wadsy, who was running out of ideas about where Sara might be. Lowell's initial irritation had blossomed into fear that his daughter might have met with ill fate.

"Your daughter, or whoever sent this to you,

put a block on it. We can't know for sure where it came from. We've checked with everyone on the list you provided and found no one who had either seen or heard from Sara, including her friend Julie in New York." The detective accepted a cup of tea from Wadsy. "We checked the records on all outbound trains the day of your daughter's disappearance and every day for a week afterward."

"Did you find anything there?"

"If she did travel by rail, she must have done so under an assumed name. We can't be sure that she would have taken the train, considering your connection with the railroad. She may have gotten a ride in a passing buggy, although that seems unlikely. I've visited the man who was working the early-morning shift at the ticket counter on the day you discovered her missing, and he said that only one girl boarded the train that morning. He was quite certain that the young lady's parents accompanied her to the station. He recalled she seemed to be greatly upset about something."

"Could it have been Sara? What did this girl look like?" Lowell leaned forward to the edge of his chair.

Wadsy, who had been twisting and untwisting her apron since Miss Warne arrived, twisted with new urgency. "Lordy, Lordy, Lordy. Where has my Babygirl gone?"

"If it was her, she's traveling under an assumed name." Kate paused and opened a folder, then flipped through the pages. "Do you recognize the name Olivia Mallory?"

"No." Lowell sank back in his chair. "And I can't imagine how Sara got to the train."

Miss Warne scanned farther down the page. "The station clerk reported that the girl boarding the train had brown hair and brown eyes and was wearing a light blue dress, but he couldn't say more about her because she didn't come near the booth. An older man and woman made the arrangements for her. He assumed they were her parents."

"Don't sound like our Babygirl—who'da gone with her?" Wadsy asked.

"No," Lowell said wearily. "Sara has red hair. The clerk would have noticed that mane." For a moment the three sat in silence. "Is it possible that she may have left the day after?"

"I talked to several men who worked the day of her disappearance and the days after, and they claim that no one matching her description bought a ticket to board the train within a week of her disappearance. I can check again if you would like."

Lowell got up and moved to the window. *Where has she gone?* Sara had never disappeared for weeks at a time. Once she'd stayed away for two days, but she'd come home when her temper had cooled and she'd worn out her welcome with whomever she'd stayed with. He didn't want to think of what could have happened to her. She might have run away with anyone—or, even worse, she might be dead. He rubbed his temples. Neither he nor Wadsy had slept much over the past couple of weeks, and the lack of sleep was beginning to show on their faces and in their tempers.

"Are you sure there wasn't anyone else boarding the train? Maybe someone they couldn't closely identify?"

Miss Warne checked her notes again. "The only other person boarding a train on the morning of your daughter's disappearance was a young man. The conductor said that he looked to be less than twenty years old, but he couldn't tell much more than that."

Lowell whirled from the window to meet Wadsy's hopeful eyes. He knew they were thinking the same thing.

"Sara's dressed like a boy to escape before. She uses Blue Boy's—Abe's grandson's—clothing. Why didn't we think of this earlier!" Striding back to the desk, Lowell sat down. "That must be it—Sara dressed like a boy. That's why no one noticed a redheaded young woman leave that morning."

Kate frowned and checked the files again. "According to the conductor, he says the boy was young, wore a hat, and kept his head down. He boarded with only one bag."

"Was it a brown bag wi' a gold clasp?" Wadsy asked.

"The report doesn't say. If you give me a description of the bag in more detail, I'll talk to the conductor again and see if he recalls. Do you think this person could be your daughter?"

"I don't know, but I want you to explore every option. My daughter . . ." Lowell paused and turned away, overcome by emotion. "We have to find her, Miss Warne."

The woman's sharp features softened for a moment. She made a few notes in a small black book as Wadsy told her about Sara's bag and a few other items that might help the detective locate the missing girl. Meanwhile, Lowell called Abe into the room.

"Abe, is it possible that Sara got into your grandson's clothes? We're thinking she might have dressed in boy's clothing that morning."

Abe looked toward the window. "Blue Boy ain't said nothin' 'bout it, but I could check if you want."

"Please do, Abe. It's the only lead we have."

The detective closed her notebook. "We'll talk to the clerk again. Perhaps we've overlooked something." She covered her mouth with her handkerchief and coughed.

"That's a nasty cough, Miss Warne. Ya want some of my cough remedy?" Wadsy asked.

The detective smiled. "Thanks, but I'm afraid syrup won't help." She got up to leave. "We'll try to find this Olivia Mallory and her parents, Mr. Livingston, to see if they saw anyone who fits your daughter's description on the train or in the area of the station that morning."

"If Sara was still in Boston, you would have found her by now," Lowell admitted. "I'm offering a five-thousand-dollar reward for anyone who can tell us where she might have gone. Someone must know something. I'd give up my railroad to have my daughter back home safe and sound."

Miss Warne extended a hand to him. "I'll make this my first priority, Mr. Livingston. You can be sure that we'll find your daughter and return her safe."

Lowell rose and shook her hand. "Thank you, Miss Warne. Keep in touch. I want to be informed of any further developments, however small."

Wadsy escorted the lady detective from the study, and Lowell returned to his desk and gazed at Gracie's picture. "Don't worry, dear. We'll find her. Even if I have to call Allan Pinkerton himself to find her, I'll stop at nothing to bring her back." Tears that had been threatening to fall all afternoon finally rolled down his cheeks, and he turned the chair to face the window. Every day he sat here, looking out at the street in the hope that somehow, someone out there knew where Sara had gone. But days passed, and still there was no word of his daughter's whereabouts.

Sara, when will you come home and put your poor old father out of his agony?

The morning after their trip to town, the kitchen blossomed with Sara's chatter. Her mind worked faster than Walker could think, and her endearing smile was quick and lively. *Nervousness*, he told himself as he sipped his coffee and absently nodded at her ceaseless prattle. It would work its way out of her once she was comfortable with her surroundings. As he smiled and nodded again, he hoped that wasn't just wishful thinking.

The truth was, Walker had begun to get used to the idea of having her around—as long as he had her around when he slipped out of his clothes at night. Already the warmth of her weight against him as he drifted into sleep felt right. Nightmares about the bull's attack had lessened. Their lovemaking was passionate; in bed she was a force to be reckoned with. Still, he shook off the idea that there might be something deeper than lovemaking that held his attention.

Sara broke through his ponderings. "Walker, do you think we could have a party? A *real* party, not just a bogus barbecue?"

He kept his eyes on the newspaper. "I don't see why not." A party seemed like a good idea, and party plans would keep her busy—and, hopefully, quiet.

"Oh, wonderful! I was thinking maybe a ball— a grand ball! Everyone could wear their finest clothes—the fancy clothes they would have worn had they known about our wedding. We could have lots and lots of food and drinks. Maybe even champagne—no—I know! A formal dinner with rich satin tablecloths—and maybe one or two of the ranch hands could serve so Sophie doesn't have to work so hard. We could serve coq au vin—"

So much for keeping her quiet. "Whoa, there!" Walker feigned concern. "We're simple country folk; we don't like anything fancy. Beef, potatoes, and slaw. None of that French stuff. Besides"—a flicker of a smile broke through—"you'd have to chop up my whole herd to feed all of our friends."

Sara fell silent and studied his face. He wondered if his teasing offended her. Like sunshine through the rain, though, her worry reversed itself.

"You said 'our friends.' " She beamed.

Walker sipped his coffee, feigning indifference. "Did I?"

"You *did*! You said *'our* friends'!" Oh, Walker, every day I feel more and more at home. First the dresses, and now the party. You've been wonderful to me. I just love it here! You'll see: I'll be the best wife ever, and before you know it, Walker McKay, you'll wonder what you ever did without me!"

I'm wondering that already. He gave her a wink, uneasy with the thought. Truth was, he was getting a little too comfortable around her.

Later that afternoon, Sophie filled a jar with chilled lemonade and wrapped it in a heavy cloth. Walker and S. H. were stringing new fence nearby, and Sara thought they would appreciate a cold drink. Though the distance wasn't too far to walk, she asked Potster to saddle one of the mares anyway. It had been months since she'd ridden, and she looked forward to the outing. She skipped upstairs to put on the new riding skirt Martha had made her.

Fifteen minutes later she was astride the mare and galloping to the south pasture. She missed Samson, and wondered if he missed her. They'd ridden together nearly every day this past year. Once she told Walker about her ruse and cleared the air, she'd ask him to send for the animal.

The lemonade swished in the saddlebag as the mare's shod feet clipped merrily along the rocky trail. Sara's heart sang as she perched on the newly polished saddle. She was married to the man of her dreams! Life couldn't get much better.

She spotted a shirtless Walker bent over a calf, and her heart speeded up. The heifer bawled for its mother, which S. H. held at bay.

Sara approached quietly in order not to startle the men. Her gaze skimmed her husband's torso, resting on the vicious scars marring his olive skin. Shivering in the heat, she had never desired him more. Reining in the horse, she quietly admired him, cattle and lemonade forgotten.

S. H. glanced up and grinned when he saw her. "That you, Sara?"

Walker turned at the mention of her name and smiled as well. "What brings you all the way out here? Did Sophie finally ban you from her kitchen?"

"No, I'm . . ." The way his eyes shamelessly devoured her in broad daylight made her forget the purpose of her visit. "I . . ."

"Came to see ol' Bessie here?" S. H. teased, slapping the cow on her side.

"No." Sara blushed. "I brought lemonade."

Both men chuckled and Walker released the calf, which ran crying back to its mother. As he lifted Sara down from the mare, their eyes met and held for the longest moment. He lightly squeezed her waist and she smiled fadishly at him.

After he released her, he took the lemonade

from the saddlebag and removed the lid. "Aren't you joining us?" he asked, pouring the lemonade into the glasses she held for him.

"I'm not thirsty." Her eyes told him that she was hungry; the need grew more urgent the closer he stood. Sara could smell sweat and a mixture of shaving soap and musk. The manly scent made her nearly faint from wanting.

"It's too hot to drink this here," S. H. said, taking a long swallow. "Think I'll find some shade down by the creek."

Walker winked at Sara. "Sounds like a good idea." When the foreman wandered off, Walker leaned closer, his mouth taking that kiss that had silently been between them. Though brief, it was no less effective. "Want to find some shade?"

Nodding, she returned the kiss, oblivious to the dirt and sweat.

Taking her hand, he led the horse down a small incline to where a stream cut through the land. His eyes skimmed her lightly.

"Is that one of your new dresses?"

She slowed, making a mock curtsy. "Do you like it?"

He shrugged. "I think you'd better take it back."

Sara frowned. She thought it was most flattering. "Why?"

"Because Martha put legs in it. Women aren't supposed to have any legs in their skirts but their own."

"Very funny." She made a face at him, twirling in her split skirt. "Just for that, I'm going to have Martha put legs in all my dresses."

Walker picked up a stone and skipped it across the water. Sara wished that S. H. weren't there so they could be alone. As if reading her mind, the old man wandered farther downstream.

Walker moved closer. "But they all come off the same." He tugged teasingly at the front of her skirt, and Sara shuddered at his touch.

Taking her by the hand, he led her closer to the stream's edge. "Look at that," he said, pointing at the rocky bottom.

"What?" Sara bent closer. She couldn't see anything but rocks and the reflection of the sun in the clear stream.

"Look closer," he said, crouching. She got on her hands and knees and peered into the water. When her head dipped near the water's surface, Walker splashed her with a handful of water. Sputtering, she wiped her eyes.

He grinned at her, obviously pleased with his prank. But the grin quickly faded as Sara pushed him into the water. The stream was deep enough to cover his head and drench his half-naked body. He struggled up and pitched his soggy hat onto the bank.

Giggling, Sara watched him shake the water out of his hair, dodging the spray.

"Think that's pretty funny, huh?" He stood up and strode back to the bank.

Sara couldn't stop laughing long enough to respond. Walker paused at the water's edge and, with one quick hand, took hold of her boot. Her laughter died in her throat as she stared at the steely grip.

"Don't you dare."

But he did dare.

Yanking her into the water, he submerged, pulling her under with him. When they met underwater, he clasped her head, drawing her to him for a long, gratifying kiss. When they finally surfaced, they met the eyes of an amused S. H.

"I heard the splash and thought someone fell in."

Walker glanced at Sara, grinning. "Sara needed cooling off."

Sara blushed, shooting him a priggish look. Gathering up her soaked hem, she tried to wade to shore, falling back into the water twice.

Walker stretched out his hand to S. H. "Pull me out, S. H.?"

Sara whirled when she heard the foreman hit the water. Yelling and sputtering, the old cattleman muttered oaths under his breath as Sara and Walker broke into laughter.

"You're terrible," Sara chided Walker as the three tried to find solid footing to wade out.

"Think so?"

Color flooded her cheeks when his eyes promised that tonight he'd show her just how bad he could be.

Sara stepped out the front door that evening, drawing her wrap tighter. The air was chilly tonight, reminiscent of Boston. Martha had included this beautiful soft wrap with the first dress she'd finished, as a wedding present, and Sara was glad for its warmth.

Somewhere nearby, a wild animal called to its

mate. Wolf? Coyote? Something she didn't know about? Ordinarily she'd be curious to learn the source, but tonight she was just plain too tired to care. Sinking down onto the porch swing, Sara thought about the long week full of learning the rules and ways of ranch life. Papa would be quick to tell her she'd made her bed and now she'd have to sleep in it.

But what a lovely bed it was.

A smile raised the corners of her mouth and she shivered from thoughts of playing in the creek and of the nights that had followed. Never in her wildest imaginings had she known the delight, the exquisite pleasure, the pure ecstasy a man could coax from a woman's body. Heat crept up her throat, and she dropped the shawl to her lap. She responded to her husband with a fervor even she found, well, distressing. What must he think of his bride who shamelessly . . . eagerly . . . encouraged his advances?

Sara quickly looked away when the screen door creaked and Walker walked out, afraid he might read her thoughts. He paused, gazing up at the star-studded sky.

"Thought you'd be in bed by now."

"No." She fussed with her wrap, determined to ignore the impressive width of his shoulders, but the familiar heat started to build in her middle. How could such an innocuous statement like "Thought you'd be in bed" ignite a response so effortlessly? Was it wrong for her to desire her husband with this seemingly unquenchable thirst, even though she barely knew him? The

Good Book commanded, "Wives, submit your-selves unto your own husbands." And gladly she would.

"Mind if I join you?"

She readily scooted aside, making a place beside her. He eased down, the swing creaking beneath his heavier weight. The aroma of soap and the sunshine scent of his freshly ironed shirt drifted to her. Sophie took care with his clothing, pressing each garment with a hot iron, hanging the shirts in neat, organized rows in his closet. Sara had stood before Walker's open closet for a long time that morning, familiarizing herself with her husband's taste. He liked blue, with just a hint of starch in his collars. Denims were his choice of work clothes, but he favored khaki for social occasions, white shirts, and brown suits. Walker McKay was fastidious about his appearance, and that suited her fine. She adored the sensual leathery smell of his toilet water in the small bottle on top of his dresser.

The swing swished quietly back and forth. Moonlight bathed the honeysuckle trail along the front porch. Sara could see a light burning in the bunkhouse. She'd yet to become friends with the ranch hands, but she would, soon. She intended to be a vital part of her husband's life in every way.

"You settling in all right?"

Sara started at the sound of his voice, pulling her back to the present. "Yes, thank you. As long as I stay far out of Sophie's way."

"I take it you haven't had much experience in the kitchen."

"No . . . well, a little." She'd watched Wadsy cook. The old nanny had tried to teach her the finer arts of homemaking, but it never sank in. She much preferred to read magazines, wedding notices, or stories about far away lands. Someday she wanted to go to Ireland, but Papa was always too busy to travel. Once he'd promised to take her, but he never had, and he frowned on her going alone. Maybe Walker would take her to Ireland someday. He appeared to be a man of great means—and even if he weren't, Papa would pay his passage, grateful to have someone escort his daughter to Ireland so he wouldn't have to.

"I thought your letter said you cooked," Walker said.

"I do. A little." Very little.

Walker's thigh rested against hers. Was it accidental or deliberate? She shivered, contemplating the latter. He had to be aware of the contact. A hot current seared through her thin cotton skirt, and she couldn't think of anything else.

"It doesn't matter. Sophie tends the house and cooking. I imagine she wouldn't be too happy with another woman underfoot in her kitchen."

My kitchen, Sara mentally corrected him. But she didn't intend to move in and abolish Sophie's position in Walker's home. She wanted to fit in, and part of fitting in was being a wife and doing the things a wife would do. But she also knew she couldn't storm in and demand that everyone change for her. Eventually Sophie would let her into the kitchen, and she'd be extra careful not to get in the way until she'd learned her way around.

The hypnotic sound of the creaking swing blended with the sounds of the mid-June evening. *This is what I've wanted all my life*, Sara thought. *Husband and wife enjoying each other's company at the end of the day.* And soon, very soon, she hoped there would be three of them. A real family. Certainly, if the intensity of Walker's love-making meant anything, a baby was already on its way. Everything was finally perfect—with the exception of two small, niggling doubts. What she'd done was deceitful. And poor Papa must be beside himself with worry. She should write the letter informing him of her marriage, but to do so meant telling Walker of her deception. Would he find it amusing, or think she was deliberately scheming against him? Fear that he would find it anything but what it was—a solution to every-one's problems—troubled her. The lie was the only fly in an otherwise blissful ointment. Once she informed Papa of what she'd done, he would forgive her peccadillo. But would Walker forgive her? Especially after Trudy's deception?

"Nice evening."

"Yes, it is." Was he eager to retire? As ready as she was to go upstairs? Certainly he must be tired. He'd left the house shortly after sun-up and hadn't returned until supper. Sophie said Walker wasn't afraid of work. Like his father before him, he put in twelve to fourteen hours a day.

"Are you tired?" she asked.

"Tired?"

Color flooded her cheeks, so aware was she that the question sounded more like an invitation than casual conversation.

"I know that you work very hard."

He smiled, inciting that mysterious need within her.

"Are you?"

"Somewhat."

The heat of his arm, now resting lightly along the back of the swing, was tortuous, and her insides curled with the thought of the approaching hour. Walker was a virile man, his needs strong. She'd spent five blissfully delicious nights now in his arms, eagerly appeasing his incessant hunger. Five deliciously happy mornings waking to his experienced caresses, the fascinating brush of stubble on her sensitive skin, her breath consumed by his demanding kisses. She sensed he wasn't looking for love, but she was. Before Walker knew what hit him, she would win his love, and there wouldn't be a thing he could do about it. She would be the best wife, the most devoted mother, and the most loyal friend he ever had. He would never let her go—even when she told him about the deception.

"Is this one of the new dresses?" His fingers lightly toyed with a lock of her hair, playfully tugging it. His reserve usually held him distant—except for that day at the creek—but tonight he clearly felt the undeniable current racing between them.

"Do you like it?"

Walker's eyes devoured her and she knew that he wasn't just admiring Martha's work.

"I love it. Think we should turn in early?" he whispered softly.

Should she play coy, and pretend she wasn't as

eager as he for what the evening promised? Coyness wasn't her way. God had answered her prayers. He'd surely approve if she honored her husband with all the love and affection she could bestow. If she hadn't met Olivia Mallory, she would be in New York now, hiding from Papa, searching for a man who filled her dreams and expectations. God had dropped Walker McKay in her lap; she could do no less than submit to her husband with a willing heart.

Turning, she looped her arms around his neck, smiling. "I was thinking a hot bath might be nice." When he drew her closer, she whispered against his ear, "With bubbles—and candlelight."

"I'll go in and tell Sophie—"

"I put the water on to heat before I came out," she replied.

"You did?" Lowering his mouth, he kissed her, deepening the embrace when she softly moaned and clasped the front of his shirt tightly. The cool night air turned sultry as his hand closed around her waist.

"And I had S. H. bring the tub up to our room."

Groaning, he stood up, lifting her into his arms. "No use wasting a good bath."

Resting her head on his shoulder, she nuzzled his neck as he carried her inside the house and up the long staircase.

They never made it to the bath.

Chapter 8

Once she got Walker's approval, Sara wasted no time arranging a lavish social with food and fun for all, without the fancy tablecloths. Since Sophie had done all the arrangements for the barbecue/wedding, Sara enjoyed the opportunity to plan something special for the ranch. It took only a week for invitations to be sent and supplies to be gathered.

By the day before the party, Sophie had invited her back into the kitchen on a temporary basis.

"Darlin', you're trying too hard. If you'll let me do the work and just help instead of taking over, we'll work better together."

This morning the two women were baking apple pies for the party. Sophie tried teaching Sara how to make a crust, but Sara's attempts turned out tough and doughy compared to the light and flaky crusts Sophie eased from the oven. With each failed attempt, Sara grew more flustered. What was wrong with her? She had been in the kitchen hundreds of times watching Wadsy and Cook prepare everything from tea biscuits to roasts. Why couldn't she make a simple pie? She'd hoped that somehow what she'd seen Wadsy and Will do would creep into her mind now.

"No, no, no." Sophie stopped slicing apples and reached over to where Sara was attempting to roll out another batch of dough. "You're pressing too hard and the crust won't be thick enough." Sophie confiscated the rolling pin and ran the pin back and forth until the dough was the right thickness.

Sara sighed. "Maybe I should just give up, Sophie. I want to be a good cook, but maybe I'm just not made for cooking."

"I thought your letter said . . . well, no matter. It takes time and practice." Sophie handed her the pin and returned to the apples. "You need to relax, enjoy your marriage. Everything will fall into place in time."

"I'm trying, but it seems like I'm going backwards instead of forward. What else needs to be done?"

"Why don't you take a little break? Maybe if you took yourself outside for a walk, you'd feel better. When you come back, we'll start over." Sophie pushed a bowl of bruised apples across the table. "The mares in the barn will appreciate a treat. There's nothing they like better than apples, and gettin' out of the kitchen for a few minutes will do you good."

Sara formed her apron into a cradle and Sophie dumped four apples into it. Sara smiled. "I suppose it would be nice to see if Diamond is about to foal."

Walker had taken her for a walk in the moonlight two nights ago, and they'd stopped at the barn to check on his personal horses. Diamond was Walker's prize mare—Sara's favorite. The horse was bred late, and Walker was anxious.

Sophie shooed her out of the kitchen and into the midday light. Sara savored the heat of the warm earth in the fields. A dozen ranch hands would be cutting hay tomorow. Walker had talked about it all week long, hoping that rain would hold off until they could get the hay down and dried. Clutching the apples to her, Sara sauntered toward the barn at the left of the house, a large wooden building with a loft on top for hay and stables below for horses that were injured or about to foal.

It took Sara a moment to adjust to the warm darkness of the interior. Each mare stuck a nose over the outside of her stall to sniff at Sara's treats as she walked by. The breath from their big, round nostrils stirred up dust when they snorted.

Sara offered an apple to the first animal, a large roan. Long lips felt around the apple and enormous teeth split it in half with a crunch. Sara jumped, laughing as the mare withdrew to chew with noisy bites. Sara held up the second half of the apple and the animal made soft nickering sounds in her long, sleek throat. Patting her head, Sara offered the other half and moved to the second stall.

Diamond's stall was larger and more open than the others. The horse raised her muzzle from the water bucket when she heard Sara approach. Diamond was a full sixteen hands high, coal-black with white markings on her forelock and front fetlocks. Sara could see why she was Walker's favorite. She had enormous brown eyes that kindly asked what Sara had brought.

"Here you go, girl." Sara lifted an apple. The horse sniffed and took it from her hand in one bite, leaving a trail of water and saliva in her palm. Sara wrinkled her nose.

"Very unladylike to drool. If I couldn't see that you obviously have found a mate, I would remind you that men don't appreciate this kind of thing. Of course, horses may be different."

Standing on tiptoes, she stroked Diamond's mane while the mare crunched contentedly. She ran her hand up and down the long nose. "Now, Diamond, you are a lucky lady. You don't have to cook or clean or worry about not being able to cook or clean. You simply have to run fast, look pretty, make babies, and eat apples. Right, girl?" Sighing, Sara stepped back to move across the aisle to the next mare. "If only I could be a horse, life might be easier."

"You'd shore be a pretty un," a kindly voice said from behind her.

Sara started, dropping the remaining apples

into the hay. Whirling around, she spotted a small, grizzled-looking man grinning at her, holding a bowl of potato peelings.

"I didn't hear you come in," she said.

"Sorry. I wasn't expectin' to find a little red-headed filly in the barn." He turned and spat into the hay. "I was enjoyin' your little speech to Diamond there. And it sounded like Diamond was enjoying it, too, wasn't ya, girl?" He moved to the mare's stall, reaching into the front pocket of his vest for a lump of sugar.

Color sprang to Sara's cheeks. "You shouldn't have eavesdropped on me. That's not polite."

The tobacco-stained grin widened.

"Sorry if I offended ya, ma'am." Removing his battered hat, he made an old-fashioned, sweeping bow, dislodging some of the potato peels. "You're Walker's new bride, aren't ya?"

"Yes, I am." Sara smiled. "And you are?"

"Potster. I'm the bunkhouse cook and all-around maid. Closer to a mother hen sometimes." He wheezed a dry laugh and returned the hat to his head. "These boys need lots of lookin' after."

Sara held out a hand. "It's nice to meet you, Mr. Potster, sir."

He frowned. *Mr.? Sir?* Honeypie, you must be from the East. 'Round here I'm just Potster, or Potsie." He bent down and picked up the scattered apples. "I believe you was in the process o' distributin' these to the mares?"

Sara took the remaining apples and tossed them into the stalls. "I have to get back to the kitchen. Sophie's teaching me how to bake pies, but I'm having a little trouble with the crust."

Potster threw his head back and laughed, slapping a thick thigh.

"Well, maybe you should just come with me. I bet I could teach ya how to make a pie that'd have Sophie jealous."

"Thank you, Mr. Potster, but—"

"Just plain Potster, honey. No 'mister' to it." Potster spat into the hay and rubbed his chin. "No offense, ma'am, but from what I hear, Sophie don't want you in her kitchen."

Sara bristled. How dare he insult her—her—her what? Culinary skills? She had none. *Face it, Sara McKay: you can't boil water.* Potster's rough honesty allowed her to drop her guard.

"It's not that I haven't tried. Honestly, I have. I just don't know how to cook."

"People ain't jus' born knowin' how to cook, honey. Ya gotta learn it."

"I'm trying. Sophie's been working with me, but I'm afraid I'll never be able to make even a decent pan of corn bread."

"Why, corn bread's th' easiest thing on earth. Here." He reached for her arm. "Help me scatter these peelin's to the chickens, and we'll go back to the bunkhouse and make corn bread for the hands tonight."

"Oh, I'd better not." Sara shook her head, thinking about the last disaster. "The men would starve if I cooked for them. Besides, I promised Sophie I'd be right back. I've got to help her finish baking for tomorrow."

"If I know Sophie, she's probably doing fine without ya, and I could use yer help. I got thirty-five hungry men to feed! You'll learn a thing or two 'bout fixin' vittles, an' I'll have a pretty face in m' kitchen for a change."

Sara thought about the request. She could help if he gave her easy tasks, and maybe if she watched him closely, she could see what she was doing wrong.

"Well, okay, but I should tell Sophie where I'm going in case she needs me."

Potster winked. "You do that, an' I'll meet you at the bunkhouse."

Potster chuckled at Sara's tale of Sophie's obvious relief upon learning where Sara would be spending the next few hours. In the ranch hand's kitchen, Sara watched Potster slice potatoes with deft precision. In front of her was a large bowl, four beat-up tin pans, and an assortment of cornmeal, lard, and other ingredients.

"I mix this all together?" Sara asked when Potster urged her to start the cornmeal mix for the party fixings. "How do I know how much to add?"

"Enough." Potster winked at her. "Just start mixin'. I'll help when you get stuck."

Sara lifted a dollop of lard and flipped it into the bowl. It landed with a splat.

"Enough?" she quizzed.

Potster looked up from his potatoes and craned his neck to peer in the bowl.

"How many you makin' this for? Two?" Potster's smile never left his face, and she noticed that the lines etched there showed signs of hard laughing as well as hard living.

"Well, *Mr. Potster*. If you know all this so well, why don't you show me how much I need?"

His laugh rang through the bunkhouse kitchen. "You got sass, girl. Ain't no doubt 'bout that. I can see why Walker hitched up to your wagon." Sara blushed when the ranch hand slapped his knee with his free hand.

"You gotta do this yourself or you'll never learn." He wiped his hands on a cloth and set the potatoes to boil. After that task was done, he turned all his attention to her.

"Now," he said. "How many are ya' fixin' for?"

Sara paused, calculating in her head. "Let's see. If I'm adding right, I'd say forty." She looked for a confirmation. "But they won't be eating this corn bread with butter—it's for corn-bread dressing. I'm cooking two turkeys. Sophie said that would be the easiest."

"Whatever." He shrugged. "Okay, so you'll need a pan for every five people and one dollop of lard for every pan."

Sara's face brightened. Arithmetic was something she could understand; it had been the easiest subject for her in school. The numbers began ticking in her head. She quickly scooped another thick lump of grease from the larder. "So cooking is all math!"

"Heavens, no! A shaky bunch of guessing at best," he replied. "Lard's the only math part. The rest," he added with a grin, "is all poetry."

Sara's sails dipped slightly, but Potster was quick to assist her, and soon she was ladling the yellow paste into pans. It oozed out evenly, the lumps smoothed out under Potster's gentle guidance.

"Now," said Potster with a grand flourish, "the greatest secret of making corn bread is . . ." He slid the pans into the hot oven and closed the door.

"Putting them in the oven?" Sara peered over his shoulder.

"No," he said, his voice a gravelly whisper. "Taking them out at exactly the right time. The Potster's secret."

Sara teasingly slapped his arm and they both broke into laughter.

The rest of the afternoon, Potster shared cooking secrets and kept Sara transfixed with stories of the West he knew—the outlaws, cowherds, dust, and ponies that dotted the beautiful, wide-open prairies. Before she knew it, hours had passed and dinner was ready, including four beautiful pans of yellow corn bread.

Sara jumped when she realized the time.

"I can't believe it's this late!" She threw her arms around a startled Potster and squeezed. "I would stay here and have dinner with you, but I have to finish the final plans for my party."

Potster unwrapped himself from her and blushed. "I understand," he said. "No tellin' how much Sophie's been missing you."

She made a face at him. "Thank you for taking the time to teach me about corn bread. Can I come visit again?"

"You're very welcome. Stop by anytime you want."

"And you will be at the party tomorrow evening?"

Potster frowned. "Do I have to wear my fancy duds?"

"Not if you don't want to." She patted his arm.

A smile lit his face. "Then I wouldn't miss it for the world!"

With that, Sara dashed from the comfort of the kitchen and back to the main house.

The following afternoon, wagons, horses, and guests eager for another McKay surprise crowded into Spring Grass. News of the latest gathering had traveled faster than Sara's invitations, and since there was barely enough room in the big dining room for the guests, the party was moved to the lawn. It was a beautiful day, the sun shining, warm breezes, perfect for an outdoor event.

Walker smoked a cheroot and leaned against a railing on the porch, keeping out of the line of partygoers filing through the house and out into the yard. In the midst of the attendees, his lovely wife eagerly made sure that all of them had punch as they drifted around admiring the house and furnishings before retiring outdoors. Sophie and Sara had the place shining. Walker had been so busy haying the past two days that he had barely seen Sara, and hadn't mustered the energy for their usual romps when he fell into bed. He had seen her disappointment when he rolled

over and fell asleep about as fast as his head hit
the pillow.

Toward the end of the week, she was up earlier
than he was, organizing trips into town and table
placement. Her boisterous chatter continued
unchecked, but she moved so quickly from room
to room and plan to plan that many times her
wonderings were aimed at no one but herself,
freeing Sophie and Walker of the need to carry on
the conversation.

Walker took another drag of his cheroot, then
crushed it out under his boot. Music filled the air
as guests mingled. He wondered if Sara had
instructed the musicians not to play "Turkey in
the Straw" and grinned. Thinking of his feisty
wife, he felt desire rise hot and unchecked in him.

He watched her carry trays of smoked ham
and cheese to the table and his desire grew. As if
she could sense his interest, she suddenly turned
from her task and met his dark gaze. An invisible
thread drew her up the steps to where he stood,
her brilliant blue skirts swishing around her legs
and satin shoes.

"Why, Mr. McKay, what a pleasure to see you
here. I'm so glad you could join the festivities."
She curtsied just low enough to expose a bit of
her chest in the low-cut bodice. Frowning, she
straightened. "I haven't seen you in so long that I
was afraid you'd forgotten all about our little
gathering."

Walker winked. "I haven't forgotten you."

She leaned closer and whispered, "You'd better
not." Their mouths were only inches apart now.

"Surely, Mrs. McKay, you wouldn't expect me to be so thoughtless as to turn down your invitation." He brushed a lock of hair to the back of her ear. "Especially when I had such a good time at your last event." He mustered a puzzled look and put a finger to his lip. "When was that? Ah, I believe it was your wedding."

Sara blushed. "Why, my dear Mr. McKay, you are being shamefully forward with a married woman. If my husband were to see me here . . . with you . . . he'd surely . . ."

"Ask you to behave yourself?" Walker smiled, pulling her close.

"Hey, McKay, remember your party?" a voice called from somewhere across the porch.

"Maybe you two should take that upstairs." Roe Masters slapped Walker on the arm as he passed on his way off the porch. "We can wait."

Everyone within listening distance broke into laughter as Walker released Sara, her face crimson down to the neckline of her dress. She returned to her hostess duties with a shy backward glance.

Walker joined a group of ranchers on the opposite side of the porch to discuss business matters, but his eyes occasionally searched the crowd for his wife. He was eager for the party to end, and tonight he wouldn't be asleep the moment his head hit the pillow.

"So, Walker, how's ranching been treating ya?" Blake Slayton asked.

"Never had a better year, Blake. To tell you the truth, it's gonna be bigger than last."

The remark brought a low, appreciative whistle from the other men. Every rancher there knew the pitfalls of a bad year, and they were quick to rejoice when one of them pulled off a good profit. Walker searched the faces of the men around him, many of them close friends of his or old friends of his parents. Rusty Johnson and his family had been on the same wagon train with Walker's parents. Rusty's sons had grown up closer than kin with Walker.

"Been the same way over at the Circle J," Rusty offered and spat a wad of tobacco over the porch railing. "Looks like good times this year. Son of a gun, we shore needed it after these last few." Everyone nodded in agreement.

"Maybe Walker should have married sooner." The men turned to see Caleb Vanhooser approaching. The accountant looked small and out of place among the larger-built ranchers, but they parted and welcomed him into their circle. He smiled nervously at the group.

"I don't know if my marriage did it." Walker clapped the accountant on the shoulder affectionately. "I'd venture to say that the good spring rains are responsible."

The men doubled over with laughter. Caleb took his glasses off, chuckled, and wiped them on his handkerchief. Walker and Caleb had attended school together, and although the two led different lives, Caleb was still one of Walker's closest friends. Walker didn't know how he would have made it through his parents' deaths if Caleb hadn't been there to help him with the financial side of the ranch.

The group soon split up, leaving Walker and

Caleb alone on the porch. They talked about the ranch and cattle prices until Sara approached with two glasses of punch. Caleb quickly excused himself and went inside.

Walker accepted the glass of punch, his eyes on his wife. The setting sun caught and framed her face, lighting her features with a bright glow. She had made good on her promise to organize the party, and she had done a fine job. He was proud of her.

Inside, the first few notes of "Turkey in the Straw" drifted out, and Walker took Sara's punch from her hand and set it on the railing.

"I do believe this is our song?"

She nodded, her eyes aglow. "I do believe that it is."

Extending his arm, he led her down the steps into the center of the lawn, where people were beginning to form lines for square dancing. Stealing a brief kiss, Walker drew his bride into his arms.

"It's a nice party," he whispered against her ear.

"Thank you," she replied. "I hoped that you would enjoy it."

For now, it was a good start.

Chapter 9

It was rare for Walker to take a day off at Spring Grass, but the hay was taken care of, fences restored, and the excitement of the party and the hours afterward left him needing a day of rest. Leaning close to the mirror, he ran the razor down a cheek, wondering what his wife was up to. She'd left the bed early this morning, murmuring something about baking biscuits.

He grinned when he thought of Sara's urgent lovemaking and what it promised. Sara was confident that she would be a mother soon. Words like "chinz" and "coverlet" and "baby cribs" filled her breakfast conversation. Each evening, she filled him in on every household activity she'd participated in that day. Every apple she'd fed every mare, the potato peelings she'd thrown to the chickens, the leftover scraps she'd fed the dogs. Every aspect of ranch life fascinated her, and nothing was an unfit topic of conversation at her table.

Sobering, he stared at himself in the mirror. The image he saw was one of a contented man. How could that be? He'd been married less than a month, and the tight lines around his eyes were gone. He studied the change, surprised at the transformation.

Whistling, he dressed and went downstairs, sniffing the air, which was laced with the smell of burning bacon. Sara's voice drifted to him from the kitchen.

"I don't have any idea when he's going to get up, but I want this breakfast to be perfect. I could go upstairs and lay out his clothes—better yet, I could catch him in bed and we could have breakfast together. Yes, that would be good. Go upstairs, lay out his clothes, and then maybe, if I'm lucky, he'll open his eyes and . . ." Her voice trailed off as she disappeared into the pantry.

Grinning, Walker paused for a moment at the top of the stairs. And what? Would his wife like a few private moments with him this morning? The idea appealed to him more than he wanted it to. Through the front window he saw Sophie weeding her flower garden, so whom was Sara talking to?

"What do you think, Brownie?" Sara's voice emerged from the pantry, and Walker realized that she'd lured one of the cattle dogs into the kitchen. Sara talked a lot, a trait he hoped she'd overcome—to no avail. His grin widened, picturing the old coonhound as a captive audience, head cocked to one side, trying to decide what the female human was trying to say. "Should I use the white napkins or the blue ones? White is more practical, but blue matches his eyes . . . those blue, blue eyes . . . and—" Sara started as Walker entered the room.

"Oh! You've ruined my surprise. I was going to bring you breakfast in bed." She bounded across the room and threw her arms around his neck. Gazing up at him, she ran a finger over the pillowcase lines still imprinted on his face.

"I didn't wake you up, did I? I was trying to be quiet—I wanted to have your breakfast ready when you came down. Sit down and I'll serve you." She quickly kissed him and was off again.

Walker sat down at the table and watched her put the finishing touches on a breakfast tray, which she carried over with a flourish. He surveyed the damage before him, then lifted a fork to run through the undercooked eggs. Jagged pieces of eggshell floated in the gelatinous whites. Black specks dotted the heavily buttered toast. Four charred strips of what appeared to be bacon took up the rest of the plate.

He smiled to hide a grimace as she sat down across from him to watch him eat. He couldn't escape.

"Where's yours?"

"I'm not hungry. I've been too busy to even *think* about eating." She grinned, propping her chin on her tented hands. "I'll just watch you enjoy your meal."

Walker took a bite of egg and toast and quickly chased it with a swallow of tepid amber liquid.

He looked inside the cup. What was it? Coffee? Hot tea?

"Where's Sophie? How come she didn't fix breakfast?"

Sara beamed. "I gave her the day off. I thought it would be nice for the two of us to spend the whole day together. Do you realize we haven't had any time alone, other than in the bedroom? You've been so busy with the hay that we've barely had time to talk about the baby."

He glanced up. "Are you . . . ?"

"I don't know—maybe."

"Isn't it too early . . . ?"

"It doesn't take any certain length of time, does it?"

"I don't know." He didn't know how babies worked. Maybe she was. The thought wasn't all that bad.

He picked up a piece of bacon and studied it. "So what's the hurry? We have months to worry about the specifics."

"Then we'll just have a nice, quiet day together."

Walker had given up hope of *ever* spending a quiet day with her. He hadn't thought about what it would mean to have someone around the house in the evening. Sara's incessant chatter was—incessant. What would it be like when babies screamed to be fed, toddlers raced up and down the hallways and older kids banged doors shut, yelling back and forth?

". . . and so I thought I'd ask you what you thought about it, because I don't know what to do." Sara stared at him expectantly, and it dawned on him that she was waiting for an answer. To what? He didn't have the slightest idea.

"You want to know what I think?" His mind raced. What *was* she talking about? Babies? The house? The new dresses?

"That's what I asked," she said, still waiting.

He took a bite of runny eggs and forced himself to swallow.

"I think your cooking is getting better every day."

Sara beamed. "You do? Potster and Sophie have been working so hard with me and I thought that I wasn't getting any better, but if you think so, then I guess I was wrong." She chattered on about meat loaf and corn bread and some cockeyed pie for the rest of the meal, pausing only to remove his empty plate and take it to the sink. He excused himself to go to the other room.

"I'll be out right after I wash the dishes," she called.

Walker entered the study and picked up his cattle register. Rubbing his eyes, he edged toward his chair, listening to the third off-key chorus of "Amazing Grace" as Sara washed dishes. He smiled when he heard the back screen door flap. Brownie had escaped to the porch.

Walker kept careful track of all his cattle in the register: when they were born, bred, and sold. It was the only ledger he didn't mind keeping track of.

Easing down, he suddenly flapped his arms wildly, searching for a seat. He fell backward as the register dropped to the floor. He lay motionless for a moment, stunned.

"Sara!" he bellowed.

She darted out of the kitchen.

He glared up at her, then asked in a calm voice, "Did you move my chair again?"

"Yes, I moved it this morning. The light is *so* much better by the window, Walker. I know you like the chair in its regular place, but I thought if you'd just sit in it once by the window, you'd love it." She started picking up the scattered mail. "See how much better it is?"

Groaning, Walker shut his eyes.

Sara offered a hand up, which he refused as he pushed himself up from the floor. Giving her another short look, he sat down in the chair, motioning for her to put the register on the table. When he found his place and started reading again, he noticed Sara was still there. He lifted his head.

"Can I get you another cup of coffee?" she asked.

"No."

"Do you need your slippers?"

"No."

She sighed. "Can I get you anything?"

"A chair. In its proper place."

"Oh, shoot. I'm *sorry* about that chair—but really, Walker, you ought to look before you sit down." She turned and went back to the kitchen, and for a blessed full two minutes, silence reigned. Walker sighed, settling deeper into the chair cushion.

Before he had finished entering information about the new calves, she was back.

"Are you going to the barn today?" She had something nestled in her apron. Walker didn't want to look up.

"I'm going to check on Diamond later."

"Good. You can take these." Sara opened her apron to reveal four bright red apples. "There's one for each horse." She dropped the fruit in Walker's lap. He stared at the deposit, thankful her aim wasn't better.

"I was going to wait until you finished working, but I didn't want you to leave and not have them. Now, Duchess likes to bite hers in half, and you have to wait until she's through chewing and then let her take the other half out of your hand. Left hand—she doesn't like the right hand. Diamond likes to take hers any way she can get it and all in one bite, but be careful that she hasn't just had a drink of water or she'll drool all over you. Also, if you scratch her precisely on the white spot on her head, she seems to like that a lot. Daisy likes it when you—hey! Did you ever notice that their names all begin with *D*? How interesting." Forgetting her original thought, Sara turned and went back to the kitchen. Walker, holding the register and four apples, watched her walk away. He stared at the study door. A few moments later, she returned.

"If you need anything, I'll be right in here. Okay?"

Walker nodded.

When her singing started up again, he quickly shut the register and rose quietly, creeping to where his boots and hat lay by the door.

He slipped them on soundlessly, keeping an eye on the closed kitchen door. As the singing rose in pitch and intensity, he quickly grabbed the apples and sneaked out the front door to find shelter in the barn.

Walker curried the last mare, then bent to check her hooves. Was he stalling, afraid to spend time with his wife? Surprisingly, he enjoyed his time with Sara, though he realized that much of it *was* in the bedroom. He wasn't sure the only reason he'd run from the house was her chatter. *Admit it, McKay: you're scared of her. You like marriage better than you thought you would—like her better than you thought you would, and the idea scares the dickens out of you.*

He brushed all four mares and put them back into their stalls with an extra ration of hay. Spending time in the barn calmed him. Here he knew what to do; with Sara, he didn't. But he couldn't spend the rest of his life in the barn, and trying to get her out of the house could be dangerous. He'd given her a few outside chores to occupy her time so he could have the house to himself, but she wasn't experienced with ranch life. Walker hung the picks and brushes back on the wall. Even simple tasks like making corn bread turned deadly if Sara was left unattended.

He took off his hat and wiped his forehead,

thinking back to an earlier conversation when
Sara had mentioned something about dime novels. Maybe he could get his hands on some. If she
was reading, she couldn't be cooking or rearranging. Or talking or singing, or the thousand and
one other distracting things she did. Until she
adjusted to the quiet workings of ranch life, she
needed something to occupy her time.

After leaving the barn, he walked to the bunkhouse, his mind on Spring Grass now. The ranch
had been his father's pride and joy and the blood
of their lives. The verdant, rolling hills stretched
for miles. He inhaled the warm air, sweet from
the newly harvested hay, and realized that he
hovered near happiness. The revelation disturbed him. Ranching he knew; marriage he
didn't. The land had comforted him since his
youth; a marriage's comforts had until now never
seemed to be satisfying.

He reached S. H. and Sophie's cabin as S. H.
was leaving for town.

"Where you off to?"

"Sophie's supplies are runnin' low. Gettin' a
late start, aren't you?"

"Sara thinks we need to spend the day
together."

The old man winked. "Now, what can two
young folks find to occupy their time all day?"

Sophie's voice sounded from the kitchen. "Git
on out of here, S. H. Quit teasin' the poor man!"

"Good morning, Sophie," Walker called into
the house. Inside, he found the housekeeper busy
making new curtains. Bolts of shiny blue material

were spread across the kitchen table, and Sophie measured squares and pinned hems with a vengeance.

"Thought you and Sara planned to spend the day together."

"We're going to. I just went to the barn to check on Diamond."

"By the way, she moved your chair again this morning."

"Thanks. I noticed."

Sophie shook her head. "She wants to help, but she don't know how."

"I don't understand it, Sophie. The ad promised an experienced housekeeper. Either her pa lied, or the Mallorys have a different idea of experienced than we do."

"Well, give her a little time. Can't ship her back, can you?"

For a moment, silence dominated the room. Walker took off his hat, absently tapping his forefinger against the crown.

"Given time, she'll quiet down and smarten up, won't she?"

"The poor thing tries hard enough." Sophie bent close to the table, her scissors rhythmically cutting the fabric. "Don't suppose you've taken a likin' to her?"

Walker turned toward the counter and poured a glass of lemonade.

Eyeing him, Sophie grinned. "Not going to answer, are you?"

"Sophie, do you have any dime novels? Sara said something the other night about liking to read them."

"I may have a few." She laid the scissors aside and disappeared into the bedroom. Walker heard her sorting through the trunk at the foot of the bed, and a few minutes later, she returned with a stack of books.

"This ought to keep her busy."

Walker studied the covers, frowning. They looked like love stories. He took one off the top of the stack, read part of a scene, then snorted and threw it back on the stack.

"Give me a seed catalogue any day."

Sophie laughed. "Men. Not a romantic bone in their bodies."

Walker took the books, thanked Sophie, and returned to the main house.

Strains of "Amazing Grace" met him at the door. He thought about asking Sara if she knew any other songs, but thought better of it. She needed about as much encouragement to sing as she needed prompting to talk. Sara was making her way down the stairs with a basket of Walker's clothes tucked beneath her arm.

"Oh, good, you're back. Is something wrong with one of the horses?"

"No, why?"

"You've been gone a long time." She spotted the books. "What do you have there?"

"Sophie was cleaning and she thought you might like to read these. They're dime novels— you might not—"

"Love stories!" Dropping the basket on the steps, she sprang at him. "That's so sweet of Sophie!"

"You read this stuff?"

She looked offended. "I certainly do! Does that bother you?"

"No—of course not. I wouldn't have brought them for you if it did."

Sara scanned the covers, her eyes alight with excitement. "I mostly read magazines back in Boston, when I had time to read."

Walker's heart dropped. Magazines? They came only once a month. He'd have to ride into town and order more books—and Denzil and Martha would raise eyebrows that he ordered love stories.

"I'm glad you like them. Sophie went through that whole big trunk of hers looking for them."

Sara regarded him questioningly. "I thought you said she was cleaning and found them."

Walker shifted to the opposite foot. "Well, she was cleaning and found . . . one of them . . . and it reminded her she had others, so she had to go and find . . . those."

"Oh." Sara picked up a book and thumbed through it. "I'm dying to read them, but it's time to fix dinner. I'm going to fry a chicken. Potster's and Sophie's chicken looks different from mine, but I'm sure they'll taste the same." She handed the book back to Walker and picked up the laundry basket. "You have time for a short nap before dinner's on the table."

"Thanks." He smiled lamely as she disappeared into the kitchen. What the hell did she mean, Sophie's and Potster's chicken "looked different" from hers?

*　*　*

The harsh light streaming through the living room window blinded him. Walker sat down, leaning his head back in the chair. The room didn't feel right. When the chair was by the fireplace, he could see out the window to the barn. This way, he couldn't see anything but inside the house.

For a moment he sat and stared.

Eventually his eyes drooped and he dozed. In his dream, swarms of children surrounded him, looking just like him but talking constantly. They chattered mercilessly until he woke with a start, sweating. Would his heirs inherit Sara's talkative gene? What if his children were never silent?

When he fully woke, he realized it was nearly time for dinner and that the house was surprisingly quiet. The only sound coming from the kitchen was that of chicken sizzling on the stove. The smell wafted through the study and he knew it wasn't Sara's cooking: the meat wasn't burned.

Sophie glanced up and clucked her tongue as he came through the kitchen door.

"Sleeping in the middle of the day. What's this world coming to?" Walker eyed the chicken, wondering about Sara, but Sophie answered before he could ask. "I sent her out to help S. H."

Walker took advantage of the silence and sat at the table, listening to Sophie cook and hum softly under her breath. His day off was turning out to be anything but restful. Before he could begin to think of what to do about Sara, she and S. H. came in the back door and Sophie finished setting the table. When the housekeeper put a plate of golden fried chicken on the table later, she leaned close to Walker and whispered, "Don't even try and identify the pieces."

Sara looked up, smiling. "What'd you say, Sophie?"

"Nothin'. Eat your dinner."

The chicken tasted better than it looked. Walker ate with a vengeance—he didn't know how long he could survive on her cooking.

While Sara and Sophie washed dishes, Walker and S. H. escaped to the front porch. The sun hung low as it found its bed for the night, bathing the two-story home in a golden light. The men sat quietly, Walker on the swing and S. H. in a wicker chair with his feet propped on the ledge. Neither spoke at first, surrounded by the soft chirrup of crickets and the horses' nickers as they settled in for sleep.

"Been quite a day." S. H. shifted, putting a pinch of snuff under his tongue.

Hat tipped over his face, Walker murmured, "Can't remember a harder day off. Not since I was a small boy and Ma made me spend Saturdays working in the house."

S. H. chuckled, settling deeper into his chair. Inside the house, dishes clattered and the melody of the women's conversation drifted to them.

Walker sat up and reached over to set his hat on the railing, barely missing a caterpillar working its way along the edge. He watched it reach the end of the post and inch up the side of the house. As it paused, a flutter of white caught the corner of his eye from the direction of the barn.

He straightened, squinting against the setting sun.

"S. H., is that a chicken over by the barn?"

S. H. sat up for a closer look. The men watched the chicken get up, walk three feet, and flop back down.

"What's wrong with it?"

"Darned if I know."

The bird staggered back to its feet, wobbled in a wide circle, then hit the ground again, occasionally ruffling its feathers.

The men got up and leaned over the railing for a better look.

Three more chickens came out of the barn, stumbling and falling against each other.

"Are they sick?"

"They weren't an hour ago."

Walker stepped off the porch as the coop door swung open, spilling a dozen more hens and the rooster, all flapping and squawking. S. H. followed him down the steps, frowning.

"I'll be ding-darned. Ain't never seen anything like it. It's almost like they're—uh-oh."

Walker turned to look at him. "Uh-oh? What's 'uh-oh' mean?"

"My mash. I put a new batch in the barn today. Gonna make some moonshine—they must've gotten into it." S. H. lunged for a chicken and the bird hopped, stumbling out of reach.

"Moonshine mash? S. H., I've *told* you to keep that stuff locked up." Wading into the chickens, Walker tried to snare one. "How did they get to it?"

"I don't know." S. H. grabbed for a hen and

missed. "We've gotta get these back in the pen. If Sophie finds out I'm makin' moonshine, she'll nail my hide to the outhouse."

The two men sneaked up on the drunken chickens one at a time. The fading light made it difficult for them to see, and Walker stumbled over a grain bucket, startling a hen he was about to nab. She bolted away, stumbling in the dirt, eyes glassy, sides heaving. He made a dive and caught her, then carried her back to the coop.

"If Sophie sees us, I'm dead." S. H. grabbed another hen by the leg and pinned her to the ground. The bird stared at him in wonder. Feathers flew and she squawked loudly as he wrestled her back to the pen.

The men froze when Sophie lifted the kitchen window and shouted, "S. H? What's going on out there?"

"Nothing," S. H. shouted back. He shot Walker a desperate look. "McKay stumbled over a bucket, that's all!"

Three hens had made it all the way to the porch and were assessing the steps. Their heads wobbled precariously on their feathered shoulders. Walker quietly approached the closest one.

"You take the other one," he whispered. S. H. reached for the first hen just as the porch door flew open.

"S. H.? What's going on out here—why are those hens putting up such a ruckus?" Sophie stood in the doorway, Sara peering over her shoulder. "S. H.?"

S. H. straightened with a sheepish grin. "Nothin's going on, sugar. We'll be there in a minute."

Sophie eyed the hen flapping behind his back.

"Why aren't those hens roosting?" she asked. "It's almost dark."

"Well, they don't seem to be feelin' too good," he said. The hens set up another squawk, feathers fogging the air. S. H. stifled a grin.

Stepping onto the porch, Sophie put her hands on her hips. "S. H. Gibson, what's goin' on out here? You two look like naughty boys caught with a hand in the cookie jar."

Walker caved in first. "They're drunk, Sophie."

S. H. glared at him. He and Walker faced her wrath, each holding a chicken that, thinking it had successfully roosted, appeared to be asleep.

"Drunk!" she bellowed.

"Drunk?" Sara echoed. "The chickens are drunk?"

S. H. tried to absolve himself. "Now, Sophie, honey, I know you're not going to like it, but I bought a little mash in town today—it's my last, sugarpie. Bought it from Babe Jensen, and I was gonna tell ya, but I didn't want ya to yell at me." He looked at Walker pleadingly. "I don't know how the chickens got into it."

"Of all the goldurned mistakes—" Sophie began. "Well, did you feed it to them?"

"Me! No, I wouldn't make a mistake like that, honeybunch. Besides, Sara fed the chickens, not me."

Three pairs of eyes swiveled to nail Sara.

Sara's hands flew to her cheeks.

Walker eyed her sternly. "Sara?"

"What does . . . mash look like?"

His eyes narrowed. "Why?"

Sara swallowed. "S. H. asked me to feed the horses earlier and . . ."

"Oh, Lord." Walker dropped his chicken. Squawking, she rolled onto her side. "Not the horses, too."

"No!" Sara exclaimed. "I know I gave them oats. I know what oats look like." Color flooded her face. "But when I was looking for the oats, I opened another barrel and . . . I may have forgotten to shut the lid."

First breakfast, then the chair. Now S. H. was in the doghouse with Sophie, and he had a barn full of drunken poultry. Walker had had enough for one day.

Sara's bottom lip quivered. She looked at the unconscious chicken under S. H.'s arms and the one lying peacefully in the dirt.

"Are they going to die?"

"Mash isn't going to kill them, but they're gonna have one heck of a hangover in the morning." Walker bent over to pick up the limp bird. "I wouldn't use the eggs tomorrow, Sophie."

Whirling, Sophie marched back into the house and slammed the door. Sara sank onto the porch swing, looking stunned.

"Guess I know where I'll be roostin' tonight," S. H. grumbled. He adjusted his hen and started for the barn.

* * *

By the look on Walker's face, he was ready to buy her a train ticket back East. Sara had taken pains not to crowd him today, had done everything she could to stay out of his way. Granted, it had been foolish of her to leave the lid off that mash barrel, but it wasn't a hanging crime. She was getting a little tired of Sophie's and Walker's insinuations that she was inept. She might not have been born and reared on a farm; she might not be the most experienced cook or housekeeper in Wyoming; but she tried, and Walker should be grateful that she loved him enough to want to learn.

She stayed in the kitchen reading by the oil lamp until Walker came through the house and went upstairs. She heard the thump of heavy boots down the hallway; then their bedroom door opened and shut.

Tucking a bookmark in her book, she crept up the stairway, straining to hear his activity. Was he so angry that he wouldn't talk to her?

She heard first one boot drop, then the other. When the bedcovers rustled, she ascended the stairs and walked into the room. Walker, sitting in bed, looked up from the journal he was reading, his eyes scanning her tear-swollen face.

"What are you crying about?"

"Nothing. Thank you." She marched to the closet and removed her dressing gown.

Laying his reading aside, he sighed. "Anyone could have left the lid off that barrel."

"No, it's my fault and I'm sorry. I don't pay enough attention to what I'm doing." She crossed the room and sat down on the bed, determined to stay calm. He hated it when she cried—she could see that.

"Don't worry about it. You'll learn. You've only been here a few weeks." Pulling her close, he whispered, "Would a hot bath make you feel better? I'll have Sophie heat some water."

Visions of previous bathtub trysts flooded Sara, eliciting a warmth she couldn't ignore. But a bath wouldn't solve the problem. They needed to communicate on an emotional level, rather than just on a physical one. The marriage would never grow otherwise, and she dearly wanted it to bloom, to thrive so that eventually, solving little problems like the chicken fiasco would be as automatic as breathing.

"We need to talk, Walker. I'm sorry if I get in the way—I only want to help."

Lifting her hair off her shoulders, he placed soft kisses along her neckline. "Your efforts are duly noted, but we don't have to talk about it right now, do we?"

Sara felt her tensions draining. He was right. It would take years to learn everything she needed to know, to develop trust and communication. But she *would* learn. She would show them all that she could be as good or better a wife and helpmate than any other woman. Ranching was second nature to Walker, and Sophie had cooked for S. H. for forty years, if not more. How could *she* expect to master in a few weeks what had taken others forty years to perfect?

She eyed her husband shyly. "I suppose a bath might be nice."

Trailing kisses along the curve of her cheek, he murmured, "Think so?" Drawing her down on the spread, he closed his mouth over hers, ending the discussion.

Settling deeper into his arms, she surrendered to the building heat.

Right now, she knew everything she needed to know to please her husband.

Lightly, Sara ran a finger over the cover of her dime novel. Walker lay beside her, drowsy with satisfaction. Her eyes focused on the horse and cowboy, and on a woman standing in the background in a long, billowing dress. She imagined that the woman was her and she was watching Walker rope a wild stallion, his arms bulging as the horse struggled to break free.

"Are you going to turn out the light?"

She gave him an absent love pat. "In a minute. I want to read a few pages of my book." She gazed at him lovingly. "Thank you for bringing these to me."

Drawing her back for another long kiss, he whispered, "You're welcome." His hand caressed her bare leg and she smiled. This was the way it was supposed to be. Husband lazy and replete from lovemaking, wife reading in bed, contented and happy.

The end of page five hooked her. The girl in the book was so like her, looking for a husband on the high plains. But the one right man hadn't come along—only a rakish, surly sort who was quite rude, in Sara's opinion. She turned the pages, eyes glued to the text, fascinated that the heroine actually liked the rogue. The girl mirrored Sara's own thoughts about love and marriage. Marriage was a treasure, and once the right man came into the picture, the heroine ceased to know anyone else was alive.

Slamming the book shut, she sat up straighter. "Walker!" She rolled toward him and he grunted. "I'm going to write a love story."

Opening an eye, he looked at her. "A what?"

"A love story! I can do it! This author is all right, but I could write it better." Hadn't she dreamed about love and marriage since she was a toddler?

"Really?"

"Really!"

He wadded his pillow beneath his head. "Have you ever written anything before?"

"I've written letters—and once I wrote a short poem. I'm good at making up stories." She paused, biting her bottom lip. Almost too good. But how hard could it be to write a dime novel? She wouldn't have to make up any of the story; she could use her own. "After I'm through with the chores in the morning, I could shut myself up in your office and no one would hear anything from me all day. Do you mind?"

Walker frowned. "Why my office? Can't you do it in the parlor or the kitchen? Or even up here, where you wouldn't be disturbed?"

His hesitation puzzled her. She questioned him with a look. "I didn't think you'd mind. The kitchen and parlor are noisy, and this room is so hot in the daytime . . ."

"My study is my place, Sara. A man's place."

He rolled over and adjusted the covers, and she knew he was thinking about his furniture. She wouldn't touch his old furniture, not for a hundred dollars.

But she decided not to push him. She still felt guilty about the chicken incident and she didn't want to spoil the memory of their earlier lovemaking. She comforted herself with thoughts of her writing.

She could see it now:

Sara McKay's (wife of local rancher Walker McKay) fourth book, Love's Eternal Flame, *has broken all sales records. The romance novel has swept fiction circles from New York to Montana with a vengeance and Mrs. McKay's fans are demanding that she write faster! When asked her secret for penning riveting love stories, Mrs. McKay says she's living her own romance, and cannot write any less.*

She dropped a kiss on Walker's forehead, then leaned over him and blew out the lamp. Settling back on her pillow, she sighed. A novelist. She was going to be a novelist!

Love's Eternal Flame—or *Flaming Love. Love With A Handsome Stranger* wasn't bad—no, *Love Burns Brightly* . . .

Burning Love had a nice ring to it. . . .

Chapter 10

‿‿◯◯‿

Sara skipped down the stairway the next morning, eager to start the day. If Sophie didn't need her and Walker wanted her out from under his feet, she'd begin writing the book today. Her eyes scanned the gleaming parlor. There wasn't a hint of dust on the cherry-wood tables, moss-colored drapes, or hand-hewed oak mantel. The open window carried the scent of lemon oil throughout the immaculate room. It was clear she wasn't needed here.

She'd woken thinking that she should write Papa and tell him more about where she was and break the news that she was married, but the idea appealed to her about as much as the thought of intoxicated chickens. Maybe she'd wait another week before stirring that hornet's nest.

Strolling back into the parlor, she paused at the

open window, sniffing. Mouth-watering aromas drifted from the bunkhouse kitchen. Maybe Potster had time to teach her to cut up a chicken in recognizable pieces. One glance at the mantel clock assured her that the old cook would be up to his elbows preparing dinner and wouldn't want to be bothered.

As she started back upstairs, she noticed the door to Walker's study was closed. Was he home this morning? She'd overslept, and by the time she'd read another chapter of the dime novel, dressed, and come downstairs for breakfast, Sophie informed her that Walker had been up for hours.

The closed door lured her back down the stairs. Obviously, if he was in, he was busy. Too busy for a brief visit from her?

Stepping off the last stair, she edged toward the study door. She knew how picky Papa was about his study, and Sophie had said that Walker was a man of habit. One of those habits, apparently, was to allow no one else in his office. But she didn't intend to stay long, just long enough for a friendly hello and perhaps a stolen kiss . . .

Research for *Love's Eternal Flame*.

Grinning, she reached out for the knob.

"Sara! The door's closed! You're not supposed to go in there!"

Sara jumped, hastily retreating. Rubbing her palm on her skirt, she turned to the housekeeper. "I wasn't. I was just dusting the doorknob."

"You know Walker doesn't like anyone bothering him when he's in his study."

"But I was just—"

"I just don't want to see you in any more trouble with Walker." Sophie eyed her sternly before returning to the kitchen.

Sara retrieved her book from her nightstand and brought it downstairs to the parlor. She'd barely read a paragraph when a ruckus in the kitchen drew her attention. S. H. burst through the doorway, heading for Walker's study in a dead run.

Sara listened as the foreman explained about a bull down in the north pasture. A minute later, the two men left the house with a flurry of clanking boots and slamming doors. Hmmmph—men! If S. H. could go into Walker's study unannounced, so could she.

Sara sat until the sound of galloping horses left the barnyard. Laying the book aside, she stepped into the hallway. Her gaze swept the deserted foyer, relieved to see Sophie nowhere around.

The open door to Walker's study called to her. Edging along the length of the foyer table, she argued with herself about the advisability of infiltrating sacred ground. Papa fussed about his study—called it his domain and allowed Wadsy to dust only once a month. Walker had told her that he didn't want her rearranging the room and didn't want her writing her book in there, but he hadn't said anything about just taking a peek inside. Besides, from the sound of things, he and S. H. would be tied up with the lame bull for most of the morning. Her slippers eased along the polished floor, encouraging her exploration with their soft, nudging sensations.

If Walker's study was anything like Papa's, it

could use a little attention. There'd be papers, books, and journals everywhere. Sophie was busy in the kitchen, and if Sara was reading in the study, she wouldn't be underfoot. She'd just step in for a moment and look the room over, to use for book reference. Her hero couldn't just ride a horse all day; he'd have to have reasonable interests, and his interests would take place in his study—his manly domain.

In a flash, she entered the study and quietly shut the door. Leaning against the wooden panel, she paused to let her racing heart catch up.

A delicious sense of expectancy washed over her as she waited for her pulse to return to normal. Her glance slid over the masculine lair with its rich furnishings: the teakwood desk, burgundy leather sofa, and wing-backed chairs sitting before a cold fireplace; heavy gold damask draperies opened to reveal a large picture window overlooking the unkempt rose garden. Closing her eyes, she released a quick breath. She was in.

Hurrying to the window, she feasted on the garden's statuesque fountains of near-naked women pouring water from the large vases perched on their delicate bare shoulders into a lovely, lily-pad-covered fishpond. What an exquisite sight it would be if anyone were to tend to it. Maybe one day she would be able to convince Walker to let her take care of it, and she would put her love into each fountain and flower.

Turning back to the room, she walked among the furniture, touching each piece, admiring the quality. Walker was most assuredly a man of considerable means. This room would please Papa, but money meant nothing to her. In many ways, she wished her husband were a struggling farmer who needed a young wife to help him make his way in the world. Money made people independent—maybe if they were poor, he would need her more.

Sitting down in his chair, she leaned back, closing her eyes. Walker's scent surrounded her: leather, soap, and musk. Images of his lovemaking filled her with euphoria.

Opening her eyes, she spotted an open ledger and a stack of unpaid bills. Moving to the desk, she perched on the side. Today must be the day Caleb came for dinner. Every two weeks, the two friends combined business and pleasure over a plate of Sophie's fried quail and hot biscuits.

Caleb Vanhooser was a strange little man. If he weren't Walker's friend, Sara wouldn't like him. He'd done nothing to her personally—he was ever the perfect gentleman. Her dislike wasn't rational; her womanly instinct kept her reserved. There was something odd about the way he had avoided her at their party, as if he hadn't particularly had anything to say to her.

Shifting the ledger ever so slightly, she scanned the columns of numbers. They were regular and even; the deposits barely fluctuated at all. She was impressed with the sizable profit the ranch made. If there was one thing Sara Livingston knew, it was numbers. A teacher had once told her she could work for the government if she wanted. Cooking and housekeeping came hard, but mathematics was easy for her.

Scanning the ledger, she felt a twinge of conscience. Maybe Walker didn't want her to know his business, yet didn't it directly affect her now? Sophie didn't want her in the kitchen, S. H. didn't want her in the barnyard, and Walker wanted her only in the bedroom—maybe she'd stumbled onto an area where she could actually be of service. She could go over Walker's figures and make sure they were correct. He wouldn't have to know—not until he felt more comfortable with her delving into his business.

Sara heard the back screen door open. Hurriedly shoving the ledger back into place, she arranged pencils the way they had been. Today wasn't the best time to start her mission, but the next time the house was empty, she would begin.

At least writing *Love's Eternal Flame* and rechecking Walker's figures would give her something productive to do.

She left the study feeling considerably more needed.

Agents Kate Warne and Frank Roche stepped onto the Mallory porch and knocked on the shanty door. A crowd of towheaded children from toddlers to teenagers stopped playing in the front yard to stare at the newcomers. All boys, Kate noticed.

The door opened, and a man with his thumbs hooked between his suspenders and undershirt met their unsmiling gazes. The tall, thick man eyed the strangers coldly.

"Jack Mallory?"

"Might be. Who wants to know?"

Kate flashed her badge. "Kate Warne, Pinkerton National Detective Agency." She waited for the usual response.

"Woman detective?"

"Yes, sir. We'd like to talk to you if you have a minute."

Mallory opened the door wider, allowing the couple to enter. Sleeping pallets were spread across the dirt floor of the small sod shack. A long eating table sat at the south end of the room. An infant nursed from a haggard-looking woman sitting in front of the stove.

"Frank Roche, my partner," Kate said.

Jack nodded toward his wife. "This here is Lorann—the missus."

Kate smiled. "Ma'am." The two detectives sat down.

"What is it?" Lorann frowned. "Has something happened to Olivia?"

"No, ma'am," Frank said. "We're just here to ask a few questions regarding your daughter's recent trip."

"What about it?" Jack sat down opposite them across the table.

"Have you heard from your daughter recently?"

"No—sent her a letter, but we ain't heard nothing back. Why?"

Kate picked up the conversation. "No reason for alarm. We're hoping that your daughter will be able to help with a missing-person's case that we're investigating."

"That right? What would our Livvy know about a missing person?"

"We understand you were with your daughter in the train depot the morning she left. Is that right?"

Jack nodded. "Me and the missus took Livvy to the station to catch the five-forty."

"Did you see anyone other than your daughter in the waiting room that morning?"

The man pursed his lips in thought, his dark brows drawn tightly against his weathered features.

"A young boy," Lorann supplied. "There was a young boy waiting for the train."

"Anyone else?"

The room fell silent. Outside, the boys' squeals filtered through the open doorway. It was several moments before Jack said, "No, cain't think of anyone."

"Are you sure the other person was a boy?"

Jack frowned.

Frank joined the conversation. "Could it have been a young woman dressed like a boy?"

Shaking his head, Jack said, "Don't rightly know—suppose it could have been. Me and Lorann weren't really lookin'. We were too busy trying to convince Livvy to get on the train."

Kate and Frank swapped glances.

"She didn't wanna to go. Got it in her head to marry some no-good gambler, Rodney Willbanks. Kids." Jack snorted. "Got her set up to marry a wealthy rancher, and what's she do? Tries to run off with a man who can't give her a roof over her head, let alone a decent life. Me and Lorann told her she was marryin' Mr. McKay whether she liked it or not. Girl's got a streak of orneriness in her a mile wide, but she ain't gonna ruin what we got goin'."

"Going, sir?"

"This McKay feller's got enough money to make us all comfortable. Livvy's not gonna ruin that for us. Marrying McKay's the only thing she can do. She's a looker, like her ma—told her she needs to put that to use. The McKay feller wants an heir, and Livvy's born for breedin', just like Lorann here."

"You want your daughter to marry for money?"

"We want her to be happy, and money goes a long way toward happiness, ma'am." Jack's rheumy eyes wandered the shanty's cramped interior, the squalid conditions. "Ain't nothing wrong in wantin' the best for our daughter."

"No, sir." Kate was writing in a small notebook. "You haven't heard from your daughter since the morning she left?"

"Like I said, we've sent a letter, but we ain't heard nothing back yet. A letter should be along any day now. Say you're looking for a missing person?"

"Sara Livingston—are you familiar with the name?"

"Livingston? Her papa the one who owns the railroad?"

"Yes, sir."

"I've heard of her—hear she's a real handful. She missing?"

Closing the notepad, Kate smiled. "Thank you for your time. We'll check back in a few weeks to see if you've heard from your daughter." She scribbled an address on a piece of paper and handed it to Mallory. "Meanwhile, if you hear from Olivia, please let us know."

"We'll be hearing from her any day now." Jack got up to walk them to the door. "Mail's slow. You know how it is. I ain't lookin' to hear anything for another week or so, but by now Livvy's married to McKay. Should be gettin' money anytime."

"Yes, sir."

"Livvy's our only girl . . . got them five boys out there in the yard and the little one the wife's nursin'. They'll make their way in the world, but you can see how we needed to make sure Livvy married well. Takes a lot of money to raise a family this size. My health ain't so good—down in the back. Ain't been able to work steady for months. It'll be a real comfort to know someone's lookin' after us."

"Yes, sir."

On that note, Kate motioned to Frank and the pair said their good-byes.

Walking back to the buggy, Kate glanced at Frank. "Isn't love grand?"

"Sounds like it," he replied.

"Are they sure it was a boy?" Lowell asked.

"That's what they said, but the Mallorys could be mistaken." Kate glanced at Frank. "They were preoccupied with making sure their daughter got on the train."

Wadsy set a tray of tea and cookies on the desk. "My poor Babygirl. Where can she be?"

"It wouldn't be the first time Sara dressed as a boy when she wanted to hide." Lowell prowled the study, lighting and relighting a cigar. Kate took out her notebook and consulted it. The telegraph at first had given them hope, but their inability to trace its sender left her frustrated. If it was from Sara, she was taking precautions not to be found. But why?

"Our next step is to check with McKay in Wyoming, see if Olivia arrived there safely."

Lowell Livingston hadn't wanted to involve the rancher, but despite an intensive search, the agency had failed to turn up anyone who had seen or heard from Sara since her disappearance. Hopefully, Miss Mallory had observed more in the train station than her parents. Kate closed the notebook. "What do you think, Frank?"

"We could send Fox and White up there, let them poke around."

Kate nodded. John Fox and John White were two of the agency's best. Short of Allan himself, there weren't any better.

"There'll be a thousand-dollar bonus for the man"—Lowell glanced up—"or woman who brings my daughter home within the month."

"That's generous of you, Lowell, but it's not necessary." Kate straightened in her chair. Allan Pinkerton hired his detectives for their character rather than for their experience. He insisted on incorruptible, courageous men, dedicated to the law: men with strong personalities and keen powers of observation. Kate was the first woman Allan had hired, and she'd talked hard and fast to convince him she was capable of filling the position. A woman could worm more secrets out of a reluctant male witness than another man could.

Women also observed what men couldn't, and were able to form friendships with wives and girlfriends of suspected criminals. She'd convinced Pinkerton and got the job. Now she was among his top four agents along with Frank, John Fox, and John White.

Chewing on the end of his cigar, Lowell stared out the window, a wisp of smoke playing through the worry lines on his brow and whitening hair. His daughter's disappearance weighed heavily upon him. Kate's heart ached for the man.

"We'll find her, Lowell. Be patient."

"If only I had listened closer, tried to reason with her. . . ." Kate could barely make out the railroad tycoon's voice, filled with pain and regret. He spoke more to himself than to her. "I'm so afraid that something has happened to her."

"You would have heard. No news is good news."

"If I were to lose Sara . . ." He shook the thought away. "Send the wire, Kate. Send McKay a wire and ask him to have Olivia Mallory get in touch with us as soon as possible."

"Yes, sir. Right away."

"And tell Allan I want him in on this."

"I'll tell him, sir, but he's busy with another case."

"Hang the other case. Tell him he can name his price if he'll drop everything and help with the search."

"I'll tell him, sir." It was unlikely the boss would comply with Livingston's wishes for any amount of money, though. Allan had been on the other case for months, consumed with apprehending the criminal. He wasn't going to be happy about this.

Kate rose, signaling Frank that the conversation was over. The two detectives left the Livingston study a moment later.

"Think we'll find her?" Frank asked.

"She has to be somewhere. We'll find her," Kate replied.

"The Eye That Never Sleeps" was the Pinkerton motto. For Kate, it meant more. She considered it a personal promise.

Chapter 11

⌒⌒

As Sara finished lacing her boots, she heard Walker come into the foyer downstairs. Her hair was pinned in a bold new upsweep Sophie had taught her that afternoon, and she wore a burgundy dress of Martha's own design: a rich polished linen that fit her curves and dips in all the right places. The Johnsons' first summer barn dance was only hours away, and she glowed with excitement. She recalled the way Walker had flawlessly led her around the dance floor at their wedding, and all eyes had followed the newly-weds at the party. Tonight would be even better.

"Sara?" Walker called up the stairway. "I have something for you."

Heat crept up her neck and spread across her cheeks. What might it be? Usually when he said he had "something for her" in that roguish male tone, it had nothing whatsoever to do with trinkets. Checking her appearance in the mirror one last time, she smiled. Maybe he had gotten her pen and ink—or new pencils. If so, she could start *Love's Eternal Flame*.

Sara flew down the stairs in time to catch Walker easing into his chair in the parlor. She noticed that he was careful these days of where he sat, no longer taking his seat for granted.

"What is it?" she asked, entering the room. She didn't see any packages; all he had was the monthly mail. "S. H. picked up the mail in town this morning," she told him. "I'm sorry I haven't had time to sort it."

"That's fine." He absently handed her a letter. "Looks like you got a letter from your father."

Her heart skipped a beat. Papa? Oh, no—*how* did he find her? Willing a steady hand, she casually accepted the missive and Walker returned to his mail. She was glad his distraction kept him from noticing her paling face.

Turning away, she stared at the envelope and nearly sagged with relief. The sender wasn't Livingston, as she had feared, but Mallory. Olivia's parents. Her fingers smoothed the seams of the envelope thoughtfully. The letter inside bulged against the thin paper. Did she dare open and read it? She glanced at Walker.

"Aren't you going to open it?" Walker finished sorting the mail and threw it on the table. He stood up and brushed past her on his way upstairs.

"Yes . . . of course."

He paused and turned to look back at her. "When?"

"Now, while you change." She grinned. "You'd better hurry; we don't want to be late for the dance."

"Right. I'll only be a minute." He kissed her before moving on. A stripe of warmth began at the spot where his lips had touched her and raced through her stomach like wildfire. He smiled in a backward glance and took the stairs two at a time. She slumped into his chair.

The letter lay like a coiled rattler in her hands. Had the Mallorys discovered the plan? They couldn't have. It wouldn't be addressed to Olivia if they had, and Olivia would never inform her parents of the switch. Not until she had to.

The postmark indicated that the letter had traveled for a month, almost as long as she had been at Spring Grass. She lifted the envelope to the light but couldn't make out the writing.

She had to open it.

No, she couldn't.

Her hands quivered and she rested the letter in her lap, pressing her fingers to her temples. Opening it would be an invasion of privacy—Olivia's. Leaving it unopened prevented her from knowing if the Mallorys suspected their daughter's ploy.

But what if the Mallorys were on their way to visit and the letter warned her of their imminent arrival?

Picking up the letter, she gingerly played with an edge of the envelope, wriggling a finger under the flap, trying to loosen the stubborn seal. She dangled the envelope by one finger, shaking it. Finally, she tore the seal away and scanned the contents quickly.

Walker started down the stairs and she sprang to her feet, cramming the letter into her pocket. When she streaked past him on her way up to their room, he reached out and grabbed the hem of her dress.

"Whoa—what's your hurry?" He turned her around by the shoulders and Sara could see his eyes appraising her hair, her dress.

"We're going to be late," she murmured.

"We have plenty of time. Everything all right?"

"Perfect. Walker, I don't want to be late." Could he see the guilt in her eyes? The deception blacker than sin? She had to tell him the truth—now, before he discovered her ruse on his own.

But she couldn't. She felt sick just thinking about it.

Leaning down for a kiss, he whispered against her ear, "I meant, is everything all right with your parents?"

"Oh—yes. Fine. Thank you."

Giving her an affectionate squeeze, he smiled. "Finish prettying up. I'll bring the carriage around front." He started down, then turned around, his eyes openly ravishing her. "You look real pretty in your new dress."

"Thank you."

She waited until she heard the back door close, then took the rest of the stairs in a rush, Walker's smile etched in her heart and the letter burning a hole in her pocket.

A few minutes later, Walker climbed into the

carriage and sat beside her. It was a beautiful evening; the sun was setting, the air cooling.

Sara loved their carriage rides together. She and Walker attended church every Sunday, and she rode to town with him occasionally for supplies. Everywhere they went, someone stopped to comment on what a handsome couple they made. Sara preened at the attention. Little gray-haired women patted her hand and assured her that she and Walker would make beautiful children. Rugged-looking men from neighboring ranches slugged Walker on the arm as they walked by, still chuckling about the wedding barbecue.

Had it been five weeks already? It seemed like only days. She snuggled closer to Walker on the buggy seat and he pressed back against her warmth. She felt him relaxing, opening up little by little, trusting her. He watched her when she walked across a room, and one night when she was doing dishes he helped, splashing her with soapy bubbles until she retaliated and they ended up soaking wet on the kitchen floor.

Guilt brought her back to reality. It was all a ruse, a scam. Her marriage was a lie, and the Mallorys' letter confirmed it.

She straightened and pulled away from Walker. If only she knew how he would react. Did he care for her enough that it wouldn't matter? Would they both laugh about it in their old age, the way the townfolk chuckled about the wedding? Or would he send her away, forcing her to return to an empty life in Boston, or worse, to a cheerless Uncle Brice? Who would want her, now that she had been with a man? The rumor would spread throughout Boston and her reputation would be sullied. No amount of Papa's money could buy back virginity.

Walker glanced at her. "You're going to make that pretty lip bleed," he said.

Sara realized she was biting her lip so hard she could feel the broken skin.

"Something bothering you tonight?"

"I'm just nervous." She hoped her face didn't reflect her anguish. "The Johnsons didn't talk to me much at our party and I'm afraid Mrs. Johnson doesn't approve of me."

"Nonsense," he said, dismissing her concerns. "They'll love you. They were probably having such a good time they didn't want to stop to chat." He switched the reins to his left hand and patted her knee with his right. "Stop worrying and enjoy yourself. You'll be the prettiest girl there."

The word "love" cut deep. She longed for Walker to tell her he loved her. But why? So she could shatter him? Break his heart the way Trudy had?

Walker returned both hands to the reins as the carriage rolled up the drive of the Johnson ranch. Ahead, she saw rows of carriages lined up in front of the sprawling farmhouse. Tantalizing sights and smells greeted them when they drew closer, and Sara's pulse quickened. She adored dancing, especially with Walker. All she had to do was forget about the letter, shove it to the back of her mind, and deal with it later. Tonight, she was going to enjoy the party.

The buggy came to a stop in the midst of a

swarm of servants and party guests waiting to greet them. Two tall, burly friends of Walker's swept her from the carriage to claim her for a dance. Walker disappeared into a flock of women who had convened to drag him into the party the minute his boot touched ground. Before she could sputter "yes" or "no," the men whisked Sara across the yard and into the open barn alight with lanterns. More neighbors moved to welcome her, and for the first time since she came to Wyoming, she felt at home.

Sara promised the first dance to Buck Whitley, a school friend of Walker's. His height and gawky legs made him an awkward partner. He hunched over, trying to accommodate Sara's diminutive frame and carry on a conversation. His bumbling but sincere attempts amused Sara.

"If you don't mind me saying, ma'am, you sure are a pretty sight. I'd venture to say about the prettiest I've ever seen around these parts."

Sally Hinter danced by close enough to overhear Buck's comment and swatted him on the arm. "You'd better be nice to us trolls"—she winked at Sara—" 'cause she's taken." Her sheer bulk forced her partner to crowd Buck. "You don't have a chance—not when she's got Walker McKay waitin' at home."

The two couples parted with good-natured laughter. Buck blushed and handed her to one of Rusty Johnson's red-haired sons, who whirled her away.

The sweet strains of fiddles and revelry pushed unwanted thoughts of the Mallory letter aside. Sara tried to bow out when the couples lined up for square dancing, but Mac Maze, whose name aptly described his dancing style, wouldn't hear of it.

"Just follow the directions," he said, leading her to the line, "and keep your eyes on me."

The dance began and those gathered in the middle separated from their partners. They folded over in a bow and Sara did the same, bowing to her left. She righted herself to see Mac doing the first step, something called a do-si-do. Her feet flew, trying to keep up with the music. After a few spins and bows and different partners, she began catching on and lifted her skirts to prance lightly around a man she'd never seen before with a grin as wide as Texas.

She traded partners again as the dance ended and found herself face-to-face with Walker. The crowd clapped when Walker caught her up in both arms and swung her around, his gaze centered on his bride.

She laughed as she flew through the air, holding tight to him. She'd watched him all night and been rewarded with only brief glimpses of him dancing with other women, chatting with friends, or being slapped on the back by other ranchers. Now she was in his arms, and the evening took on a magical glow. Pulling her close with one hand around her back, he met her eyes, and the desire she saw there took her breath.

"You're the belle of the ball," he teased.

"And you're the prince," she teased back. He kissed her briefly, then twirled her around for a promenade.

The fiddles slowed and Sara recognized the

first strains of a waltz. As Walker moved her easily around the floor, his gaze met hers again. It was as if she were the only woman in the world, and he the only man. Pressing his mouth against her ear, he whispered, "You're beautiful, Sara McKay."

She floated in a sensual cocoon for the remainder of the evening. Walker brought punch, and they sat on the sidelines holding hands, watching the merriment. Other men stood back, now that Walker had claimed his bride.

Sara observed occasional glimpses of envy from the local girls, but for the most part, the single women of Laramie had accepted her. One by one, they stopped to say hello. Rolene Berry asked her to the quilting bee the following week, and, smiling, Sara accepted.

Lanterns burned low when Walker finally lifted Sara into the buggy, his eyes dark with the promise of pleasures yet to come.

Snuggling close to him, she sighed. Her feet throbbed from the hours of dancing, but she felt hope. Hope that Walker was falling as deeply in love with her as she was with him; hope that when she told him about her silly ruse, he would forgive her. How could he not? They were a match made in heaven, and after tonight, even he knew it.

"That wasn't so bad," he remarked.

"It was wonderful—the best dance I've ever attended."

"And I'll bet a pretty woman like you has attended her share," he whispered, lowering his mouth to take hers. The intensity of the kiss incited a fire in her only he could quench. Drawing her onto his lap, he effortlessly managed the reins as the kisses grew longer, deeper, more provocative.

"How much farther home?" she murmured between snatches of heated passion.

"Five hundred miles," he groaned, hungrily capturing her mouth.

S. H. had waited up for them. He took the reins as Walker lifted Sara off the buggy seat and held her in a passionate clinch.

"Have fun?" the foreman asked. He glanced at the couple; then red crept up the sides of his face and he hurriedly looked the other way. " 'Pears so."

Unhitching the horse, he led it to the barn.

An hour later, Sara dropped back against the pillow, damp with perspiration, her breath coming in ragged gasps. Walker's lovemaking had been different tonight, more intense. He lay beside her, his breathing gradually returning to normal. Dear God, how was she going to tell him?

He traced his fingers lightly along her bare thigh, "What did the letter say?"

"Letter?"

"From your folks."

That letter.

"Oh . . . nothing much. They miss me . . . hope everything is going fine."

Rolling onto his back, he leaned over and lit the lamp. "Read it to me."

"Oh, Walker, it's so late, and you have to get up early in the morn—"

A finger to her lip quelled the protest. "I realized tonight that I don't spend enough time with you. I haven't taken an interest in your life, and I'm going to do better. Read me your letter so I'll know a little about your folks." Kissing her lightly on the nose, he released her, propping a pillow behind his head. "We'll have them for a visit this summer. How does that sound?"

Disastrous. Horrifying. The ruination of everything she'd tried to achieve these past few weeks.

"Hey?" He gazed at her, a smile touching the corners of his mouth. She loved it when he smiled. It softened his features and made his eyes even bluer.

"Tomorrow we'll have more time—"

"Tonight. Get the letter, sweetheart."

Sweetheart. He'd never called her sweetheart. Why did he have to now? Now, when she was about to tell him the biggest fib of all? Why was he putting her through this? Couldn't he leave the subject alone? Sliding out of bed, she got the letter and climbed back under the sheet.

She stared at the written albatross, turning it over in her hands. She had no choice. Walker wouldn't give up until she opened the envelope. Closing her eyes, she lifted the flap and eased the letter out.

"Does it bite?" he teased.

It could. It could devour her if she weren't careful.

She opened the envelope and hurriedly scanned the opening salutation.

"Dear Olivia."

Sara took a short breath, stalling for time, then quickly reviewed the body of the text.

Dear Olivia,

We hope this letter finds you well. We are worried about you. Has the wedding takn place? You have had pleenty of time to become Mrs. Walker McKay and get that dreadfool Rodney Wilbanks out of your head. I'm sure you kin now see the wisdom of our decisheen.

Sara read on, eyes widening. Mrs. Mallory told about the hard times on the Mallory farm, how Mr. Mallory had to sell some of his chickens at market to buy supplies for planting and now they were low on eggs. Mr. Mallory hadn't worked in months, and they were about to lose the homestead.

The entire letter was little more than a plea for money and a demand for Olivia to supply it.

The six pages showed little concern for their daughter's happiness. The final lines read, "We deeply hop that this letter finds you well and that you have come to adjust to your situation in a manner befitting a lady. Sincerely, Mother and Father."

She rested the letter in her lap. That was why Olivia had been so upset on the train. Her parents were marrying her off to Walker to save their farm. They'd sent their only daughter to marry for money, caring nothing for her happiness. Relief filled Sara: she'd saved both Olivia and Walker from a loveless arrangement.

"Well?"

Starting, Sara came back to the present. Lifting the letter, she read aloud:

Dear Olivia,

Everyone's happy and well and we hope you are, too. We've missed you dearly on the farm— ranch—and are glad that you made it safely to Mr. McKay's house. Things are going well with us. We have more money than we could ever imagine, so we surely don't need any help from you.

Sara paused and bit her lip. Improvising wasn't her strongest suit.

She returned to the letter:

In no time at all we're sure you'll be pregnant and then we'll have a grandchild to love, and maybe much, much later we can even visit. We are terribly busy now, so please don't ask us to make the long, tiring trip to Wyoming. We just in no way could do it at this time. But we really miss you and are glad that you are happy and well. Tell us when the baby comes.

Love,
Mother and Father

Walker looked at her. "That's pretty brief, isn't it? Glad you're happy and we can't come and visit now."

Sara consulted the missive again. " 'P. S. We got a new cow last week.' "

"Well, a new cow, huh? Did they say what kind?"

She skimmed the letter. "A black one." Yawning, she shoved the letter back in the envelope. "My, can you believe how late it is? We'll never get up in the morning." Crawling across the bed, she kissed him good-night and blew out the lamp. When he pulled her down to him, she grinned. "You're insatiable, you know that?"

Wrapping her in his arms, he rolled her over onto her back, and the question—like so many others—was never addressed.

Chapter 12

Stirring, Sara slowly opened her eyes the next morning. The force that could bring her world crashing down around her lay on the bedstand beside her. Swallowing against the tightness in her throat, she shoved the sheet aside and sat up as the door opened and Walker came into the bedroom. She smiled when he bent and kissed her, nuzzling her sleep-warm cheek.

"Anyone ever tell you that you're beautiful first thing in the morning?"

"Just you."

Their mouths drifted together for a long, unhurried good-morning kiss. *Tell him, Sara; tell him right now, while he's in a charitable mood. Last night was so wonderful he can't deny that fate had brought us together.*

"S. H. and I are going into town," he whispered against her mouth.

"What about breakfast?"

Rumpling her hair, he gave her another brief kiss before he sat down on the side of the bed. "Breakfast was two hours ago."

"What time is it?" Sara hadn't thought to look at the clock, and the curtains were still drawn.

"Eight o'clock. S. H. and I are getting a late start, so don't expect us back until supper."

Sara lurched upright. Eight o'clock? How could she have slept so late? Swinging her legs over the side of the bed, she leaned down to retrieve her nightgown off the floor.

Walker watched her, grinning, his eyes traveling the length of her nakedness.

She glanced around at him, not the least embarrassed by his slow and thorough masculine perusal. "What?"

"I know why you slept so late." His grin was as smug as his conceit.

"Turn your head," she sniffed.

"Why? I like looking at my wife."

"Just turn your head, you cad." Reaching for her gown, she faced him again. "Are you peeking?"

"Yes, ma'am, and enjoying every minute of it."

"Shame on you."

Leaning over, he pinched her on the fanny. "Shame on *you* for making me late. What am I going to tell S. H.?"

She gazed back at him innocently. "About what?"

"About this." Catching her in his arms, he

tossed her onto the bed and dove after her. Drawing her arms over her head, he gazed at her, his eyes darkening with passion. "You know what?"

"What?" She whispered.

He sobered. "I never thought . . . after Trudy . . . I figured I'd spend my life alone."

Her heart ached, treachery a bitter taste in her mouth. "And now?" she whispered, both fearing and desperately needing the answer.

His mouth captured hers with such urgency, response wasn't necessary.

But she knew the answer. Dear God, she knew the answer, but she didn't have the strength to shatter his illusion.

Later, snuggling deeper into the rumpled sheets, Sara listened to the buckboard rattle out of the barnyard, wondering what excuse Walker had given S. H. for his delay.

When she wandered downstairs in search of breakfast, Sophie was standing at the kitchen counter mixing a chocolate cake.

"Thought you'd grown to the bed."

"It's shameful, isn't it? We didn't get in until late, and—" Sara paused, color flooding her cheeks when she saw Sophie's sly grin. "I'm starved. Is there any bacon?"

Sophie motioned toward the warming oven. "Saved you a cinnamon bun. Had to nearly beat S. H. to keep him from eatin' it."

"Thanks." Sara poured a cup of coffee, then moved to stare out of the window. It was hot this morning, barely a breeze stirring. Clouds were building in the west, and she wouldn't be surprised if it rained.

"Did you have a good time at the dance last night?" Sophie scraped the thick, rich batter into two round baking pans.

"Wonderful. I learned to square-dance."

"That right?"

"I still don't understand why you and S. H. didn't go. You would have had a good time, and everyone asked about you."

"Me and S. H. cain't stay awake past eight." Sophie slid the cake pans into the hot oven and closed the door. "Walker said there was a letter from your folks in the mail?"

Sara lifted the cup to her lips, closing her eyes. How much longer could she keep up this deplorable pretense? "Yes."

"They doin' all right? Must be hard on 'em, having a daughter living so far away. My pa woulda never sent me cross-country at your age." She chuckled. " 'Course, Pa didn't necessarily want me marrying S. H., either."

Small talk was lost on Sara as she berated herself for how lies rolled off her tongue like honey. She had to tell Walker about the ruse—today. The sun couldn't set on the McKay household until he'd been told of the deception. Shivering, she brought the cup back to her mouth and drank without tasting. *Today, Sara. When Walker comes home tonight. You will tell him and then beg his forgiveness, and then you will get down on your hands and knees and pray that he will somehow find it within him to overlook your foolishness.*

Sophie slid the cinnamon roll onto a plate and set it down on the table. "Guess you'll write your folks and let them know that you got here safely.

S. H. can post the letter for you when he goes to town next week."

"Yes, I need to do that," Sara murmured. After she told Walker, she would write to Papa. She wanted this awful treachery to be over.

She ate the roll, thinking about the long day that stretched before her. She'd start the book, her tale about a girl in love with a man she was deceiving. It shouldn't be hard to write; she knew the story by heart. The only thing she didn't know was the ending.

"Sophie?" Sara carried her cup to the sink. "Where can I find some paper and a pencil?"

"Walker's probably got some in one of his desk drawers. Want me to get them for you?"

"I'll get them." Sara excused herself and left the kitchen.

She hadn't been in Walker's study since the day she saw his ledger. She opened the double doors to the large, manly room with its shelves of thickly bound books and dark leather furniture.

Moving quickly to the desk, she searched the drawers until she found the paper. Walker's ledger lay on the desktop, open. Tomorrow was Caleb's day to come and look at the records.

Sneaking a hurried peak, she scanned the pages. The columns were long and precise; nothing seemed out of place; yet habit made her want to check the additions and subtractions for accuracy. Caleb appeared competent, but Papa said a man should always know his personal business, especially in monetary matters. Her eyes darted to the open study door.

It would take only a few minutes to check the

tallies. Sophie would be occupied in the kitchen until the cake came out of the oven—the pleasant aroma of baking chocolate filtered in from the other room.

The foyer clock struck nine as she edged around the corner of the desk and sat down, drawing the ledger to her.

Row after row of entries filled the pages. Frowning, she studied the columns, occasionally encountering Walker's chicken scratches questioning Caleb about a certain entry.

She turned another page, her eyes running down the columns. The numbers were too consistent, too regular. The deposits never fluctuated, even though she had heard Walker talking to S. H. about how well the ranch was doing this year. Where were the receipts? Papa kept his receipts with his records for future reference.

The entries went back at least a year. She located the most recent additions, and compared the totals to those of the accounts. The totals matched in all columns. The straight edges of the numbers showed how meticulously accurate Caleb was. Every month, the same deposit total, the same payroll deducted. Household expenses in one row, farm expenses in the next. Sara smiled, proud of how well her husband managed the ranch. His earnings were consistent, spring, winter, and fall.

She ran her fingers up and down the numbers, and at the beginning of the entries for the past spring, she paused. Too consistent. Too even. Something wasn't right. Several dinner discussions had revolved around how well the ranch was doing this year; profits were expected to increase more than they ever had. But the numbers entered remained even. Sara understood profit from her discussions with her father, and from her father's discussions with others.

She grabbed a pencil and started calculating.

In the kitchen, Sophie hummed under her breath while she browned a roast, then checked on the cake. Good thing S. H. and Walker wouldn't be wantin' dinner on the table at noon.

Reaching for the clothes basket, she eyed the flies on the screen door. A body couldn't keep up in this house. In addition to everything else, she'd have to stop by the study and ask Sara if she wanted chocolate or vanilla icing on the cake. Walker favored fudge and S. H liked raspberry, but Walker had asked that the icing be Sara's favorite. Lord, it was impossible to keep everyone happy. She glanced out the back door, frowning when she saw the boil of dust. How was a body expected to hang wash if Potster was gonna beat rugs on the clothesline?

Twenty minutes later, she'd shooed Potster back into the bunkhouse and hung the last of the towels to dry in the hot sun.

A waft of cool air washed over her when she returned to the house. When she saw Sara sitting in the study, head studiously bent over Walker's ledger, she stopped dead in her tracks. When the girl realized she was standing in the doorway, she offered a quick smile.

Sophie frowned. "What are you doing?"

"Helping Walker with the books."

"Sara . . ."

"Sophie, if Walker gets angry—which he won't when he sees how much I've helped out—I'll tell him it was my idea, not yours. Please let me help. I won't get in the way doing this. I'm really good at math."

Sophie's forehead furrowed in a frown. Walker was finally adjusting to Sara, but she doubted he had adjusted this much. Still, there was little else she could do other than lock Sara out of the office.

Sophie remembered her question. "Do you want chocolate or vanilla icing on that cake?"

"Pardon me?"

"The cake. Chocolate or vanilla icing. Walker told me to ask you, but I forgot."

"Chocolate . . . isn't that Walker's favorite?"

"Yes." Sophie's eyes skimmed the young woman. Why was Sara going through Walker's books? Caleb came to dinner twice a month to do the bookkeeping. There'd be no reason for Sara to be prying—unless she wanted to know Walker's financial worth. Her gaze returned to Sara's and the young woman looked away.

"You need anything washed?"

"There's a few things in my dressing room. Do you want me to get them?"

"No." Sophie backed up, uncomfortable with the encounter. "I'll go get them myself." She left the room and started up the stairs.

She had no call to meddle in Walker's business, but he ought to know that his bride was snooping around the study. Entering the couple's bedroom, she started gathering clothes.

Walker was starting to trust again. It'd be a

shame if his trust were misplaced a second time. Sara seemed to be his perfect match, yet what did they really know about her? She came from somewhere near Boston, and her ma and pa must have been anxious to marry her off, to have agreed to let her be a mail-order bride. Sophie threw a shirt into the basket.

She'd never seen Walker happier than he'd been with Sara the past few weeks. His smile was back, and he walked with a lighter step. Marriage agreed with him, and she'd hate to think Sara was in the marriage for reasons other than honest ones. Could she possibly be one of those gold diggers, out for Walker's money and nothing more? Sophie would hate to think that—real bad.

Spotting Sara's hastily discarded dress flung on a corner chair, she stuffed it in the basket. *Young'uns.* Even though it was one of Sara's new frocks, she figured it could use washing after the dance last night.

She moved to the bed, straightening the covers. Young folks these days weren't taught to make a neat bed. Nothing bothered her more than— She looked over her shoulder when she heard something drop to the floor. An envelope?

She bent to pick it up, checking the postmark. Mallory. Sara's folks.

Sophie turned the letter over in her hands, studying it. Did it bring bad news? When she glanced over her shoulder at the open bedroom door, her teeth worried her lower lip. What did the Mallorys have to say? Were they worried about their daughter—afraid she wasn't gettin' enough to eat? Enough sleep at night?

Hurrying to the door, she turned the lock, then opened the letter and skimmed the body of the text. The more she read, the madder she got. Flushed with heat, she refolded the papers and shoved them back into the envelope, then grabbed the remainder of the dirty clothes and stuffed them into the basket. The Mallorys were schemers. They weren't interested in a good marriage for their daughter; they were interested in Walker's money.

What could she do about this? She didn't have the heart to tell Walker the Mallorys were out to take him, and witness his disappointment a second time.

She was torn between anger at Sara and pity for Walker. She'd keep quiet about the letter until she talked to S. H. and they confronted Sara. Though, Lord, she didn't know what good that would do. Maybe S. H. could talk sense into her; the girl didn't seem materialistic—nearly the opposite at times. Maybe Walker wouldn't care; he'd married Sara to produce an heir. Maybe he was willing to pay whatever price she asked.

Then again, maybe Walker McKay didn't have an inkling that Sara Mallory had married him to provide an income for her shiftless family. Sinking to the side of the bed, Sophie stared at the basket of dirty clothes. There was gonna be trouble over this; she knew it as well as she knew her own name.

Five new books for Sara, a box of pencils, and two hundred sheets of white paper were tucked safely in the supply box, so Walker guessed the whole day wasn't a wash. He smiled, liking the thought of having a famous author for a wife. Chances were, nothing would come of Sara's efforts, but if her literary aspirations kept her out of trouble, he'd encourage the endeavor.

He could smell supper as S. H. wheeled the buckboard into the barnyard.

"Pot roast," S. H. remarked.

"Meat loaf."

The two men backed up their bets, and S. H. unhitched the team and walked the horses to the barn. When he returned, they headed for the house.

Sara, curled up reading in Walker's chair, paused to look up and smile when they came into the foyer.

"Research?" Walker teased over his shoulder as he climbed the stairs to wash up.

Sara grinned. "No, I'm saving that for later."

"I have something you might like," he called.

"I like everything you have!"

He laughed at her almost childlike devotion, deciding a little girl with curly red hair might be nice. A boy would be fine, someone to carry on the McKay name, but he'd have no objections to a girl with Sara's laugh. Or her smile. Or anything about her. Truth was, he liked everything about his wife. Maybe marriage wasn't so bad. Once the baby came, they would be a family. He hadn't known until now that he'd missed that aspect of life . . . a family to come home to. Christmas and Thanksgiving hadn't been the same since Pa died. When the baby was born, he and Sara could put up a tree and decorate it with ornaments Ma had stored in the attic. Sophie did her best to keep the holidays festive, but Walker hadn't cooperated. This year would be different.

Sophie had supper on the table when S. H. and Walker took their seats.

"Sophie, if you weren't already married, I'd marry you again," S. H. said, licking gravy from one finger.

"If I weren't married, you'd play heck catching up with me, S. H. Gibson. Get your elbows off the table."

S. H. spooned green beans onto his plate, winking at Walker. "You let Sara talk to you this way?"

Walker winked at Sara as she handed him a plate of roasting ears. "My wife has respect for me, S. H. Yours, on the other hand, is out of control." He took an ear of corn and handed S. H. the plate.

"The roast should be delicious. I didn't go anywhere near it," Sara said quickly.

Walker grinned. "I can see that. Thanks."

Sara picked up the plate of meat and forked three thick slices of beef onto his plate.

"Look at that, Sophie." S. H. grabbed Sophie's behind as she bent to serve the potatoes. She swatted his hand away with a dishcloth. "Why don't you fix my plate? Sara fixes Walker's."

Sophie ignored her husband and sat down. "S. H., it's your turn to say grace."

Waker noticed that the two woman refused to look at each other tonight. What was going on?

The meal proceeded with friendly chatter, except for Sophie, who ate without looking up.

Sara buttered a piece of hot bread, smiling. "How was your trip into town?"

"Wasted a whole ding-dong day," S. H. said. "Didn't get half done what we needed to do." He glanced at his wife. "You're awful quiet tonight, sugarbunch. Something put you in a bad mood?"

Picking up her fork, Sophie met Sara's eyes pointedly. "Just you, S. H. You always put me in a bad mood."

S. H. winked at Walker. "Tart little heifer. I wouldn't trade her for a California gold mine."

"A California gold mine?" Walker reached for the cream pitcher. "I'd have to think about that one."

After supper, the men insisted the women could wash dishes later. They led the two women onto the porch and handed them packages, which, by the look of them, they'd wrapped themselves. Walker couldn't take his eyes off Sara as she shook the gift, trying to guess what the box held. She hadn't been far from his mind all day. The way she felt in his arms, and the feelings she evoked inside him when she slid beneath the cool sheets, her skin soft against his.

Fireflies darted around the porch, flashing among the bushes.

"Go on," S. H. urged Sophie, his brown eyes sparkling with mischief. "Open yours first."

His wife eyed the ill-wrapped package. "S. H., what'd you do? Wad this paper up and stomp on it?"

"That's a first-class wrapping job, Sophie Mae."

"It's a downright disgrace." Sophie tore into her package, gasping with delight when she held up a new dress. "S. H., you old goat. You can't afford this!"

"Honeybun, I'm rich in every way that matters. Just stuck a little extra money away in my sock each payday—weren't nothin' much." He reached for her hand, and gave her a kiss as gallant as any knight would his lady. "Worth every penny to see the look in yer eyes right now," he said softly.

Sophie's eyes misted, and she leaned over and kissed his cheek. "That'll have to do until I can thank you properly."

S. H.'s face lit up.

Walker draped an arm around Sara's waist. "You're next."

"Oh, Walker, you shouldn't. You bought me all those lovely dresses—"

He silenced her with a brief kiss. Sara squealed when she opened the parcel of pencils and paper. "My paper! Thank you so much." She jumped up and threw her arms around his neck. "Now I can start that book."

"I thought you were going to start this morning."

Sara glanced at Sophie. Walker watched the exchange, wondering why there was an underlying tension between the women. "No . . . I didn't get around to writing—but I will. Tomorrow." She hugged the paper and pencils to her chest. "Thank you. I've never had a nicer gift."

"Are you gonna write love scenes?" S. H. teased.

Sara turned a deep shade of crimson. "Of course not, S. H. My books are going to be fun and exciting and . . . well, I'd never—"

"Oh, S. H., leave her alone," Sophie said. She gathered up the wrapping paper and headed back into the house.

"Hey, where ya goin'?" S. H. sat up in his chair. "Aren't you gonna model yer new dress for us?"

"Not tonight, S. H. Those dishes won't wash themselves."

The screen door flapped shut, and S. H. turned to Sara. Shrugging, she handed the pencils and paper to Walker. "Guess I need to help."

Walker looked at S. H. when she disappeared into the house. "What's that all about? Did the two of them get into it?"

S. H.'s features sobered. "Darned if I know."

Walker barely glanced up when Sophie poured his coffee the next morning. "Do you want more eggs?" she asked.

Shaking his head, he scanned the sheaf of papers he was reading.

Stock ledgers. The man never read anything interesting. Sophie started to clear the table.

"Noticed in the paper that Lowell Livingston's daughter is missing," she said.

"Who's Lowell Livingston?"

"Who's Lowell Livingston?" Sophie sighed. "That wealthy railroad tycoon up in Boston? You've heard of him—everyone's heard of him. Got more money than a body ought to have."

Walker shook his head. "I haven't heard of him."

"Well, you know why, don't you?"

"Why what?"

"Why you've never heard of anyone."

Walker closed the journal, reaching for the cream pitcher. "No, but I suppose you're going to tell me."

"You never read anything interesting. Just that old stock journal."

"I read all the time, Sophie." He reached for a piece of toast and buttered it.

"Farm journals. Seed catalogues. What can you learn from them?"

"What to buy and when to plant it. You ought to try it sometime, and then you wouldn't be worrying over some Boston man's troubles. Haven't you got enough of your own?"

"Poor soul. The paper said his daughter's been missin' over nigh onto six weeks." Sophie shook her head. "Don't see how a body could stand not knowing where their child was—suppose Mr. Livingston can't sleep a wink at night for worryin'."

"Do the authorities suspect foul play?"

"They don't know what to expect. Seems Livingston's daughter, Sara"— Sophie paused. *Guess all Saras were bound to cause trouble*—"just up and ran off. No one's seen hide nor hair of her."

"Having money doesn't keep trouble off your doorstep." Walker stuck a piece of toast in his mouth and reached for his hat. "I'm late, Sophie. Any chance we can have pork chops tonight?"

"As good as any." Sophie watched him leave the dining room, still shaking her head. Money *didn't* keep trouble off a body's doorstep. Fact was, it seemed to cause more.

When she'd told S. H. about catching Sara reading Walker's financial records, and about the letter from her folks, he hadn't been too excited. He said she didn't need to be stickin' her nose into other people's business, but Sophie didn't like withholding information from Walker. Especially this information. If Sara was up to something she shouldn't be, Walker needed to know.

When Caleb rang the bell later that morning, Sara invited him inside. As always, he carefully stepped around her, avoiding her direct gaze and fiddling with his glasses.

"Since you're a bit early, Walker's not in from his morning rounds yet," Sara explained as she escorted him into the parlor. "Would you like something to drink? Coffee or tea, perhaps?"

"Well, uh, yes, coffee would be nice, I suppose." He smiled, but the effort seemed insincere. Sara left to fetch the coffee while Caleb eased uncomfortably onto the couch. Sophie wasn't in the kitchen when Sara got there, but the coffee from breakfast was still warm on the stove. She poured two cups, placed them on a tray, and went to retrieve the sugar from the pantry.

Playing hostess to Caleb was not exactly the perfect way to spend a morning, especially with pencil and paper awaiting her to begin the book. She sighed. Returning from the pantry, she placed the cream and sugar bowl on the tray and lifted it, balancing them precariously. With slow, sure moves, she navigated back into the parlor.

Caleb shot off his seat the moment she came through the doorway. His hat, which he had taken off and placed on the chair beside him, tumbled onto the floor, by the satchel he carried with him to each meeting with Walker. Sara set the tray on the table and moved to gather his things.

"Here," she offered. "Let me take your things into Walker's study so you won't be tripping over them." She picked up the hat and reached for the satchel.

"No!" Caleb shouted, startling her. They stood for a moment, Sara still bending over to reach for the case and Caleb snatching it to the other side of the couch. "I mean, I'll just keep it here with me. I don't want you to have to go through all that trouble."

"Suit yourself," she said, sitting down. The man certainly was an odd duck. She watched his hands fumble with the sugar spoon, nearly shaking all of the sugar off onto the tray before he managed to dump it into his cup. Rather than let him make a similar mess with the cream, Sara intervened.

"Let me serve you." She took the pitcher from his hand. Despite the warmth of midmorning, Caleb's touch chilled her. She poured cream for both of them and settled back into her chair. Why was the accountant so nervous around her? He certainly didn't have any way of knowing she had been looking through Walker's books. And even if he did know, why would that knowledge make him so uncomfortable around her?

She took a sip of coffee. She didn't want to accuse Caleb of anything right now; she *couldn't* accuse him with anything. All she had were suspicions of misconduct, and that certainly wouldn't hold up for long if she were to confront him. Thinking of her own lies, Sara realized she couldn't make any bold statements until she had told Walker the truth about her own situation. But that shouldn't stop her from finding out what the little man was about—for he *was* about something.

"So, Caleb," Sara asked sweetly, "how long have you been taking care of Walker's books?"

The man looked at her as if it took a moment for him to realize that she was talking. "Uh, well, I suppose since Mitch and Betsy died, which would be a few years ago now."

"Oh, you didn't do the books before that?"

"No. Mitch took care of everything. Cattle. Books. Everything."

"But Walker never has anything to do with them?" Sara took another sip of coffee and chided herself for pursuing the questioning this far. *Be careful, Sara. This isn't the Inquisition. Just act curious, that's all.*

"No. Not really." Caleb adjusted his glasses and sipped from his shaking cup. "I suppose he may look them over once in a while, but there really is no reason for him to concern himself with finances when he has so many other things to think about on the ranch."

"Yes, he does." Sara said, placing her cup back on her saucer. "Especially with the ranch making such a huge profit these last few months."

Caleb smiled. "Quite true. The growth of his estate has been astounding. Mitch taught him well."

"But not everything, obviously," Sara said teasingly, "or Walker would keep his own books."

Her meager attempt at humor fell to the floor, and silence took over. She wanted so badly to ask about the books, but she didn't dare. She needed to talk to Walker about the issue before she ran around accusing anyone of anything.

Just then Walker came barging in through the front door, shaking dust everywhere.

"Caleb! Sorry I'm late. Things were a little hectic around here this morning." He smiled at Sara and her heart fluttered. "Luckily you were in good hands."

"Yes, excellent hands," Caleb agreed meaninglessly. He immediately got up and reached for his things. Before anyone could say any more, he had disappeared into the study, apparently relieved to be away from Sara. Walker followed and Sara slumped back in her chair.

What had gotten into her? Questioning Walker's best friend as if he were a common thief. Her teeth worried her bottom lip. But what if he *were* a thief—what if the books and her suspicion proved to be accurate? She couldn't know for certain, since she'd only skimmed the surface of the books, but there had to be something behind

Caleb's nervous manner. What, she didn't know, but she intended to find out.

Sara climbed into bed that night, pencil and paper in hand. Walker rolled over and tried to take her in his arms, but she stopped him. He leaned back, disappointed.

"I've started."

"Started what?"

"My book. Listen." Leaning over him, she slid the lamp closer. "It isn't exactly Bret Harte, but I think it's good. Now mind you, it's only thoughts so far, but see what you think."

Pages rustled and he sensed that she awaited his cue. "I'm listening."

"Well, okay . . . but it needs work. Maybe I shouldn't read it to you yet—tomorrow might be better."

He reached up and tugged the front of her gown down to expose the swell of her breast.

"Walker," she chided, pulling the fabric up. "I'm trying to read this. Be serious."

"I am serious." Reaching for her hand, he strategically placed it to show his earnest intentions.

"Stop it; you said you wanted to hear this."

"I did?" He grinned. "I do. Go ahead."

"You're not concentrating."

His eyes returned to the swell of her breast. "I am, too."

"Okay." She moved his hand again. "It's a story about a girl who wants nothing more in life than to be married. She falls in love with one man after another and none of them ever work out. She keeps getting more and more frustrated because she thinks she'll *never* get married. Her father tries to help—somewhat—but none of the men he chooses ever work out because there's always something wrong with them. They don't want to get married or their mothers tell them they can't."

Walker listened with one ear, his mind on the curve of her back. Sara's description of the girl's father reminded him of his own father, and their last few conversations about Walker's finding a wife and leaving the ranch in McKay hands. Mitch McKay would love Sara. In many ways, they had the same free spirit.

"So this girl—this foolish, foolish woman—decides to run away. She boards a train to Wyoming and on the train she meets . . ." Sara paused, taking a breath.

Walker's eyes skimmed her. "Meets?"

"I haven't decided who she meets . . . yet."

"Then what? The train derails? That won't be much of a story if she dies in the first chapter."

"No, the train doesn't derail." Sara shuffled the papers. "That's about as far as I've got right now. I can't decide where to go from here." She caught his wandering hand in midair and gave him a warning smile.

"So," he teased, easing the gown lower, "who does she meet on the train?"

"I guess you'll just have to wait and see."

She giggled as Walker took the pages from her hands and tossed them to the end of the bed.

Rolling her on top of him, he met her playful gaze. "What was that all about last night?"

"Last night?"

"Between you and Sophie. Did you two have a fight?"

Sara blushed. "No . . . I must have gotten underfoot again."

He raised his brows. "Sophie wasn't herself last night, and she didn't say a whole lot at breakfast. What's going on?"

"Walker . . ." She caught her breath as he softly kissed the nape of her neck.

"Hmm?"

"There's something . . . there's something I need to tell you . . . I've been meaning to . . ."

She whispered his name when his mouth took hers. His hand freed the bodice of her gown, his long fingers exploring her pliant warm flesh.

"We're through talking," he whispered.

"Walker, I . . ."

The light went out a moment later. Conversation was over.

Chapter 13

Walker was starting up the stairs with a tray for Sara the next morning when she descended. He had planned on surprising her with coffee and muffins in bed . . . and maybe a few other dalliances. The only surprise now was Sara's early rising.

"Oh, Walker, how nice of you!" She stood on tiptoe to kiss him. Her face glistened with cleanness and her smile melted him. "I'm sorry I spoiled your surprise," she whispered, kissing him again.

"Why don't we eat upstairs anyway?" he suggested, winking at her.

"What about your morning chores?"

"They can wait."

Laughing, she turned and sprinted back up the stairs, clutching handfuls of her dress before her.

In the bedroom, he rested the tray on the night-stand and they sat down on the bed. Sara picked up a muffin and pulled a piece off the top, offering it to him. For a few moments they said nothing, just fed each other bits of muffin and tried unsuccessfully to twine their arms together as they sipped the scalding-hot coffee. Eventually they exploded with laughter.

"I'm so happy here, Walker."

But behind her happy declaration he detected something else. She set the coffee cup on the nightstand. What could be bothering her on such a wonderful morning? He took her hands in his and began kissing bits of muffin from her fingertips. Her beauty made him forget about the muffins, and he began kissing his way up her arms.

"Is there something on your mind?" he asked. Sara's happiness at Spring Grass had become one of his top priorities these days, and until now, everything seemed to be going well.

Sara stared at him as if her soul were struggling to break free. She started to speak, but managed only a "Well . . ." before falling silent again. Her tongue worried her lower lip.

"Sara, nothing could be that bad. What is it?" His heart began pounding. What was wrong? Was she sick?

"It's Caleb."

"Caleb?" He frowned. "What about Caleb?"

"I . . . I don't think he likes—no—trusts me."

Walker laughed. "Caleb? Why would you say that?"

"He seems . . . uncomfortable around me, Walker. Do you know why?"

That seemed an odd thing for her to say. Chuckling, he drew her back to his chest. "Honey, if I hadn't known him since we were barely old enough to speak, I'd think he didn't like me, either."

Sara pulled away and the tension in her mouth softened.

"Actually"—she bit her lip again, deep in thought—"I've been meaning to ask you something about Caleb."

"What is it?" He reached again for his coffee. If Caleb was the only thing bothering her, he could quickly put her at ease.

"I know you know Caleb well, but how well? I mean, how much attention do you pay to his accuracy with your ledgers?"

Walker's hand paused as he brought the cup to his mouth. What was she talking about? What did she know about the ledgers?

"None. I don't pay any attention to them. That's what I pay Caleb to do." Why the uneasiness about his finances? Had she been snooping? Not that it mattered; she was his wife—but why would she be interested in his ledgers? "He's one of my best friends and a fine accountant to boot. Why the concern?"

Sara blushed. "No reason, really. It's just that my father always took care of our business . . . ledgers and all, so I was wondering if you ever looked at them."

Walker grinned. She was worried about money, although he didn't know why. They had more than enough to last them as long as they would ever need. "Well, you have nothing to worry about. I trust Caleb completely. And we have more money than you've ever seen."

"I'm not worried about it," she scoffed. "I'm not worried about money at all."

"Good," he said, "because I don't want you to have to worry about anything ever again."

He laid her down on the bed and began undoing the buttons she had fastened just minutes before.

When he saw her frown, his fingers paused. "What's wrong?"

"I *am* worried."

Concern darkened his eyes. "About what?"

She giggled. "About what you're about to do to me."

"Good," he murmured, his hand easing the dress off her shoulders. "You have a right to be."

Potster cracked another egg into the bowl, eyeing Sara. "Clean as a whistle."

"Cleaner," Sara agreed. Sniffing the aromatic air, she wondered if she'd ever cook as well as Potster. She bent her head and sighed, writing another sentence in the notebook. After her morning tryst with Walker, she'd thrown herself into writing, angry with herself for not coming clean with him as she'd intended to. At the last minute she'd weakened and allowed Walker to think that Caleb's coldness had been affecting her instead. Finally, to ease her distress, she'd sought refuge in Potster's kitchen.

"You spend all yer spare time writin' in that book. What's it say, anyway?"

"You wouldn't like it, Potsie. It's about love."

He frowned. "What's that supposed to mean? Love's my specialty—know a lot about the subject." He doused a chicken leg in a bowl of batter. "Name me one stronger love than man and his food, and I'll eat my hat."

Sara scratched the sentence out and wrote another. "It's not that kind of love; it's about a girl from the East who runs away to the West and finds the man of her dreams."

"Oh, that kind of love." Raising a cleaver, he split a chicken breast with one swift motion. "The lovey-dovey kind that makes the ole heart go pitter-patter."

Sara laughed as the old man picked up a whole chicken and started waltzing it around the kitchen, cleaver still in hand. He cooed to the plucked bird, giving it loud, smacking kisses, calling it "milady" and "madam."

Sara shook her head at his shenanigans. "Go ahead, make fun of me. You'll be sorry one day when I'm a famous author."

Potster deposited the chicken on the counter and affected a sweeping bow. "If you think you can write anything more romantic than that in your book, Mrs. Famous Author, I'd like to hear it."

Sara consulted the sketchy chapter. She'd been working on the part where the heroine switched places with the girl on the train. The more she wrote, the more the story became autobiographical, and her carefully crafted story had her waking up in the middle of the night drenched in a cold sweat. She dreamed she was carried off by an angry mob, publicly humiliated for her treachery. She'd plead with Walker to save her, but he would turn away, calling her Trudy.

Then he would look her right in the eye and say something derogatory about hats.

Yet writing came surprisingly easy to her, as if she'd been born to pen fanciful, romantic stories.

"Are you sure you want to hear this?"

"Fire away. I'm all ears."

She took a deep breath, then started to read.

The train, a massive, domineering beast with an engine full of coal as black as Elizabeth's heart, crept through the hills and valleys, destined to meet the end of the track and take her to her one true love. But who was that love, that knight, that chivalrous man who would be forever hers; the man who would whisk her off on his polished steed into the bright Western sunset? Who was this man whom she risked her future to marry? She did not know, nor had she any idea of his means or ways. Once she had secured her place as Emma Lowery, she knew she could not turn back. She could know but one life, a dreary existence of deceit, longing, desire, but also one of true and unabashed love.

Sara paused. The following paragraphs dealt with her arrival at Spring Grass. The characters so closely mirrored Potster, S. H., and Sophie that she was afraid to read it; afraid the old cook would catch on and discover her guise.

Potster glanced up. "Ain't bad . . . a little rough around the edges. Go on."

Tears welled in her eyes, blurring the pages. Potster was so trusting, so gentle and kind; he had been her best friend since she'd met him that day in the barn. If she lost his respect, Spring Grass would be a lonely place. She'd had few close friends in her life and she couldn't bear to lose him. What would he think when he found out that she was deceiving Walker, that she had been all along? And Sophie? Would she regret the day she'd taken Sara under her wing? Was the housekeeper beginning to suspect that Sara was a fraud? She'd been distant since she'd caught Sara looking at Walker's books, and Sara knew Sophie was suspicious of her intentions. With each passing day, she could feel herself getting snared deeper and deeper in her web of lies. She wanted more than anything for the deception to be over.

Potster saw the tears and frowned. Laying the knife aside, he approached her, squatting to kneel beside her chair. "Here, now, it's not that bad. I don't know anything about writin' books; you shouldn't take to heart what some ol' farm folk say about yer writin'. It's gonna be a fine book, rough or not."

His remark was more than she could bear. Dropping the pages, Sara buried her face in her hands and whispered brokenly, "It's me, Potster. It's me, and it's all true! The story is about how I traded places with that girl on the train and made

Walker believe that I'm Olivia Mallory, when I'm really Sara Livingston. I've meant to tell Walker— every day I think I will, and then something happens and I don't. I love him so much, and I truly think he's starting to have feelings for me—but I'm afraid once I tell him what I've done, he'll hate me and he'll send me away. Oh, Potster, I don't know what to do!"

Potster drew back, his eyes bewildered. "Whadda ya mean it's you? It's just a story."

"No!" Sara cried. "It's about me. I'm Elizabeth. I'm the black heart. I'm only pretending to be Emma."

He stared back at her blankly. Chicken popped in the hot grease, shooting across the room. He jumped up and shifted the iron skillet to the back of the stove.

"Honey, you're workin' too hard. Maybe you should go to the house and lie down for a spell." He turned the pieces of crusty brown chicken, scowling worriedly at her.

"No. You don't understand. I'm . . . I'm . . . not Olivia Mallory."

"Well, you have to be Olivia Mallory. Who else can you be?"

"Oh, Potster, forgive me. I didn't mean to hurt anyone."

Sara related the whole sordid story: running away from her father, meeting Olivia on the train, how they hatched the foolish plan to switch identities. She told him about the Mallorys' letter, and how they wanted Olivia to marry Walker only for what he could provide.

Potster sank into a chair opposite Sara, the frying chicken forgotten. "If that don't beat all. Have you told anyone else about this?"

"I can't tell Walker, and Sophie already thinks I meddle too much." The sobs began again, unchecked. "Walker will send me away, Potster; I know he will. He'll never forgive me for deceiving him, and who could blame him? I should have told him the truth from the beginning, but I was foolish. So very selfish and foolish."

Potster awkwardly bobbed his head. "No one's gonna hate you, and no one's gonna send you away, but you're gonna have to tell Walker what you've done. The longer this goes on, the worse it'll be. He's a fair man. He'll be mad as a hornet, ain't gonna try to kid you about that; but he'll listen to your side of the story."

Sara shook her head. "I can't. I love him, Potster, and if he sends me away I'll die. I didn't mean for it to go this far. I thought I would have been able to tell him by now. I thought once he fell in love with me, he'd find the ruse laughable."

Reaching across the table, Potster wiped her tears with the edge of the tablecloth. "Walker's had worse news—and he's got a heart bigger than you think. You got to tell him, young'un, and you got to tell him before another day passes." He bent to retrieve her fallen papers and put them back into her hands. "You got to tell him before he finds out on his own. That'd make things a heap worse, child—a whole heap of a lot worse."

Sara knew Potster was right. Not another day could pass without Walker's knowing the truth.

She dabbed her eyes on the edge of her sleeve. "I'll tell him today."

"That's my girl." Getting up from the table, he went back to the stove and turned the chicken again.

Sara felt surprising relief, and Potster's quiet reassurances gave her the courage she needed. It wasn't going to be pleasant, but as Wadsy always said, correcting a lie was never easy.

She got up from the table, grasping the edge when her head spun wildly. It took a second for the room to come back into focus. Potster glanced around at her.

"What's wrong?"

"Nothing. I felt a little light-headed," she said, her head slowly clearing. The dizziness passed, but the smell of hot grease made her queasy. "I'm all right now."

"You best go to the house and lie down a while. Sophie'll fix you something cool to drink. I ain't got nothin' but coffee out here."

Releasing the table's edge, she tested her legs and found them surprisingly weak.

"I'll be glad to help if you need me."

"Child, do you know how many times I've fried chicken? I can handle a few more. You go on now, take care of yourself." His smile gradually faded. "The minute Walker rides in, you tell him, young'un. Don't waste a minute of time. If you need me, you come and get me, and we'll tell him together."

Sara crossed the room to give him a grateful hug. "I'm glad you're my friend."

The old man awkwardly patted her back.

"That's good, Sara girl . . . because you're gonna
need one."

Sara paused when she stepped out of the
bunkhouse, allowing her eyes time to adjust to
the bright sunlight.

A commotion in the barn caught her attention.
She could hear the thump of sharp hooves hitting
wood. When she walked into the barn she discovered Diamond down in her stall, legs flailing
against the wooden cubicle.

"What's wrong, girl?" Sara unlatched the gate
to look at the mare. The animal gazed up at her,
nostrils flared with pain.

Potster burst into the barn after her, wiping his
flour-covered hands on his stained apron.
"What's going on in here?"

"I think Diamond's about to give birth. Oh,
Potsie, what do we do?"

He quickly assessed the situation. "Run down
to the north field and see if you can find Walker
or S. H." Potster knelt to comfort the animal.
"Walker said he wasn't stopping for dinner, but
he might be working nearby."

Sara flew out of the barn and ran toward the
field on shaky legs. She spotted Walker and S. H.
on horseback, riding slowly across the meadow
from the north. Waving her arms wildly, she tried
to catch their attention.

The men saw her and kicked their horses into a
gallop. Sara waited until they were close enough
to hear her.

"It's Diamond! She's foaling! Hurry!"

The men galloped to the barn and Walker

jumped off his saddle, dropping the reins. Sara ran to catch up as Diamond cried out again.

"How long has she been foaling?" he asked.

Sara struggled to match his long-legged strides as they entered the barn. "I don't know; I found her a few minutes ago and she was already down."

Potster massaged the horse's belly, trying to keep her from thrashing her head into the side of the stall. Diamond's eyes were wide, her mouth foaming.

"It's breech," Potster warned as Walker came into the stall. "Poor girl's in a lot of pain."

"Easy, girl, easy.". Walker knelt, running his hand down the animal's heaving sides. "Keep her still, Potster. Sara, get me a bucket of water. She's going to need some help."

Sara grabbed a bucket from the wall and rushed to the pump. Latching onto the handle, she pumped furiously, impatient with the small trickle. Potster said it was breech—what did that mean? She'd heard Wadsy discussing births with other women, but she had never been daring enough to ask how that worked. Though she dreamed of having children, she had never thought much about how they got here.

Water trickled slowly into the pail, and she pumped harder, using both hands now. Sophie came out the back door, shading her eyes.

"What's going on?" she hollered.

"Diamond's colt is breech!" Sara stopped momentarily to catch her breath. "What's breech?"

"Backwards." Sophie approached, commandeering the pump handle. "Here, I'll bring the water. You go and see if Walker needs help."

"S. H. is with him."

"Go on—but don't get in the men's way."

Sara raced back to the barn. On the way, she noticed black smoke rolling out of Potster's kitchen window.

"The chicken!" she cried. "The chicken's on fire, Potster!"

Potster darted out of the barn, his eyes following Sara's finger.

"Dadburn it! Sara, go help Walker!" Potster sped off to salvage his kitchen as Diamond's whinnies filled the air.

Hurtling toward the barn, Sara ran inside to Diamond's stall, where Walker was calmly stroking the mother's back with one hand.

"Where's the water?"

"Sophie's bringing it." Her chest heaved, trying to pull in more oxygen. "Is she okay?"

"It will be close, but I think she can deliver it." Walker spoke softly to Diamond and she nickered lowly, her eyes wide with fright.

"What can I do?" Sara asked.

"It's all up to Diamond now. Come on, girl, give me a push."

The horse's sides heaved. Sara climbed the side of the stall and leaned over the railing to watch. Diamond's coat shuddered under Walker's hand.

"Almost there."

Diamond pushed and rested, panting.

"Attagirl." Walker moved and Sara couldn't

see him. Maneuvering along the railing, she spotted him crouched behind Diamond.

The horse gave another gallant push and two tiny hooves popped out, a little bigger than the size of silver dollars. A set of legs followed. Walker held them steady as he reached with one hand to coax the back end of the colt from Diamond. Sara caught her breath, realizing that she was witnessing a live birth.

The mingled smells of sweat, horse, and blood filled Sara's nostrils. Diamond rested and Walker patted her side.

"Good girl, good Diamond." Sara noticed that he had taken off his field gloves and was holding the colt with his bare hands. It was covered in a thin, slimy substance traced with specks of bloody foam.

Diamond gave another push and half of the colt was out. The mare heaved and nickered, but calmed as Walker continued to speak in soft tones. With each push, more liquid coursed from her, covering the stall floor and Walker's chaps.

The stall suddenly tilted, and Sara lifted her hands to her head. She saw Potster enter the barn and say something to Walker, but the blood pounding in her ears blocked out the words. Potster placed the bucket of water beside Walker and glanced up at Sara, mouthing words that looked something like "far to."

What was he saying? Sara scowled, shaking her head to clear the fuzz. The stall was spinning out of control. Spinning, whirling—then it went black.

*   *   *

"Sophie!" Walker lurched through the back
door carrying an unconscious Sara.

Sophie appeared in the kitchen doorway,
shock registering on her face. "What's happened?"

"She's fainted. Send one of the men for the
doctor."

"Doc's over in Dexter County. Effie said he'd
be there all week if there wasn't an emergency."

Walker took the stairs two at a time, covering
the distance to their bedroom in record time.
Kicking the door open, he carried Sara to the bed
and put her down. Momentarily stirring, she fluttered her eyes. Smiling, she lightly touched his
cheek before sinking back into unconsciousness.

Sophie rushed in carrying a pan of cold water
and cloths. By the time she wet the cold compress, Sara was coming around.

"Walker . . ."

He gently pressed the cloth to her forehead.
"Hold still; you've fainted."

She gazed up at him, eyes melting into his.
Desire raced through him, startling him with its
intensity. Gently removing her arms, which had
crept back around his neck, he wet the cloth
again.

"Swooned?" Sara murmured.

"You were looking at the colt one minute, out
cold the next." He grinned, gently smoothing a
lock of hair off her face. She tried to sit up, pushing his hands aside.

"Is Diamond's baby here?"

"She has a fine little filly."

Sara wilted back to the pillow, her eyes drifting shut. "I'm so glad. I've never swooned in my life."

"I'll get her something cool to drink," Sophie offered, turning to leave.

When the door closed, Sara looked at her husband. "I'm fine, Walker. Really."

"You don't look fine."

Reaching out, she traced the outline of his cheek, smiling. "Apparently breakfast didn't set well with me."

"Doc Linder's working in another county this morning, but if you think you need him—"

"I'm all right, really." Swinging her legs off the bed, she tested them, then slowly got up. Moving to the washstand, she groaned when she encountered her image in the mirror. "Is the foal all right?"

"Healthy as a horse." He met her eyes in the mirror, wondering how a woman could be so pretty. Even now she had a freshness about her he'd seen in few women. Sara's hair reminded him of summer evenings when he and Pa rode out to Box Canyon to watch the sunset blanket the valley in a crimson robe. He would sit on his horse trying to identify colors: glowing reds, brilliant oranges, and pinks so vivid he couldn't find a name for them. Then the sky darkened, and stars came out. Pa would challenge him to a contest to see who could count the most, but he knew there were too many to count.

On nights when he rode the range, he still looked up, wondering if Pa was up there, counting.

Sara returned his gaze in the oval mirror as if she could read his thoughts and knew how to bring back the boy who'd once tried to count the stars.

Sophie interrupted the moment when she returned with two glasses of lemonade. Placing the tray on the bedside table, she clucked. "What are you doing up? You should lie flat for a while."

"I feel better, Sophie. Thank you."

"Well, you're not going anywhere until you've had something cold to drink and been off your feet for at least an hour."

Sara glanced at Walker, grinning. "Yes, ma'am."

"I have to check on Diamond," he said regretfully, backing out of the room. His eyes still locked with Sara's. For some crazy reason, he hated to leave her.

When he'd gone, Sara lay on the bed, eyes closed. She'd promised Sophie an hour of rest, but she was having difficulty keeping still. Outside the window, she could hear the ranch going about its daily business. Walker was home. She had to tell him. She had to clear her name and prove her trustworthiness before she could talk to him again about Caleb. She'd promised Potster, and this was one promise she intended to keep.

She savored the last few blissful moments of Walker's innocence. After today, nothing would ever be the same, regardless of how Walker took the news.

Blinking back tears, she recalled the feel of his

arms at the dance, the sensual brush of his hand on the small of her back as he helped her into the buggy—the way he'd made love to her twice this morning before the sun was up.

She kept her eyes closed against a swell of dizziness. Her stomach rolled, and she wondered if she needed to empty it. Those awful eggs at breakfast—she shuddered at the thought.

Sliding off the bed, she washed her face and straightened the pins in her hair. She couldn't put it off any longer. Walker was in the barn; they would have a few moments of privacy—enough for Sara to tell him the truth about their marriage.

Sophie was bent over the sink, scrubbing pots, when Sara crept down the stairs. Unlatching the front screen door, she looked over her shoulder as she slipped out, letting it softly close behind her. She wondered if this was how men felt facing the guillotine. It couldn't be much worse than the mission she was about to embark upon.

When she turned around, she jumped as she came face-to-face with Olivia Mallory. The blood drained from her face, and she couldn't find her voice.

Olivia broke the strained silence. "Hi." She smiled. "Guess you didn't think you'd ever see me again."

Chapter 14

Sara grabbed hold of the porch railing, staring at Olivia as if she were an apparition. "What are you doing here? You're going to ruin everything!"

"Ruin what?"

"Ruin *what*? Ruin the plan! If Walker sees you, he's going to want to know who you are."

Jaw set, Olivia sat her valise down. "I didn't marry Rodney."

This can't be happening. Not now, when she was about to tell Walker—why couldn't Olivia have stayed away one more day? "Why not?"

The girl shrugged. "For a while everything was wonderful, but then I got to know him. . . . He started going out every night drinking, coming home early in the morning, smelling of beer and other women. He swore that he loved me,

222

but, well, money was always so tight. There wasn't enough for our room, let alone the things I wanted."

Sara slumped against the railing, too weak to argue. She wanted to feel sorry for the girl, but she couldn't.

"Why didn't you go home? Why did you come here?"

"Go home?" Olivia raised her chin. "And tell my parents what I'd done? I couldn't do that. Besides," she said, "I have a contract to fulfill. I promised that I would marry Walker McKay, and after considerable thought, I realized I can't, in conscience, go back on that promise."

Sara stared at her, speechless. Why the sudden sense of right and wrong? Why hadn't she thought of this earlier? Why hadn't they discussed this on the train; why hadn't Sara been smart enough to ensure that the deal was final and not subject to Olivia's whims? A million "whys" tormented her. She had to get rid of the girl before Walker discovered that she was here; she couldn't let Olivia Mallory ruin her marriage. Collecting her wits, Sara straightened.

"I'm sorry, but I'll have to ask you to leave. Walker McKay is my husband and I won't let you walk in here and threaten my marriage."

Olivia eyed her smugly. "Actually, he's not your husband. Legally, he's married to Olivia Mallory, and that's me, not you."

"No!" Sara cried, yet she knew that Olivia spoke the truth. She was not Walker's legal wife. Fear, rage, and humiliation coursed through her. Never once had she considered the legalities of the marriage. The hours in Walker's bed—the nights she'd enjoyed his unchecked passion. They were *never* married.

"What do you want from me?" Sickened, she clung to the porch railing, waiting for the other shoe to drop.

"I want you to tell Walker the truth—he doesn't know about the switch, does he?"

Sara shook her head, unable to think.

"He has to be told. Then you will leave and I'll fulfill the contract."

"You can't—it's too late. Walker will be furious when he learns what we've done—he'll send us both away. You don't know him, Olivia; he isn't a man who'll take lightly to being tricked by two women. He'll not want either one of us."

The idea of Olivia replacing her in Walker's bed, in his arms, in his life, churned the white-hot pain in her stomach.

"I'll risk his anger. He still needs an heir, doesn't he? He'll be angry for a few days, but that'll pass. He sent for a bride, and I'm that bride."

Sara simply stared at her, wondering how anyone could be so coldhearted.

"Why now?"

Olivia's features hardened. "I made a mistake, and now I'm here to correct it."

Sara turned as the front door opened and Sophie appeared, holding an armful of dirty sheets. Sara could see from the look on her face that she had heard too much.

"What's going on out here?"

Olivia promptly extended her hand. "Olivia

Mallory," she said, her head held high. "Walker McKay's expected bride."

Sophie glanced at the extended hand, then at Sara. Sara felt tears welling in her eyes. She couldn't bear the look of shock and disbelief on Sophie's face. Brushing past the bewildered housekeeper, she grabbed her skirts and flew into the house and up the stairs, weeping.

Nausea overcame her flight and she slumped on a step, not sure if she could go on. Her head spun, and she laid her head down, sobbing. Part of her wanted to die. Then she wouldn't have to face Walker, wouldn't have to witness his anger. Gathering her strength, she covered the last of the stairs and ran down the hallway, slamming the bedroom door a moment later.

Sophie listened to the flight, wondering if the world had gone mad. First Sara fainting, now this woman claiming to be— She turned to face the young woman standing on the front porch looking very much at home.

"Who'd you say you were?"

"Olivia Mallory."

"That can't be. Sara is, or was, Olivia Mallory."

"No, she isn't, or wasn't." The girl squared her chin defiantly. "I am."

Sophie's eyes swept over her. Where was S. H.? "You stay right here." She reentered the house and marched up the stairs, sheets trailing behind her. If Sara wasn't Olivia Mallory, then whom had Walker married? She grimaced at the thought of Walker facing yet another deception. Pausing in front of the couple's room, she pressed her ear against the closed door. She could hear the sound of vomiting. Dropping the sheets, she entered the room without knocking.

Sara was hunched over the chamber pot, heaving. Sophie bent to help, holding the sobbing girl until the retching gradually eased. The old woman gently brushed the damp tendrils of hair out of Sara's face. "Land sakes, this has been quite a day for you, young'un. What in the world is going on?"

Sara slumped to Sophie's shoulders, crying. "I've done a terrible thing, Sophie."

Sophie held her tight, gently rocking back and forth. "Is the girl downstairs really Olivia Mallory?"

"Yes." The sobbing made Sara's answers difficult to decipher. "It's all true. I'm not Olivia Mallory; my name is Sara Livingston."

Sophie brushed her hair, fingers untangling wet strands off her cheeks so she could see her face.

"I don't even pretend to understand," Sophie admitted. "But you're going to make yourself sicker if you don't get yourself under control." She sat Sara up, wiping at the tears coursing down her cheeks. When the girl had gained control of her emotions, Sophie said softly, "Now tell me what's happened and we'll see what we can do about it."

The story slowly unfolded, and Sophie listened intently as Sara revealed that she was the daughter of a wealthy railroad magnate, Lowell Livingston. There'd been an argument, and Sara had run away. During the journey, she'd met

Olivia and the two girls had agreed to trade identities. But the plan backfired, and Olivia was here to claim a husband. Sophie had never heard such a story. The ramifications of the girls' whim were unthinkable.

"Why did you run away? Certainly some fine young man in Boston would have married you; your father is a rich man."

"I don't want someone to marry me for my father's money. I want them to marry me because they want *me*, because they love me!" Suddenly pulling out of Sophie's arms, Sara leaned over the chamber pot and emptied her stomach again.

Sophie waited until the retching had eased. A fainting spell . . . nausea. The signs could mean only one thing.

"Sara, have you had your monthly?"

Sara looked up, pale and weak from the violent episode. She shook her head.

"How long have you been sick?"

"I don't know—three or four days."

"Could be that you're expectin', then."

"No." Sara shook her head, wiping her mouth with a cloth. "That isn't it, Sophie. It's nerves, the fear of facing Walker with the truth, nothing more."

"The fainting spell in the barn . . . are you prone to fainting spells?"

"No, that was my first."

"You're with child, young'un. You got to tell Walker."

Sara sat back on her heels, closing her eyes in despair. "I *can't* be, Sophie. And even if I were, I wouldn't tell Walker—not until I've seen a doctor and confirmed the suspicion. He'd only think I was lying to him."

Sophie remembered the days following Trudy's departure. Walker hadn't slept or eaten, prowling the house at night, snapping at anyone who crossed his path. This wasn't going to be an easy time in the McKay household.

"I don't envy you none," she conceded. "Not a'tall."

Covering her face with the cloth, Sara murmured, "What about Olivia? She's downstairs . . . if Walker sees her . . ."

"Don't worry about her. I'll keep her out of the way until you can talk to him."

Sara gave her a grateful look. "Thank you, Sophie. I'll change my dress and go find him."

Sophie turned to leave, absently gathering pieces of wash on her way out.

"Sophie?"

"Yes, honey?"

"You know I love him, don't you?"

Sophie nodded, smiling at her for the first time in days. "Yes, I know."

God help them all. Anyone with a lick of sense knew that Sara loved Walker McKay.

When Sophie walked into the parlor, she noted that Olivia had made herself at home. Hands clasped behind her back, the young woman prowled the room, closely examining the craftsmanship of the grandfather clock Grace had given Mitch fifteen Christmases ago.

She turned and smiled when she saw Sophie come in. "What a lovely clock. Is it very old?"

"I don't know. If you'll excuse me, I have to take these sheets to the washroom."

When she returned a few minutes later, Olivia had moved from the clock to the mantel and was holding a porcelain vase in both hands. Sophie plain didn't care for the girl's audacity. Bold as brass, she was. Rude.

"Are you the maid?" Olivia asked, carefully scrutinizing the vase.

"I wouldn't say I'm a maid. I tend to Walker and Sara." Sophie didn't like the tone of her voice, condescending and uppity.

"What's your name?"

"Sophie."

"Sophie. My father had a dog named Sophie." Olivia gently placed the vase back on the mantel. "It wasn't with us very long."

Sophie wasn't sure how to take the observation, so she pretended to straighten a doily on the table by Walker's chair.

"Is Walker handsome?"

There was something about this girl Sophie didn't like. She was too nosy as she waltzed around the parlor, eyeing the furniture, running her hands along the polished tables as if she owned the place.

"He must be very rich to have all of these nice things and such a big house!" Olivia sat herself down in Walker's chair, testing the comfort, tilting her head at Sophie. "Is he a kind man?"

Sophie stepped over and jerked a pillow from behind the girl's back. "Always treated me good."

Olivia clearly didn't appreciate the pillow's sudden departure. Touching a hand to her hair, she said shortly, "I sincerely hope this matter can be straightened out promptly." Sophie could practically see dollar signs in her eyes. "I'm tired of traveling and I want to marry Mr. McKay as quickly as possible. My parents are expecting . . ." She paused, looking hesitant for the first time. "My parents expect to visit soon, and I don't want to disappoint them."

Sophie remembered the letter in Sara's room. Relief filled her when she realized that she'd misjudged Sara. She wasn't after Walker's money at all; Olivia Mallory was the culprit.

"Miss Mallory, I don't like your attitude, and if you think for one minute that I'll stand by and watch you or anyone else make a fool of Walker McKay—" Sophie heard the kitchen screen door slam shut and whirled to look over her shoulder.

"Sophie! You got any leftover roast? I'm hungry."

Walker.

Olivia straightened her skirts, giving the housekeeper a cool smile. "Well, we'll see how Mr. McKay feels about you talking to me this way."

"On the counter, Walker!" Sophie turned back to Olivia. "You're on your own, missy." She bent close as she walked past the young woman. "Don't expect any support from this corner."

Walker had found the meat by the time Sophie reached the kitchen. He bit into the beef, washing it down with a swallow of milk.

"Let me fix you a plate. Got some beans and corn left from dinner."

"No time, Sophie. I got to get back to work."

Sophie wrapped the plate of meat in a cloth and put it back on the counter.

Walker cut a hunk of bread. "Sara feeling any better?"

"Ask her yourself. She wants to talk to you."

Walker swallowed another bite. "Where is she?"

"Upstairs."

"She'll have to make it quick. Diamond's foaling early put me an hour behind." Picking up the pitcher of milk, he strode through the kitchen into the hall foyer.

Sophie saw him glance into the parlor as Olivia slowly got up from her chair, smiling. He nodded. "Afternoon."

"Good afternoon, Mr. McKay." Olivia snapped a fan open, her eyes bright with excitement as she cooled her flushed features.

Sophie hurriedly diverted him toward the stairs. "Hurry along. She's waiting for you."

Walker proceeded up the stairs, eating roast.

Chores forgotten, Sophie returned to the kitchen to await the explosion.

"Sara? You up here?" Walker paused at the bedroom door.

Sara froze when she heard his voice, forcing back another bout of queasiness. "In here, dear . . ." Dear? She never called him "dear." He would know something was wrong!

The door opened, and Walker stuck his head in. "Who's the girl in the parlor?"

Sara swallowed. "An acquaintance . . . someone I met on my way here."

He frowned, sticking a piece of bread in his mouth. "Why aren't you in the parlor visiting with her?"

Sara looked away, unable to meet his eyes. He would know all too soon that Olivia Mallory was no one's friend.

Entering the bedroom, he kicked the door shut with the heel of his boot. "Sophie said you wanted to see me?"

Unable to find her voice now, she nodded.

Chewing a piece of beef, he winked at her. "Lonesome?"

"No . . . not lonesome."

Concern clouded his features. Her face was flushed and tear-stained. "Are you still feeling bad? Why don't I send one of the—"

"I'm not ill!" The denial came out harshly. She bit her tongue, willing her tears at bay.

"Okay," he said softly. "Maybe a kiss will put some color back into those cheeks." He walked over, trying to embrace her.

Any other time she would welcome his advance. But not now, when she was about to destroy their world. She left the washstand to put distance between them. *Why* hadn't she told him sooner? Now she'd waited too long; Olivia was here, threatening to destroy the union that had just started to form between them.

Following her across the room, he made a second attempt to take her into his arms, failing again.

Shrugging his efforts aside, she said shortly, "There's something I have to tell you."

Their eyes met and locked. Setting the milk

pitcher aside, he said quietly, "I can think of better ways to spend my break than talking."

Memories flooded her. Heated, exciting, gentle, and passionate memories. Dear Lord, how she loved him. What if he insisted that she leave today, insisted he'd bargained for Olivia Mallory and that he was obligated to keep the commitment? Her heart broke when she remembered Olivia's words: "You're not his wife."

She wasn't his wife legally, but she was his soul mate in every way that counted. Maybe the marriage wasn't sanctified, but that was easily corrected. They could remarry and continue as if nothing had happened.

Foolish Sara. Such thoughts are wishful thinking. Walker will be so furious when he hears what you've done, he'll order you out of the house and out of his life. He'll say you have tricked him as surely as Trudy had betrayed him earlier.

But it wasn't the same. She wasn't Trudy, and she loved him with every fiber of her being. Couldn't he see that?

Twisting the hem of her apron, she tried to organize the confession in a sane manner.

You're not going to believe this, but a funny thing happened to me on the way here—

No, that would never work. He'd see right through that.

I should have mentioned this earlier, darling— you'll laugh when you hear it, but I'm not Olivia Mallory. Isn't that hilarious?

He wouldn't find it mildly amusing, let alone hilarious. The certain knowledge crowded her throat, threatening to cut off her air supply. Nausea turned her stomach to an angry, churning pit. *Please, God, don't let me faint now. Give me the words to make him believe what had started as deceit quickly turned into a deep love.*

Walker's voice came to her through a fog. "So what's so important that you need to talk to me in the middle of the day?"

Sucking in breath, she willed her voice to be steady. "I . . . you'll never guess—actually, I know you'll find this really odd, even amusing. . . ." She paused, taking in another deep breath. How could she say it?

I tricked you, played a cruel hoax on you—jeopardized what might have been a glorious marriage between us, all in the name of selfishness.

He would never forgive her. She knew that as surely as she knew her knees were about to give way again. Heading toward the bed, she swallowed against the rush of bile in her throat.

"Sara?" New concern tinged his voice. "Are you going to faint?"

Grasping her by the shoulders, he eased her down on the side of the bed.

"Sophie!"

"No!" She didn't want Sophie here when she told him. One pair of accusing eyes was enough. "I don't need Sophie," she murmured. "Please, Walker . . . let me say this."

Walker leaned close, his breath warm against her cheek. "What is it, sweetheart? Sara . . . what's wrong?"

Tears brimmed in her eyes and she lay back on the pillow, aware it would be the last time he would look at her with love and caring in those blue, blue eyes. Never again would he see her as the woman who shared his bed, his heart, the one and only woman he'd dared to trust after Trudy.

"I don't know how to tell you this."

His eyes met hers, grave now, as if he knew their idyllic world was about to collapse. "Just say it."

Clasping his face between her hands, she said softly, "I'm sorry, Walker. I'm not Olivia Mallory."

His penetrating gaze held hers as the words sank in. Long, agonizing moments passed. She saw fear, disbelief, betrayal, pain, and then gradual acceptance play across his features. Had she honestly expected him to laugh it off, to compliment her on her extraordinary theatrical abilities?

The moments between her revelation and his reply stretched into days. She couldn't read his eyes for the torrent of conflict that waged there.

Straightening, he released her shoulders, and she fell back onto the pillow. "Who are you?"

The coldness in his voice hurt, but she deserved it. The sensual teasing was gone, the husbandly banter, the intimate whispers between a man and woman in love. Vanished. In their place she heard the voice of a stranger.

"My name is Sara Livingston." When she saw confusion cloud his eyes, she prayed it wasn't too late to make him understand. Sitting up, she held out her arms, willing him to return. "What I've done is inexcusable, but I can explain if you'll only let me."

"Sara Livingston. Livingston. You're the girl who ran away?" For a moment she thought he might allow her to explain herself. Her heart soared, then plummeted when his eyes hardened, his jaw clenched. "Why should I allow you anything?"

"Because I am your wife—in every sense of the word, Walker. I love you." When he swore, she went on. "The paper we signed may not be legal, but in God's eyes we are man and wife."

Uttering a black oath, he cupped the back of his neck, pacing the room. "Who are you?"

"I told you, my name is Sara Livingston." As briefly as possible, she explained the ruse and the reasons behind it. Even to her own ears her words sounded lame and incredibly childish. "I meant to tell you—I tried to tell you this morning. I've thought about how I would tell you every day, but there just hasn't been a proper time. I was on my way to the barn to explain when Olivia came. Please, don't hate me—"

He paused before the window, staring at the activities below. Normal sounds drifted up, but the day was anything but normal. "Did Sophie know about this?"

"No, she didn't—not until this afternoon. I had to tell her what I'd done a few minutes ago."

He turned to look at her. "Olivia Mallory is *here*?"

"Sitting downstairs in the parlor. She's the . . . acquaintance I mentioned."

"I don't believe it." Resuming his pacing, he ran his fingers through his hair. She knew he was trying to make sense of what she'd done. But if *she* couldn't, how could he?

Sliding off the bed, she approached him hesitantly, as if she were cornering a wounded animal. "I know it's upsetting, but all is not lost. All you have to do is void your contract with Olivia, and we can marry. Olivia will go home, and nothing will change. I'm happy being your wife—I don't *want* to change anything."

He shrugged her hand aside and her heart broke. All the love he would ever need was in her eyes—couldn't he see that? Didn't he know by now that she'd never pretended feelings she didn't have—that she adored him? No woman without love could ever respond to him the way she had.

And he wouldn't respond to her the way he had if she were merely a convenience, a broodmare, someone to bear his name and children. Love could be theirs again if only he would forgive her.

He might send her away, convinced that his feelings for her ran no deeper than a need for an heir. But there was more to his embraces, much more than mere obligation. She *knew* there was.

"Upsetting?" He could barely look at her now. "You lied to me, made me think you were my *wife*, and you think it's upsetting to me?"

"Devastating," she amended.

He glared at her.

"Insidious," she murmured. "Judas-like, actually."

His look nearly felled her. "Try infuriating. Deceitful."

"But not unforgivable," she pleaded. Please, God, he had to forgive her. She would die if she lost him because of one foolish lie.

Stalking to the door, he refused to answer. She

followed him, begging now. "Not unforgivable, Walker. I know you're upset—I understand you think I've betrayed you. First Trudy, now me. But I swear, I never intended to hurt you—I don't want to leave you; I love you—you must believe me. You're the only man I want, the man I've dreamed about since I was a young girl. Please, let me be your wife; let me show you that I can be trusted. I shouldn't have lied and I'm paying the price, but I've kept the bargain. I've looked after your house, tried to be of help, done everything I *know* to make you happy. Please, Walker—"

"You've made a mockery out of this so-called marriage, Sara. How do you expect me to feel?"

She stepped back as he slammed out of the bedroom, the noise jarring her teeth.

Blinking back tears, she bit her lip and sagged against the closed door. "Just say you'll at least think about it," she whispered brokenly.

Olivia's fan paused, and she brightened as Walker came downstairs. Half rising out of her seat, she smiled. "Mr. McKay—"

The rancher strode past the parlor and disappeared into his study, slamming the door behind him.

As she sank back to the sofa, her fan fluttered harder.

Chapter 15

The foyer clock struck seven. Sara sighed, her gaze returning to the study door. Walker hadn't come to bed last night, and the closed door was a stark reminder that her husband's anger had yet to run its course.

Olivia Mallory shifted in her chair, eyeing her empty plate.

Eggs, sausage, and cold biscuits sat untouched on the table. No one ate until Walker took his chair, which he apparently didn't intend to do this morning.

The minutes ticked by. The women avoided eye contact, focusing instead on their plates. How long could Sara keep up the pretense that Walker would join them? Breakfast was served at six. If he wasn't speaking to her, he wasn't taking meals with her. Like an ostrich, he'd stuck his head in the sand and pretended the past seventeen hours hadn't happened.

"I'm positively faint from hunger," Olivia muttered. "Doesn't the man eat?"

One hour passed, then two.

How long did it take to starve? Sara wondered. Her gaze slid to Olivia, her thoughts anguished. Wadsy's voice flashed through her mind. *Shame on you, Babygirl! You're jest as much to blame in this mess as that Mallory girl!*

The dining room felt as if every window were closed and air were a priceless commodity. Sophie stepped to the doorway, glancing anxiously toward Walker's study.

"No word from him?"

"None. Sophie, maybe I should—" Sara started to get up, but the housekeeper leveled a warning finger at her. "You stay put, young lady. You've caused enough trouble." The old woman disappeared back into the kitchen, where the smell of hot grease permeated the air. Sophie had given up on breakfast and Sara could hear her getting ready for dinner.

Closing her eyes, Olivia sniffed the air appreciably. "Is that chicken I smell?"

"Quail, and it's not for us. It's for Walker and his guest."

Olivia opened her eyes. "The housekeeper doesn't like you, either, does she?"

Why didn't Olivia give up and go home? Walker might be furious with her, but he certainly wasn't going to allow Olivia to infiltrate his home.

"Sophie likes me just fine."

"She doesn't sound like she likes you."

Sara bristled at her smirk. The girl had more temerity than a hound on a fox. "I wouldn't laugh if I were you. Walker's just as upset with you as he is with me."

Olivia fussed with her hair, clearly sure of herself. "How could he be? I didn't come here pretending to be someone else—I didn't marry him under false pretenses."

"You're as guilty of this lie as I am." How dare she insinuate this was all Sara's fault? If she hadn't agreed to the ruse, Sara couldn't have pulled it off.

"*You* were the one who suggested it."

"*You* were the one who wanted to marry Rodney Willbanks."

Both women sat tall in their chairs to face off.

"If you think you can waltz in here and take my husband, *Miss Mallory*, you have another think coming!"

"He's not *your* husband!"

"He *is* my husband. Maybe I don't have a legal document to prove it, but we took our vows before God—"

"You lied to God."

"I did *not*!" Sara would never lie to God!

But that was exactly what she'd done. She'd stood before Reverend Baird and taken sacred vows, knowing full well that she was perpetrating a fraud. What had she been thinking? A scream of fury stuck at the back of her throat. She wanted this woman, this Jezebel, this home wrecker, out of Walker's house and out of her life. Olivia wanted him only for his money and what he could do for her family. Sara would die before she'd hand him over to the scheming likes of Olivia Mallory.

"I want you to leave, Olivia—now, today."

"You can't order me to leave. You have no authority."

"I'm Walker's wife, and this is my home."

"Is not."

"I'll make you leave." Sara pushed back from the table, prepared to do battle.

Olivia snatched a biscuit and hurled it. Sara gasped as the bread ricocheted off her right cheek.

Grabbing the bowl of gravy, she hurled it at Olivia.

Eggs flew, then china cups. Jam and coffee splattered the tablecloth. The dining room erupted in a full-scale assault as the women threw dishes and screeched in outrage.

"Girls!" Sophie burst from the kitchen and waded in to separate the warring factions. It took a minute for the housekeeper to gain control and get the girls back in their seats. Sopping gravy off the front of Sara's blouse, she tsked.

"Never saw such goings-on in all my born days. What are you, a bunch of hooligans?"

"Sophie, she just wants—"

"I don't want to hear it!" Sophie left Sara and moved around the table to see about the ugly stains dotting Olivia's blouse. The young woman's hair was loose from its pins, and she had a big gob of grape jam above her left brow.

"Lord have mercy. Have you two no learnin'?

Throwing food like unruly children! You ought to be ashamed of yourselves."

Sara reached for a napkin, wiping greasy spatters off her skirt. "She has to leave, Sophie. This is an impossible situation. Walker will never come out of the study while she's still here."

"I'm not leaving," Olivia announced. "Not until I talk to Mr. McKay and see how he feels about the matter." She brushed food crumbs out of her hair. "You think you're so smart—you'll be attending my wedding, Sara Livingston."

"I hope you like barbecue," Sara grumbled.

"What?"

"I want this catfight to stop, you hear me?" Crossing her arms over her chest, Sophie looked at the two girls sternly. "I'm going in that study and get this mess straightened out. You sit right here, and I don't want to hear a peep out of either one of you! Do you understand?"

Both women nodded in unison.

Sophie disappeared around the corner and Sara hazarded a quick look at Olivia, who promptly stuck out her tongue.

Looking in the other direction, Sara licked jelly off her lips, ignoring the infantile gesture. It would be a cold day in Hades before she let that woman—or any other, for that matter—get her clutches into Walker McKay.

"Walker?" Sophie tapped softly on the study door.

"I'm busy, Sophie."

"You're not that busy, and if you're not decent,

you'd better say so, because I'm comin' in." She waited for a moment, then turned the handle. Walker gave her a dirty look as she entered the room.

"Can't a man have his privacy around here anymore?"

"Ordinarily, but these aren't ordinary times. And cowards don't get special privileges. Hidin' away in here ain't gonna solve a blessed thing." She walked to the window and opened the drapes. Sunlight poured into the cluttered study. Walker, with hair tousled and a day-old beard, sat at his desk, feet propped up, smoking a cheroot with a half-empty brandy container in front of him. He'd obviously had a dandy night.

"Are they gone?"

"Who?"

"Miss Mallory and the other Miss Mallory."

"At least you still have a sense of humor."

"Who *knows* their names?"

"They're still here, big as life, sitting at your breakfast table waiting for you to come out."

"Inform the ladies they'll be sitting a long time."

Sophie straightened a stack of books, absently wiping the desk surface with her apron hem.

"Can't blame you for being upset—who wouldn't be, under the circumstances? Marry one woman and find out she's not who she says she is. But the problem isn't going to be solved by you holing up here, refusing to eat or sleep or even discuss the matter. I can't have those two girls sitting at my table all day. Got food all over my clean floor, the tablecloth's a mess . . ."

Giving her a questioning look, Walker tossed down a half glass of brandy.

"Don't ask."

Boots hit the floor, and he got up to prowl the room. "Why did she do it, Sophie? Why didn't she just tell me about the switch? At the time, it wouldn't have made any difference. One woman was as good as another."

At the time, that might have been true. But not now. As much as Walker vowed he'd never fall prey to another woman's treachery, Sara had wormed her way into his heart, and that made Sara's actions even more painful than Trudy's betrayal.

"I can't answer for Sara, Walker. She tells me she's sorry, that if she had it to do over again, she'd never deceive you. She's young; she goes on feelings instead of sound judgment. She realizes she's done wrong. She can't understand why you can't forgive and go on."

He snorted. "Who is she, Sophie?"

"Tells me she's Sara Livingston. Her father is that wealthy Bostonian I was telling you about. She's Lowell Livingston's missing daughter."

He shook his head wordlessly. "Good Lord. How blind can a man be? Then why, Sophie?" Walker paused before the window, his eyes fixed on the rose garden. Sophie knew the reminder was yet another knife to the heart.

"She says she made the switch because she wants to be married. She's stayed on because she loves you."

"She needed a stranger to fill her needs?"

"Does seem peculiar, a pretty little thing like

Sara. Who knows why anyone does anything? But she seems sincere enough. Still . . ."

Walker turned to look at her. "Still what?"

Sophie hadn't wanted to mention it; she'd seen no need until now. But if Sara was in the marriage for anything other than what she claimed, then Walker needed to know. "I found her going over your books here a while back."

"My financial ledgers?"

"She said she was trying to help you. Said she was good at math. When I mentioned it to S. H., he didn't think it was anythin' to get upset about. Could have been idle curiosity—you know how fascinated Sara is with ranching. Besides, she comes from a wealthy family. I wouldn't let it overly concern me, but you need to know."

Rolling the cigar around the corner of his mouth, Walker turned back to stare out the window.

"What are you going to do about the situation?"

He simply stared at the flower garden as if the answers lay somewhere between the roses and the fountains.

"S. H. should have plowed that garden under two years ago."

He still didn't answer.

"You can't just ignore the situation. There's two women sitting out there waiting on you to decide who is going to be your wife."

Snorting, Walker returned to the desk.

"She's gone about it the wrong way, but Sara's suited for you, Walker." Sophie treaded lightly, fearful of upsetting him further. Lord have mercy on them all if he chose that money-grubbing hussy, Olivia Mallory. Judging by the Mallorys' letter to their daughter, they thought they had a money horse, but she knew Sara's feelings ran deeper. Even before Trudy, Walker had needed a woman, a woman who'd put a shine in his eyes and a bounce in his step. Trudy never did either, but Sara filled the bill. Walker was a proud man, though, whose blind pride would be his downfall.

She could see she was getting nowhere with him. Walker had to work this out on his own. She just hoped it didn't take all day.

"Caleb will be here any time. S. H. went for him this morning. You ought to be good and hungry by now." By the looks of the half-empty bottle on the desk, he'd drunk his supper and breakfast.

"I don't know who else to ask about this, Sophie. Caleb will know what to do."

She edged toward the door. "Do you plan to stay in here all week?"

He reached for the brandy bottle. "I might."

Not if I have anything to say about it. She closed the door behind her.

Caleb was already at the front door with S. H. Both men looked worried, questioning Sophie with their eyes when she answered the door. She shook her head and nodded toward the dining room. Olivia and Sara still sat in their chairs, the length of the dining room table separating them. It was going to be a long day.

Caleb stepped into the foyer. "Walker in the study?"

Sophie inclined her head toward it. "He's expecting you."

Caleb smiled nervously and breezed by the dining room, pausing to tip his hat. "Morning, ladies."

Cold silence met his cordial efforts.

Sighing, Sophie hurried on to the kitchen.

A second knock came minutes after Sophie had left.

"Go away!" Walker bellowed.

"I'd like to, but you asked me to come."

"Caleb?"

"How many people did you send for?"

The door opened a crack, and Walker allowed him entrance. Caleb stood by the doorway, looking at the jumbled room. "Have you been ransacked?"

"Worse. I've been lied to."

Walker slammed the door, and resumed pacing.

The two men were the same age, but the years had been kinder to Walker. Caleb's gray suits and dark shirts made him look sallow, washed-out, and overly weary.

Walker's boyhood friend frowned. "You look as if you haven't slept in weeks."

Running a hand over the back of his neck, Walker muttered something about years, then sat down at the desk.

"Is something wrong?"

Walker picked up a glass and tossed down the contents. Sara's deception went so deep, he hadn't realized how much he had grown to . . . love her. Love. The very thing he'd told himself he would never do. "I've been lied to."

Caleb's eyes shifted to the open ledger on the desk. "Who's lied to you?"

Walker swiveled around to face him. "Sara lied to me."

"Sara?" The accountant sat in the wing-backed chair in front of the desk and removed his wire-rimmed glasses, absently polishing them on a hankie. "Sara lied? About what?" His eyes casually returned to the ledger.

Walker lit another cheroot, then drew on it. Blowing smoke toward the ceiling, he said quietly, "She tricked me, Caleb. She switched places with Olivia Mallory."

"Switched places?"

"The two women switched places. Olivia Mallory went off on some jaunt to marry a man she wanted, and Sara agreed to stand in as my bride."

"Merciful heavens. What could they have been thinking?"

"That I was a fool and I'd never know the difference, and that even when I did, I wouldn't care." He drew on the cigar again, thinking of how easily he'd fallen for it. Why? But he knew why. The moment Sara Livingston got off that train, she did something to him, something he hadn't wanted to acknowledge. When would she have told him about the switch? Tomorrow? The week after? Never?

"How did you discover the deception?"

"The real Miss Mallory is sitting in my parlor. Seems she's had a change of heart and she now wants to keep her end of the bargain."

Caleb hooked the sidepieces of his glasses behind his ears, frowning. "Merciful heavens."

The two men sat, mulling the situation over in their minds.

"What does Sara have to say about her actions?"

I'm sorry, Walker. I love you. Please let me be your wife, let me show you I can be trusted. The knife twisted deeper.

"She says she intended to tell me about the switch."

"When?"

"I don't know, Caleb. Does it matter?" He reached for the brandy container, but Caleb's hand stopped him.

"Why don't I have Sophie bring in a pot of hot coffee?"

"Coffee won't help."

Replacing the stopper in the bottle, Caleb moved the liquor aside. "So Sara lied. She could have done worse."

Giving him an impatient look, Walker got out of his chair and returned to the window.

"You didn't know Olivia Mallory. You didn't know Sara. You were willing to marry a stranger in order to produce an heir, so I hardly see where you've been wronged."

"She *lied* to me, Caleb."

"True, but she hasn't run off with another man."

Maybe it would have hurt less if Sara had run

off with another man. Then she wouldn't be waiting in his dining room. Drawing on the cigar, he
studied the garden.

"Sophie said Sara's been going through the
books, trying to help."

Caleb sat up straighter, color draining from his
face. "Why would she do that?"

"Who knows why Sara does anything?"

Loosening his collar, Caleb shifted in his chair.
"There'd be no reason for her to look at the
books—do you suspect she's after your money?"

"She shouldn't be. Her father's one of the rich-
est men in America."

"Could she be lying about her identity?"

Walker turned to give him a wry look.

Caleb reached for the brandy snifter and
poured himself a drink. The burgundy liquid
spilled on the desk and he absently blotted it
with a piece of paper. "Perhaps I should check
the books—make sure she hasn't tampered with
them."

The statement irritated Walker. "She hasn't
'tampered' with them. She can't even manage a
meal, much less swindle me out of money. She's
not a thief."

"You didn't think she was a liar."

The observation was met with stony silence.

Sara *wasn't* a thief. Walker would stake his life
on that, although at the moment, he was helpless
to know why. She'd lied about her identity, lied to
him, lied to Sophie and S. H. and Potster, but her
explanation was so cockeyed he almost believed
it. He'd never met a woman who could get herself in so much trouble with so little effort.

Caleb downed the liquor, his eyes returning to the ledger. Sweat covered his thin upper lip. "I'll take the books home with me. Until this matter is settled, you can't be too careful."

"That isn't necessary. You and I are the only ones with access to the funds." Walker thought about telling Caleb about Sara's earlier questions, but decided not to. One crisis at a time was enough.

"I still want to go over them carefully." Caleb put his glass on the desk, pressing the handkerchief to his upper lip.

"There is something you can do." Sitting down again, Walker reached into the desk drawer for the signed agreement between him and Olivia Mallory. "Can you read this lousy thing and tell me what I signed?"

Caleb's brows lifted. "You don't know?"

"At the time, I thought I did. Back then, I didn't think it'd make a whole lot of difference."

"I'll give it a look." Caleb took the papers and the two men fell silent.

Walker poured another drink. Maybe the contract would take the choice out of his hands.

Sara watched the clock, resting her head on the dining table, nausea building at the smell of frying meat. The mere thought of food made her shudder, yet she knew she should eat.

Her head shot up when she heard the study door open. Walker and Caleb emerged, grimfaced and looking anything but happy. Her hand automatically reached out to touch Walker when he walked past her chair, but he brushed it aside.

The two men sat down at the opposite end of the table.

Walker refused to meet her eyes. "Where's Sophie?"

"Hanging wash. Olivia is taking a walk."

"Caleb, tell Sophie and Miss Mallory that I want to see them."

Sara searched for a hint of forgiveness and found none. He looked tired, disappointed, and she longed to take him in her arms and comfort him. But the look of desperation on Walker's face held her silent.

Caleb returned with Sophie and Olivia in tow. Olivia chose the seat closest to Walker, murmuring a shy hello. Walker acknowledged the greeting. Barely.

Sophie sat next to Sara, reaching for her hand beneath the table and giving it a squeeze.

Caleb flipped through the contract, scanning various sections. Pausing, he glanced up, clearing his throat.

"Walker has asked me to review the contract he and Miss Mallory signed prior to her arrival. Walker, is there anything you want to say before we proceed?"

Sara slid to the edge of her chair, holding tight to Sophie's hand. She hadn't been aware there was a contract. Walker had never mentioned it.

Walker finally looked at her, and the pain in his eyes drove deep into her heart. It was a devastatingly fit punishment for her sins.

"I was foolish," she said softly. "Please forgive me, Walker."

"Actually, it was my fault," Olivia said. "I

shouldn't have agreed to the plan, but Sara was so desperate. I'm terribly sorry, Mr. McKay. I wasn't thinking clearly, but once I realized we had a binding contract . . ."

"Miss Mallory, the reason doesn't matter. I'm bound by what the contract stipulates."

Olivia looked momentarily flustered. "Well . . . yes, of course, but I'm sure this can easily be straightened out."

"Caleb, what're my options?"

"Well, it's rather complicated." Caleb studied the document. "Of course, there's no clause relating to the present circumstance, mind you, and I'm not a lawyer—but I believe, if I read this correctly, Miss Mallory is legally entitled to enforce the contract."

"That's not fair!" Sara cried. "Walker is married to me!"

Caleb received the outburst coolly. "Technically, you are not his wife. The marriage certificate bears the name Olivia Mallory—though not her signature. You are Sara—is it Livingston? But by the contract, Miss Mallory would be the legal party who—"

"She forfeited that right when she allowed me to take her place." Sara turned to Walker, her eyes silently pleading while Caleb continued to recite contract clauses. The accountant's voice faded and she was aware only of the man who until yesterday had been her husband in every way except legally. He couldn't let this happen. He had to put a stop to this madness.

Her gaze locked with Walker's and she saw

not pain but a kind of powerlessness he seemed to accept.

"Like Caleb says, he isn't an attorney," Sophie reminded them when Caleb finished. "Might be Estes Knolls would have a different opinion about the document."

Walker broke Sara's locked gaze. "Estes won't be back from Portland until next month."

"That's right. The lawyer is visitin' his daughter." Sophie squeezed Sara's hand.

Olivia looked relieved. "I trust Caleb. If he says the contract is binding, then I guess there's no choice. Sara can either go home or join her friend in New York. You and I can be married, and we can put this whole unpleasant thing behind us."

Sophie's jaw firmed, and she cleared her throat. "It's none of my business who you choose, Walker, but before you make a fool of yourself a third time, you'd best take this into consideration." She took from her pocket the Mallory letter.

Sara gasped. "Sophie, no, don't—"

"Sara, you may have lied to us, but it would be worse to have a thief to carry on the McKay name." The housekeeper handed Walker the letter.

Walker scanned the missive and Sara held her breath. Olivia's face flushed crimson when he finished and fixed angry eyes on her.

"Who wrote this?"

"I believe that would be Miss Mallory's mother," Sophie replied.

Tossing the papers down on the table, Walker

stood up. "Miss Mallory, S. H. will take you to the train tomorrow morning."

Olivia sprang to her feet. "What does the letter say? You can't do this—we have a binding agreement! Why . . . my pa won't hear of this! You'd best give this more thought, Mr. McKay." She whirled on Sophie. "Where did you get that letter? How dare you read my mail!"

The housekeeper shrugged.

Olivia whirled back to face Walker. "You can't do this. I won't permit it."

Walker met her eyes coldly. "You'll be leaving tomorrow. I'll see that your ticket is paid for."

"While we're on the subject of who's stayin' and who's goin'," Sophie added, "there's another thing you should know."

The baby. Sara shot the housekeeper a warning look. If Walker decided to forgive her, she wanted it to be because of love and not because of obligation.

"Sophie, please don't. If Walker wants to send me away, I'll go."

Sophie continued as if she hadn't heard. "You'd be a fool to send Sara away. You're mad right now, but you'll get over it. Don't do anything until you're thinking straighter."

"Sophie, I am capable of defending myself," Sara murmured, her cheeks hot.

"Walker, the contract says . . ." Caleb opened it again.

Sara glared at him. He was on Olivia's side. This didn't surprise her. Caleb Vanhooser was cool to her now, suspicious. She'd thought it was resentment because she consumed more of Walker's time, but considering his curt reaction to her questions about Walker's bookkeeping, she wondered if it wasn't more. Caleb and Olivia argued with Walker, Sophie chiming in with her opinion until the room rang with voices.

"Enough!" Walker threw his hands up. The room's occupants fell silent.

"The contract is void. If Miss Mallory wasn't interested in me from the beginning, then she invalidated it herself. Tomorrow S. H. will take you to the train, buy your ticket, and give you fifty dollars for your time and effort."

Olivia glanced from Sara to Sophie, then whirled and marched out. "You can't do this and get away with it," she declared over her shoulder.

Sophie shoved back from the table. "Now you are finally making sense. Dinner will be on the table in ten minutes."

Sara slumped in relief, closing her eyes. Walker hadn't asked her to go, but he hadn't asked her to stay. He walked past her chair, hardly sparing her a glance. She opened one eye a moment later and found a tight-lipped Caleb staring at her.

Shuffling the papers, he folded them neatly and left the room.

Early the following morning, S. H. reined in the team just short of the train station. Not a word had passed between him and Olivia Mallory on the way into town.

Olivia reached for her bag before the wagon

came to a complete stop. She was furious with Walker's decision and even more upset about facing her parents back home.

"I'll get that." S. H. set the brake and bounded off the wagon, coming around to help her down. She gave him a cold look, stepping down on her own.

He hoisted the bag and carried it to the train platform. "Have a pleasant trip, Miss Mallory. Do you need any help with arrangements?"

"Just leave."

Tipping his hat, he said pleasantly, "Have a safe journey."

The buckboard rolled off and Olivia quickly crossed the street and went into the telegraph office. Approaching the counter, she pulled the fifty dollars from her purse, peeling off a bill.

"Can I help you, ma'am?" the man behind the window asked.

"I want to send a telegraph."

"Yes, ma'am. Who should I address it to?"

Olivia smugly glanced over her shoulder. The dust from the McKay wagon had yet to settle.

"Lowell Livingston, Boston, Massachusetts."

Chapter 16

"**S**ara? A thief?" S. H. looked at Walker as if he'd lost his mind. "That little gal might use poor judgment occasionally, but she ain't no thief." He handed Walker a leather strap and Walker attached it to the halter.

"Then why was she going through my books?"

"Cain't say, but I'd bet my last dime she don't care if you got a dollar to your name. She ain't that kind, son. And I've known a few women in my younger days."

Walker grinned, binding the leather. "I've heard rumors to that effect."

S. H. slapped another strip of leather in his hand. "Notice you're a little testy these days. Haven't seen much of her lately, have ya?"

Walker hadn't seen Sara since Olivia had shown up a week ago. Sophie said she was under

259

the weather and hadn't gotten out of bed the past few days. Finishing the harness, he reached for another one. What ailed her? Guilt? Or was she really ill? He pushed the bothersome thought to the back of his mind. Sophie would have told him if Sara were in any danger.

"Wouldn't hurt none to check on your woman, would it? Sophie says she's a pitiful sight, eyes nearly swollen shut from cryin'."

"She's not my woman, S. H. Not since she lied to me."

"Could be that you're bein' a little bullheaded about this. The girl's crazy about ya, Walker. Any fool can see it."

"Implying that I'm one fool who can't?"

"If the boot fits."

Walker wanted to go to her. The nights were long without her body warm and sweet in his arms. He missed her smile and the sound of her laughter, the way she looked early mornings, warm and willing. Sleeping in the spare room wasn't his idea of paradise, but every time he reached her bedroom door, he remembered that she had lied. If a man couldn't trust a woman, all the lovemaking in the world was useless.

S. H. stoked the mare's neck. "You keepin' this hardhead company, ole girl?" Diamond threw her nose up in the air and tossed her head as if denying any involvement with Walker's mulishness.

Walker gritted his teeth and bore down to tighten the finishing knot on the halter. "Maybe I should send her home, S. H." The thought had been at the back of his mind for days. He couldn't forgive her, and wouldn't stay in that guest room forever. Sara should be home with family, people who loved her. Yet that idea appealed to him less than facing her.

S. H. snorted and tore a piece of leather in two. "If that's what you really wanted, you'da sent her home with that other gal."

Walker threw the harness over a stall door, then reached for a saddle that needed mending. S. H. had a point. Trudy had left him with no choice; with Sara he still had options. He could marry her, move on. Until a week ago the marriage had been good, nearly ideal for a while. Sara was good company, easy on the eye, easy to be with. There wasn't a man in the county who didn't look twice at Sara McKay. Only she wasn't Sara McKay; never had been. A dollar and five minutes with Reverend Baird would correct that, but somehow he now wanted more.

A man didn't have to love a woman in order to live with her. He was in the marriage to sire an heir. Personal feelings hadn't counted when he'd ordered a bride and they needn't count now. So why did her deceit stick in his craw? Why did he lie in his bed sleepless nights, his mind going over the hours she'd spent in his arms, the taste of her mouth, the way she made him feel nine feet tall inside, the way she curled around him like a playful kitten?

"So what are you gonna do? Not speak to her until the baby's born?"

"There isn't going to be a baby, S. H."

"Oh . . . open yer eyes, Walker." S. H. glanced up, his face coloring.

Walker's saddle slipped from the stanchion

and into the hay. "What's that supposed to mean?"

Color dotted S. H.'s cheeks and he busied himself with the mare.

"S. H.?"

"What?"

"What does 'open your eyes' mean?"

Head bent, S. H. eased behind Diamond's flanks and began checking her hooves.

"Do I have to come over there and beat it out of you?"

"I cain't tell you, Walker. Sophie'd kill me. I already opened my big mouth too much."

A chill ran up Walker's spine despite the extreme heat. Sara's sickness, her wan features— three days spent in bed. Sara was scatterbrained, but she wasn't sickly.

"S. H., is Sara carrying my child?"

"Don't make me tell ya, Walker. I wanna be able to eat and sleep in my own house."

"S. H.!"

"Walker!"

The two men stood at an impasse. Neither spoke, as if trying to wear the other down. Finally Walker broke the silence, leaning over to jerk the saddle back on the post.

"She can't be. If she was, she would have told me." She would have used it as a tool to trap him. What better way to bind him than to produce his heir?

S. H. took off his hat and wiped his temples, shaking his head. "Son, don't you know nothin' 'bout havin' babies? The woman don't know right away, and the way you two was goin' at it, I'm surprised you don't have a houseful a young'uns by now."

A baby. The heir to Spring Grass; Mitch McKay's grandson. Something leapt inside Walker at the thought.

"You said Sophie would be mad at you—has Sara told Sophie that she's pregnant?"

S. H. picked a rock from Diamond's hoof.

Walker stepped around the front of the mare to confront him. S. H. glanced up, his ears coloring. "If you want to know, why don't you ask yer wife?"

"She's not my wife."

"Well, another barbecue would take care of that."

"Blast it." Walker sank into the hay bale, swearing under his breath. "She's pregnant?"

"Well . . . maybe. How can ya not be tickled plum to death about a young'un? That's what you've wanted all along—that's what started this whole mess."

"No, *you* started this whole mess."

"I ain't the one with enough money to buy California. When I die, someone will have to take up a donation to bury me. Besides, why are you complainin'? You want a son or daughter, don't ya?"

"I thought that's what I wanted." Right now, he was trying to make sense of it all. Sara was expecting his child. Elation warred with his hurt pride, confusing him.

S. H. finished with the mare and closed the stall door. Storing the tools, he said quietly, "You can do what ya want. It's yer woman and yer business; I just think you're being a dern fool about the whole thing. Ya could be happy 'n' married and havin' a baby together, but you're out here fixin' straps and sleepin' on an old bed in the spare room because of some misplaced pride ya think is more important than yer feelin's for her." The old man grabbed the cattleman's shoulders. "Do yourself a favor. Let it go. Ain't nothin' nicer than wakin' up to the woman you love in yer arms. Makes up for a heap of mistakes, son." His tone dropped lower. "You could be sleeping in her bed tonight, 'steada by yerself."

The sound of a carriage pulling up to the house drew Sara away from the vanity, where she'd been absently brushing her hair and grieving Walker's rejection. When she lifted the bedroom curtain aside, her heart sank. Papa, accompanied by a man and a woman, climbed the porch stairs. That rotten Olivia had wired Papa and told him where she was! She'd gotten her revenge. Taking a deep breath, Sara prepared for battle.

She quickly changed into her best dress, listening to the familiar murmur of her father's voice downstairs. When Lowell spotted her coming down the stairway, his face crumbled. Her heart ached for him; he'd aged ten years in the months since she'd last seen him.

"Hello, Papa."

Instead of the anticipated explosion, Lowell's shoulders slumped, his eyes bright with emotion.

"Dear God. I feared that I might never see you again."

Sara stepped off the last stair and into her

father's arms, hugging him tightly. It felt so good to hold him. When had he gotten so old? Was she responsible for the new lines beneath his eyes, the fatigue in his strained features?

"I'm so sorry, Papa."

"Are you all right, child?"

"Fine, Papa. And you?"

"Better, now that I know you're safe."

Stepping back, Lowell cleared his throat, eyes brimming with unshed tears. "Daughter, these are Pinkerton agents Kate Warne and Frank Roche."

Sara shook hands with the tall woman and her male companion.

When the introductions were over, Sara wrapped her arms around Papa's waist. "Let's all go into the parlor—"

Sophie cleared her throat from the stairway.

"Oh, I'm sorry, Sophie. I was so happy to see Papa that I neglected you." Sara introduced her to Lowell and the detectives.

Sophie nodded. "You'll be needin' privacy. Use the study." She smiled at Lowell. "You must be dry as a bone. I'll fix a pitcher of lemonade." She hurried off, discreetly pulling the double doors closed behind her.

Lowell sat down on the sofa, rubbing his forehead. Sara had witnessed the anxious gesture a hundred times over the years when Papa was upset.

"Sara Elaine, what have you done?"

Standing behind Walker's desk for comfort, Sara clasped her hands, gathering strength. Marrying Walker was much more serious than any of her other schemes, and the implications affected more than just herself. She wasn't proud of running away, but given the choice, she'd do it over again for just one hour in Walker McKay's arms.

"I know you feel that I've done a foolish thing, Papa. I married a man I didn't know. He could have been cruel or a drunkard, but fortunately, he wasn't—or isn't. He's a wonderful man, and I've hurt him deeply." Lifting her chin, she drew a lengthy breath. "I love Walker McKay with all my heart, but he doesn't seem to feel the same. We've lived together as man and wife for two months now, Papa—without the benefit of marriage."

"You married a total stranger—switched places with another woman. You lied to McKay, betrayed me, and made a mockery of the sanctity of marriage. Are there no limits to your absurdity, Sara?"

Focusing on her hands, Sara forced back tears. "It seems there isn't, Papa."

Shaking his head, Lowell sank back against the sofa. He closed his eyes and she wondered if he wished he hadn't come.

"Then you are aware that you and Mr. Walker are not legally married?" the woman detective asked.

Sara turned to meet Kate Warne's eyes. "I have been so advised."

Pain flickered briefly across Lowell's face.

"What do you intend to do about this situation?" he asked quietly.

"I'm not sure."

"Do you think you can put it off until someone

rescues you? Don't you think about what you've done?"

She resented the disdain in his tone. She *had* thought about it—day and night—but she still had no solution. She didn't want to go home; she wanted to stay here with her husband, her child; with the new life she'd begun. "I want to stay, but Walker refuses to discuss the matter with me. When he is speaking to me again, we'll decide what to do about the situation."

She missed her husband lying beside her at night, his hard, warm body next to hers, his sweet kisses that drove her out of her mind. Did he miss her even a little? Was Diamond's company preferable to hers? She ached to be back in his good graces.

Getting up, Lowell walked to the window. He stood there for a moment, staring at the overgrown rose garden.

Sara watched his changing expressions. *It isn't fitting that Walker leave the beautiful flowers unkempt to represent women's betrayal*, she thought. Surely each time he looked at the garden, the sight reopened old wounds. Why didn't he destroy the hateful reminder, cut it down, cut it out of his life the way he had her pleadings? Sighing, she looked away. If she knew Walker, he would simply plant another bush in honor of Sara Livingston.

"You will come home with me, Sara. Mr. McKay has been through quite enough because of you."

"No, Papa, I can't come home with you."

"You have no other choice, daughter." Lowell turned from the window, his face blotched with anger. "You can't expect Mr. McKay to marry you now, to go on as if nothing has happened. You lied to the man, misrepresented yourself. Surely you don't expect him to turn a blind eye to your whims!"

"I *don't* expect that, but you don't understand. I've been a good wife—I've tried to help around the house, make friends with his ranch hands, and dutifully fulfill my wifely obligations—" She broke off, blushing when he winced at her openness. "Walker's angry right now, but he'll cool down, and when he does, I know that I can make him love me again."

"Your rosy perspective implies that he loved you before. Is this true?"

"I don't know if he loved me—but he liked me, and that's the first step to love. Given time, I know I could have made him love me. You can't ask me to go back to Boston, Papa. I have to stay here until I know there's no other choice."

"I'll not have you throwing yourself at a man's feet, clinging like a pathetic, love-starved pup. You will come home, Sara, and, Brice willing, you will spend time in Georgia trying to rectify this mistake. We'll keep the details a secret and eventually people will forget . . ."

"I can't do that, Papa."

"You can and you will."

"Miss Livingston, your father is offering you a reasonable way out of an unfortunate situation," Kate put in. "We can say you ran away to live with friends in the West. You can leave here today, join your uncle, and no one will be the wiser."

Sara paced the study. *Everyone* would be the wiser, especially Uncle Brice, when she delivered Walker's baby seven months from now. She'd missed her monthly; Sophie was right, she was expecting a child—Walker's baby.

The McKay heir.

If she could only hold on long enough for Walker's rage to subside, she would tell him about the child, and his broken heart would mend and accept her again. If not . . .

"There's no other way, Sara. Now, pack your things. We're leaving immediately. My private rail coach is waiting at the station."

"No—you don't understand. I can't leave because I'm expecting Walker's child."

A cannon shot would have been less explosive. The two Pinkerton agents flinched; Lowell's eyes bulged and the color drained from his face.

"That's not possible."

"Not possible? Papa, I have been married to Mr. McKay for almost two months now. We've—"

Lowell threw up his hands. "No, no, you're imagining things. It's too soon—you're upset about the situation and you—"

"Papa, I'm going to be a mother. I'm sick to my stomach, I've missed my last two monthlies, and I faint at anything. Sophie says I'm with child, and I'm scheduled to see the doctor next week."

"Dear God." Sinking back to the couch, Lowell mopped his brow. Kate and Frank exchanged resigned glances.

"So, you see, I can't leave." Not that she would

if she could. However feeble the possibility, she still held out hope for a reconciliation.

Lowell absently stuffed the handkerchief into his pocket. "Does Walker know?"

"Absolutely not!"

"Thank God—then all is not lost. A baby makes it even more imperative that you leave. No daughter of mine is going to trap a man into marriage."

"Trap? But, Papa—"

"Is this what you want, Sara? To offer him no way out? Do you for one moment think a marriage could survive if based on treachery and manipulation?"

Sara didn't know what she thought. She would never *trap* Walker. She wanted his whole and undivided love. Anything less would be an abomination, a festering sore incapable of healing. Turning soulful eyes on Papa, she started to cry. "I love him, Papa. I don't want to leave him."

"You cannot make a man love you, Sara. And you cannot put Walker McKay in a position where he has no choice. My heart breaks for you and the child you're carrying, but we can't heap trouble on top of more trouble. Arm-twisting is never the answer, and if you bind Walker to you by obligation, you will forever regret it."

"Has Sophie told him about the child?"

"I made her promise she wouldn't."

Silence fell over the occupants of the room. Sara paced yet again, praying for a miracle, knowing one wasn't likely.

"I'll arrange for Brice to assist you through the pregnancy. When the child is born, I'll have it brought to us in a few months, saying it's a foundling and we have chosen to raise it. No one need ever know that it's your child."

"You would allow me to keep it?"

His shoulders slumped. "It's my grandchild— my flesh and blood. I'm not an ogre, Sara. I grieve for the circumstances your reckless behavior has brought upon this family, but I love you dearly, and I'll love your child. We will get through this, and someday you will thank me for saving you from a loveless existence. A fate far worse, child, than admitting a wrong."

"But I love him, Papa." Sara wept openly now. How could she leave Spring Grass, bear Walker's child, live with a visual reminder of the man she loved day after day after day? Where would she find the strength to walk away from Walker McKay, to never again experience the heat of his embrace, the touch of his lips, the passion that threatened to consume them both?

"What if I tell him about the baby and he asks me to stay?" She was grasping at straws, but once Walker had calmed down, he might see the situation more reasonably.

"Can you trust the invitation won't arise from need or from a sense of duty? If McKay is an honorable man, he can do no less than ask for your hand in marriage. The man is trapped, whatever else he might imply."

Sobbing harder, she buried her face in the front of his shirt. The familiar scent of tobacco reminded her that he was Papa, reminded her of crawling onto his lap as a child when some other hurt found her. As he was then, he remained her one source of security. He was right; she could not, would not, trap Walker. She had done enough already.

"I will always love him."

Awkwardly cradling her in his arms, Lowell said gently, "Love can be overcome, Sara. We'll get through this."

It was close to suppertime when Walker finished up in the barn. Diamond nuzzled her sleeping foal to her feet to nurse. The filly was dark and had the height of her mother, but the markings and spirit of her father.

Mother nickered quietly to her baby and baby responded by starting to nurse. The sight calmed Walker. He was going to be a papa. Would the child have Sara's features, be delicate and winsome, or stubborn like his own pa?

After tossing hay into the other two stalls, he exited the barn, his gaze drawn to a buggy sitting in front of the house. Company? Who would be visiting at this hour?

When he came in the back door, Sophie put a finger to her lips, her eyes motioning to the study. He continued through the kitchen and into the hall, pausing in front of the study door. Three pairs of eyes focused on him as he removed his hat. One belonged to a tall lady in a gray dress; the other two were of businessmen of some standing. The older man extended his hand.

"You must be Walker McKay. Allow me to introduce my companions and myself. I am Lowell Livingston, Sara's father." He turned to the woman. "This is Kate Warne and her associate Frank Roche, of the Pinkerton detective agency."

The agents shook hands with Walker and stepped aside. Mr. Livingston remained in the doorway.

"Mr. McKay, I was wondering if I might have a word with you alone."

Walker's gaze traveled across the small gathering. "Of course."

Kate and Frank left the study and Walker closed the door behind them. The setting sun threw the room into partial shadow, so he lit a lamp. Sitting down at the desk, he motioned Mr. Livingston to take a chair across from him. Lowell wasted no time in coming to the point.

"I must apologize for my daughter's behavior. I can only say I deeply regret any inconvenience Sara might have caused. I realize an apology is weak in view of the circumstances, but I can assure you, Mr. McKay, Sara and I find the whole episode highly regrettable."

Walker removed his hat and laid it on the desk. "My name is Walker."

"Thank you. Please call me Lowell." The older man smiled and Walker saw a strong resemblance between him and his daughter. "By now you're aware that my daughter has a stubborn streak the likes of which few have ever witnessed. But she's a good girl, Walker—admittedly the apple of my eye."

Lowell rubbed his hands together, forming his words carefully. "I'm afraid after her mother died I indulged Sara more than I should. I accept full responsibility for her behavior; we argued fiercely the night she ran away. I've wished a thousand times I had been more patient with her—tried to understand this need she has for a family of her own. But I wasn't, and the last two months have been extremely difficult. I've been worried sick about her, and when Miss Mallory wired, informing us of Sara's situation, I came immediately."

"Olivia?" It made sense; the girl had found a way to strike back. Walker forced back a spurt of anger. Sara had befriended her and this was the thanks she got.

"Miss Mallory sent a telegram last week and we got here as quickly as we could. Miss Warne and Mr. Roche have been looking for my daughter since her disappearance."

Walker leaned forward, opening the cigar humidor and offering Lowell one. The older man declined. Sara's father looked as if he hadn't slept much lately. Walker sympathized with him; he hadn't been doing a whole lot of sleeping himself.

"I'm sorry, Lowell. If I had known, I would have sent word . . ."

"I don't hold you responsible, Walker. On the contrary, I'm deeply indebted to you for looking after her."

Walker struck a match, meeting his gaze. "It was not an imposition."

"Yes . . . she tells me that she's never been happier . . ." Lowell paused, clearing his throat. "We will be leaving for Boston immediately."

Walker's heart skipped a beat as he touched the match to the tip of his cigar. "Leaving?"

"Yes, my rail coach is waiting. Sara is packing as we speak. Again, I hope that in time you will be able to forgive her. She isn't mean-spirited, Walker, only misguided and impetuous. Wadsy, her nanny, says she'll outgrow it. I hope I live to see the day."

Walker drew on the cheroot and rose from his desk. "Did she tell you that she's expecting my child?"

Lowell paused. "Then you know about the baby—she thinks that you don't."

Walker moved to stare out the window. "I didn't, not until a few hours ago."

Lowell leaned forward. "I'm a man of great means; the child will want for nothing. Sara will spend the next few months with her uncle in Georgia. Once the baby is born, she will come home, and a few months later, I'll send for the child. You needn't worry about its welfare."

"*Its* welfare?" Walker repeated, closing his eyes. The situation had come to this? His child was an "it"? Something to be discussed in whispered innuendos, with a sense of shame?

"Sara's baby," Lowell corrected himself. "My grandchild."

Walker bit into the cigar, crushing it between his teeth. "My son or daughter."

"Yes—but under the circumstances, I don't hold you responsible for events beyond your control. I understand your hesitancy about letting the child go. Any man worth his salt would struggle with the dilemma, but let me assure you, we are open to an amicable agreement. Once the child is born, you will be allowed visitation rights, if you so desire."

"That's not acceptable."

Lowell shifted in the chair, his eyes focusing on Walker. "Do you have a better suggestion? If it's a matter of money, I have more than—"

"Money has nothing to do with it." Walker ground out the cigar in an ashtray on his desk. "The child is mine as much as Sara's."

Lowell shook his head, uncertainty filling his eyes. "Then what do you propose?"

"Sara stays here and I marry her."

Color flushed the older man's cheeks.

"That is out of the question. I won't permit it— I will not have my daughter in a loveless marriage, McKay. Sara worships you. If I were to agree to a marriage, she would inevitably end up hurt, and I will not allow that."

"Shouldn't Sara be the keeper of her future?"

"Sara isn't thinking clearly; she would jump at the chance to stay. But once the child was born, she would be forced to live with a man who doesn't love her."

"You don't know that!"

"Do you? Are you capable of absolution, of complete forgiveness? Because I'll have it no other way—"

Sara burst through the doorway, her fists clenched. Startled, Walker and Lowell turned to face her.

"How dare you bargain over me like some—

some—broodmare! It's my child and *I'll* make the decision of whether to stay or go!"

"Sara," Lowell chided, "we're only trying to do what's best for you and the child."

"You're not doing what's best for either of us, Father. I've made my decision."

She then addressed Walker. "With your permission, Mr. McKay, I'd like to remain at Spring Grass until I have the baby and sufficiently recover from the birth."

Their eyes met and held. The fire that had consumed them both in their months of lovemaking burned strong in spite of the pain.

"Then what?"

"I'll return to Boston and resume life at my father's house."

Her sudden strength surprised him. "What about the child?"

Sara bit her lip. "The baby is your heir, as you wanted all along; I'll have no claim to it. When he or she grows up, you can tell him or her I'm dead."

Lowell interrupted. "Sara, you're talking nonsense! This child is a Livingston—*my* flesh and blood—the heir to the railroad. I'll not hear of you giving it away. You need to be with family during your confinement. Wadsy would have a fit if you didn't come home. I can't permit this. You've inconvenienced Mr. McKay enough."

Ignoring her father, Sara held Walker's gaze. "Is that acceptable to you, Mr. McKay?"

"You are willing to abandon your child?"

"No, but I am capable of keeping my word,

Walker. Maybe I lied in the beginning, but I knew what I was agreeing to: to provide you with a child." Her hand moved to her stomach and his eyes followed. "This is your child, Walker. I will carry it, nourish it with my body, and deliver it safely into your arms. I only ask that the child be born in tradition, here at Spring Grass."

Lowell sprang to his feet. "You propose to carry that child beneath your heart for nine months and then walk away? You have no idea what you're saying. That child will wrap its arms around your heart and never let go, Sara. That child is part of you—part of me."

"And part of me," Walker reminded him.

Sara lifted her chin, squaring her shoulders. "Do you accept my proposal?"

"Don't be foolish, Sara. I've told your father that I'm willing to marry you."

Her chin rose higher. "I heard. I was listening outside the door."

Their eyes clashed.

"Sara, your father's right. The child is heir to both fortunes. Maybe we should marry—"

"I don't want to marry you, Walker. Papa's right; I won't live in a loveless marriage." Her bottom lip quivered. "I'm fully aware of how difficult it will be to leave my baby, but I will have your child, and then I will leave. Do we have a bargain?"

It was the worst bargain he would ever make; Walker knew it. But Sara would not be moved.

"You have a deal."

She extended her hand and they shook on it.

Lowell shook his head. "I have never witnessed anything like this."

"Well, now you have, Papa." Sara gathered up her skirts. "And if you'll excuse me, I'm going upstairs to lie down. I'm not feeling well."

"Walker, if you'll excuse us for a moment, I want to speak to my daughter in private." Lowell started to follow Sara out.

Walker nodded.

Within moments, Lowell returned, beaten.

"It seems Sara will not be persuaded to go back to Boston at this time. With your permission, she will remain with you until the baby arrives and then return to Boston alone."

Getting up from the desk, Walker ran a hand over his face. He couldn't send the man away thinking he was allowing Sara to stay only out of a sense of obligation to his child. It went much deeper than that.

"Lowell?"

"Yes, son?"

The two men looked at each other, both loving the same woman, but in a different way.

"I'll see that she's well taken care of."

Lowell's shoulders slumped. "If you should need anything—anything I can do . . ."

"I have enough money to buy her whatever she wants. What I don't have," he said quietly, "is the ability to change her mind."

Later that evening, Sara sat on the porch swing, praying for the proper argument to convince Walker that she wasn't a schemer, that she'd always had his best interests at heart. She'd bought herself time, but if she weren't able to convince him of her true motivations, she would lose the child she carried. The thought was inconceivable.

The sun rimmed the tops of the clouds, spreading reds and golds across the barn lot. Occasional lightning flashes raced through the building clouds forming in the west.

Walker came out of the barn and strode toward the house. The wind picked up, whipping his clothes around his tall, rugged frame. Sara shivered, images flashing through her mind: pictures of how lonely Papa had looked when the train pulled out earlier, how big and incredibly lonely her bed was without Walker.

She rehearsed her apology under her breath as he walked toward her, unaware that she was waiting. *Give me the words to soften his icy reception.* Either she made amends for her error now, or they continued on with this deplorable game. Sliding off the swing, she met him at the foot of the porch steps.

"I want to talk to you."

Ignoring her, he reached for the screen-door handle. Desperate now, she threw herself between him and the doorway.

"Just *listen* to me. If you'll give me half a chance to explain . . ."

The coldness in his eyes stopped her. Within the blue depths she saw the pain she had caused, and she longed to erase it. It was never her intention to hurt him or cause him unhappiness. *Foolish girl. You've ruined it all with your lie.*

He stepped back as if debating whether to move her aside by force. Sara swallowed against her dry throat, determined to stand her ground. The air crackled with the building storm both within and without. He was still attracted to her; she could see it in his indecision. Part of her wanted him to grab her, to thrust her out of the way if only for physical contact, that wonderfully delicious connection she felt when she was in his arms.

"Don't do this—don't shut me out. We have to talk about this, Walker. It won't go away."

Turning on his heel, he started back to the barn—his sanctuary, the one place he could wrap himself in his misery and refuse to face the problem.

She pursued him across the dusty barn lot, unwilling to let him walk away. Dark clouds swallowed up the sun as she picked up her skirts and called out after him.

"It isn't fair! You've never once asked why I was driven to such desperation. You have to believe that I would never hurt you." The first wet drops struck the dusty ground as she followed him into the barn. "Answer me!"

"I don't care why you did it." He disappeared into the recesses of the barn and a lantern blazed to life.

"Well, that's a horrible attitude." Shaking the rain off her blouse, she sat down next to Diamond's stall. Walker might not care why she'd lied, but he *was* going to hear her side of the story "I am a most privileged child. My father is extremely wealthy, able to provide anything I've ever wanted. The trouble is, all I ever wanted was a husband, my own family and children. Papa has never understood that need. Truthfully, he's spoiled me shamefully, partly because Mama died when I was born, and partly because I know how to wrap him around my little finger."

She probably shouldn't be telling Walker that, but she refused to tell another lie. Never again. "This whole fiasco began the day Papa intended to send me off to live with my uncle Brice in Georgia. He said a few months with my uncle might get my head on straight, but a few months with my uncle would have been the death of me. So I ran away—and not for the first time. I've run away more times than I care to admit this past year, but only because Papa refuses to cut the parental strings. When I almost married the dockworker, he blew up."

Walker glanced at her over his shoulder. She met his eyes defiantly. "If Abraham hadn't happened along, I would have married Hank that day."

Clearing her throat, she continued. "Papa and I quarreled, and the next morning I left the house and boarded a train to New York. I intended to live with my friend Julie until I could find suitable employment. Olivia was on the train and she was unhappy about being a mail-order bride— and getting married was the only thing I wanted. Well, before we knew it, we'd traded places so she could marry Rodney."

He looked back at her again, then away.

"Rodney Willbanks is the no-good gambler she was in love with. Olivia had cried herself dry when I sat down to eat breakfast with her that morning. One thing led to another, and Olivia made it plain she didn't intend to marry you, Walker. And since you were willing to marry a stranger anyway, I thought, well, now, this could be the answer to my prayers. And it was—until you found out."

She could see his silhouette against the glow of the lamp. His face was hidden in the shadows.

"When were you going to tell me?"

She slid to the edge of the bale. "I've thought about it every day. At times, I had my mind made up to tell you the moment you got home, but then something always happened to change my mind."

"In five years?"

"Of course not—not five years! I couldn't keep a secret that long—ask anyone who knows me. I tell everything I know."

"Except this time."

She studied her hands. "Except this time. Oh, Walker, I'd never leave you. I wouldn't walk out on you like—" She caught herself when she felt him tense.

"Like who?"

"Like . . . Trudy."

She didn't have to see his eyes to know they had turned to granite. "So you know about her. You know and still you deceived me."

"I didn't deceive you—well, I did, but I was going to tell you the truth. Why can't you believe me?"

"Sara, I trusted you. I was—" He stopped, turning back to the rigging.

What had he been about to say? That he thought he was falling as deeply in love with her as she had with him?

"I adore you," she whispered. "I love living at Spring Grass, and I love our home. I've wanted to tell you so many times, but I was afraid—I knew the lie was between us and it tormented me day and night. I was afraid that when you knew, you'd react exactly the way you have. And the thought of losing you—" Tears welled to her eyes and her voice trembled. "I couldn't bear it. But I also can't marry you if you aren't in love with me. I won't marry out of obligation."

Thunder pealed in the distance, but the weather was of little concern. His reaction was utmost in Walker's mind. Why didn't he comfort her? Why couldn't he accept that she loved him more than anything in this world?

Lightning flashed outside the barn. Sara slipped off the bale and approached him. "Walker, I love you."

Walker turned and their eyes met. For a brief, euphoric moment she thought he was going to take her right there in the hay. Passion and anger warred on his features. Sara held her breath, trying to read his response. Pain and desperation battled between them.

"We can start over—I promise I will never lie to you again. However painful or awful the matter might be, I will not lie to you again." When he still didn't answer, she pleaded softly, "Say something."

Tossing the bridle over the stall, he brushed past her. "You should have married Hank."

Dumbfounded, she watched him walk away. Suddenly anger replaced desperation.

"Well, maybe I should have! At least he wasn't so pigheaded!"

When his tall form disappeared out the doorway, she turned to Diamond, stroking the mare's head while a clap of thunder shook the ground.

"Hank *couldn't* have been that pigheaded."

Nor could she have loved Hank even a fraction of the way she loved Walker.

Chapter 17

Days folded into weeks, which folded into months. October arrived. Sara stood at the parlor window, admiring the glorious fall colors. Warm sunshine filtered through tree branches of oranges and golds; the scent of burning leaves a pleasant reminder of nature's cycle. The land was dying—so very pretty, yet a stark reminder that soon snow would fall, blanketing the fields with an icy coat of white.

She sighed. She'd been so certain that it was only a matter of time before she would be back in Walker's good graces, yet her time at Spring Grass waned. Nothing she said or did had made the least difference to Walker. At times, she'd caught him looking at her, studying her rounding belly, his face an emotionless mask. Her love would not die; his would not resurface. Pride kept them in separate beds. The lonely nights made her love burn hotter and it grew quick and impatient inside her, like Walker's child. His unconditional love would be the only tie to keep her in Wyoming, yet his favor was slow in coming.

Sara rose early to eat with Walker. At first, he refused to sit at the table with her. He'd stride straight through the kitchen, reaching for a biscuit on his way out the back door. Sometimes he acknowledged her; more often he didn't. Eventually, hunger got the best of him and he began eating suppers in the dining room. She cherished those brief interludes because they represented one of the few times she was alone with him. Communication was limited to Sophie's acting as mediator. Walker wasn't rude; he just wasn't there. Somehow he'd removed himself from the situation, and she envied him. She wished she could do the same, but day in and day out, memories of their love haunted her.

The crisp fall air and her rapidly expanding middle made it hard to get out of bed. She dressed in half darkness and as she slipped into her boots, she realized that before much longer, Sophie would have to help her lace them. Happiness bubbled inside her as she felt the growing roundness of her stomach, the tight skin covering the child being formed. Then the futility of the situation hit her, and she lay across the bed, Papa's stern warning in her ear. *You will never be able to walk away from that child, Sara Elaine. Never.*

But she would. As much as she cherished the new life growing inside her, she was strong, capable of keeping the promise. It would be better for the child to think he or she didn't have a mother than for Sara to remain and have her son or daughter witness their loveless marriage. The realization brought tears to her eyes and the bed shook with the force of her sobs. By the time she could control herself to rise and leave the room, she was exhausted from her emotional burden.

Sophie was scrambling eggs when Sara rounded the kitchen corner. Sara was ravenously hungry these days and as she lumbered into the kitchen she eyed the mound of sausage and biscuits. The aroma of eggs fried in butter, and of sausage, captivated her.

"What smells so good? I'm famished." She plucked a biscuit from the pile and peeled apart a hot, flaky layer. Steam rose from the bread and she sniffed appreciatively. "Who would think that it took this much food to feed one little baby?"

Sophie smiled and ladled eggs into a white bowl. Sara downed the biscuit and reached for a second one.

"Your eyes are red as a beet. Have you been crying?"

Biting into the biscuit, Sara nodded. "I think something's wrong with me. One minute I'm happy, the next I'm crying. I can't stop once I get started, and I never know what's going to set me off. Yesterday I was watching Potster carry eggs from the chicken house into his kitchen, and all I could think of was how those mother hens would never know their babies because they would be eaten even before they hatched. I couldn't stop crying about it. Don't you think that's strange?"

Sophie chuckled. "All part of having a young-'un. You cry and laugh at the same time. There's no particular reason for either, and when you aren't sleeping or eatin', you're generally trying real hard not to kill the man that did this to you."

"Does it get any better?"

"Eventually, though never soon enough."

Sara tried to laugh, but ended up bursting into tears. Sophie laid the spoon aside and stepped around the table to embrace her. Sara sank into her warmth, grateful for the kindness. It seemed like years since she'd had any physical contact with another human being, and Sophie's hug was like manna from heaven. The older woman stroked her hair lovingly.

"Sophie, will he ever love me again?"

"I don't know, Sara. I really don't know. I've never seen Walker this stubborn about anything. You've got to hold on to hope. If you lose that, you don't have anything."

After drying her eyes as she went to the dining table, Sara prepared a plate heaped with eggs and sausage, glancing up as the object of her misery strode in, yawning. She sank into her chair, avoiding his view, feverishly stuffing eggs into her mouth, trying to satisfy an insatiable hunger. Former concerns about baby chickens and their unfortunate demise forgotten, she used the edge of a biscuit to herd a few stray pieces of egg onto her fork.

Walker sat at the far end of the table, as distant

from her as possible without eating in the foyer. She'd realized what he was doing a few weeks into the game, and tried sitting at different areas of the table. He would take the seat farthest away. Once she had tried removing all of the chairs except the one next to hers, but he only picked up the chair and carried it to the farthest end. She finally gave up and let him sit wherever he wanted.

"Walker, don't forget Caleb is coming today," Sophie called as she scoured a skillet at the kitchen sink. "You'll need to leave the study key."

Walker dug into his pocket and produced the long skeleton key, laying it before him on the table. He'd taken to locking the study. Sara had avoided having another discussion about Caleb. But the locked study door hurt her almost as much as Walker's locked heart.

The key sat there, taunting her. The food suddenly tasted bitter. How dare he lock her out of his study, his room, and his life? She'd done nothing but love him, and now she wasn't worthy of his trust. Use her to have his baby, then send her away, withholding his love while his precious friend manipulated the books! Had Walker even noticed? No, he couldn't have—he was too busy fueling his anger at her. Resentment bubbled in her throat and before she could check them, the words were out of her mouth.

"Still letting that weasel Caleb steal money from you?"

Walker's fork hovered halfway between his plate and his mouth. He studied the utensil as if it were a foreign object. Sara heard Sophie cease scrubbing for a moment, then slowly resume. The silence at the table was deafening. Walker slowly lifted his head to look at her.

"Are you talking to me?"

"Caleb's stealing from you blind." She bit her lip, wondering if she'd lost her mind. She suspected the accountant was tampering with books, though she had no proof. But given a few hours alone with the ledger, she was certain she could back up her claim.

Walker calmly picked up a biscuit and lathered butter on it. "What makes you think he's stealing from me?"

"Have you looked at your books lately? Really looked?" Now she'd done it. She wasn't going to win points on this one, but if he was so blind that he couldn't see what was going on under his own roof, he shouldn't accuse her of bad judgment.

Walker slid a forkful of eggs into his mouth. "Snooping again, Miss Livingston?"

"I have no reason to steal your money, Mr. McKay. You're in such an all-fired hurry to believe the worst of me, why doesn't that apply to others?"

"Like Caleb?"

"Like Caleb."

Sara knew she was out of bounds, but she didn't care. Frustration drove her. Leaning closer, she quietly asked down the long table length, "Why doesn't he let you keep the receipts?"

Walker took a moment to answer. "For safety, I suppose. I don't need to see the receipts."

Sara scooped up the last bit of egg. "Because he doesn't want you to know how much he's taken." Careful, Sara, you have no proof of this accusation, just a gut feeling, which has rarely proved to be wrong. Papa contended she had some sort of built-in mechanism to sense trouble, and the uncanny device was working overtime.

Walker locked gazes with her. "Bull, Sara."

"Scared you'll find out your best friend is cheating you?"

"Bull!"

"You two knock it off in there!" Sophie yelled from the kitchen.

Sara ignored her. "What, too much of a coward to prove me wrong?"

Sophie stuck her head around the doorway. "Sara, those are mighty strong words."

The warning only stiffened Sara's resolve. "I know the books have been tampered with and I can prove it."

"You're talking nonsense."

"Prove me a fool."

Glaring at her, he grabbed the key and rose from the table, the chair scraping behind him. Sara rose also and followed him out of the room.

Sophie trailed behind, whispering, "You better be able to back this up, young lady."

"Or what? Lose his favor?" Sara laughed, suddenly light-headed with power. She had to prove it, but could she? And would Walker believe her if she did?

Walker strode through the hallway. Inserting the key in the lock, he gave her a dark look, then opened the study door.

Sara's heart was trying to escape her chest and she was short of breath by the time she approached the desk. She didn't have much time to prove her theory. Caleb would be here by eleven, and there were pages and pages in the ledger. Pushing Walker aside, she sat down and opened Spring Grass's financial records. Her hand shook when she realized that she had just touched Walker for the first time in weeks. Her hand burned from the explosive contact and she fought the heat of passion.

Reaching for pencil and paper, she started adding and subtracting, examining the columns of numbers for discrepancies. Walker stood behind her, his eyes fixed on the paper.

"I don't know why you're doing this."

"I hate to see anyone cheated." She rebuked his impatient sigh with a warning look.

Caleb Vanhooser had honed the art of embezzlement. Proving that his numbers were off was going to be more difficult than she had anticipated. Were there two sets of books? The ledger looked surprisingly clean today, as if he had tidied his dirty work.

"Has Caleb worked on the books recently?"

"He works on them twice a month—you know that."

She could feel him watching her, and she dared not look up for fear of losing her place on the columns of numbers. Walker edged around the desk as if trying to get a better look, and he accidentally brushed the side of her chair. She glanced up, realizing that he was studying her, not the numbers. She blushed with heat, and for a mere second she considered dropping the pencil and reaching for him.

He turned toward the window, clearing his throat. Sara dared not take time to breathe. She found a mistake, and she circled it with a pencil.

She had reached the last page when a soft rapping at the closed study door made her start. Caleb's knock. Her heart leapt to her throat. She was so close! Walker glanced at her as the knock came again, more persistently.

"Don't answer it. I'm nearly finished. Just a few more numbers . . ." She hurriedly tallied the last three columns, praying that Walker would allow her sufficient time to finish. From the corner of her eye she could see him walking toward the door.

A moment later, Caleb's thin frame appeared in the doorway. The accountant's smile faded when he saw her, and his eyes moved to the open ledger.

"What's going on here?"

Closing the door, Walker returned to the desk. "Sara thinks there is an error in the books. Is that possible, Caleb?"

Caleb met Sara's eyes. His normally pallid features flushed and his gaze pinned her. "I don't believe so, but I'll be happy to go over the entries in question."

"Some of your entries don't make sense, Mr. Vanhooser."

His left brow arched. "Are you an accountant, Miss Livingston?"

Sara blushed. "Of course not, but I've always been good with numbers."

Caleb forced a smile, giving Walker a pitying look. "Of course. Perhaps your condition has you . . . imagining things? I know when a woman—"

Sara sprang out of the chair. "My condition has nothing to do with it, and I want everyone to stop saying that!" She threw her calculations at him. "Check the addition yourself."

Caleb reached out to catch the fluttering sheets.

"Walker," Sara pleaded, "this isn't the same ledger I saw when I first looked at it. The one I saw had dozens of discrepancies. This ledger is a book of lies."

Papers collected, Caleb glanced at Walker. "I don't know what she's talking about. Perhaps she's detected a slight miscalculation. Regrettable as it is, these things happen. I'll be happy to go over the figures with you and explain anything in question."

For a moment Sara was almost swayed by his sincerity. Dear Lord, had she made a mistake? *Was* her condition making her utter these wild accusations? But she'd *seen* the mistakes! The receipts were the only way to prove her claim. She snatched the papers out of Caleb's hand and scanned the long rows of numbers again.

She glanced at Walker, who said nothing. His grave features chilled her.

Caleb smiled, taking the papers back. "After dinner? We'll come in here and I'll explain whatever's bothering you."

"No. That won't be necessary." *He's lying,* Sara realized. *He's lying about something and he's desperate. And desperate men are dangerous.* He met her gaze and she wasn't sure what she saw. A warning? Fear?

Walker broke the silence. "Sophie will fix you something cool to drink. Caleb and I will finish up in here."

"Walker—"

Walker took a step toward her, and for a moment she thought he wanted to comfort her. Instead, he took her gently by the arm.

"Sara, go cool off. You are out of order."

Sara's eyes shot white with anger. How dare he! How *dare* he not believe her?

"Get a cold drink, Sara." Walker opened the door and gently ushered her through it.

Over Walker's shoulder she saw Caleb's cold, hard face. "Don't mess with me, Sara," he mouthed. Although he didn't make a sound, she knew exactly what his warning implied. That confirmed she was right; he was cheating Walker blind—and she couldn't do a thing about it. Oh, he had cleverly covered his tracks, but someone with more knowledge about numbers could catch him.

A moment later, she was out in the hall, the door closed behind her.

"Don't be so smug, Caleb," she told the closed door. "You haven't won yet."

After supper, Sara avoided Walker, going instead to the front porch. The encounter with Caleb had left her numb. Gazing at the stars, she wondered why she allowed herself to be ridiculed. Walker didn't believe a thing she said. She wasn't sure she cared any more. Her eyes traveled the darkened bunkhouse. The ranch was remarkably quiet tonight. During supper, Sophie had mentioned a Grange dance that she and S. H. planned to attend. Apparently the ranch hands had taken advantage of the monthly social as well and left the bunkhouse early.

Drawing her wrap closer, she leaned against the railing, picturing herself in Walker's arms, swirling to the music of banjos and fiddles. She imagined his scent, the feel of his thick, springy black hair.

Sighing, she opened her eyes, aware her dreams were as hopeless as the relationship. She would give everything she had to start anew, but she couldn't. After today, he would never forgive her for accusing Caleb of cheating him. Maybe the time had come for her to go home. There, Papa and Wadsy and Abe would love her. When the baby came, Abe could deliver the child to Walker and . . .

Her hand slipped to her stomach, where part of Walker McKay grew. The baby kicked, a butterflylike flutter, reminding her that if anyone had been wronged, it was this innocent child who was created in love—if one-sided—and desire.

Stepping off the porch, she meandered to the side of the house and entered the rose garden. Sitting down on a bench, she stared at the neglected bushes—painful reminders for both her and Walker. Did he keep them to bolster his belief that all women were schemers? Her gaze swept the light that burned in Walker's study, then returned to the roses. The flowers were almost gone, the vines withered and drawn. What must Walker think when he looked at the shriveled tokens of his and Trudy's love?

Her conscience nagged her.

Hadn't she hurt him even worse?

Hopeless tears swelled to her eyes. One moment she was reasonably optimistic that Walker would forgive her; the next, she wallowed in a pit of despair. Both Doc and Sophie had assured her that mood swings were normal, but tonight they didn't feel normal. They felt hateful, strange, as if someone else occupied her body—someone who felt even worse than she did. Tears ran down her cheeks. Her breasts were sore to the touch, her ankles puffy and swollen. She must weigh ten pounds more than she did last week, even though she'd passed on Sophie's chocolate cream pie tonight—a pie with heaping mounds of evenly browned egg whites. . . . She shook the vision aside, her eyes roaming the garden, switching back to the study light.

Why did she let Walker get away with treating her like a criminal? He had no right at all to treat her this way. Shoving herself off the bench, she gathered her wrap and marched around the corner of the house.

He couldn't treat her like this—barely speaking to her, ignoring her when she walked into a room, locking himself away in that hateful study every night, refusing to go to town socials. He made them live like hermits, and she wasn't going to put up with it any longer.

Walker dropped the journal he was reading when Sara pushed through the study doorway.

"You can't treat me this way!"

Retrieving the magazine, he grunted. "Ever hear of knocking?"

Striding across the floor, she cleared the top of his desk with a defiant sweep of her hand. Papers, journals, and blotters fell to the floor in a heap.

Shoving back from the desk, Walker stared at the carnage. "Good grief, woman—are you in another one of those *moods*?"

"I'm not in a 'mood' and you listen to me, Walker McKay. Trudy might have betrayed you, and you might think I'm just like her, but I'm not! Do you hear me!"

He tried to straighten the papers. "The whole town can hear you, Sara."

She leveled a finger at him. "Don't you patronize me."

"I'm not patronizing you, I'm just telling you, everyone in a ten-mile radius can hear you."

"Good. Then maybe they'll listen to my side of the story."

Getting up, he fetched the brandy decanter, but she stepped in front of him before he could pour a drink. They faced off, neither giving an inch.

"You're in my way."

"You are not going to fix me with brandy. You're going to talk about us whether you want to or not."

Grasping her by the shoulders, he set her aside. She dogged his attempts to pour a glass of liquor. "Trudy ran off with another man. I didn't."

"At least I knew Trudy's real name."

"All right—I deserve that. What I did was wrong, but how many times do I have to say I'm sorry? What you're doing is worse. You won't even try to understand—I lied in the beginning, but only about who I was, never about what I intended. I vowed to be *your* wife, forever. Never did I intend to be anything else!"

Walker sipped the brandy, refusing to argue.

"Just because I'm not Olivia Mallory, and you should be down on your knees thanking the good Lord that I'm not, doesn't mean I'm bad. What I *did* was terrible and, for the hundredth time, I'm sorry. But if you're so pigheaded that you can't see that you and I belong together, then I don't know what to say to you."

"I understand what you're saying, Miss Livingston." He tossed the drink down. "And it still stinks."

Tears surfaced to her eyes. "You're not ever going to forgive me, are you?"

He moved to the study window and looked out, mindful of the despair in her voice. God, *could* he ever forgive her? The thought plagued him day and night. At times he wanted to, wanted to go back to their earlier days. Then reality would set in. Sara had made a fool of him. Had he learned nothing? He was in agony, with no relief in sight. Sitting each night at the dinner table with her, watching his child grow in her body, the body he'd touched and caressed, drove him mad with anger. He should have sent her away with her father, but he'd refused to take the coward's way out. He studied the dying bushes within the study light. Blast it all! Every time he looked out this window he saw those damn roses.

"It's late, Sara. Go to bed."

"Come with me."

The words hung between them. Desire rose hot and strong, but Walker shoved it aside.

"Go to bed, Sara." He stared at the garden, eyes fixed, jaw set. As much as he ached to make love to her, he would not.

"Oh, Walker." Her voice caught. "There comes a time when you have to forgive or be eaten alive by bitterness. You stare at those roses and you won't allow yourself to forget. Did you love her that deeply?"

The accusation in her voice surprised him. Love Trudy? He almost laughed. No, his proposal was built on lust. In time he might have grown to love her, but he hadn't appreciated being made a fool of and he wasn't about to let Sara do it a second time.

"Did you *love* her, Walker?"

Sara's voice drew him back, and he turned to face her. "You're having one of those mood swings, aren't you?"

She picked up an ashtray and hurled it at him. He ducked, barely avoiding a hit. "Sara—you throw one more—"

A vase sailed by his head, smashing against the opposite wall. He lunged too late for his cigar humidor, and she upended it and stomped the smokes into the rug.

"Sara McKay!"

"I'm not Sara McKay—remember? You won't *let* me be."

He lunged for her and she darted away. Bolting into the foyer, she picked up a vase and threw it. He sidestepped it, chasing her. She was going to hurt herself—or worse, hurt the baby. "Sara!"

She dashed outside and down the front steps. Racing around the corner of the house, she fled with surprising swiftness. He watched her skirt fade into the darkness.

Swearing under his breath, he went back into the house, slamming the door behind him. The woman was out of hand!

"Good Lord in heaven. Did a cyclone go through here?" Sophie, hands on her hips, stood at the study door surveying the aftermath the next morning.

Walker looked up from pouring a cup of coffee. "Sara wanted to talk."

Shooting him a dirty look, Sophia picked up tobacco ground into the rug. Setting the humidor back into place, she shook her head. "Darn shame you two fight all the time. You could both put the energy to better use."

"Talk to her, not me."

Sophie scooped the remains of the ashtray into the trash. "A few more months of this and you won't have a lick of anything left. Anyone ever mention that you're hardheaded as a gourd?"

"S. H. has mentioned it. Open the drapes, will you, Sophie?"

Tsking, the housekeeper shuffled across the floor. Sunlight streamed into the study when she parted the heavy fabric, and Walker glanced up at Sophie's soft gasp.

"What?"

"Uh . . . have you seen this?"

"What?" Walker got up from the desk and walked to the window. Stunned, he viewed the carnage. Not one rosebush had escaped the bloodbath. Uprooted plants and clods of dirt filled the fountain. The rose garden was no more.

"What in the . . . ?"

"Looks like the cyclone was still on the ground when it left the study."

Whirling, Walker strode out of the room and took the stairs two at a time.

Sophie, hand over her heart, stood at the bottom and yelled, "You harm a hair on that young'un's head and you'll answer to me, Walker McKay! A body doesn't feel like herself when she's in the family way! She's done you a favor by destroying those damn plants!"

Sara whirled when Walker burst into the bedroom, hiding her battle-scarred hands behind her. She started backing up when he advanced on her, his face a thundercloud. "I'm sorry—I don't know what got into me. I saw those roses and something came over me—" She edged toward the door and he lunged for her, missing by a fraction. Racing down the stairway, she shouted, "Sophie! Help!"

Walker boiled out of the room, taking the stairs three at a time. When he reached bottom Sara was crouched behind Sophie, who planted herself in the middle of the ruckus, arms crossed, daring Walker to come any closer.

"You leave this poor little darlin' alone, Walker McKay."

"That poor little darlin' just tore the *hell* out of my rose garden, Sophie!" He glared at Sara; she glared back.

"Needed to be done ages ago," Sophie said. "Now get on out of here. I've got work to do."

"I want to speak to Sara."

Sophie's face hardened. "Why? You haven't wanted to talk to her before now."

Swearing, Walker turned and walked into his study, slamming the door behind him.

Sophie shook her head, wiping her hands on her apron. "Hard to believe he once entered and left rooms like a normal person."

Sara stepped out from behind Sophie, smoothing her hair. "Thanks, Sophie."

"Girl, you'd better watch your step." Sophie eyed her. "What in the world possessed you to tear up those rosebushes?"

"I hated them, Sophie. Every time Walker looks at them they remind him of a woman's betrayal." Brushing her skirt, Sara said softly, "I'm reminder enough."

"Lordy," Sophie said. "I'm too old for this."

Later that afternoon, Sara saw Walker come in from the barn. By the looks of his clothes, he'd been treating cattle, and she knew it wasn't the best time to approach him. Still, she felt compelled to apologize again for her behavior. Tapping lightly at the study door, she entered without invitation. He glanced up, his face darkening when he saw her. "What have you torn up now? The left forty?"

"Top of my list tomorrow." She offered him a timid smile. To her surprise, he returned it.

"You have one heck of a temper—anyone ever tell you that?"

"Papa tried. I'm sorry about your rosebushes."

Removing his gloves, he laid them on the desk. "I always hated those roses."

She released a quick breath of relief. "I want to replace the plants, if you'll allow me. I'm thinking some nice perennials, maybe a few flowering bushes."

He nodded, absently sorting through a stack of papers. "Talk to S. H. He'll get you anything you need."

"Fine, but I want to purchase them."

"You bet your life you will." He grinned, and she was relieved to see the plants didn't mean a thing to him. "You didn't hurt yourself, did you?"

"No." She eased her hands behind her back.

"Sara." He moved closer, gently taking her by the shoulders. He wanted to shake her; he wanted to make love to her. She created feelings within him that he didn't understand or appreciate, yet they were there, strong and undeniable. He wanted to ignore all the reasons he couldn't have her. She gazed up at him, her eyes openly apologetic and vulnerable. How easy it would be to let what he desired overrule what he most feared.

"I'm sorry that you would believe I would ever lay a hand on you."

"Oh, I knew you wouldn't."

"Then why did you hide behind Sophie?"

"Because I was frightened. You burst into my room and I was startled." She laid her hand on his arm. "I'm sorry about my behavior."

Drawing her to him, he looked at her as if he were baffled by her charm. "Truce?"

"Truce," she conceded with a soft, tentative smile. A tortuous sound slipped from her throat when his mouth lowered to cover hers. The kiss was intimate and deep and roused primal emotions she couldn't deal with, not if he continued to keep his distance.

Slowly backing away, she smoothed his lips with the tips of her fingers. "We're making progress."

His hand refused to release her, and she thought that his eyes held more of a promise than she'd seen lately. "How do you figure that?"

"I haven't thrown anything in the past few minutes."

Sobering, he looked at her, his hand still in contact with hers. "What is this thing about Caleb? He's been a good friend, Sara. I'd trust him with my life."

"I'm sorry, Walker. Maybe I'm mistaken, but I don't think I am. I'm very good with numbers, and the ledger I saw on your desk a few weeks ago was filled with inconsistencies."

"I don't know how that could be."

"Do you look at the books? Go over Caleb's figures?"

"No. I'm not good with numbers. I run the ranch and I employ Caleb to take care of the financial aspects."

"Is that wise? Papa says a man should never trust anyone with personal matters."

"I wouldn't have an employee I couldn't trust, and Caleb has given me no reason to question him. No one has ever disputed his work."

But there wasn't a suitable explanation for what she'd seen, and if he was innocent, why had he been so hateful earlier? His ominous warning to stay out of his way had come as no surprise. Yet if Walker trusted the man, she had little choice but to back off.

She sighed. "He doesn't like me, you know."

"I can't imagine why. You question his work, call him a thief and a liar to his face—what man wouldn't be flattered?"

Her head drooped. "I'm sorry if I upset him—I'll apologize for my accusations."

He squeezed her hand, his eyes darkening with respect. "Give me a little time, Sara."

Nodding, she backed away, afraid that if she stayed she couldn't grant his request. When he was near she lost her ability to reason. Their fingertips strained, stretching the contact as long as possible. When distance forced them to separate, she felt miserable. "I'll see you at supper."

"I'll be there," he conceded, his eyes still locked with hers. He seemed to war with his emotions, but feelings won. Covering the short distance between them, he drew her mouth to his and kissed her. Briefly, then longer, then deeper. When their lips parted many long moments later, he whispered, "Stay out of trouble."

Chapter 18

Sara's spirits were high the next morning as S. H. maneuvered the buckboard around potholes. "I don't want to jar the baby too much, hon," he said, frowning with concentration.

"S. H., you can go faster. You don't have to worry about me. I'm fine." She was better than fine. For the first time in weeks, she and Walker had actually carried on a conversation at the breakfast table.

"Best quit that squirming," Sophie warned, winking at S. H. "You'll have the baby spittin' up."

"Spitting up?" Sara looked at her skeptically. "It can do that?"

Sophie and S. H. laughed, and Sara realized she'd fallen for the joke.

Twenty minutes later, S. H. wheeled the

wagon to a stop in front of the mercantile. Doc's office was on the opposite side of the street, so Sara would make her ten o'clock appointment easily.

S. H. tied the mare to the hitching post, then extended Sara a helping hand. Moving was troublesome now that Sara had gained weight and girth. Sophie said she already looked like she was about to burst, even though she was barely into her fifth month. There was a hint of snow this morning and Sara sucked in the crisp air, enjoying the smells of approaching winter.

"Careful, little mama," Sophie warned as S. H. carefully lowered her to the ground.

S. H. groaned with the effort of holding her in midair while she found safe footing. "Dear Lord, what're ya havin', a heifer?"

"Sizemore! You don't tell a woman that!" Sophie snapped.

"Aw, she knows I'm jest teasin'." S. H. winked at Sara, helping Sophie out of the wagon. Sophie's joints were giving her fits and though she never complained, Sara noticed that she was in pain this morning. How long would Sophie be able to help care for a child? She was nearly as old as Wadsy. Wadsy always said, "God shore knew what He was a-doin' when he gave little folk to the young. A body my age is too old to be running after young'uns."

"I'll be getting supplies," Sophie said. "S. H. can help you across the street."

"I know how to cross a street," Sara protested. "I can still do some things by myself, you know."

"I'm goin' with ya and that's that," S. H. said. "You might trip and fall."

"S. H., I'm not an invalid. I'm just having a baby."

"Yes, ma'am, I know it. Walker's baby, and he'd expect me to look after ya."

"I'm not going to get hurt. You can stand right here and watch me. You'd think you were my papa, the way you fret over me."

Lifting her skirts, Sara glanced both ways for S. H.'s benefit. A driverless wagon sat at the end of the street. No imminent dangers awaited her. "I'll be back in a few minutes."

"Watch yerself. Look both ways! Don't walk too fast!" S. H. hollered. Sara turned and waved him off.

Sophie disappeared into the mercantile and S. H. joined a group of friends farther up the sidewalk. If S. H. and Sophie had their way, they'd keep her in a glass box for the length of the pregnancy. Rarely a day went by when Sophie wasn't coddling her with blueberry muffins or hot tea or another pillow. When her back ached, S. H. was there with a hot compress. She accepted their pampering with a smile, grateful for the affection. If only Walker would show the same concern.

Sara looked up when a shout broke through her thoughts.

"Sara! Look out!" S. H.'s warning was drowned out by the sound of hoofbeats bearing down on her. She froze midway across the road as a wagon bore down on her with frightening speed.

Shouts sounded, and before she could gather her wits, someone grabbed her arm and jerked her clear of the buckboard, the wheels brushing the hems of her skirts. A pair of strong arms swept her up onto the porch and out of danger.

"Someone get the doctor!" The male voice sounded familiar, yet in her confusion Sara couldn't place it. The street tilted lopsidedly, and from a distance she saw S. H. sprinting across the street. She looked up to identify her rescuer, and saw Caleb.

Sophie ran out of the mercantile, yelling, "Sara! Oh, land sakes, are you all right? I knew we shouldn'ta let you cross the street!" The housekeepeer approached, reaching for her hand. Sara couldn't feel her arms; they hung limp from her body and she lacked the energy to raise them.

The excitement drew a crowd. Men stepped to the door of the saloon; women pulled small children across the street. She could hear Caleb calmly assuring the onlookers that everything was fine, and asking them to stand back. Sara could hear the curious departing, murmuring under their breath about how lucky she was.

"Can you sit up?"

Nodding, she allowed the banker to lift her upright. Caleb felt her pulse with cold precision. Of all the men in town, why did *he* have to be her knight in shining armor?

Brushing his hands aside, she straightened her blouse, embarrassed by all the fuss. "I'm fine, really."

Caleb smiled, but the effort didn't quite reach

his eyes. "That was a close call, my dear. You have to be more careful." The smile widened. "You could have been killed."

"I'm always careful, Caleb." She found her strength and stood up, her legs wobbling beneath her.

Doc Linder rushed across the street, his long strides eating up the ground. After a cursory examination, he straightened.

"S. H., we'll need to get her over to the office. I want to check the baby and make sure she's suffered no ill effects."

"Shore thing, Doc."

Caleb and S. H. escorted the expectant mother across the street and into the doctor's office. Excusing himself, Caleb then left, saying he had a customer waiting in his office.

Doc took Sara into the exam room and put the stethoscope to her stomach. Drawing a deep breath, she closed her eyes, praying the baby was fine.

He listened, stepped back, frowned, and moved forward to listen again. Sara shrank against the table. The doctor moved the stethoscope back and forth across her protruding stomach.

"Is there something wrong with my baby?"

"No, no, the baby's fine." He listened again, frowning. "But there's a lot going on in there."

Sara's head came off the table. "What do you mean? Something awful?"

The doctor picked up Sara's chart, his eyes scanning the information. "Not awful. Hmmm."

Sara waited, holding her breath.

"Well, can't say for sure, but with this weight gain, I'd say twins are a definite possibility."

Sara's heart leapt with joy. Two babies? Papa and Wadsy would just spit! "Are you sure?"

The doctor lifted her to a sitting position. "No, can't say for certain, but seems to me I might hear two heartbeats. Now, I wouldn't get excited about it yet. Sometimes stressful situations can make a baby's heartbeat irregular, and that's what I could be hearing. But everything else checks out okay. You need to be careful for a few days, pamper yourself a little."

"Doc, may I tell Walker about the twins?"

"No need to count your chickens before they hatch." Doc Linder patted her on the back. "We wouldn't want to get his hopes up only to disappoint him, would we?"

Sara felt deflated. "No, we wouldn't." But he hadn't bargained on two heirs.

Doc ushered her to the waiting room, where S. H. and Sophie were sitting. Sophie shot to her feet. "Is everything all right?"

"Everything's fine." The doctor winked at Sara. "You'll need to take special care of this little lady for the next few days—make sure she gets lots of rest."

"We'll do it," S. H. declared, reaching for Sara's hand. "I told you you ought to let me help you across the street."

"What difference would that have made? We both might have been killed."

The three left the doctor's office and returned to the wagon. Due to all the excitement, Sophie had cut her shopping short, and the wagon was only partially loaded with supplies.

"Aren't you going to finish your shopping?" Sara asked.

"Heavens, no! We're going to get you home. I'll ask Denzil to send the rest with Caleb when he comes to supper tomorrow night."

Sara glanced toward the bank and saw Caleb leaning against a post, watching her. His earlier warning rang in her ears. *You might have been killed.*

Was he responsible for the near fatality? The thought seemed preposterous, yet the odd way that he had smiled at her chilled her, as if warning her that he could be dangerous.

"Why is Caleb coming to supper tomorrow night? He eats dinner with Walker twice a month."

"I don't know. Guess I mentioned I was fixing roast and he kinda invited himself."

Sara met the accountant's eyes from across the street. "I think he just tried to kill me."

"Kill you!" Sophie stared at her. "What a thing to say. Why, he saved your life, young'un. Why would he pull you out of the way if he were trying to kill you? That's ridiculous. Caleb wouldn't hurt a fly."

Maybe not, Sara thought. But she was sure he'd tried to hurt her—and, worse, Walker's child.

S. H. hoisted Sara into the buckboard and Sophie climbed up behind. They settled in for the drive home, and as the vehicle passed the bank, Sara glanced at Sophie. "I don't want him at the ranch tomorrow."

"Sara Livingston. I think that brush with death addled your brain."

Sara settled back on the seat, adjusting her skirts. "Caleb resents me, Sophie. Why, I don't know, but he does and I'm afraid of him."

The ride home did nothing to lighten Sara's mood. The only conversation took place between S. H. and Sophie. Denzil had raised the price of sugar another penny, and S. H. wanted pork chops instead of chicken and dumplings for supper.

Shortly after arriving back at the ranch, Sara excused herself. "I think I'll lie down for a while."

Sophie looked relieved. "You do that, young'un. I'll send up a tray of tea in a bit."

Sara went to her room and stretched out on the bed, but sleep eluded her. No one could make her sit at the table with Caleb Vanhooser. She'd promised Walker after the garden incident that she would apologize for her accusations, but the words lay like granite on her tongue.

Sitting up, she glanced out the window. There must be a way for her to prove that Caleb was manipulating the books, and that he had arranged today's accident as a warning. But how?

Rolling onto her side, she cupped her stomach tightly. "It's true, babies: Caleb is not your father's friend. I may anger him so that Walker will never forgive me, but I'm going to prove my suspicions." When a soft knock sounded a few moments later, she called softly, "I'll be down very soon, Sophie."

She slipped out of bed as the door opened. Releasing her hairpins, she freed the long strands of fiery tresses.

"While you're here, could you help me with my—" She turned to see Walker standing at the foot of the bed holding a tray. His eyes clearly appreciated her state of undress.

"Sophie thought you might need a cup of tea."

"Thanks. It was thoughtful of her, but I was dressing to come downstairs." Sara watched him place the tray on the bedside table, his eyes drawn to her breasts spilling out of the chemise.

"Care to share a cup with me?" she ventured.

"Thanks, I'll wait." In spite of his refusal, he pulled up a chair and sat down, taking a cheroot from his shirt pocket.

Her cheeks warmed under his intimate perusal.

"I wasn't sure I'd join you for dinner tonight."

"Why not?" Striking a match, he lit the cigar. Their eyes met and held.

"I'm not hungry. It's been a big day."

Did he know about the accident? Had S. H. told him of her newest charge against Caleb? She was nearly naked, with only the thin chemise covering her. She should put on a dressing gown, but she didn't want to. She liked the way he looked at her, the way his eyes darkened with desire. "I'm not decent—I'll put on a gown—"

His hand blocked her halfhearted efforts. "Please don't." Their eyes met again.

Lifting her hand to his mouth, he kissed her fingertips. Sara shivered, closing her eyes. This was the passionate Walker, the Walker she adored.

"S. H. said there was an incident in town this morning?" he asked.

"A wagon almost ran me down—" His mouth set off explosions in her body.

Concern flared in his eyes. "Did you see the doctor?"

"The baby's fine. As a matter of fact . . ." She paused, tempted to mention Doc's suspicions. How would he feel about twins? "He or she is perfectly healthy."

As if to prove the declaration, one of the babies put a foot into her rib. "Oh." Sara laughed, holding her breath. A baby lay against her diaphragm, making it difficult to breathe.

Walker frowned. "What's wrong?"

"Nothing; the baby just kicked, that's all." She sat down on the edge of the bed, cradling her stomach. "Do you want to feel?"

"Feel what?"

"Your son—or daughter." She was pleased by his interest. She often wondered if he had personal feelings for the child—or children. She'd caught him looking at her stomach sometimes as if he felt fatherly pride. But did he? Did he feel anything other than relief that she was carrying his heir?

She reached for his hand and placed it on her stomach. "Feel."

He examined the rounded stomach much as he had Diamond's that day. The baby responded to the gentle pressure. A slow smile spread across his face and warmth flooded Sara. His hand tenderly explored the new life, the pressure of his touch comforting.

His eyes locked with hers. "Feels like a strong, healthy boy."

"Or a feisty, healthy daughter."

"Like her mother."

He kept his hand in place, smiling when the baby made its presence known. The moment was magical. Mother, father, child. The moment contained everything Sara ever wanted, except for one missing ingredient. A man who loved her, a man with whom she could share this child instead of relinquishing it to him in a few months. Would he allow her to see the children through the years? She longed to see them grow, experience their first haircut, first tooth, and first tentative smile. She'd use every cent she had to travel the long distance that separated them, as often as Walker might allow.

"Sara." Walker's features sobered.

"Yes?"

"Exactly what happened this morning in town? Sophie said you thought Caleb was responsible for the accident."

She looked away. "I don't want to argue, Walker."

"I don't want to argue, either; I want you to tell me what happened."

"I was crossing the street and this wagon started toward me. A moment earlier, it was driverless."

"Caleb was driving the wagon?"

"No, of course not. I didn't see who was driving it."

"But you think Caleb was responsible for the accident?"

"I . . . don't know, Walker. Yes, I think he is, but I have no proof."

Walker leaned back, drawing on the cheroot. His expression gave no indication of his thoughts.

"You don't believe me, do you?"

His gaze moved back to hers. "I want to."

"You want to?" Her heart tripped.

"Give me the proof, Sara. Produce the second set of books you accuse Caleb of keeping. Show me the evidence that says he was driving the wagon this morning."

"I can't," she admitted.

"What would you have me do? Throw away twenty years of trust and friendship on speculation? You're a fair woman, Sara. You tell me. I don't profess to be good with numbers. I can only rely on people I trust, and without evidence, I'm left with conjecture."

He was right, of course, but she had no evidence, just a growing conviction that she was right. She would bet her life that the books she saw yesterday were not the ones she'd seen months ago. Caleb was too smart for her; he could look her in the eye and lie, and she was powerless to do anything about it.

"He's not your friend," she said, getting up from the bed. The magic had disappeared with Walker's blind refusal to see Caleb for what he was. "He . . . threatened me, Walker."

"Threatened you?"

She could see she was only making it worse, heaping accusation upon accusation as if driven by madness. But she knew something was terribly wrong, and the wrong involved Caleb.

"Sara, he saved your life."

"If it wasn't for him, my life wouldn't have needed saving." Her cheeks burned. Why did every conversation between them evolve into a quarrel?

Sighing, he got up. "The tea's cold. Come downstairs and eat. You'll feel better."

She reached for the hairbrush, and despondently pulled it through her hair. Walker's loyalty to Caleb clearly overshadowed any feelings he might have for her.

He paused at the doorway. "Sophie said that Caleb is coming for dinner tomorrow night."

Brushing her hair, she pretended to not hear him.

"Did you hear me?"

"Perhaps it's time I leave, Walker." The impasse was too difficult; she couldn't go on. It was upsetting her and the babies. Motherhood was all she had left; she had to protect that.

"Leave?" His features darkened.

"Return to Boston, to my father. I've been rethinking the matter and I feel that it's best that I have the baby there. Wadsy will be there to help—and Papa."

His features closed. "What about our bargain?"

"I'll honor the bargain." Her eyes met his in the mirror. "If that's your only concern."

"I have many concerns—one is that the McKay

name isn't disgraced. The town doesn't know about our situation, and I don't intend for them to find out."

"They'll find out everything, anyway. And you can't stop me from leaving."

"If you leave I will fight you for custody of the child, Sara. Sole custody."

He didn't have to spell it out for her. "If I stay?"

"Once the baby is born, we'll set up reasonable visitation rights."

She yanked the brush through her hair, glaring at him in the mirror.

"And you will be at supper tomorrow night. Is that understood?"

She continued to glare at him. "I'll be there."

When the door closed a moment later, she muttered, "But you won't like it."

Sara was up early the next morning, eager to begin the day. That darn Caleb was lower than a snake, but she was smarter and she was going to prove it. After breakfast, she pulled out the good silver and began to polish it. Sophie watched the activity with raised brows.

"All this work for Caleb's benefit?"

"You know, Sophie, I've been thinking, and I realize how foolish I've been acting toward Caleb. I should be *thanking* him instead of persecuting him." She glanced up, smiling. "It's my condition, you know. And I want supper tonight to be special, a celebration."

Sophie eyed her skeptically. "All right. Then don't forget the soup bowl—we're having Caleb's favorite cheese soup."

Naturally. Sara polished a knife, then held it up to view her reflection. What else did you feed a rat?

That afternoon she visited Potster and asked his help. The old cook, elbow-deep in pie crust, gave her a wary eye but promised to do what he could. But he didn't like it.

When she came downstairs that evening, Walker's and Caleb's voices drifted from the study. S. H. and Sophie were in the kitchen, banging pans. Sara could hear S. H.'s teasing banter as the housekeeper dished up potatoes.

The study door opened and Sara smiled as Walker and Caleb appeared. "Caleb. I am so glad you could join us tonight." She stepped off the stairway to give him a brief embrace.

Caleb glanced at Walker. "I hope you haven't suffered any from yesterday's unfortunate incident. I've been worried that you wouldn't be able to join us tonight."

She tilted her head skeptically. "Why not?"

"I thought the accident might have left you too shaken."

"Goodness, no. Everyone's made too much of the whole incident." Looping her arm through the accountant's, she smiled, trying to look behind his back. "I see you aren't carrying your briefcase—that's encouraging. Tonight is social only, no thoughts of work?"

"No. The briefcase is in the buggy."

"Good. You and Walker work much too hard. Tonight we visit and get to know each other better."

Caleb gave Walker a helpless look when Sara drew him into the dining room. Sophie appeared from the kitchen with the silver soup tureen. When she saw Caleb, she smiled. "Perfect timing."

S. H. blessed the food; then the men picked up their napkins as Sophie spooned soup into Walker's bowl.

"Oh—before we start." Sara cleared her throat. "Caleb, I want to apologize for my atrocious behavior. I've made unforgivable accusations recently, statements that I don't understand myself. But as you know, I'm not myself these days."

Caleb glanced at Walker. "No apologies necessary. I understand, and all is forgiven. As I've said, I will be only too happy to go over the books with you, to explain—"

"Goodness, no." She snapped her napkin open, smiling. "Walker has complete trust in you, Caleb. And since you saved my life yesterday, how could I feel otherwise? Please forgive me if I have hurt your feelings in any way."

Caleb nodded pleasantly to Sophie as she filled his bowl. "Ah, cheese soup. Sophie, you're the greatest."

"And I just want to say that I've been lashing out at everyone, simply everyone. I am most genuinely, sincerely sorry." Sara reached for a roll and butter. "I don't even feel like myself. I have all these odd feelings that S. H. and Sophie and even the doctor assures me are normal, but still, they're there, and sometimes I'm unpleasant. Isn't that true, Walker?"

She met Walker's guarded look with a warm and friendly smile.

Caleb seemed embarrassed by the subject. "Don't worry about it. Everyone has bad days." He accepted the basket of rolls from S. H. "What did you ever do about that lame bull, S. H.?"

As they ate their soup, conversation circled around issues at the ranch, but eventually returned to the puzzling near accident.

Sara picked up the butter dish and offered it to the accountant. "You didn't happen to see who was driving that wagon, did you, Caleb? It was so strange—when I looked a moment earlier, the wagon was sitting in front of the blacksmith's with not a driver to be seen."

"No, I'm afraid I didn't," he said.

"Why, you could have been killed yourself," Sara said.

Caleb seemed relieved when Sophie served the roast.

"When you pulled me from the path of that wagon—you know, I've been thinking. Isn't it odd that wagon was coming at such a fast clip the very moment I was trying to cross the street? Don't you find that just the oddest thing? Usually there are hardly any wagons—and if there are, it's mainly families coming to town for supplies. But lo and behold, here comes that wagon out of nowhere, clipping along so fast. Why, it was almost as if the driver had deliberately set out to run me over. Me—an expectant mother! You'd think the person responsible had no shame." Cutting a piece of roast, she innocently met Caleb's eyes.

"Sara," Walker said, "Caleb isn't able to eat his supper for all the chatter."

"Really odd." Sara slipped a piece of meat into her mouth. "As you said, a person needs to be careful. Why, I *could* have been killed."

"Sara." Walker lay his fork aside. "We're indeed grateful that you are still among us. Now, will you please let our guest eat his meal?"

"Oh, certainly." She took a bite of potatoes, her eyes going back to Caleb. "But don't you find it all really peculiar?"

Murmuring an appropriate response, Caleb struck up a conversation with Walker, and the diners made it through the rest of the meal with idle talk.

Sophie was serving dessert when a noise caught S. H.'s attention. Turning in his seat, he cocked an ear toward the barn. "It's Diamond again. She's been throwin' fits ever since we took her colt away this mornin'."

Walker pushed back from the table. "I'll check on her before she hurts herself."

Caleb half rose from his chair. "Do you need my help?"

"No, S. H. and I can handle it. Enjoy your cake and coffee."

The two men left and Sophie started gathering up dirty plates. When she disappeared through the kitchen doorway, Sara looked at Caleb, who was defenseless now.

"Really odd. Don't you think?"

His eyes met hers now with no attempt to conceal his animosity. "I've heard of more bizarre things."

"In Laramie? An expectant mother being nearly run down? It's almost as if someone wanted me out of the way. Like I might be getting too close to something—but what that is, I can't imagine. What could I possibly know?" She handed him the pitcher of cream for his coffee.

The anger in his face chilled her blood, yet the quest to reveal his ugly nature was stronger than common sense.

"Your condition, Miss Livingston, not only has left you delusional, but you're in dire need of a straitjacket."

"Do you think so?" She took the last bite of cake, removing remnants of fudge frosting from her plate with the tip of her fork. Rising from the table, she picked up her plate and bent close to his ear on her way to the kitchen. "Don't suppose for one moment, Mr. Vanhooser, that I don't know what I'm doing," she said in a voice as sweet as honey. "I know what you're doing, and I will expose you." Patting his shoulder, she moved on.

When she heard Walker and S. H. come in from the barn a few minutes later, she lifted the pot of fresh coffee. "I'll refill the cups, Sophie." She entered the dining room and, after serving the men, sat down and listened to Walker and S. H.'s discussion concerning the mare, ignoring Caleb's attempts to catch her eye.

"The poor ole girl's sufferin'," S. H. said, sipping his coffee. "I'm afraid she's gonna break outta her pen and try to get to her baby."

"She'll come around by morning." Walker finished his cake and shoved the plate back. He looked at Sara. "There's a full moon tonight. Why don't we get a breath of fresh air?"

She wanted nothing more than a walk in the moonlight with him. Upstairs yesterday, she'd heard a softening in his tone, almost a signal that he was willing to try again. But it was a temporary truce if she couldn't gain his trust, and the only way she could gain his trust was to prove that her condition had nothing to do with her suspicions. Meeting his eyes, she declined softly. "Thank you, but I'm going to retire early." Her heart tripped a beat when she realized her refusal disappointed him.

"Caleb?" She turned to smile at their guest. "Why don't you accompany Walker?"

"You miss the point," Walker grumbled.

S. H. laughed, getting up to remove the dishes. "I think he wants to be alone with ya, honey."

Any other time, Sara would leap at the chance to be alone with him. But not tonight. Not with Caleb's buggy so conveniently parked in the front yard. She met Walker's eyes and silent looks passed between them.

"I would like nothing better than a walk in the moonlight with you. Perhaps we can tomorrow night."

Walker winked at her. "Your loss."

"It's warm in here, Sophie. Are the windows open?" Caleb mopped his brow, then absently returned the hankie to his pocket.

Sophie looked over her shoulder. "Yes, they are, Caleb. Must be that hot coffee making you sweat."

Walker got up, glancing at Caleb. "If the lady prefers her bed to my company, I guess I'm stuck with you. My new plow came this week. Are you interested in seeing it?"

"Of course."

Sara excused herself and slipped through the kitchen. Sophie was busy at the sink and didn't notice her entry. Tiptoeing to the open window, she lifted the curtain and watched Walker and Caleb leave the house and walk toward the shed.

Sophie glanced over her shoulder. "Why don't you go with them? S. H. will help me clean up."

"Thanks, Sophie, but I think I'll sit on the porch for a few minutes, then go upstairs."

"Go right ahead, but take a wrap, because it's chilly."

Sara grabbed her cloak and went out to the swing. Soon she heard Walker's and Caleb's voices in the shed. Slipping off the porch, she hurried around the corner of the house. Caleb's polished surrey glistened in the moonlight.

Running her hand under the interior seat, she found nothing. It *had* to be here; Caleb said he'd left it in the buggy. She stepped into the carriage and groped around the pleated upholstery, searching for openings. The buggy must have cost a handsome price. Had Walker's money bought it?

Nothing. The briefcase wasn't here. She sat back on the seat, breathing hard. Once she'd read a story about a man who hid things in secret compartments. Tapping her feet along the floorboard, Sara noticed that the thud that her left foot made was more hollow than that of her right foot. She leaned down in the semidarkness and felt along the floorboard, her pulse thumping when her fin-

gers encountered a leather latch. She lifted it up—
and inside was the briefcase! Pulling it out of the
hole, she slid down from the carriage.

She raced to the bunkhouse and knocked softly
at Potster's kitchen door. It seemed like an eter-
nity before he let her in, taking the case from her
immediately and holding it up to the candlelight.

"I haven't seen one of these in years," he whispered.

"You can pick it, right?"

"I'd remember how to do this in my sleep."
The old cook chuckled. "Spent my share of time
behind bars to prove it."

He located his tools, and Sara held the briefcase steady as he went to work on the lock.
Uneasy, she glanced out the window, praying
that Walker wouldn't see the light and come to
investigate. The stubborn lock refused to budge.
If Walker caught them breaking into Caleb's
briefcase, she could forget about a truce. He
would have her on the next train to Boston.

"What is it you're looking for?" Potster
strained against the lock, and they finally heard it
click and the latch opened.

Sara unfastened the case and hurriedly shuffled through papers. "I'll know it when I see it,"
she said, opening a contract, scanning it, and
folding it back exactly as it had been. The evidence *had* to be here.

"You think Caleb's stealing from Walker?"

"I know he is. But if I can't find what I'm looking for, I have no way to prove it." She picked up
a small book wrapped in a leather band. When
she untied the strap, the ledger fell open. In the

flickering light she could see numbers written out. A depositor's book! The dates went back several years and the notations showed both deposits and withdrawals.

"This is it, Potster. If I can show that Caleb's deposits are different from Walker's books, then I can prove once and for all that Caleb keeps two sets of books."

"Girl, you gotta be careful. It's hard to believe that Caleb would do such a thing. I have faith that you know what you're doin', but you better be sure about yer facts."

Sara hugged the old man's neck. "Thank you for your trust. You're the best friend a person could have."

"Think so?" He rubbed his whiskered chin. "Wonder if my ex-wives would agree with you."

Sara tucked the bankbook into the front of her dress, rearranged the papers, and latched the case. Potster put the lock back into place and fastened it.

"*You're* the one who's really saved my life," she whispered.

"You just git that case back into the buggy before Caleb knows what you've done."

Sara opened the door and slipped out of the bunkhouse. She could hear the men coming back from the shed. Easing into the shadows, she waited for Walker and Caleb to pass. They passed so close she feared they might hear her breathing. After they went inside, she slid the briefcase back in the buggy and latched the trapdoor.

When she crept back into the house, Sophie heard the screen door. "That you, Sara?"

"Yes, Sophie. I'm going to bed now. Would you please say good night to Walker and Caleb for me?"

"All right, dear. Good night."

"Good night."

Once inside her room, Sara drew the lamp closer, her eyes scanning Caleb's entries. She was tempted to take the evidence directly to Walker the moment she heard Caleb's buggy leave the yard, but she didn't dare. She had to make doubly sure she had the proof needed to convict Caleb.

Footsteps sounded down the hall, then paused in front of her door. Scrambling under the blanket, she slid the book under her pillow.

Please don't let Walker come in.

But the door opened softly and he stood in the doorway, his tall frame illuminated by the hall lantern. She lay still, affecting a steady rise and fall of her chest. Finally he closed the door, and she released a whoosh of air when she heard his boots fading down the hallway.

Sleep wouldn't come. Her chest pounded, and she knew that it would leap from her chest if she lay still any longer. When she was sure the coast was clear, she got up, slipping the bankbook into the front of her dress.

Leaving the bedroom, she crept downstairs and out the back door. Diamond's restless nickers sounded from the barn.

When she entered the stable, she saw the horse milling about in her stall, searching for her foal.

She put the lantern on a barrel and reached to comfort the mare.

"I know, girl," she soothed. Soon she would be leaving her own baby, or babies. She would leave Spring Grass and return to Boston and an empty existence. Even if she proved her accusations, it wouldn't change her and Walker's situation. It would only be one more of life's disappointments; one more betrayal for Walker to learn that his best friend was cheating him.

"Oh, Diamond, I know how you feel. When I told Papa and Walker that I could leave the baby here, I didn't know it would be so hard." She choked back the hard knot crowding her throat.

Diamond rested her head over the stall, her brown eyes shimmering with grief. She snuffed at Sara's dress, and Sara realized that she was looking for sugar. Smiling, she let the horse nuzzle her belly.

"Do you want some sugar? I suppose I could sneak into the kitchen and get some. Wait here; I'll be right back."

She picked up the lantern and started toward the door, then remembered why she was here in the barn. Removing the passbook from her bodice, she looked around for a protected hiding place. Her eyes lit on the tool bin and she slid the book behind it, lodging it between the bin and the rough wall. Turning to leave, she noticed the barn door was closed.

When she pushed against the heavy planking, it wouldn't move.

Standing back, she tried to remember if she

had closed the door. She hadn't; Diamond's cries had drawn her, and she'd left the door open. Had the wind blown it shut? She shoved, but the door refused to give.

And then she smelled the smoke.

Whirling around, she beat against the door, looking over her shoulder to see the first flames lick through the rear wall.

She pounded harder as gray haze filled the barn. Diamond whinnied, thrashing against her stall. The other horses nickered, shifting around nervously. Smoke bellowed throughout the rafters, and flames jumped from the back wall into the hayloft, trailing a stream of red flames.

The heat intensified, and Sara put the hem of her dress over her mouth. The fire roared like an angry beast, picking up fury. She pounded, screaming now.

Why couldn't they hear her?

Beating her fists, she yelled, black smoke clogging her throat. Her eyes ran and she couldn't get her breath. Finally, she slumped to the floor, the sound of Diamond's frightened cries ringing in her ears.

Twice in two days, she thought as fire consumed the hayloft. Dear God, someone *was* trying to kill her.

Chapter 19

Tossing his sheet aside, Walker rolled out of bed. Sleep was slow to come tonight; his mind kept going over the dinner. Sara was unusually cheerful in Caleb's presence. What had happened to change her mind about him? She'd been so adamant the day before that Caleb was cheating him, yet tonight she was friendly. Overly friendly, not like her. She was a woman with clear convictions, and she was convinced Caleb was embezzling from him. Was that possible?

The problem was easy enough to correct. He'd take the books to Pete McKinley and let him go over them. Pete was discreet; Caleb would never know his work was in question. But Walker would know, and that was the sticking point. He ran his hand through his hair, wondering if Sara could be right. Caleb had been a loyal friend through the years. He'd listened to his problems, been a solid supporter during Pa's death. What was it about Caleb that put Sara on edge? She might be given to theatrics on occasion, but fantasies? He'd seen no indication of that. The least he owed her was an impartial look at the books. First thing in the morning, he'd take them by Walt's and get his opinion. If Sara was right, he owed her a debt of gratitude. If she was wrong, it would only deepen their rift into a chasm.

Lighting a cheroot, he moved to the window, enjoying the smoke. Moonlight illuminated the barn. Inside, he could hear Diamond mourning the loss of her foal. His eyes traveled the deserted barnyard as a matter of habit. Everything was quiet, the bunkhouse dark. The men had been asleep for hours.

Cocking his ear, he realized that Diamond's whinnies were different from a moment ago. Nervousness tinged the animal's cries now. Lifting the window, he studied the barn, searching for a source of concern. There was no wind tonight; a full moon mantled the farmhouse in mellow rays. Then he smelled it. Smoke.

He ground out the cigar and swiftly reached for his pants. Damn—had a careless hand dropped a lighted cigarette on the ground? That could spell disaster.

By the time he reached the barn, flames were licking through the roof. Pounding on Potster's door, he yelled for the cook to wake the men, then grabbed a bucket and raced toward the rain barrel. Within minutes, the barnyard teamed with bare-chested men, still half asleep, racing against time. Fire shot out of the barn roof and spread to the back of the building.

Unlatching the door, Walker lunged inside to free the animals but stumbled, dropping to his knees when he encountered an obstacle blocking the doorway. Black smoke belched from the blazing interior and he grabbed a nearby rag to protect himself from the smoke. Coughing, he tried to shove the object aside, but he came into contact with a feminine hand. He strained to see whose it was. Sophie's? What would she be doing out here at this time of night?

The draft shifted, sucking the flames to the rear of the barn. Lifting the inanimate form, he carried her outside, laying her on the ground. S. H. ran up, out of breath, tucking his shirttails into his pocket.

"Sara!" the men exclaimed in unison.

Jerking the rag off his mouth, Walker covered hers, shielding her from the rolling smoke. Her eyes flickered briefly and he saw recognition before they closed.

Sophie darted out the back door, her unpinned hair streaming down her back. The old woman knelt in the dirt, cradling Sara to her ample bosom. "What's she doing out here? She was in her room when I went to bed."

Walker scanned the area. Chaos reined as men shouted, racing back and forth with water buckets. What *was* Sara doing out here at this time of night? Even worse, why was the barn door locked? Spring Grass didn't have any trouble with theft—nothing was locked up at night except the house.

Lifting Sara into his arms, Walker carried her to the house. When he placed her in their bed, her eyes fluttered and she moaned, coughing. Reaching for him, she clung tightly.

"You're all right, you're safe now," he soothed her.

"Fire . . . the door was locked . . . oh, Walker!"

"It's all right," he murmured, gently stroking her back. He could feel her trembling beneath his hands.

"What if you hadn't come . . . I called for you . . . but no one came."

What if he hadn't gotten out of bed to smoke? The ramifications chilled him more than the cool November air. He could have lost her. He had no way of knowing she was in the barn, caged like a wild animal. If he hadn't smelled the smoke . . .

Holding her close, he inhaled her scent, tainted by smoke, but still very Sara. "Why were you in the barn this time of night?"

"I couldn't sleep . . ." She coughed, still trying to catch her breath. Gently wiping her mouth, he eased her back onto the pillow. "I couldn't sleep," she whispered. "I heard Diamond crying for her baby and I went out to keep her company."

Another spasm of coughing hit her. When it passed, she lay back, her eyes meeting his wearily. "It was Caleb, Walker. Caleb locked me in the barn, then set fire to it."

Walker checked his temper. She had almost been killed twice now and she'd been through enough, but it made him mad when she talked like this. "Caleb left hours ago."

"He left the *house* hours ago. He didn't leave the ranch, Walker." Her eyes were brimming with tears.

"Are you saying he waited in the shadows until everyone was asleep and then just happened to be around when you decided to check on Diamond? Come on, Sara, do you know how insane that sounds?"

"I know . . ." She coughed again, struggling to sit up. He helped her, tucking the pillow behind her head. "I *know*, Walker, but I know it was him, just as I know he's responsible for the incident in town yesterday. Caleb wants me out of the way."

"You're talking nonsense." He poured water into the basin and wet a rag. Wiping her face, he cleaned the smoke away, his eyes locked with hers. "If you want me to believe that my best friend is cheating me, trying to kill the mother of my child, give me *proof*, Sara. Rock-solid proof."

She moaned, closing her eyes. "I had proof. . . . It's gone, burned up in the fire."

"What proof? Caleb's written confession? He didn't appear to be a man on the verge of a confession during supper."

"A bank ledger—with recorded amounts of what he's stolen from you."

"He wouldn't write that in a bank ledger."

"I know it sounds crazy, Walker! You don't know this man—this evil man. He was only pretending to be nice to me tonight. He didn't mean a word of it. You'd know that if you could have

seen the way he looked at me yesterday—
friendly, as if he cared, when he knew he'd
nearly succeeded in having run me down."

"But you were so charming to him tonight, I
was starting to think he was *your* best friend!"

"I am a very good actress."

He stared at her. "Where did you get this passbook?"

"From Caleb's briefcase. When you and he visited the shed, I searched his buggy and found a
trapdoor. That's where he keeps the records,
Walker."

"You *searched* his buggy? My friends are subject to searching before they can leave the ranch?"

"If Caleb is the friend in question."

"Sara." He stood up, shoving his hands
through his hair. How did a man deal with this?
If what she was saying was true, there'd be no
point in taking the ledgers to Walt, because
apparently there *was* a second set—or so Sara
implied.

"You'll defend Caleb to the death! What about
me? What about your child? If Caleb had succeeded tonight—"

"You're talking crazy, Sara. This pregnancy,
our situation—it has us confused. Sophie says
your frustrations are normal, nothing to be concerned about. She says they'll pass when the
baby's born."

"I may be a little moody, but I'm not
crazzzzzzzy." Burying her face in her hands, she
sobbed.

Walker returned to the bed, taking her back

into his arms. Smoothing her hair, he gave her a handkerchief and said quietly, "Don't put me in this situation, Sara. The Caleb I know is a loyal friend. He has his faults, but show me a man who doesn't. Give me solid proof that Caleb is betraying me, and I'll listen. What do you want me to do, Sara? Have the man arrested on the suspicion that he's cheating me? If you're wrong, I've betrayed him."

"Potster saw the book."

"*What* book? How can you be sure that this book you claim to have seen is what you think it is? Did Caleb write in bold letters, 'This is the amount I'm stealing from Walker'?"

"No—but I know that's what it is. A neat column with dates—and a lot of money involved, Walker. A lot. Maybe he intends to pay it all back, but that doesn't excuse the fact that he's stealing from you."

"Why, Sara? Caleb makes a decent salary. Why would he steal from me?"

"You can ask Potster if you don't believe me. He saw the book."

"What's Potster doing helping you force open someone's briefcase?"

"I asked him to help—he didn't want to, but he did because he's my friend." Her eyes turned on him accusingly. "He doesn't think the idea is so far-fetched. He was a criminal once—and I should think it takes one to know one."

"Can't you find enough to keep you busy without playing detective? What happened to the book you're writing?"

"I haven't worked on it lately." She doubled the handkerchief and wiped her eyes. "Every time I write a new scene I start crying."

He clamped a hand to the back of his neck. She cried over chickens, eggs, for Pete's sake! "For crying out loud—why?"

She wiped her nose. "It's just too painful. The story reminds me of you and me, and how we were so happy for a while. Just ask Potster about the depositor's book if you don't believe me."

"I concede Potster saw some book, but neither you nor he knows what it was."

"I know," she said stubbornly.

Walker turned and left the room. He had a barn on fire. At least that was something he knew how to handle.

Sara opened her eyes the next morning, awakening slowly. Her hand automatically searched for Walker's warm body beside her. Filled with the usual sense of disappointment, she got out of bed and padded across the floor. She couldn't go on this way. Her stomach hurt, her eyes were swollen from the smoke, and the whole situation had her worn to a raveling. Walker wouldn't believe her or forgive her, so what was the use of staying? She wanted to go home, home to Wadsy and Papa and Abraham, who cared if she lived or died.

By sunup she had dressed, drunk a cup of hot tea, and packed her valise. Hitching the buggy wasn't easy, but she'd seen S. H. do it numerous times. She found extra tack in a small shed near the house, and the carriage rattled out of the courtyard before anyone in the main house stirred.

The private ledger was the key to the mystery, but it was gone. Maybe Walker was right. Maybe she should have stayed and written her book and forgotten all about her suspicions.

The train station was deserted when she pulled up. Unloading her valise, she stood it on the platform and purchased a ticket. "What time does the train arrive?"

The clerk consulted his pocket watch. "You got about half an hour."

She walked back to the buggy, wondering what to do with it. She supposed she could tie the mare to the bank post. Caleb would notice it and see that it was returned to Walker.

Her gaze moved to the bank. Or, she could tell Caleb that he'd won; that she was leaving. Wouldn't he be pleased? He might have the last laugh, but she could confront him with her knowledge of the second book—let him know that he might fool Walker, but he couldn't fool her.

The McKay buggy was waiting in front of the bank when Caleb arrived. The whistling banker turned the corner, his jaw dropping when he saw Sara. Color drained from his face. "You're not . . . ?"

Sara smiled. "Dead? Nope, sound as a dollar. Sorry."

A shutter closed over his features. "Hallucinating again, Sara? Perhaps the doctor can give you something to ease your discomfort." A sly grin crept across his face. "Why don't you cross the street? Doc will be in his office at any time."

"You'd like that, wouldn't you?" Climbing out of the buggy, she followed him into the bank.

"The bank doesn't open until nine," he said, trying to shake her.

"My train leaves in twenty minutes. I can't wait for business hours." She followed him to his office and watched as he stripped out of his coat and loosened his tie.

Seating himself behind the desk, he glared at her. "Dare I hope you're leaving?"

"Ooooh. The real Caleb surfaces." She perched on the edge of his desk. "Yes, I'm leaving."

"Does Walker know?"

"He wouldn't care if he did."

"How sad." The banker looked anything but remorseful. "What do you want, Sara?"

"What do you think I want?" He knew that she knew; the guilt in his eyes was proof enough. Should she tell him how she knew, or just let him wonder?

Perspiration beaded his upper lip, although the room was chilly. "I'm a busy man. State your purpose." He checked his watch. "Didn't you say you had a train to catch?"

She met his cool appraisal. "You win, Caleb."

Leaning back in his chair, he smiled. "Of course. When did you finally realize it?"

"Last night when you locked me in the barn. I thought I was going to die."

His smile never wavered.

"And I would have, if Walker hadn't heard Diamond's cries and come to investigate."

Caleb shrugged. "Walker's always been lucky. What is it you want, Sara? Surely you know by now your efforts to convince Walker that I'm stealing from him aren't going to work. He doesn't believe you."

"No, he doesn't. You're right. He accepts your word over mine. It's hard to find friends like that."

"Yes, it is." Caleb turned to the stack of papers on his desk.

"But when I show him the depositor's book, I imagine he'll change his mind."

Caleb glanced up.

"You know, the private ledger you keep in the secret compartment of your buggy." When he paled, she smiled. "Oooh," she mocked. "That ole book."

The banker's eyes hardened. "What do you want, Jezebel?"

"Ahhh, Jezebel." She pretended to ponder the request. "Correct me if I'm wrong. Just a few days ago, wasn't I 'dearest girl' and 'my sweet'?"

Shoving away from the desk, Caleb got to his feet. His hand hovered near the middle desk drawer and for a fleeting moment she wondered if he had a gun. It was a little late to think of that, but she supposed it was possible; a banker would be prepared to defend his establishment. Keeping an eye on his right hand, she said softly, "Last night, when you and Walker went to the shed, I searched your buggy and found the briefcase."

"So? My briefcase is always locked." He patted his vest pocket. "The key never leaves my person."

"True, but Potster knows how to unlock things without a key."

Eyes narrowing, he took a threatening step forward. She backed a step away. "I have the ledger, Caleb. You're stealing from Walker."

The ledger was burned cinders, but he would never know. She would simply let the knowledge of his sins eat away at him day by day, until he was driven mad with wondering when and if she would hand Walker proof of his crime. She, on the other hand, would be eating Wadsy's cherry pies and growing fat and lazy with Walker's children. She might not have Walker McKay, the home she wanted, the babies she carried within her, or the man she loved, but she would have the satisfaction that Caleb would never have a moment's peace.

He lunged at her and she jumped back, fear rippling through her. He was stronger than she was; he could overpower her—shoot her, if he dared, then take her somewhere outside of town and bury her body. No one would ever know what had happened to her. His powers of persuasion were immense.

"Tell me what you want," he gritted between clenched teeth.

"I want you to tell Walker the truth. That you're embezzling money from him—that you have been for years." If nothing else came of this madness, Walker would know that she hadn't lied to him. And she *was* in her right mind, baby and all.

Turning back to the desk, he rested his hand on the top drawer.

"I'll do nothing of the sort."

"Then you admit that you have been stealing from him?"

"I admit *nothing*." Pulling the drawer open, he removed a small hand pistol.

Sara swallowed. Should she run? Scream? It was early; no one was moving about yet. *You're foolish, Sara. You shouldn't have come here alone just to prove a point. You should have gotten on the train and gone home.*

Leveling the gun at her, Caleb motioned her out the doorway.

"Don't be a fool," she warned. "Walker will be here any moment—I lied—he knows where I am."

Shoving her out of the room and into the bank foyer, he glanced out the front window, apparently gauging his next move. "Open the door."

Shielding her stomach, Sara edged backward. "If anything happens to me, Walker will know that you're responsible. He might not care what happens to me, but he does care about his child. You destroy this child, and you'll have the devil to pay."

"Shut up. You talk too much." He backed her through the door, pausing to look up and down the deserted street. Nothing stirred.

She had one choice, and that was to make a break for it before he could stop her. She was fast, able to outrun all the other girls in her boarding school. In her room in Boston, she had an array of blue ribbons from sporting events. But now she was thirty pounds heavier and with child—or children.

She whirled to run, but Caleb was faster. Pinning her squirming body against the wall, he pressed close, his breath hot on her cheek. "Don't *mess* with me, Sara." Jerking her arm tighter behind her back, he hissed, "I'd just as soon shoot you right here, woman."

"You wouldn't dare." She moaned as he twisted her arm tighter.

"What do I have to lose?"

"You're still able to convince Walker that you're innocent. If you shoot me, there'll be witnesses. You won't be able to talk your way out of this one."

"Witnesses?" He pretended to assess the danger, then grinned. "Seems the town is deserted this morning. Pity." Thrusting her away from the wall, he herded her out toward the waiting buggy. She struggled to break his hold, but he was stronger than his physical stature indicated.

"Why, Caleb? Why would you do this to Walker?" She panted, almost out of breath. "He's your best friend—he won't hear of you deceiving him. He's willing to risk his future happiness because of you."

"You're breaking my heart. If I had a violin, I'd play it."

"At least tell me why—what can that hurt? You're obviously a big, mean brute who's going to do me harm."

"It seems certain bank funds are missing—funds I am held accountable for. I intend to pay Walker back—don't fret your pretty little head about that."

"When?" She grunted when he shoved her up

into the buggy, tipping her cumbersome body onto the seat.

His face closed. "I've incurred a few gambling debts lately. But that will change—and soon. When it does, I'll return the money and Walker will never be the wiser."

"He's not stupid." She twisted to release his hold. "If anything happens to me, he'll have his books audited."

"My dear, when word of your demise reaches him, nothing will matter for a time. By then the money will be replaced with no one the wiser."

"Walker doesn't love me! He isn't going to mourn my death!"

"You little fool. You think you're so smart, but you know nothing. He loves you—I can see it in his eyes." Caleb sprang aboard the buggy and reached for the reins.

"You're wrong—he only wants the baby," she murmured, fighting against the temptation to believe him. Was Caleb right? Did Walker love her, and only foolishly clung to his stubborn pride?

Caleb slid her a sideways glance. "In another few minutes, it won't matter."

Across the street, Denzil Mitchell yawned, scratching the top of his head. The wiry shopkeeper's hair stood up like a porcupine. After the next spat with Martha, *she* was sleeping in the back room—breaking her goldurned back on the board floor. Yawning again, he caught sight of a buggy wheeling out of town. Now, who'd be leavin' in such an all-fired hurry this early?

Straining to see out the window, he frowned. Walker McKay's rig—with Caleb Vanhooser and McKay's bride in it.

"Don't that beat all," he said, absently rolling a cigarette. He could already tell it was going to be an interesting day.

Chapter 20

Walker squinted against the bright sunlight, groaning when he realized that he'd overslept. The fire had kept him up most of the night; he'd gotten to bed only a little before sunup.

He lay there for a moment thinking about his dream. In it he was holding his son, standing beside Sara and looking out over Spring Grass. It was summer and the grasses were blowing, the sun hot on his face. He held Sara's hand, and the baby she was holding was laughing up at him. A little girl with Sara's eyes.

His hand absently felt Sara's side of the bed. Lately his anger came less frequently. He thought about the opportunities that he'd had to end the dispute, the way the baby felt kicking against his hand. Sara's smoky cheeks, him wiping the soot from her tear-stained face. The feel of her dancing

351

against him, her quick and easy smiles, the burned corn bread and drunken chickens. Her bulldog tenacity and how much she wanted to make the marriage work.

He thought about the two near-fatal accidents coming one on top of the other. He could have lost her. Would his righteous anger have been worth it? She'd done wrong; he'd done wrong by not forgiving her. She wasn't at all like Trudy. Sara had a heart of gold, and if he continued to hold her at bay, he would be a fool.

The hall clock struck eight when he came downstairs—midmorning for him. Sophie was busy in the washhouse, her face flushed with early-morning heat.

"Where's Sara?"

The housekeeper doused a shirt in the rinse water. "Still asleep, I imagine. You're gettin' a late start, ain't you?"

"Yes. I'm going to fix a tray, maybe have breakfast with her."

"Suit yourself. Want me to fry bacon?"

"No, I'll find something."

Later, he rapped at their bedroom door, balancing a tray in one hand. When Sara didn't call out, he rapped again. Still no answer.

Pushing the door open with his boot, he was surprised to see that the bed was made. His eyes scanned the empty room. Maybe she was with Potster—but he'd seen the ranch hand cleaning windows earlier, alone. He stepped into the dressing room. It was in disarray, but she wasn't there.

Walker carried the tray back to the kitchen, glancing up when Sophie came in.

"She wasn't hungry, huh? That's not like her. Are you two quarreling again?"

Walker shook his head. "She wasn't there. You haven't seen her this morning?"

"No. I assumed she was plumb worn-out from all the doin's. Are you sure she isn't in her room?"

"She's not there."

They searched the house, to no avail. Walker caught a glimpse of S. H. from around the corner of the house, heading for the barn. He opened the back screen door and called, "S. H., have you seen Sara around anywhere?"

"No—been inspecting the damage."

"What did we lose?"

"Everything's gone—the hay, the tack, and the buggy. At least the horses made it out safely. Barn's gonna hafta be rebuilt."

Walker frowned. How could they have lost the buggy? It wasn't in the barn last night. He'd taken it out to mend the top, and hadn't put it back.

"Are you sure about the buggy, S. H.? It shouldn't have been in the barn."

S. H. shrugged. "Well, it's not here."

"What do you mean it's not here?"

"If you didn't put it in the barn, I don't know where it is."

Sophie came out on the porch, wiping her hands on her apron.

Walker glanced at her, then turned back to

S. H. "Check the shed and see if the extra tack is missing."

"Why?" the foreman asked.

"Maybe she decided to use the buggy this morning." That seemed unlikely; she never ventured anywhere on her own. Unless she had decided to run away. His stomach churned at the thought.

Sophie frowned. "Where would she have gone?"

"Check on that tack, S. H."

S. H returned in a few minutes, shaking his head. "You're right, the tack is gone. She must've took the buggy."

"Does one of the men have an extra saddle and bridle?"

"Imagine I can scare up one—where are ya goin'?"

"To town. I'm afraid she might have decided to go back to Boston."

"Land sakes!" Sophie exclaimed. "Why would she do that?"

"Because I'm a blind fool, Sophie. I just realized that."

S. H. disappeared and returned with a saddle, a blanket, and tack. Walker saddled Diamond and swung aboard, allowing the animal free rein. Dread washed over him as he rode out. Where was Sara? They weren't on the best of terms, but she wouldn't have left without telling him.

The fall wind cut through his light jacket when he tethered the horse at the train station. Eldon Snides looked up, grinning when he saw him.

"Walker. What can I do for you today?"

"Did my wife board a train this morning?"

"Mrs. McKay?" Eldon scratched his head. "I just came on duty." He peered over the passenger list. "No, I don't see a Sara McKay here."

"Try Livingston. Sara Livingston."

He scanned the list again. "Oh, yes. Here it is: Sara Livingston."

Walker swore under his breath. "Was the ticket to Boston?"

"Yes, sir—'pears it was. Train left an hour ago."

Walker turned away from the window. "Why would she leave without telling me?"

"Pardon?"

"Nothing. Thanks, Eldon."

When Walker reached the Mitchells' store, he realized that he was walking the horse instead of riding her. He secured the animal, then sat down on the bench outside the mercantile to gather his thoughts. Should he go after her? Ask her to forgive him?

Lowell Livingston would fight tooth and nail before he let Sara return after all that Walker had said to her.

He heard the door open and hoped Denzil would leave him alone with his pain.

"Mornin', Walker."

"Morning, Denzil." He started to get up, but Denzil motioned him back down.

"Sit a spell." The storekeeper sat down beside him, taking out cigarette papers.

"I'm not good company right now, Denzil."

Denzil eyed him knowingly. "Woman problems, huh?"

"What makes you think that?"

"Well—" Denzil rolled a cigarette, licked the paper, and sealed it shut. "You know I'm not one to pry." He struck a match, letting it burn. "It's just a damn shame that it had ta happen to ya twice."

Bad news spread quicker than poison ivy. Before long, the whole town would know about Sara's sudden departure. Folks laughing behind his back, snickering. *McKay can't keep a woman*, they'd say. *Wonder what's wrong with him?* Worse yet, he'd lost the only woman he'd ever loved.

"If a man cain't trust his best friend, what's the world comin' to?"

Walker frowned. "My best friend? What's Caleb got to do with this?"

Denzil shifted on the bench, fanning the match out as it seared his fingers. "Now, you know I don't want to get into your matters, but when I saw your buggy with Caleb and your missus leaving town this morning, I couldn't help but take notice." He leaned closer, whispering. "Martha and I had a little squabble ourselves and—"

"Caleb?" Walker interrupted. "Caleb was taking Sara to the train station?"

Denzil pulled the cigarette from his mouth and studied the cold tip. "Train station? No, they left town in your buggy."

Why would Sara be with Caleb? She'd never go to him for help.

"Are you sure it was Sara?"

A match flared. "Yeah, it was your buggy, all right, and Caleb was in it with your wife."

Caleb and Sara. Impossible.

"You can never tell about women these days. One minute a man's minding his own business, the next he's sleeping on the floor of his store."

Walker rose from the bench and began striding toward the bank.

"Good luck," Denzil yelled, flinging the flaming match to the ground. "You never know about these females."

Sara wouldn't be caught dead with Caleb. What was going on here?

Walker walked into Caleb's office without knocking. The banker glanced up, surprise registering on his face.

"Denzil said he saw you with Sara early this morning. What's going on, Caleb?"

Caleb swallowed, his eyes darting past the open door. "Saa . . . er . . . she asked me to drive her to the train station—"

Walker faced him coldly. "Why would she ask you to drive her to the train station? And when would she have asked you? Last night? Hardly— she accused you of locking her in the barn and starting the fire."

"I know . . . but she had a change of heart."

"Where did she go?"

"Er . . . back to Boston. She said she thought you'd be happier this way . . ."

The answer didn't surprise him. Back to Boston. She'd left without saying good-bye to him or to Sophie. His behavior the past few weeks had come home to roost. Why shouldn't she leave? He'd all but shoved her out of the house.

"Calm down, Walker." Caleb's features softened. "I know Sara's departure comes as a shock, but it's the best for all—"

Turning around, Walker strode out of the office. He walked out of the bank, determined to act as if the world went on. Like Trudy, Sara had proved to be more fluff than substance. For some reason, he had thought she was different—yes, he'd kept her at bay to punish her for her lies, but deep down he knew she was different. He'd known it from the day he married her—didn't marry her— She had him so confused, he didn't know *what* he was thinking anymore. *Let her go*, a voice in his mind demanded. She'd been nothing but trouble since she got here. Yet he rebelled at the thought. He didn't want to let her go. Mounting Diamond, he picked up the reins.

Then it hit him.

If Sara had taken the train, where was his buggy?

Swinging off the horse, he strode back into the bank. When he reached Caleb's office, he asked, "Where's my buggy?"

"Buggy? Er . . . well, I . . . I suppose it's . . . maybe you should ask Tom Howell—"

"The blacksmith? Why would he have my rig?"

"He could have . . . I wasn't sure what Sara wanted to do with—" The banker fidgeted with a stack of folders. "Sometimes, Walker, things happen . . . things we don't want—"

A large hand slammed over Caleb's, pinning the banker in place. "Where's my *wife*, Caleb." It wasn't a question, it was a demand.

"I . . ." Caleb's eyes beseeched him. "God knows . . . I wasn't going to hurt her."

Leaning over the desk, Walker grasped him by the collar. For the first time in his life, he wanted to hurt Caleb—badly. Fear constricted his throat. "What have you done with Sara?"

"She's . . . not hurt. She's . . ." Caleb's voice broke. "I didn't know what to do with her, so I locked her in a bedroom at my house." Breaking into tears, the accountant clutched Walker's shirt-sleeve. "I wouldn't have hurt her . . . I've ago-nized over what to do with her from the moment I took her this morning—I snapped, Walker. When she came here accusing me of stealing from you, saying she had my book to prove it—you're my best friend, you know how I am when I get nervous. If she'd only left it alone! She snuck into my buggy last night and found the ledger. I planned to pay you back, Walker, every cent. I've borrowed money from you before—when have I ever failed to pay you back?"

Walker shook his head, sick at heart. Sara was right; Caleb was doctoring the books and he had refused to believe her.

"Haven't I always paid you back?"

"You always asked me first, Caleb." He took off his hat, running his hands through his hair. "Why now? You know I would give you any-thing you asked."

"I'm in deep, Walker. Deeper than I've ever been in my life. I haven't known where to turn—but my luck's changing! I'm playing in a high-stakes game Saturday night—you'll see, I'll win it all back and more. Then I'll—"

Releasing Caleb's collar, Walker pushed him back into the chair. "If you've harmed Sara or my child in any way—"

"I haven't." Caleb wept. "I wouldn't do that, Walker. I know that you love her."

The realization hit Walker like a ton of bricks. That was exactly what it was. He didn't just need her; he wanted her, *loved her*. And he had done everything within his power to drive her away. The baby was important, but without Sara it would be only half a family. His existence would be as empty as it had been since he left Sara's bed.

"Walker—"

"I'll deal with you later, Caleb. I'm going after my wife."

Sara was locked in some room, scared half out of her wits. Striding through the bank, he bounded aboard Diamond and spurred her flanks.

Denzil rolled another cigarette, his eyes trained on the bank. Judging from the way McKay had taken off for the bank, Caleb's life wasn't worth a buffalo chip. Wasn't fair that Walker had two women walk out on him. Trouble was brewin'.

"Martha," Denzil shouted, keeping an eye on the bank.

Martha poked her head out the door. "Stop yellin'. I ain't deaf."

"Shhhhh . . . look over there. An ill wind's brewin'."

Martha glanced at the building across the street. "What's going on?"

"McKay and Vanhooser are goin' at it." Denzil lit a match. "McKay's in the bank with Caleb right now and it's gonna git nasty."

"Caleb's Walker's banker. What's suspicious about Walker being in the bank?"

Denzil turned to give her a pitying look. "Because Walker's gonna kill the man, Martha."

Martha frowned. "Have you lost yer mind? Walker and Caleb? Those two have been friends since they was kids."

"Might be, but they ain't now." He fanned the match out, the cigarette forgotten. "Caleb's messin' with his wife."

"With Sara?"

"None other." He struck another match on the bottom of the bench.

"And I suppose he told you that he was going to kill Caleb?"

"Not in so many words." Denzil drew on the cigarette and a whiff of smoke struggled to life.

Martha rolled her eyes. "Why on earth would you think that Walker was gonna kill him?"

"Because." Denzil fanned out the match. "I saw Caleb and Sara leaving in Walker's buggy this morning."

"Going where?"

"How should I know? I jest saw them, I didn't ask any questions." He struck another match. "Seemed to be in a big hurry." He held the match to the tip of the cigarette and inhaled. "You know how I don't like pryin' in other folks' business, but when Walker asked, I felt obliged to tell him."

"That poor man!" Martha lowered herself onto the bench, which groaned beneath the added weight. Denzil crouched to one side, fanning out the match. "That poor man. Imagine. Two women low enough to do the same thing to him."

"It ain't right. Jest a dad-gummed shame. Wonder if there's somethin' wrong with him."

"Dad-gummed shame," Martha echoed. The couple swapped speculative looks.

Walker emerged from the bank and swung aboard his horse. "Look at his shoulders all slumped over like that," Denzil whispered.

Martha nodded. "Did you hear gunshots? I didn't hear gunshots."

"Of course you wouldn't hear *gunshots*," Denzil kept an eye on the bank as he sucked on the cigarette, coaxing a flame. "McKay's too smart for that. Musta killed him with his bare hands."

"Oh, dear, one of us oughta go for the sheriff," Martha said. Before Denzil could answer, Walker swung off the gelding and headed back into the bank.

"Oh, Lordy," Denzil breathed.

Martha fanned her apron in front of her face. Pitching the cigarette butt aside, Denzil rolled another one. Folks went about their business, oblivious to the unfolding drama.

"He's returnin' to the scene of the crime." Denzil shook his head and rolled the paper with shaking fingers. "If he read more of those mystery novels, he'd know that the worst thing he could do is to go back inside. If Sheriff Perkins was to come along right now, he'd catch him red-handed."

"And he's so young and handsome, too. Pity that he'll have to hang for this." Martha shook her head. "Jest a real shame." The couple sat up straighter when Walker bolted from the bank a second time, landing astride his horse. The animal galloped off, kicking up dust in his wake.

Martha gasped. "I'll get the sheriff—he's gettin' away!"

Before she could untangle herself from Denzil, Caleb emerged from the bank, disheveled but otherwise unharmed.

For a second they sat in silence as if they were looking at the living dead.

Suddenly Martha sprang off the bench and grabbed the broom. "You numskull! Walker McKay didn't kill anybody!" She took a swing at Denzil's head.

Denzil ducked, and the cigarette flew out of his mouth. "Martha, I swear!" he yelped, shielding his face and neck from blows. "I saw it with my own two eyes. Caleb and the McKay woman . . ."

She gave him another whack, then spun around and stormed back into the mercantile.

Denzil bent down to retrieve his cigarette, casting a murderous look at the closed door. He *knew* what he'd seen—and there *was* gonna be trouble. Straightening, he searched his pockets for a match.

Shoot. He was out again.

Squinting, Sara leaned down, closing one eye as she jiggled a hairpin in the keyhole. Potster had made it look so easy, but she'd worked for an hour and hadn't cracked the rigid lock. If she didn't get out of here soon, she was going to burst. Hours had gone by without the use of a necessary, and she was desperate.

Rattling the handle, she gritted her teeth with frustration.

How long would Caleb leave her here? And what then? Would he actually do away with her? Questions flashed through her mind. How would Walker know what had happened to her? Would he be so angry because she'd left without telling him that he'd think it was good riddance? Giving the handle one last vicious shake, she slid down the length of the door, sobbing.

Then she heard a horse pounding along the rutted drive. She jerked upright, listening. Someone was coming. Caleb was coming back.

Springing to her feet, she yanked so hard that when the door opened, she flew backward, landing on the wool rug with a jolt. Grabbing her belly, she lay there for a moment, assuring herself that the impact had not hurt the babies. They kicked, then settled down.

Crawling on her hands and knees, she closed the door, her eyes searching for a weapon. The bedpost. It was long, angular, and loosely attached to the bedstead. When she heard the banker's footsteps coming down the hallway, she was waiting by the door, club extended over her head.

The door flew open, and Sara swung the makeshift weapon with all her might. Her abductor caught sight of her from the corner of his eye and quickly sidestepped the blow. She shot out of the room, bouncing off the opposite wall, knocking vases and knickknacks off a polished table.

Hands shot out to support her. Strong, familiar hands. Wonderfully familiar hands. Opening her eyes, she met a man's blue, blue gaze.

"Walker! How did you know—?"

His mouth captured hers in a hungry, urgent kiss that sent her head reeling. It was many moments before she could break the embrace long enough to ask, "How did you know where to find me?"

"Caleb told me."

"Caleb? But he—" A second, more urgent kiss prevented her from asking the myriad of questions swirling in her mind.

"Sara," Walker murmured, holding her close as he stroked her hair. "I should have listened—"

She stopped him, her fingertips tracing his mouth. Oh, how she loved him, more than she thought she could ever love anyone except Papa. But she didn't want him if her word would always be in doubt. She'd had a taste of real happiness, the kind of joy between a man and a woman when it was right, and she wanted it more than anything she'd ever wanted in her life. Their relationship had started under a shadow, and she wasn't sure if the sun would ever shine upon it again.

Straightening her dress, she backed away.

"Sara—sweetheart—"

"I'm going home, Walker."

"Sara, I know I've been hard on you the past few months. I'm not proud of my actions. Can't we put this thing aside?"

"You've been terribly unfair, Walker. The least you could have done was given me the benefit of the doubt. You didn't believe my motives for marrying you, and you didn't believe me when I warned you about Caleb."

"I deserve your anger. I haven't been reasonable. We should have talked it out, tried to reach common ground. I'm willing if you are. Can you get over your anger, Sara?"

"I'm not angry, Walker. For the first time in my life, I'm finally thinking straight. I can't make you love me, though Lord knows I've tried. Until the day you do, I won't beg for your crumbs any longer."

His eyes softened. "What would I have to say in order to make you stay?"

"If you don't know, you're in worse shape than I thought." She brushed past him before she started crying. Not so long ago, she would have accepted any terms he offered, but the stakes had changed. Now she wanted more.

"I'm going home. I'm going to the necessary first—then I'm going home."

He trailed her down the hallway. "What if I told you that you're going to break Sophie's and S. H.'s heart if you leave? They're real attached to you."

"Wouldn't work."

"What if I told you Potster thinks of you as a daughter? You're not going to leave the old man without saying good-bye, are you?"

"Potster's my friend. He knows the situation." She hurried down the stairway, determined to stick to her guns.

"What about Caleb?"

"What about him?"

"If there's a trial, you'll be needed to testify."

"Are you pressing charges?" She stepped off the porch and ran to the necessary. Walker's long-legged strides kept up with her.

"Well?" she asked.

"Well, what?"

"Are you pressing charges against Caleb?" She'd bet her last dollar he wouldn't. Walker would be angry with him, but he would never send Caleb to jail.

"Sara—"

"That's what I thought. You weren't willing to forgive me, but you will forgive Caleb." She disappeared into the privy and slammed the door.

Leaning against the outhouse, he said softly, "What if I say I forgive you? We can start over, Sara. We've both made mistakes—"

"No."

She emerged shortly afterward and walked toward the buggy.

"This isn't all my fault," he said. "You could have told the truth and this wouldn't have happened."

"Could have, should have, might have, needed to. What difference does it make? I didn't, so here we are." She swatted his hand as he tried to help her into the buggy. She lurched aboard and picked up the reins, meeting his eyes for the first time. "No, I will not forgive you. None of these reasons you have stated are good enough to make me stay." Her gaze softened. "I want what S. H. and Sophie have—what Papa had with Mama, and your parents had with each other. That kind of relationship doesn't come around every day, but I'll continue to search until I find it, Walker McKay."

"Sara—" Pride kept him from begging, but he wanted to—wanted to with every bone in his body. He wanted to tell her how much he loved her, but the words stuck in his throat.

Snapping the reins, she drove off, leaving him standing in a swirl of dust.

Sara Livingston cried all the way back to Boston. Thirty-two pounds heavier and a whole lot smarter, she knew the remaining months of her confinement would be a picnic compared with what she faced once the babies came. She chided herself for her inability to accept Walker's roundabout apology. Wasn't that what she'd wanted? Yet he hadn't stated one good reason to make her stay. Oh, how she wished he had. She wouldn't be crying her eyes out over a man who didn't give a whit about her.

Stepping down from the train, she shaded her eyes, wondering how she would get home. She'd thought about wiring ahead but decided against it. How could she possibly explain in a few short, staccato sentences why she was coming home? Her eyes traveled the terminal, pausing on Walker, then moving on. They switched back.

"Walker?" she murmured. Her heart sprang to her throat.

Pushing away from the post, the tall, good-looking rancher walked toward her. Stopping a few feet from her, he said, "Sophie needs you in the kitchen."

She raised her chin. "She does not—she hates me being underfoot."

"Doc says it's not safe to travel. You could hurt the baby."

She put her hands on her hips—or where they used to be. "You haven't talked to the doctor."

"I have. He said you're not to travel."

"If you had talked to Doc, you would know there's two babies, not one."

Walker's jaw went slack.

"So there."

"You're lying."

She glared at him. "That is not the way to win my affections."

"Two babies?"

"Probably."

"Then you can't leave, Sara. Two babies? Sophie can't take care of two babies."

"Not good enough. *How* did you get here before me?"

"I was on the train—rear coach. What if I said I'd rethought this, and— *Two* babies?"

She picked up her valise and hailed a driver-for-hire. Walker trailed her out to the wagon and helped her onto the front seat. He stored the valise, then climbed into the rear of the conveyance.

She pivoted in her seat to glare at him.

He glared back. "There isn't a train home until tomorrow."

The couple rode in silence as Sara searched her mind for an explanation of her sudden appearance. What would she tell Papa? That he'd been right all along? That she should have accompanied him back to Boston weeks ago? Walker just plain didn't love her, and he never would.

When the wagon drove into the courtyard, Abraham stepped around the woodpile and came to greet the newcomers, a smile breaking out when he recognized Sara. "Sara girl!"

"Hi, Abe." Sara smiled as the old servant lifted her out of the wagon and set her on the ground.

Holding her away from him, he examined her. "My, oh, my, Babygirl is surely fillin' out."

Patting her burgeoning load, she sighed. "Aren't I, though."

Walker jumped down from the wagon and reached for her valise. Paying the driver, he turned to Sara and the servant.

"Abe, this is Walker McKay."

Grinning, the white-haired servant gazed up and down at the rancher. "So this is Mr. McKay. Lordy, Lordy, Lordy."

Sara picked up her valise and started off toward the house. Walker caught up, taking the bag out of her hand despite her protests.

"I am capable of carrying my own luggage."

"No wife of mine is carrying her luggage."

"I'm *not* your wife." Wadsy's rotund bulk appeared in the doorway. "Oh, praise the Lord! Is that you, Babygirl?"

"It's me, Wadsy!" Sara gave the nanny a big hug.

Walker tipped his hat. "Walker McKay, Wadsy. Nice to meet you."

Wadsy turned to watch his swift passage into the house. "Pleasure to meet ya, sir."

"Papa? I'm home!" Sara announced as she breezed past the study. Lowell choked on the sip of coffee he'd taken, whirling to see the back of Sara going up the stairway. Scrambling out of the chair, he followed her.

"Sara Elaine? What are you doing here?"

"I live here, don't I?" She walked down the hallway to her bedroom, with Walker in close pursuit.

"Is that Mr. McKay with you?"

"It is, sir. We'll be down in a minute. I'm trying to talk sense into your daughter."

"Well, really!" Lowell stiffened and retreated back into the study. "Who isn't?"

Sara reached her bedroom and turned the doorknob. Walker's hand blocked her. His breath was warm on her neck. "What if I said that I need you more than I've ever needed anything in my life? That life won't be worth living if you're not the first thing I see in the morning and the last thing I see every night?"

The implication of his statement left her helpless. He'd never once ever said that he needed her. Her eyes gave away her indecision, and he took full advantage.

"Not just need you, but that I love you, and I've been a fool." Turning her slowly around to face him, he tilted her chin, kissing her lightly on the mouth. "I want what we first had, Sara. I want it worse than I've ever wanted anything in my life. I love you, so will you please forgive me so we can get married and start over? I've got sick cows, a bull down, a heifer in heat, fence to mend, and hay to be cut before the next rain, sweetheart. Will you listen to reason? I can't be traipsing all over the country courting you."

"This is your way of courting me?"

"It's my way of telling my woman that I love her." His mouth closed over hers a second time.

Closing her eyes, she tasted him, so warm, so Walker. It had been ages since he had kissed her. Even longer since she'd felt this sense of renewed hope. Their mouths brushed, lingered, and then consumed each other.

It was long minutes before she could bring herself to ask, "Another barbecue?"

His fingers cupped the sides of her breasts with an intimacy that stole her breath. "This time we're doing it right." His lips toyed with the nape of her neck. "Your papa will be there to give you away, and Sophie and Wadsy will both help you dress." Their lips drifted back together. "I love you. Will you marry me, Sara Livingston?"

He'd finally said the right thing.

"Of course I'll marry you, Walker McKay. What took you so long to ask?"

On the landing below, Wadsy, Lowell, and Abraham breathed a sigh of relief.

Abe smiled. "Looks like you got yerself a son-in-law, sir."

Lowell nodded, grinning from ear to ear. "It does at that, Abe. A fine son-in-law. Maybe now we can all rest."

Epilogue

It was simply a glorious Wyoming morning. Sara breathed deeply of the springlike air, silently thanking God for her bountiful blessings—far too many to list. Beside her, Walker handled the buggy reins as he drove to the church services. Reverend Baird's sermon this morning was going to be on forgiveness.

Now, *that* was a subject that she and Walker knew a lot about.

Not much had changed in the past two years, yet everything had. Abe had gone to be with the Lord, and Papa and Wadsy had moved to Wyoming to help care for the children and be cared for themselves. Sara turned to watch them in the backseat, trying to keep the twins out of trouble.

"Lawsy me, I never heard such chatterin' in all

my born days," the old nanny chided.

"Just like their mama," Papa added, drawing one of the two identical carrot-red-haired girls to his chest for a big Grandpa hug.

"Land sakes, you're sweet as honey," Wadsy said to the child on her lap, "though I would appreciate a decent night's sleep. When do you think these children'll start sleeping all night, Babygirl?"

Sara grinned at Walker. "We were hoping you could tell us, Wadsy."

"Maybe I could watch them for a few nights," Papa suggested. "Take them off your hands for you."

"Mr. Livingston, these girls would run you to bits. You gotta remember your health."

"Wadsy, don't start with me . . ."

Sara grinned at Walker, listening to Wadsy and Papa good-naturedly argue about who would take care of the girls that night. Leaning closer, Sara whispered, "I haven't had the nerve to tell them we're expecting again."

Winking, he grinned at her. "I don't think they'll mind."

"What's you two a-whisperin' about up there?" Wadsy asked as fourteen-month-old Millie scrambled from her lap to the floor of the buggy. Molly extended her arms to the nanny, and Wadsy and Papa traded children.

"Nothing much," Sara said. She squeezed Walker's arm.

"Have I told you how much I love you today?" Sara teased.

"I don't mind hearing it again."

"I do—with all my heart."

His affectionate squeeze told her all she needed to know. He was always reserved around Wadsy and Papa, but he made up for it when they were alone.

Sara Elaine Livingston McKay's dreams had all come true: she'd married the man of her dreams. The second ceremony had been large, with baskets of flowers, and family and friends in attendance. Everyone thought a second wedding was appropriate, since the first one had got off to a shaky start.

Today, she was the mother of two perfect little redheaded girls who, as their father had feared, had indeed inherited their mother's tendency for gab. S. H. and Sophie were happy there was an heir, so there was little to fuss about at Spring Grass these days. These happy, glorious days.

Only Caleb concerned her now. She had long ago forgiven him; Walker was still working on it. He had pressed charges against Caleb in his anger, and Caleb was now serving a sentence for embezzlement and attempted murder. Hopefully he'd learned his lesson, and would be released early for good behavior. *Everyone deserves a second chance*, Sara thought to herself. And everyone needs forgiveness.

All in all, Sara was happier than she'd ever dreamed possible. If anyone were to ask, she'd still say you should dream big and shoot for the moon. Reaching for Walker McKay's hand, she sighed, admiring the simply marvelous day.

She couldn't be happier, and that was the honest truth.